STEVE TILSTON

Steve Tilston was born in Liverpool, raised in the Midlands and has lived in London and Bristol. A recording artist and folk musician of international reputation, his songs have been recorded by over a hundred performers. A keen archer and hill walker, he now lives in the Yorkshire Pennines.

All For Poor Jack is his first novel.

No man can regard the way of war as good. It has simply been our way. No man can evaluate the eternal contest of weapons as anything but the sheerest waste and the sheerest folly. It has simply been our only means of final arbitration. Any man can suggest reasonable alternatives to the judgment of arms. But we are not creatures of reason except in our own eyes.

Robert Ardrey   The Social Contract

STEVE TILSTON

All For Poor Jack

Best Steve Tilston

ISTHMUS

First published in Great Britain 2010 by
Isthmus books.
38 Eldon Terrace,
Windmill Hill,
Bristol BS3 4PA

www.isthmusbooks.co.uk
mail@isthmusbooks.co.uk
www.stevetilston.com

ISBN 978-0-9565122-0-8

Designed by Jerome Dineen Graphic Design

For my mother Bettine
and the stories she read to me

Author's note

A few years before starting this story, I came upon the following passage in William Cronon's ecological history of New England *Changes in The Land.*

When the Pilgrims first landed on Cape Cod in 1620, they discovered "a place like a grave" covered with wooden boards. Digging it up they found the many personal possessions that the natives ordinarily buried with their dead: mats, bowls, dishes, a bow and two bundles. In the smaller bundle, amidst a quantity of sweet-smelling red powder, were the bones of a small child. More disturbing for the graverobbers were the contents of the larger bundle. There in the same red powder, were the bones of a man: some of the flesh remained on the bones and they realized with a shock that "the skull had fine yellow haire still on it." With the bones, "bound up in saylers canvas Casake, and a payre of cloth breeches," were a knife a needle, and "two or three old iron things," evidently the dead man's most personal belongings. A fair-haired European sailor, shipwrecked or abandoned on the New England coast, had lived as a native, probably fathered a native child and had been respectfully buried in a native grave.

This unknown man's set of circumstances may or may not have been unusual, but they illustrate an already long established contact with the coast and natives of the New World.

For centuries English fishermen had been fishing for cod (Poor-Jack) in Icelandic waters. The Hanseatic powers were unhappy with the English reaping the rewards of these waters without payment of tariffs. Consequently a prohibitive treaty was imposed in 1450. The merchant mariners of Bristol opposed this treaty and the seas around Iceland became a battle zone right up until nearly the end of the 15th century.

In those days, long before refrigeration, salted cod was an essential staple item and the cessation of the main supply a near disaster. It was imperative that a new source of the fish be found. The preservation of cod was a relatively straightforward matter of gutting, salting, laying out and letting the dry, windy weather work its bacterial action in a process not unlike cheese making. The other essential item was dry land on which to build the drying platforms where this could be done. I believe they found that land on the north eastern coast of America.

On July 6th 1481, two ships, part owned by Bristol Merchant and Collector of Customs Thomas Croft (one of this story's main characters), ventured westwards into the 'Ocean Sea,' ostensibly to search for the fabled island of Brasil. Both ships were mysteriously laden with 40 bushels of salt. This was more than just a voyage of discovery. Evidence suggests that they discovered the grand banks of Newfoundland and a source of codfish that dwarfed the previous Icelandic source. Incidentally, in 1490, when a treaty between King Henry V11 and the Hanseatics freed up the Icelandic waters, the Bristolians were virtually begged to renew their old trade. For some unexplained reason they declined to do so.

This is a tale of Old Bristol, its merchants, mariners, outcasts, of shipwrecked sailors cast adrift on those New World shores and the native peoples they encountered. The year is 1485.*

Of the many native peoples that occupied the north eastern part of North America, this novel is mainly concerned with two tribes: the Pennacooks and the Paquatuogs (Pequots), both members of the most widespread linguistic stock, the Algonkians. The Pennacooks, as part of the western Abenaki** group occupying parts of what is now Vermont and New Hampshire; and the Paquatuogs, further south in what is now Connecticut. All these tribes were warrior societies and by their very nature spent a considerable amount of their time revelling in being warlike, war being the most important rite of passage for young males; they regularly practised ritual torture of captives . All accounts of the Paquatuogs point to them being the most numerous, powerful and the most feared in the region. Known far and wide as the 'Destroyers,' they demanded tribute from neighbouring, less numerous tribes. As is so often the case in history, these subject tribes clamoured to join another powerful and warlike people (the English) in ultimately destroying the 'Destroyers' at their fort on the Mystic river in 1637.

An equally powerful and, in some respects, even fiercer tribe were the Maquack, or Mohawk. People of Iroquoian speech and part of a league of five nations, they formed a wedge against the Algonkians, ultimately pushing them further north and eastwards.

There are many difficulties in writing about a native people - and about a history which, for the most part, is written by the very people responsible for its destruction. How to do justice to such a rich and complex culture? To depict all natives as either the bloodthirsty 'Red Indians' of folklore and celluloid fiction, or 'Noble Savages,' in the Rousseauan mould does them a disservice. For example, there has been much heated argument as to the practice of scalping and whether or not it was an ancient native ritual or introduced by Europeans.

However, I believe it would have been impossible for Europeans to teach it to so many different tribes over both Americas in the absurdly short time after their arrival. It would have been equally impossible for these tribes to so deeply embed in their cultures all the elaborate and varied ceremonies with which they surrounded it. Without a doubt, Europeans were guilty of countless barbarities in war and peace. In the 16th and 17th centuries burning at the stake, hanging, drawing and quartering were commonplace in public executions and war, but no observer ever described them scalping their victims during that period. But what is without doubt is that Europeans introduced the practice of paying for scalps.

*1485 was the year when the Battle of Bosworth was fought, thus bringing an end to the Wars of the Roses and heralding in the Tudor dynasty. Recent archaeological research has, literally, unearthed much evidence of the impact firearms played in the battle, finding "more than all the lead roundshot from all the other battlefields of 15th and 16th century Europe put together." The technology was certainly advanced for incorporating a tricker (trigger)mechanism on handguns, having long been an essential part of Crossbow design.

** An aide-de-campe under Marquis de Montcalm described the appearance and equipment of the Abenakis in the mid-1700's. Heads were shaved except for the crown, with scalp locks plaited and adorned with deer-hair roaches, feathers, and wampum. Their noses and ears were bored to be hung with silver pendants, wheels, and "ball-and-cones." Their faces and exposed skin were painted with cunning and terrifying designs with pigments of red, black, and white mixed with bear fat.

I'm deeply indebted to my wife Margaret for her help and encouragement. Special thanks to John Hopwood for his patient editing, and to my agent Lorraine Carpenter.

I am also indebted to the authors of the following works:
Colin G. Calloway *The Western Abenakis Of Vermont. North Country Captives.*
GR Crone *The Discovery Of America*
William Cronon *Changes In The Land.*
Patrick M. Malone *The Skulking Way Of War.*
Francis Parkman *Pioneers Of France In The New World.*
Howard S. Russell *Indian New England Before The Mayflower.*
A.C.H. Smith *Sebastion The Navigator*
William S. Simmons *Spirit Of The New England Tribes.*
Ian Wilson *The Columbus Myth.*
Ruth M. Underhill *Red Man's America.*

PART ONE

CHAPTER 1
Shipwreck and Savage Men

Twice the cracked looking-glass saved Tyrell's life.

Raising the mirror high above his shoulder to see how the latest carbuncle was progressing, he had glimpsed the painted man emerge from the thicket, and dived aside as a whirling blur rent the air. Then, a second time, as he cowered in a shivering clench, the painted man had lowered the same ball-headed club, only to snatch the shaking mirror and postpone murder in favour of magic.

Tyrell's stare was drawn to the eyes. They suddenly appeared ready to explode from the painted mask, the whites huge against the blackened face. A sound midway between a wail and a groan blasted from the spittle-soaked lips, and then in an instant the face changed. The fearsome sneer became a wide grin, the eyes no longer bulged but flickered bright with a child's delight; and the pounding of the surf, the war cries, the shouts of desperation from his comrades beyond the dunes were lost in the belly rumble of a painted savage's laughter.

The savage's tongue curled, probing sensually at the hard surface of the glass, the belly laughter becoming squeals of delight, and the ball-headed club thumped the sandy earth like a drum. Tyrell was aware that he, too, had laughed a fool's laugh, nodding hysterically in time to the pounding, grinning a mimic grin. He clutched at the swishing skirts of relief that flashed with a childhood image of his Mother's face, as it changed from sweetness to sour over an upturned milk pail. He did not question the long-forgotten image or its absurd connection with present events. He was so taken aback with how - like the rising steam from the warm, wet patch spreading in his breeches - all control had seemed to evaporate, and he was left as helpless and confused as that long-ago child.

He had then seen the line of blood appear on the savage's tongue and his own false smile froze. There was a smear of blood-stained spittle on the mirror where the cracked glass had caught the tribesman's flesh. A hiss escaped between grinding teeth. How white they gleamed, a shark's grin. The probing tongue thrust forward to examine the nick, but the accompanying rush of breath clouded the image. Again the savage eyes bulged, but as much with confusion as ferocity. The looking-glass was dropped like a hot faggot to land face down on the coarse grass. Please God, don't be broken! Tyrell instinctively snatched it up, receiving a hard rap on the shin for his trouble. Once again the club was raised above his head.

"No wait! Wait, wait. Sweet Jesus! Please, please... Look!" He choked and winced. "Wait! Look here!"

His left arm rose to fend off the threatened mortal blow, whilst his other hand furiously rubbed the glass against the leg of his coarse, sail-cloth breeches. Grinning, panting triumphantly like a lap dog, he proffered the polished glass to the painted man once more, and once more the laughter returned. It did not last. From the beach came the boom of one of the company's two matchlocks, followed immediately by a loud wail of anguish. Tyrell sucked in a deep draught of air, held his breath and waited. The savage sprang to his feet, the obsidian centres of his eyes sweeping from side to side. Around his neck the string of animal claws clattered nervously. Tyrell rubbed his bruised shin-bone and inched backwards.

The coarse grass rasped his palms. The savage seemed not to care nor notice Tyrell's slithered retreat, but concerned himself with drawing a stone-headed arrow from a well-stocked quiver, sniffing deeply at the tainted air. Stealing another breath, Tyrell noticed it too - the sour taint of saltpetre and brimstone. The other matchlock boomed again. The savage flinched, struggling not to parade the uncomprehending dread that threatened to undermine his mask of ferocity. Then, crouching low, nocking the arrow to the string of a powerful looking bow, the painted man loped off towards the barrier of sand dunes. Tyrell let the captive breath burst forth, then filled his lungs with the sweetest air life had yet seen fit to bless upon him.

"Devils... Demons... Satan's spawn, Oh sweet Jesus. Sweet Jesus, deliver me!"

Tyrell's fears writhed like a river of eels. It was plain that he could not remain cowering in a piss-damp heap for long. But what to do? Where to go? Again a gun barked and he was up and hopping, rubbing at the bruised shin, then breaking into full pelt towards the wind-swirled dunes. He raced diagonally, away from the path taken by the savage, away from the sounds of firing. The thoughts unfolding within his mind were first to reach the comparative safety of the hillocks, then to work his way around to see with his own eyes what his ears had led him to believe was happening.

From the beach the high-pitched whoops of triumph seemed to confirm what that last gun shot had told him. It had not been a thunder-crack issuing from the muzzle, but more a weak squib of a sound, like a drab's fart, as if the charge had been hurriedly, fumblingly placed and not rammed firmly home - as if time had finally run out for his shipmates.

Tyrell's hurtling took him up between two mounds, down into a dip and halfway up a much larger escarpment. The momentum slowed and he was caught like a drunken dancer, wildly clutching at handfuls of the coarse grass, tearfully squinting through the blast of disturbed sand. Collapsing near the dune's summit, panting, spitting, his tongue teasing the particles of salty grit from his teeth, he was fastened to the sand, unable to peer over the top. Eventually his breath returned and with it some of his customary boldness. His racing mind toyed with a set of jeering faces, enemies and friends alike, crowded together in a reeking, Bristol tavern. It was as if somehow the judgement of these misbegotten figures of fancy was all-supreme and that God had been banished to a backroom to bless the new ale.

"G'warn, my piss-stained babby. Show they painted Gypoes y'aint frit!"

The voice had growled somewhere inside his head and stung into action, he crawled forward. Tentatively, like a maggot squirming forth from a swollen plum, Tyrell raised his head. Again a blast of sand forced him to retreat and shield his eyes. In that first briefest of glimpses he had located the Swallow, the fractured masts of the broken ship, and there on the beach the blurred movements of men. Once more he raised his head and between the filter cracks of his fingers he began to absorb the scene.

Along the wide strand, barely half a longbow shot away, Tyrell could make out a mix of men - the ragged-clothed and ragged-bearded drabness of his shipmates contrasting with the emblazoned dash of a handful or so painted men. All were standing, intermingled in a near casual display, like figures at a fairground. What was afoot? Where were the dead? He scanned the beach for broken, crumpled shapes. Where were the dying, the dead men? Had he not heard men fighting, men screaming? Beyond these dunes a battle, or rather a skirmish, had raged - guns had been discharged. Was it three or was it four times he had heard their bark?

Tyrell heard the laughter, and from that alone he knew it to have sprung from the throat of a Christian man. Even at this distance - though no discernible words reached his hiding place - Tyrell immediately recognised the owner of the laughter. John Pugh, the big Welshman, was always laughing. Even when pummelling men's faces he would chuckle as if inviting his victim not to take the thrashing personally, but to share in the jest. There was no love lost between Pugh and himself, but for Tyrell now, the sing-song lilt of the Welshman's laughter was sweeter than a mermaid's call.

Emboldened, heartened by the somewhat confusing evidence indicating that his comrades and that his ears had somehow deceived him, Tyrell raised himself to his knees. In doing so, he was able to make out others of the ship's company as they mingled with the painted men. What did it mean? He was prepared to forego the sounds of men's voices in conflict. After all, the surf still pounded - even though the day was moderately calm - and the sounds of men's true intent could often be gagged because of it. But the bark of black powder? The rasp of brimstone? No, it would take the crash of a storm-tossed sea to ridicule the evidence that still resounded in his head. Both matchlocks had been fired and then one of them loaded and fired again. Nothing could dissuade him from that opinion. But had they been fired in anger? Now it appeared not. It was this confusion that held him back and restrained him from rising there and then to go hurtling through the dunes to join his countrymen on the beach. For the time being he was content to stay put, to look and listen, hoping the painted men would soon melt away; and hoping the tell-tale piss stain would hurry up and depart his breeches. How could he possibly make an appearance in that state? The men would never let him live it down.

But more than all the mockery, more than the inevitable nickname that would be mercilessly bestowed upon him, it was these tall tribesmen, with their swagger and their coxcombs, that unnerved him so. He would never have thought it possible for men to look so strange. They were men-killers and no mistake. Even when that one with the looking-glass had laughed fit to burst, Tyrell had smelt the bloodlust on him, mixed in with the greasy red and black paint. No wonder they and Big Pugh seemed to be getting on so well. Yes, these ones bore a very different stamp from the people of the Stock-Fish stations far to the north. They were tall men also, but gentler creatures, with big, wide faces - good fishermen too, venturing far out into the sea in those strange, bark craft that rose to a point midship, requiring a large slab of stone to keep them balanced. In part they reminded everyone of Gypsies, both in appearance and their light-fingered ways. "Boat-Hooks" the men called them, on account of their habit of banging their chests and mouthing the two words or some suchlike expression whenever they approached. There were also fewer of them than these fierce predators he now beheld. In the whole two months in that foggy northern land Tyrell had never seen more than a handful of Boat-Hooks gathered at any one time, but already on the beach these painted ones evenly matched the eleven surviving crew members.

Something made him turn then and look back across the apron of grass where the looking-glass had saved him. A movement caught his eye and sure enough, out of the wide band of wind-tilted trees, another group of the tribesmen spilled forth, dashing, crouched low, the sunlight catching their greased backs as they advanced.

Once again he was held fast, unable to move other than to shiver with terror. He had never known fear like this before. Even when on the graveyard watch, lashed to the mainmast with the full force of an ocean storm raging all around and every fibre of wood keening out in agony, nothing compared to the sight he now beheld.

Surely these were not human men? They looked like no men he had ever seen or heard tell of. They were as fantastical demons spewing out from a fissure in the earth's crust. What else could they be but evil? He noticed, too, the long powerful bows that they all carried and wondered if his countrymen on the beach had had the foresight to string up the five yew bows that had been borne ashore from the wreck. They were mariners, fishermen foremost, but most amongst them had seen as much strife as any soldier and had fought against Moors, pirates, Frenchmen and those Hanse robbers who had driven all the fishermen of Bristol from the waters of Iceland. Tyrell, too, had put his time in at the butts - as was the law for every able - bodied Englishmen - and was once an able shot with a longbow. However, since taking to the high seas and having his hands on one of the ship's handguns, he had let the skill slip and when back in 'dry dock' had gladly paid the farthing fine, putting time in at the Marsh Street cider houses instead. Surely someone would have had the foresight to string them up and have a sheaf of bodkins handy, he asked himself? Razor-sharp, armour-piercing bodkins - Frenchy widow makers - nothing could match a well-cast yew bow. Leastways nothing a painted savage could fashion. "Piss-all use if they aint braced," he hissed in frustration, knowing that this would most likely be the case.

Another blast of sand had finally cleared the trance and soon he was clasped tight to the side of the dune, screwing his eyes, trying not to sneeze. However, cowering face down, blind, imagining what course fate would take, induced more fear than witnessing the reality. So, no sooner had the desire to sneeze passed, than he once again ventured his head above the swirling parapet.

The swarm of savages was making towards the group on the beach. They too were concealed from view by the barrier of dunes. Tyrell marked how - in time to their silent tread - they flexed the tension of their bows with already nocked shafts, as if the weapons were vibrating wings and the long arrows poised to strike like the fatal stings of a deadlier breed of wasps.

"A trap!... A foul bloody trap!" he moaned.

Tyrell knew that there was only one course to take. He would have to warn his comrades of the impending ambuscade; but try as he might, neither his legs would bear him up nor his dry mouth produce sufficient spittle to utter ought but a feeble croak. Tyrell felt like a man fallen overboard, unnoticed, unable to do anything other than tread water and watch as the ship sails away.

Once more John Pugh's laughter resounded. Tyrell's eyes again lighted on the figures on the beach. They had parted now into two distinct groups; naked and clothed - if the tatters of wool, sailcloth and leather could be described thus - and, standing alone in the middle, was the braggart Pugh, singing at the top of his voice, beating time with the ramrod as he plunged it in and out of the long barrel of a matchlock.

"Why him? Not him! He can't fire off a gun! Give it to Dodds or Langleg, you fool! Someone who knows how to shoot! Sweet Jesus!"

Tyrell hissed with frustration, squeezing handfuls of sand between his fingers. Nevertheless, he was much relieved that he had been mistaken about a fight and that the handguns were apparently making such an impression on the savages. He only hoped the ones who now lurked behind the dunes - seemingly intent on committing treachery - would be equally impressed and decide to stay put.

It was God's doing that the ship's owner saw fit to include the handguns in the Swallow's ordnance. Some of the men said it was Thomas Croft himself who insisted they be carried, having had the bell-makers copy them from a captured Hanse design. There had been grumbled resistance in the taverns, saying they were cumbersome, took too long to load and were inaccurate. The voice of Pugh had been loudest in proclaiming them no match for a longbow, a Welsh longbow if you please, and him swearing the English national weapon had been conceived in those misty, damp valleys. Yet here he was about to demonstrate the power of the very weapon he had earlier decried with such vehemence. What wouldn't he do for an audience? Tyrell mused that it would not be rotten eggs and mouldy fruit that were thrown - should the painted ones feel the need to show their displeasure.

Even at this distance, Tyrell caught the whiff of excitement.

"Go on then, you great dolt, show us all!" He threw a handful of sand in disgust.

And then it happened. Pugh chuckled, blew the taper in the serpentine aglow, laid the long, heavy barrel on the rest, aimed at an object that looked like a sailor's red cap all of twenty paces beyond, and lowering the smouldering taper with a simple twitch of a finger on the tricker, discharged the gun.

The dull boom that seemed to shake the ground indicated the placing of a much too heavy charge. Tyrell saw Pugh jolt back with the recoil. At the same instant he noticed with amazement the cap shudder as if a rat were trapped inside.

"God's Holy Hooks! He hit it...! No I don't believe it!" he heard himself exclaim.

From out of the cloud of gunsmoke he also saw the groaning savages scatter, heard his own countrymen cheer. Then all was still as young Smithey, the ship's boy, dashed towards what must have been his cap. He picked it up, shaking off the sand, and with a whine of protest, thrust his arm through the gaping hole.

"Pugh, you gurt Welsh tosser, my Mum'll kill me for this!" The lad's voice rose to a near shriek. "And she'll kill you an' all when I tells 'er!"

Pugh had fallen to his knees, doubled up with laughter. The matchlock and rest clattered around him. The others looked at each other and started to join in the merriment. The boy was beside himself, arm outstretched, jumping up and down like a rat on hot coals. And then the lad's adolescent shriek rose once again, this time like the keenest stiletto. Tyrell also found his voice at that same moment and it too rose in tortured unison - none paid him heed.

First to come was a stone-beaked flock of arrows, their long rigid necks stretched out to catch the sunlight. Upwards they soared and the squint-eyed gawkings of the seamen strained to trace their flight. For the briefest moment there was no utterance from the open-mouthed crew, but in the final dipping of this deadly descent, all remained rooted to the spot. The wild yelps from amongst the dunes signalled the springing of the trap, as over the crest the hidden tribesmen poured.

Tyrell did not mark where the arrows fell. Like his companions on the beach, he remained frozen, mouth agape, eyes drawn to the hideous surge. He shivered as the cries of forlorn hope mingled with the war cries in a cruel dissonance, and watched as, to a man, the doomed mariners turned and scattered in every direction. Tyrell saw too the vaned shafts that now trailed from each of their bodies, bobbing up and down like tail-feathers as they ran the pitiful rings of headless chickens.

Onward charged the newly-swelled body of the painted men, horizontal sheets of missiles spitting from their ranks. A loud moan of anguish, unlike any sound Tyrell had ever uttered, erupted from deep within his belly as he thought he recognised helmsman Holdbush, John Whitt and Sam Dodds go down. He screwed his eyes tight as the clubs rose and fell.

Before he knew it, Tyrell was up and running, stumbling, then tumbling head over heels into a damp, shadowy hollow. Covered head to foot, he shook and beat his way up the other side, grinding his teeth, growling like a wild dog. The terror that had frozen him had gone, giving way to a maddened, burning rage. Tyrell had grown up with Whitt, and the older man, Dodds, had been like an uncle to him, 'shown him the ropes'. It seemed inconceivable that they had been snuffed out, swatted like bugs, as if the distance had conspired to reduce his comrades to naught but mere insects. Now he felt drawn to share their torment. His place was amongst them. There was no space left in his mind for any alternative.

In his wildest fancies, Tyrell would never have imagined that he would welcome martyrdom, but here, as he blundered through the dunes down onto the beach, he found himself like a latter-day Saint Sebastian, welcoming the bite of the arrows. Headlong he dashed, lurching forward, flailing the air with windmill arms, his mouth stretched wide with the screams of a falling man.

"JJJJJJJEEEEEEEEEEEEEEEEEEEEESSSSUUSSS!"

But the moment he left the dunes, the self-destructive resolve began to diminish with every stride. He was now fully exposed, the blast of air from the ocean undermining the frenzy and muting his cry. The scene before him began to tug at his innards until he felt sure that his entrails were about to unravel and drag him head over heels.

Barely a hundred paces ahead, isolated groups of savages were clustered around the remains of his fallen comrades. Only Pugh seemed to show any sign of life. From the centre of one of the groups Tyrell could hear the unmistakeable voice... surely not singing? No, not singing, but begging, screaming in an eerily melodious manner. Then he too was silenced and only the triumphant howls of the savages swept the beach, harsh sounds with a bragging tone to them, like gambling drunkards on a winning wave of fortune.

Had they not heard his demented screeching above their own cries? Was he of so little significance that he did not warrant a glance? His mouth remained open, fish-wide and, like a fresh landed Poor-Jack, made no utterance.

Tyrell was no longer hurtling the path of a berserker. The paces were now reduced to tiptoes, like a child crossing a frozen pond. His course had abruptly changed, taking him away from the slaughter, drawing him diagonally towards the only piece of cover on the beach - the ship's boat. He was aware that soon the skiff would draw the savages to it. At best it would buy him a few moments respite. If only he could swim more than a few feeble strokes, maybe he could have made for the stranded Swallow - she appeared deceptively close. Then he saw the line of froth just beyond where the breakers smashed relentlessly into the long sandbar that had been her undoing. It would not be long before they breached the hull and then that would be an end to her. Tyrell thought briefly of the cargo of salted Poor-Jack, flake upon flake of it, pressed tight under great slabs of stone. All that labour for nothing - bound back to the sea whence it came. He thought also on the men – including Ross the Master - who did not make it to the shore. Maybe they had been the more fortunate ones after all.

Tyrell was but twenty paces from the row-boat. Stooping low, he dashed onwards, both arms wrapped around himself, his face screwed into a grimace as if those bodily contortions were somehow granting him a degree of invisibility. So intently were his eyes drawn to the prow of the craft, that he had not the slightest inkling that, lurking in the shadows by the stern, was another fugitive. With pounding sea matching the pounding of his heart he crept forward, fighting the urge to fling himself across the remaining distance. Slowly his arms uncurled, his fingers stretching out to caress the prow. First, fingertips touched, then his hands became talons that clawed and grasped the rim. The boat shuddered a little as he let himself down beside it.

"Sweet Jesus! Jesus, Jesus! Thank you!"

No sooner had he sat down in the hard, damp sand, his lungs pumping furiously, than the boat lurched again. He sat bolt upright, aware that the force that had just rocked it was not of his own making.

Suddenly, the blur of an up and running figure sent him reeling with shock. The running man looked over his shoulder twice. On the second time, his eyes met Tyrell's and he came to an abrupt halt. The tense set of both their faces was allowed the brief flicker of recognition. It was Sam Dodds.

"But Sam, you're dead!"

Tyrell mouthed the accusation in a silent scream, stabbing the air with a pointed finger. The sweating apparition mouthed back,

"Oh no I ain't, Matty! Come on! Come on now!"

A cupped hand beckoned Tyrell to join him. Without waiting to see if indeed Tyrell did follow, the figure hurtled off along the beach.

Again Tyrell found he was not the master of his own body - his legs were imbued with a will of their own and at their bidding he was obliged to follow. He would have preferred it had Dodds returned to the shelter of the boat, even for a few brief moments, to allow him to catch his breath and see for himself if indeed this was his friend and not some ghost he was chasing. Hadn't he seen both the skewered Dodds and John Whitt go down under a rain of arrows and clubs? Now the man appeared unharmed and moving faster than Tyrell deemed his squat body capable of. He realised Dodds was not wearing his usual leather jerkin, and then remembered his losing it to the equally bald, squat Jim Harvyson in a wager. Harvyson wore it still, pierced with arrows now and stained red with gore.

The joy he experienced in knowing that he was not blindly chasing an apparition, knowing that he was not alone on this foreign shore, was short-lived The chorus of yelps that rose from behind told him that they had been spotted. The chase was on, and he too ran faster than he thought himself capable of, swifter than the wind could blow a spore of pollen.

They raced along the marble-smooth sand that the receding tide had lately relinquished. Always Dodds stayed ahead, but looked around often, scooping with his arm and calling over his shoulder "Come on, my babby! Come on, Matty lad!" Inevitably Tyrell gained on the older man, but by then he was barely a dozen paces behind when he too was forced to look round, and in doing so, gave ground both to the one he followed and the pursuing horde.

He had known before turning that the sound like a spade slicing turf was that of the arrows biting close to his heels. It was small comfort to see that the rude shafts fell short and that their owners would slow their pace to retrieve them, with what appeared to be over-exaggerated clumsiness. Even so, the horde seemed to be gaining. Was it jeering laughter he could hear, mixed in with the cries for blood? Tyrell could not then rid himself of the feeling that the savages were not really trying, but enjoying the chase, playing with their prey as a cat plays a mouse, seeing how close they could shoot without actually drawing blood - wanting the game to last.

A long-bladed knife fell from Dodds' belt and slapped the damp sand. The older man stopped, hesitated, then retracing the handful of paces, scooped it up. Four arrows landed, ringing the spot where his fingers had gouged the sand. With a succession of leaps, Tyrell was placed right beside his friend. Another snatched glance passed between them and suddenly Dodds' grabbed Tyrell's arm, wrenching him into a diagonal course across the narrowing strand towards the band of scrubby trees. Tyrell did as he was bidden, ignorant of the fact that the beach they raced along did not, as first appeared, stretch uninterrupted to the distant headland. The more experienced Dodds had realised that, a quarter of a mile further on, there was a channel, maybe a river mouth that would have been impossible to ford. It seemed that the pursuers were making no special effort to cut across their path, but seemed content to doggedly follow in their tracks.

As they mounted the rise in the beach, their progress in the fine, dry sand became as a blind man's shuffle. But even though they lurched from one pace to the next, their bare feet held the advantage over the hide-covered feet of their pursuers. Without looking, Tyrell knew that the gap had been widened. He looked back, fleetingly at first, then, still moving, turned his whole body around and noticed with a little satisfaction that the tribesmen were making harder work of it than themselves. There were still the whoops and screams, but they were fewer and not so triumphant in tone. In the immediate present a glimmer of hope seemed to flicker.

Why didn't they shoot them, fill them with shafts as the others had been? Tyrell had no doubt that, if used to their full effect, the arrows would have no trouble in reaching them. He also knew that they were the easiest of targets. Hadn't he witnessed the full power, only minutes earlier, at the scene of treachery? Yet somehow they seemed to be holding back from skewering Dodds and himself.

And then the answer came. It came in a roar of many throats whooping as one. It rose up in front of them, stopping the two dead in their tracks, making the short hairs rise on their necks and their bowels turn to froth. Before they had time to think or call to the Almighty, they became engulfed, transfixed in the centre of a roaring, savage throng.

CHAPTER 2
In Savage Hands

"Hi-Yi! What a chase! I enjoyed that. It was so good. They thought they were getting away, then all of a sudden the rest of us are right in their faces. Did you see the looks? Did you smell them shitting themselves? What do we do now though, knock their heads or take them with us?"

A painted man with large, protruding ears, that flapped in dangling loops of stretched lobe and shell pendant, peered down at Tyrell and Dodds, and snorting the air as if they were beings of no consequence, laughingly jabbed at them with a dirt-encrusted fingernail.

"If we take them along they will hinder our progress. We have a long journey ahead of us."

"Wadawagwa speaks sense. Remember, these are enemy lands and we are not many."

Another paint-smeared face peered down and spoke.

"They do not look very strong, these two. Listen, their hearts are pounding like frightened birds. I think the older one will fall down dead at any moment. It would be a good thing to crack open his head and have done with it. Why, look, it is smooth like an egg with no hair, useless... See, it begs to be cracked open."

The throng rumbled with laughter. Shoulders shook. Encouraged, the first speaker continued, "Ah, but Managnon, see! The other's hair is the colour of ripe corn and see, it curls like a young fern. I would like it for my woman's girdle."

He grabbed a handful of Tyrell's hair, twisting it, forcing him down to his knees.

"See how easy he submits... No, they would not keep up with us."

"So you say, Wadawagwa, but they ran fast enough by the edge of the salt water."

With a wide sweep of an arm, this third speaker gestured towards the ocean and continued, his words bearing the weight of some authority.

"The older one was in the lead all the time. And what is more, I heard your own heart beating like a flock of pigeons. No, I think that they are stronger than they look. Not much, but a little." They all laughed. "Besides, this younger one did reveal to me a wondrous thing."

"What wondrous thing, Tidesso? When did you see this one before?" Wadawagwa released his hold on Tyrell's hair. Tyrell slowly regained his feet.

"Yes, what magic thing? Don't keep it to yourself. Show us!"

"Yes, show it to us," came the clamour of many voices.

"Hi-Yi! Look at this one now, Tidesso. Look now, see the colour of his eyes, they have in them the colour of the sky. Just look at them, look at them! He smiles at you like one who is touched in the head, one who did not return whole from a dream journey. Yes, I think he knows you. How can this be?"

Wadawagwa was hopping from leg to leg and jabbing with his finger at Tyrell's back. Tyrell gasped as the inflamed area around the carbuncle was touched. Again the savages all laughed. Wadawagwa leered maliciously, withdrew an arrow and began to prod and twist at the infected area. Tyrell wanted to scream, but a look from Dodds made him clamp his jaws tight. The one called Tidesso held up his hand and with a final twist from Wadawagwa, the arrow was reluctantly removed. Tyrell lurched forward, gasping.

"Yes, I did see him before when I came over by the sand hills. But I think I will not show you my trophy yet. It might be bad for you to see yourselves as the Manitous see you."

He chuckled to himself, heedless of the groans of disappointment and playfully stroked Wadawagwa's shoulder.

Wadawagwa stopped prancing.

"What do you mean, 'as the Manitous see us'?"

"Yes... Hey, Hi-Yi! Come on, you must show us. It's only right," came a voice from the group's midst.

"Oh I must, must I? Who are you to say that I must?" Tidesso did not bother to turn as he spoke.

"Don't be this way, Tidesso," said Managnon, his voice assuming a tone of feigned hurt. "We know that it was your dream that told you to put this raiding-party together and that you are the chosen leader and your dream-picture is strong. No one has gone under. We all of us know this. No one forced us to come along. But where would you be without the rest of us? A fine raid you'd lead on your own. You need us to carry all these trophies you have dreamed about."

Again they all jeered, some rattling shafts against bows in mock applause.

"Do you forget the thunder-makers so soon? Did we not all cower like puppy dogs because of the big roar they made? Look closer at the red bonnet you have in your belt."

Wadawagwa took young Smithey's red woollen hat from a his belt and, poking the arrow through the bullet hole, raised it aloft. The hat slid down the shaft to come to a halt covering his fist. Again they all laughed.

"Don't you all see, if we had not pretended friendship, but attacked them head-on, like some of you were eager to do,"

Tidesso paused, looked around the attentive faces then continued, "some of us would be this very moment lying punctured and leaking into the sand. And the red of this bonnet would not appear so attractive."

In disgust, Wadawagwa cast the red cap aside. Tidesso continued, "They might appear puny and pale, like fish dragged straight from the water, but it is undeniable that they have powers. I think that they are Mystery-men like our Mateoulins. I also think that we have slain enough of them for the while. We have plenty of their straw hair already. It is my wish that we take these two back with us to show the people."

"Pha!... Not only do these Wobigen look like fish, they smell like them too!"

Again the one called Wadawagwa brought his long nose close to the ear of Dodds and snorted with disgust. Others followed suit, sniffing and coughing with exaggerated distaste.

"Then what, after we have brought them back to our lodges?" asked Managnon.

Tidesso shrugged his shoulders.

"Cherish them, torment them, caress them with fire? I don't know. We'll let the great Sachem and the Mateoulins gaze into their pale, fish faces and see what must be. Let it be their decision."

He waited whilst the words sank in, and concerned himself with ridding his moccasins of sand.

"So, now we'll go back and join the others at the place of blood spilling. There are many trophies to be taken with us. Who will be first to have the honour of carrying the thunder-makers when we retrieve them?"

They were quite the biggest, fiercest men Tyrell had ever seen. The tufted crests of hair, some stiffened with red painted clay, rose from their shaven heads like the manes of mules to

32

give them the appearance of being even taller than they were. There was, too, an overpowering smell off them of rancid grease, woodsmoke and hide that stroked at Tyrell's gorge, only fear stopping him from openly retching. Then, slowly, like the lifting of a sea mist, the uniformity of the hide breechclouts, tufted locks and painted faces began to reveal differences that were not at first apparent. One of those who came close to sniff at them had wrinkles at the corner of his eyes and deep lines from his nose to the corners of his mouth. He also had a fuller belly and though his firm chest glistened with grease, it revealed the ribs beneath less readily. He was obviously the oldest, maybe even close to Dodds' age, but nonetheless in superb physical shape. The others were all young, none older than Tyrell's own twenty years.

He experienced a bitter, salty taste as a horny thumb was pushed into the corner of his mouth, forcing him to open his jaws wide. The owner of the probing talons, the same older savage, commenced running a finger across both rows of teeth. Back and forth the finger ran, as if tempting Tyrell to clamp his jaws tight. The fingers were finally snatched away. Tyrell glimpsed them, and knew that the red that stained them, and that covered the hands of all these savages, was not paint, but blood - the grease-mixed blood of his comrades. He opened his mouth to retch, but a score of eyes as unforgiving as quartz reduced the action to a helpless groan.

"Something troubles you, Alaskana? I would hear you speak, uncle."

The one called Tidesso lightly brushed the older tribesman's arm.

"I sense you don't think we should have attacked these Wobigen at all?"

The older man cleared his throat and spoke. His voice revealed a deeper tone than his younger companions.

"This is your warband, Tidesso. I will offer advice if I'm asked. I would have wished to observe them for longer."

There was a snort of derision from Wadawagwa. Alaskana turned towards him and continued. "Are they not considerably different from any others we have seen? I would have liked to have learned more about them. Where they came from, for instance? What brought them here? And, most important, these thunder-lances - I have never seen their like before." Pausing, he turned once more to Tidesso.

"I think it's a good thing that you keep these two alive to take with us."

Although not a single spoken word was remotely familiar - indeed he would not have deemed it possible for the human throat to reproduce such sounds - nonetheless, Tyrell had guessed by the bodily gestures and the general tone of the jumbled sounds that his and Dodds' lives hung in the balance. Most of the terrifying throng had wanted to tip it over, of that he had not the slightest doubt, but by a stroke of good fortune, the older tribesman and the one who now had possession of the cracked looking-glass were amongst the group that declared themselves in favour of life; and by his bearing the younger man seemed to be in a position of some authority.

Tyrell gazed across at Dodds. There was a fresh criss-cross of bloody score marks on his cheeks where one of the tribesmen had scratched with a crab-claw. Dodds shrugged his shoulders and gave a resigned smile. Tyrell managed the flicker of a weak smile in return. He felt guilty in being too concerned with his own wretchedness not to have noticed his friend's torment. Being reunited with Dodds, just having him near, had given Tyrell much succour. He suspected that had he been alone amidst these painted men, alone in the alien, grease-ridden stench of their bodies, his mind would have snapped asunder.

When death did not come and he had recognised the one with the looking glass, Tyrell had found himself nodding and smiling as if greeting an old friend on Touker Street back in Bristol. The tribesman, despite the impassive mask of paint, had made the slightest flicker of an eye and nod of the head in reciprocation. Investing in this meagre acknowledgment all the significance of a kinsman's reunion, Tyrell had felt almost triumphant. He had wanted to blurt to Dodds that he had indications that things would be all right, but words would not form. Instead he managed a wink, hoping that it would convey some of his returning confidence.

The feeling did not last. Their wrists were tightly bound with rawhide thongs, and they were bundled back along the beach in the opposite direction to the one they had just run, caught in the centre of a jogging phalanx of chanting, whooping tribesmen. Every step was loaded with dread, knowing that soon they would be amongst the remains of their comrades, maybe themselves destined to be bludgeoned and hacked to pieces.

"Whatever these painted buggers 'ave done up ahead lad, don't let 'em see you blubbin." Dodds had managed to utter the first words that had passed between them. The chanting stopped. He was tripped over, sent sprawling headlong in the surf, pulled back up and thrashed with bow-staves and javelins for his pains. But when they reached the scene of the massacre and were triumphantly paraded from one sorry corpse to the next, Tyrell did not weep. He puked instead, and one of the captors laughed and pressed his face into the gritty mess, squealing with delight at his new-found mask.

Then suddenly a hush descended and with it came a brief respite for the two captives. The young leader of the tribesmen had picked up one of the matchlocks, and cradling it across his arms, had begun to sniff and examine it closely with barely contained awe. The other tribesmen gathered round him in reverential silence, gingerly poking at the strange weapon, swiftly withdrawing their proffered fingers as if the long iron barrel had returned to its molten beginnings, or the serpentine firing mechanism was indeed a snake ready to strike. With the realisation that no serpent lurked, fingers became more emboldened and were soon snatching and tugging at the gun. Grasping the gun to his chest, the leader laughingly brushed the others aside. Then, turning to Tyrell and Dodds, he bade them come near as if they were a pair of slinking dogs. When they were but a couple of paces away, he reached out, and grabbing Tyrell, proceeded to undo his bonds. Tyrell had barely a moment to flex his fingers before, to his surprise, the gun was flung at him, sending him off balance and onto his knees. Hands grasping the gun, he used it to right himself and was confronted by the tribesman, standing with flexed bow and an arrow pointing at his face.

With painfully tingling fingers, Tyrell wiped the stinking puke and sand from his face, revealing an expression of anguish and confusion. The young leader barked something at him. Tyrell turned to Dodds.

"What's 'e want?"

"Wants you to fire it off! Can't you see?"

Stung at the irritation in Dodd's tone, Tyrell went into a flurry of over-exaggerated activity and stepping over to Pugh's corpse, retrieved the bullet pouch and powder flask. With shaking fingers he began to load the gun, not daring to look at the throng that surrounded him. Down the barrel he poured a measure of blackpowder, spilling some in the process. Then he proceeded to ram home a lead ball and then ripped a piece of his shirt-tail for wadding.

"What about the fuse? I need to light the fuse."

Dodds saw Tyrell's shoulders sag.

"Calm down, lad."

Even though his wrists were bound, Dodds proceeded to mime the actions of flame. Tyrell, too, joined him and giving a curt nod, the young leader made it known he understood. In a twinkling a grooved fireboard and kindling was produced and with the furious friction of a pointed stick, a flame was skilfully conjured and the gun's fuse set to smouldering. Pushing the serpentine forward, Tyrell carefully spilled some black powder into the priming pan and the gun was now ready to fire. He offered it to the leader, thinking that he would want the privilege of shooting it, but the tribesman haughtily gestured that Tyrell was to be the one. He also made it known that the corpse of Pugh would be the target. Horrified, Tyrell turned to Dodds for guidance.

"Just do it lad. Pugh's past feelin it. We ain't. And watch where you point it… They'll make an 'edgehog of ye."

With some effort, Tyrell shouldered the heavy matchlock. The tribesmen all took a step back but continued to train their arrows on him. He pulled the tricker. Down came the smouldering serpentine into the priming pan and with a thunderclap roar the gun was fired. Before the shroud of smoke descended, he saw Pugh's corpse shudder and a gaping, fist-sized hole appear. Deafened by the blast and feeling numb, Tyrell turned his face to the sea and sank to his knees. From the tribesmen's throats came a communal groan, followed by a triumphant howl of bravado laced with fear and then back up onto his feet he was dragged.

It was the incoming tide that put a halt to the grisly celebrations. Tyrell and Dodds had been made to strip until they were as naked as worms. Their clothing and that of their dead companions was shared amongst the tribesmen, who pranced and shrieked in a ring, their appearance even more like demons. Into the midst of this throng they had been dragged and made to dance and sing at the top of their voices. For both the hapless survivors however, the worst horror was seeing the freshly peeled scalps and other, more intimate, parts of those they had known being passed and examined like prized bargains at a market.

The malevolent one, with the slashed ears that stuck out like moth's wings, had noted Dodds' look of particular dread when he caressed the fine, sandy hair that had belonged to Smithey, the ship's boy. Stalking over, braying like a mule in heat, he took great delight in rubbing the reeking scalp round and round Dodds' face. Dodds sat unmoving, as if carved from a block of limestone. Even when the flies singled him out for their own particular brand of torture, all but obliterating his features, he did not move.

"Hi-Yi! Look at that Wobigen. He has a piece of shit for a face. Hey shitface! shitface...! You, I talk to you."

Still Dodds did not move. The tribesman lifted his breech-clout, and even before the jet of urine hit Dodds full on, the flies had vanished in a cloud.

"See, I give you back your Wobigen face!"

Then, as the sea-water licked his toes, Tyrell heard a sound like the groan of a great, wounded beast come rumbling across the surf. He stole a glance and saw the broken Swallow shudder. Was the swelling tide attempting to float her free of the sandbank? What cruel mockery it would be if the craft was freed. The yearning in his breast opened like a deep gash. Beside him Dodds' resolve wavered and he moaned like a doomed soul. He saw, too, the uncomprehending looks on the savage faces, as if they were noticing the ship for the very first time.

"Ship!... Ship!" he croaked from the depth of his heart, forcing a false smile and jabbing his re - bound wrists seawards. What a sorry, broken jumble she was becoming. Several of the tribesmen nodded and grinned back and, apparently amused with the word, repeated it over and over with exaggerated sibilance, slobbering between their lips as if humouring the speech of imbeciles, but none seemed impressed by the wreck.

"Ship...Ship!"

Then the smiles vanished and Tyrell and Dodds were hurried away from the shore. Through a saltmarsh and into the cool of the forest they were led, the burning skin of their backs prodded with the stone tips of javelins and arrows if they once showed signs of faltering or dared to look back.

CHAPTER 3
Into The Wilderness

For eight days they were pulled and prodded through mile upon dreary mile of the eternal forest. Along the tops of ridgeways they trudged, where the view was of yet further ridges rolling back into hazy blue, stacked like waves waiting to engulf them with hope forlorn. Down into the troughs of stinking marshland they were dragged, where the grey, fractured fingers of drowned trees scratched at the air and the air was stagnant with mosquitoes and menace. Around lakes and ponds, over rivers both sluggish and wild and stony, where, with bloody knees and toes they slithered and stumbled, to be fetched up on dry land again, wheezing and retching as their captors stood over them, hissing with contempt. And always when they looked up to see if their God should somehow display a sign of pity, the heavens were masked by leaves and the silent light that filtered down to them held no succour or acknowledgment.

Due west then north-west was their course, sometimes crossing well-trodden trails, but mostly confined to faint traces no wider than a man's single foot. They were sustained on naught but a greasy, yellow mush that was slopped into their gullets down chutes of bark, devoid of either salt or savour. For always with the mush came torment as the bugs, discovering the caked lips, and emboldened by the absence of flailing arms, hummed around their heads in droves.

It was on the afternoon of the eighth day that Tyrell and Dodds tasted meat. One of the savages had proudly appeared with a young doe slung across his shoulders. Without a word he had let the animal fall, and motionless as the surrounding trees, remained standing whilst his kinsmen butchered the carcass with flaked, stone blades and Dodds' long knife, all the while muttering their thanks to the generous beast.

Earlier that day they had skirted the edge of large clearings of cultivation and had heard the hot breeze rustling through the ranks of ripening maize like a child's shaken rattle. The high-pitched laughter and squeals of children playing in the distance had drawn them closer. The unmistakable sound of women's voices had sent a ripple of carnal eagerness coursing through the band. Like the fingers of a malevolent hand they had begun to fan out, intent on mischief, whatever the cost. With barely contained fury, Tidesso and the older tribesman had rushed ahead and turned them around. Back towards the trees they petulantly moved, to take out their resentment on Tyrell and Dodds with kicks and buffeting. It was then that the tribesman with the slain deer had arrived and, much to their relief, their torments were suspended at the imminent prospect of fresh meat.

Back in the depth of the forest, all welcomed the kindling of the first fire. Both captives were so ravenous that they eyed the meat like worm-riddled dogs, hoping that a piece would be earmarked for them, not caring if it be mostly gristle and bone - anything to break the tedium of the leaden mush. The pieces of venison were placed on the doe's own spread skin, and there they lay gathering flies until the standing hunter had consumed the raw heart and liver. Then the war-captain, Tidesso, rose and with a javelin as sceptre, a hand over his eyes so that none could accuse him of favouring one above another, pointed out which gobbet of meat was destined for which mouth. Over the flames the skewered hunks were suspended, and when barely singed, were crammed down eager gullets, with only the most cursory chewing.

After an age of exclusion, where the savoury aromas subjected them to yet more exquisite torments, both captives were relieved to see the one with big ears toss them over a single yard length of slippery intestine. He guffawed as the snake-like morsel purposely landed short, becoming garnished with rotting leaves, pine-needles and bark in the process; and as Tyrell and Dodds banged heads in their wrist-bound scrambling and tugging, he laughed aloud until censured with a grunt from the leader. As if in the most casual of afterthoughts, their bonds were released, both men nearly crying out with the agonising surge of the unrestricted blood flow. Again the big-eared one slapped his greasy thighs with laughter as the barely singed piece of gut slipped from their clumsy fumblings. Afterwards, when the bonds were again replaced, they were much loosened, a luxury for which they were both grateful.

The general mood perceptibly lightened. A sliver of whispered conversation and hushed chuckling insinuated its way between the gnaw and snap of feeding. Tyrell tentatively tried whispering to Dodds, but the older man's eyes spelt danger; and on turning round, Tyrell saw one of the savages shake his head and raise a club as warning. They contented themselves with silently savouring the respite, however brief it was destined to be, hoping that some other crumb of comfort might soon pass their way

"That was funny. Did you see the Wobigen eating the piece of gut - their noses were pressed together like a couple of beaver making heat."

"Yes, Wadawagwa, we all of us saw it. It was very funny, but is that reason enough to make so much sound? If the people of the Nipmuck are near and they have heard your laughter, they would want to join us for the feast - and if I'd let you go ahead and take their women, they'd be roasting us by now."

A residue of irritation was apparent in the otherwise easy tone of Tidesso.

"Ha, they would be thanking us for planting little Pennacooks in their women's bellies. Besides, the Nipmuck are few; we would have been doing them a service."

Wadawagwa waited for the flutter of amusement to subside before continuing the airing of his thoughts.

"I wish I had my woman here now."

A hush ensued, on some faces a barely concealed flicker of youthful envy. Wadawagwa was the only member of the band to boast a wife. His boastings continued. "I'd make such heat with her that flames would burst from her crack! It would take my mind off my belly, which, by the way, still rumbles with hunger. Such a small deer."

"Ha, would you set fire to the forest with your mating and send words of smoke up into the sky to say to the Nipmuck... 'Here we are Nipmuck. Here are the Pennacooks, the True people... we are but small in number here in the midst of your lands. Come and be our friends, gentle Nipmuck.' Do not forget, we are a war band in these lands. We are here for trophies and prisoners. I know that the great Cautantowit has smiled upon us so far in delivering these pale - skinned ones and their thunder-makers unto us, but I want more than this. My dream-picture has told me that there will be more. It has told me that in a handful of sleeps we will pay the Cowasuck a surprise visit and with our broad smiles and war-clubs entice some of their women back with us. All know that Cowasuck women are more pleasing to behold than the women of the Nipmuck."

A long silence followed whilst all, still on haunches, either sucked stubborn meat fibres from teeth, rubbed greased fingers on skin and breech-clouts, or simply stared into the forest, gripping their bows and clubs tightly.

Mateguas, the young man who had slain the deer, broke the silence with a grunt. "I too have seen the sign of other ones, Tidesso. I think these ones are more fierce than Nipmucks, though. When I stalked the deer, its spoor led me down to a big piece of water. I slew it there, then I saw many beached canoes, cumbersome dugouts from the south country." Mateguas's hand shot to his mouth to suppress a fit of giggles. "I crept down and managed to release a few of them. I pushed them out into the lake."

He stood up, puffing out his chest. "Was I not courageous to venture there and return without these Paquatuogs seeing me?"

A murmur arose from all present. Some sprang to their feet, withdrawing arrows from quivers, fitting them to taut bowstrings.

"It is very good of you to share this knowledge with us, Mateguas." Tidesso spoke, the hushed tone of his voice masking the growing unrest that all were beginning to feel. "Paquatuogs? Why did you not reveal it sooner?"

"I did not wish to spoil your digestion of such sweet meat."

The savage youth's smile vanished. Any hopes he may have had of them appreciating his jest disappeared also. The sudden rise of Tidesso's larynx as he swallowed hard was the only outward sign of his discomfort.

"It was a sweet-tasting deer, well taken. Even though it may prove to be the last flesh we partake of for many suns, it was good. And you must stay to hang the bones high in a tree so that the deer's spirit smiles upon us. Stay, then mark our shadows. See if these Paquatuogs think to follow... Join us in two suns, we go north by the big clear water, around the western edge."

Tidesso lightly touched the shoulder of Mateguas. It was a show of affection to part way ameliorate the discipline that he as leader was bound to show. The youth had expected applause to be his reward, but the prank had rebounded. The meat had been welcome, but the Paquatuogs would be this very moment looking for those who had released their canoes. All knew that the young man might never be seen again, but he had eaten the deer's heart and if his medicine was strong, then all would be well and in two days he would be amongst them once again and all would be forgotten.

The abrupt change of the capricious band's mood once again hovered, like a black-bellied cloud, above the heads of the two captives. They grinned and nodded like buffoons, as if a thousand forced smiles could somehow ward off the cloud's inevitable descent. It fell upon them in the shape of Wadawagwa, who, having readily assumed the mantle of their savage Nemesis, took obvious delight in prodding them to their feet with the inevitable razor points of arrows. As they moved swifter than ever now beneath the broad-leaf canopy of white oaks, hickory, maple and beech, it was as if by cruel example their toes had assumed the silent tread of their captors, each footfall leaving behind the scales of those they once had been, whilst by sorcery masquerading as sustenance, snakes and worms of uncertainty began to uncoil and slither deep within their bellies.

The next morning, both woke in their bed of leaves, semi-delirious, shaking with fever, and only able to move when it became certain that their skulls would be split there and then if they delayed or resisted. There was, however, some consolation. Their wrists were unbound whilst they puked and shat. They were also allowed to exchange a few brief words under the guise of incoherent babble, as if the savages considered it to be the release of the evil spirits that had caused their malaise.

"Thee 'as the same sickness? Does it burn, lad?

"Mm, it burns. I wished I were dead. Hell could be no worse. These are the Devil's spawn. Only eighteen of 'em though… Thought there was more."

"Me too. They don't look so Devilish without no paint, though."

"Did you see 'em last night though, lovingly strokin' our shipmates' hair, like they had puppy dogs on their laps. See that bastard Big Ears's still got 'is paint on. Who are they? Where are they takin' us?"

"Shush! Don't say such a thing, the Lord might deliver us yet. And don't turn around when you speak, these buggers be like fire-crackers waitin' to go off."

"Ha! God holds no dominion over this place…"

They started to move on. Dodds continued, but at a whisper. "He 'olds no dominion over 'alf of England or most lands I've set a foot on…'ere watch out, old Sail Ears is waftin' this way… give the bastard one o' your winnin' smiles, Matty, an' 'e might give us another length o' raw gut for supper."

The savage in question overtook them, hissing and grunting, lightly scoring Tyrell's arm as he stalked past. Despite his wretchedness Tyrell laughed, each burst interspersed with a wince of pain, followed immediately by a volley of uncontrollable flatulence. Wadawagwa, allowing himself a vicious grin, strode back and pricked the young man again, and again a fart ensued. He brayed like a donkey, then holding his nose between thumb and forefinger he made some pertinent comment that spread along the line, each savage's shoulders shaking as the jest was received and passed on.

"It appears our big-eared friend is a joker, Matt."

"Remind me to laugh when next he sticks me with his arrow. Anyway, I have to go again, even if he kills me."

"Go on then, behind that tree. I'll try an' keep 'im 'appy. I'll sing 'im 'Summer is a comin' in'."

Tyrell bolted from the line to relieve himself behind a tree. The affronted Wadawagwa snarled, spat out a tirade of abuse and, striding over to the tree, made ready to strike out with the flat of his bow. Dodds moved to intercept him.

Not thinking of the consequences, Dodds grabbed the end of the bow, wrenching hard, pulling the savage off balance over onto his back. Wadawagwa sprang up, hissing like a wildcat, his hand still firmly gripping the bow; and around they spun, twisting and wrenching, each trying to wrest the weapon from the grip of the other.

Within a matter of moments the savage onlookers had formed a ring of scorn and encouragement, grunting approval whenever their kinsman seemed like gaining the advantage, hissing when it seemed that Dodds gained the upper hand.

At first glance the contest would have seemed a foregone conclusion - the sun-blistered, insect-tormented captive of middle years pitted against a taller, younger man of the wilds. For most of his life, though, Dodds had been a mariner, both in Icelandic waters and lately the new found Cod banks around the 'Isle of Fogs'. Hardly a day of his thirty-nine years had passed where he had not been employed heaving on hand lines, on anchors, on sails, clambering aloft, manning the pumps, the windlass. Even splitting and salting the Stock-Fish used and honed muscles that were as much a mystery to his savage opponent as Caxton's printing press would have been.

His copper-skinned adversary, however, was more than a head taller, imbued with a different strength - strength to withstand extreme heat or cold, to paddle a canoe from dawn to dusk without once stopping, to keep following the spoor of beast or man for days on end with naught but a pouch of parched maize as sustenance. But the hand that coaxed that maize, the arm that wielded the digging stick, the fingers that plucked the ripe ears and the back that bore the load belonged to his woman, not to him. To turn his hand at that kind of labour was beneath him. His true strength lay in stealth - the stealth to give him the advantage to surprise his supper, to surprise his enemy. Having that edge was everything to him, but it hung by a tenuous thread; a whiff of death in a dream, a face-picture in a cloud formation, standing in the shadow of a menstruating woman. The catalogue of taboos was a thousand strands of doubt waiting to tangle his mind.

The adrenalin pumping through Dodds' system banished all thought of sickness. The aching left his muscles and limbs. It helped that he had grown to feel hatred for this painted man who now snarled and spat at the other end of the bow. He snarled and spat back like a bear-baiter he had 'cheered on' once in the Forest of Dean. They stood firm, staring hard, each trying to wrench the wrist of the other with a twist of the bow's limbs. The twisted sinew cord bit into the flesh of both of them.

Despite his better judgement, Dodds could not rid himself of thinking that, like a bout of arm wrestling on a cider-swilled table, once the bow had twisted sufficiently his way, he would be proclaimed the victor to the cheers of all. But it did not happen like that. The antics with the bow were just a prelude to a full-blown combat. But Dodds was not the only surprised one. Once it dawned on Wadawagwa that the Wobigen - the pale-skinned one - possessed the stronger grip, he quickly snatched a ball-headed club from an onlooker and whilst trying to extract his right hand from the bow, proceeded to clumsily cleave the intervening air with his free hand. Having made a wrong assumption once, Dodds was not about to make another mistake, and, if he could help it, he was not about to let Wadawagwa extract his wrist from the snare.

Twisting, thrashing, like a shark on a line, Wadawagwa tried to get his arm free from the bow-wood and sinew cleft. The more he thrashed, the more Dodds played him.

Even the savage throng was beginning to display an undercurrent of appreciation in Dodds' skill at both dodging the club, yet keeping his adversary ensnared, and they demonstrated it with low-pitched grunts and rumbles. Dodds, sensing that it was only a matter of time before Wadawagwa broke free, suddenly charged with him in tow. Through the ranks he hurtled, sweeping the trapped man round in a dizzy arc. Wadawagwa could not help himself from screeching out like a falling man. Snared by the right arm, which was now pulled across his chest, spinning him round, he tried his best to run backwards. His legs could not keep up and his body was tipped back, head first, unable to see the looming tree. Skilfully judging the exact moment, Dodds let his end of the bow loose. Wadawagwa was catapulted into the trunk of a hickory with a head-cracking thud.

Suddenly it was quiet but for the sound of Dodds' heaving lungs and the dissenting screak of a single crow vacating the upper boughs. All eyes were on the crumpled heap of Wadawagwa. The heap groaned and stirred. The eyes sprang open, bloodshot pink in the smudged band of red and black paint. The bruised, bloody head slowly turned, taking in the scene, the expression in the eyes one of bewilderment, until, alighting on the ridiculous, naked figure of Dodds they narrowed and blazed with hatred. An arm prised itself from under the twisted torso. All eyes were drawn to the club. Crab-like, the fingers clawed at it, caressed it, then, grasping the haft in a knuckle-whitened grip, the body shuddered and in the blink of an eye, was on its feet.

From the savage ring there was an enlivened rumble of throats. Furiously, Dodds snatched at one of the onlookers' clubs. It was snatched away even before his hand made contact. He stared into the hard, black eyes of the next man. They revealed nothing, neither enmity nor succour, but as he reached for the man's club, it too was withdrawn from his touch and like a leper begging to be let in the city gates he had his answer.

"Come on then, thee gurt big bastard. I'll show 'ee!"

He spun round shouting, his body instinctively assuming the pose of the wrestler with arms and legs akimbo, knees bent, ready to spring.

"Come on then. You wan' some more attention, do you?"

His adversary was prowling the other end of the ring, mumbling to the gathering, raising a few nods and grunts of encouragement, occasionally swinging the club in a windmill arc. Not once during this performance did he deign to look at Dodds.

"Come on then, Big ears, wha's a matter wiv' you?" Dodds was becoming unnerved by the wait, his voice rising in frustration. "Come on then!"

It was then that Wadawagwa turned and faced him full on. Once again the eyes glared with contempt and Dodds braced himself for the rush. It did not come as expected. Wadawagwa leered maliciously, said something loud to his companions and pointed with his club at the bare loins of the naked Dodds. The laughter was deafening, Dodds looked down at the object of their amusement and derision. Not even when pissing over the side in an Icelandic gale had he known his member become so shrivelled; he could barely see it over his belly. He felt betrayed, as if by his closest friend. Instinctively, one of his hands darted down to cover himself and the jeering rose again. The earlier flash of exhilaration that Dodds had experienced was now exhausted and to the stranglehold of fear was added humiliation. He began to feel vanquished even before the final bout had begun and to his further torment, the nag of sickness rumbled in his bowels and loudly announced its intention of returning.

"Ha! See this insignificant creature with the snail that retreats into its shell announces his presence with a fart. This is fortunate. How else would I see him to crack his skull open? It saves me the trouble of looking under the stones for him."

Wadawagwa threw his head back in a scoff, made as if to pounce, but again the rush did not come. Something strange revealed itself in his eyes. One moment they burned with contempt and supreme confidence, the next they looked completely mystified, the pupils jerking as if a hornet buzzed inside the skull. Sensing something was wrong, Dodds took a step forward. But Wadawagwa did not seem to notice. Instead he appeared to be trying to focus on something way in the distance, as if the wall of trees was no longer there and he was able to gaze across an open plain. Even the crows were silent as all present watched and waited. The eyes of the savage seemed to suddenly make contact with something of great import. The expression of bewilderment was wiped away, then they flickered and closed. All saw the club fall from his hand and then both hands rose to hold his head. For a moment he staggered, knees bent, as if taking the first shuffling steps of a dance, then over he toppled, hitting the ground with a loud thud.

Confused laughter arose and then a communal groan, followed by a brief but angry murmur, then all was still once more. Was it a jest? Wadawagwa often played tricks, he was well known for being a trickster... Soon he will spring up and from his club will drip the brains of the captive. Wadawagwa lay still. His mouth was full of dirt. For a handful of leaden moments all stared down at the fallen man. At first the body did not stir, but when it became apparent that breath still entered it, a great sigh of relief issued from the tribesmen.

Tidesso was the first to move. Stooping beside Wadawagwa, he heaved the fallen man over onto his back. The expression on the unconscious face was one of the utmost contentment.

"Pha! I think he dreams of mounting his woman."

An irritable leader shook his own head, then brusquely pinched the fallen man's cheeks. The expression changed to one of bewilderment before reverting to one of serenity, but still he remained unconscious.

"You laughed when I said that there was more to these Wobigen than first meets the eye." Looking up, the frustration barely concealed, Tidesso addressed the others. "I think that when he wakes he will see the sense in my words."

"Yes... when he wakes. But that might be a long time... or maybe never."

Managnon spoke. "Do we wait or carry him with us?"

Tidesso gazed upwards through the gap in the trees, as if searching for some divine clue in the cloud pattern. He finally spoke, with his face still upturned. "We'll stop here and eat and cut saplings. If he still sleeps, we'll carry him."

"And what of these two?" It was Managnon again. "What of this one who caused this?"

"It's simple. If Wadawagwa dies, then, when we get home, the hairy-mouthed one with the bare head follows his shadow into the sunset, but his journey would take longer. Much longer."

The young war-captain paced around. He was plainly agitated by events and did not attempt to rest with the others. Instead, he strung his bow and vanished without a word. He knew that, not far away, two trails converged. It was always best to go ahead and check such places. Maybe he would catch a glimpse of Mateguas? It unsettled him that he had been forced to make an example of the youngest member of the band. Tyrell and Dodds became somewhat alarmed at Tidesso's disappearance. Both had the wit to understand that his voice alone had kept them alive in the first place. They sat there in the midst of a ring of solemn hostility, listening to the distant hack and twist of saplings being fashioned for a carrying device and the low chant of the oldest of the savages as he leaned over Wadawagwa, blew a dust-like substance into his nose and shook a nerve-jangling, turtle-shell rattle.

From the throat of the unconscious man came a different rattle sound. A groan of alarm spread around. Tyrell knelt up and without thinking, pushed his way to the fallen man.

"We've gotta' get him on his side. He's chokin'... Can't you hear him chokin'?"

Tyrell nudged the chanting tribesman aside. Appearing much affronted by the intrusion, he hissed like a serpent and made as if to strike with the rattle. Tyrell grabbed his own throat and mimed choking. The man, seeming to understand that Tyrell was trying to help, lowered the rattle and assisted him in prizing open Wadawagwa's jaws.

"God's breeches! Bastard's tryin' to swallow his own tongue."

"Let the bastard swallow it. Now what you gonna' do?" asked Dodds, insinuating his body next to Tyrell's.

"How in God's name do I know? I just know tha' when... er... wha's 'is name, you know, Tommy Cahill, that Irishman, fell from the mizzen, this is what we did and he was all right. Couldn't stop him chatterin'! Mind you, he had a belly full o' cider, no wonder he didn't feel a thing."

Taking a deep breath, Tyrell plunged his fingers into the gaping mouth and retrieved the slippery tongue. Then as he was rolling the savage over, a jet of puke gushed forth, narrowly missing his legs.

"Good God...Well, sing some'ing or say a prayer!" Tyrell shouted.

"Wha', ask the Lord to spare the evil bastard for our good Christian sakes?" enquired Dodds.

"Yes...Quick! Do some'ing! Sing!"

Hark and listen Gentlemen,
That be of freeborn blood,
I shall you tell of a good yeoman
His name was Robin Hood.

"Not that Sam!...Sing something spiritual tha' the good Lord himself can 'ear."

"Well he likes it. Look at him stirring they evil eyes of 'is... Maybe he's heard o' Robin Hood even in these woods?"

Dodds began to sing again. Tyrell winced. Suddenly Wadawagwa opened his eyes and sat bolt upright, his thunderous brow lending him the appearance of a sore-arsed bear, who, having been roused from a winter-long slumber, demands nothing less than the blood recompense of the ones responsible for the disturbance.

The singing stopped. Wadawagwa growled and shook his head, his face a greasy smudge of black and red daub. The badly buckled, turkey tail-feather in his scalp lock drooped over his left eye. Blowing it aside, he got to his feet and with not a single word, passed through the assembled group, like Moses through the Red Sea. Straight ahead he strode until, face to face with the returning Tidesso, he stopped and let spill a jumble of sounds from somewhere in the back of his throat.

"...Yowige, yowige.. Hai ge hai!"

It was the turn of Tidesso to look dumbfounded. Firmly grabbing Wadawagwa by the upper arm, he steered him around and guided him back to the now standing group. Wadawagwa was still mumbling. Everyone looked askance at him, as if he displayed some hitherto unknown secret.

"What words are these? They are not the words of the true people. We do not speak words this way, from the back of the throat, like an old man trying to clear the damp from his lungs. This is the talk of enemies. How did this thing happen?"

"It is not the speech of our people, it is the speech of the flint people, the Maquaks," said Alaskana.

Some immediately nodded assent, while others shook their heads in disbelief. Tidesso shuddered; a look of distaste spread across his face, followed by a fleeting look of fear. The Maquaks, the eaters of human flesh, were a fierce and numerous people, aligned with four other strong tribes, who called themselves the Hodenasaunee, the people of the longhouse. It was these Maquaks who, in the time of the grandfather's fathers, had moved into the good flint lands across the Big Long Water, far to the west. They organised big war bands that roamed further than the men of other nations in search of plunder and prisoners to take back to their longhouses, to torture and eat. All knew, though none of the 'true people' cared to admit it, that the Maquaks were the main reason why they now lived further to the north, away from the 'place of many flints'.

"The Maquaks! Yes, I thought it was. How could this be? What sorcery is this? When did he awaken? How was it done?"

"It was the young, curly Wobigen. He put his hand down Wadawagwa's throat, made him empty his belly. Then the other one sang a spirit song to him, and up he got a Maquak. It's sorcery!"

Tidesso flexed the tension in his bow and stared suspiciously at the two prisoners. He was unsure of the course to take. It was as if he hoped somehow that the strength and decisiveness of the broad hickory limbs would pass into him and the path of action would be revealed. He could not display his doubt to the others. Vacillation was not what was required. He was the chosen war-captain of this band. His vision had brought them thus far unscathed.

Were they sorcerers though, these pale-skinned ones? Would they be his undoing? He had seen their magic. The two hollow sticks that made fire and thunder were safely in his possession, as were the pouches of black seeds, the food that must be poured down the cold, hard, muzzles, pounded and ground with a rod, just like a woman pounds the corn - only then could they belch their deadly fire. And what of the ice-picture that made laughter, the Looks-Back? What would the people make of these things? Nothing like them had been seen before. His name would live in all the mouths of the people and in the mouths of the yet-to-be people. But, what if he were to slay these two hairy faces? True, he would derive a certain power from doing it, but the real worth would be much diminished. The two live pale skins were every bit as important as the booty. The triumphant return to the hearths of his people was everything. As a boy he had seen too many war band leaders take to the trails with their boasts and defiance still ringing in the lodges, only to slink silently dejected through the stockade gates, with nothing to show for their journey but the wrapped bones of their slain brethren, sometimes not even this much. And instead of feasting, pounding drums, dancing and whoops of joy, there would be the empty-bellied wailing, the slashing of thighs and fingers, the smell of singeing hair, and above all else, the shame that descended like a shroud to cover all of the people, from the youngest to the oldest. He had known disgraced leaders who had been slain or, even worse, had suffered banishment. His elder brother had been such a one. He shuddered at the memory. No, this could not be his fate, the dreams had foretold triumph. He had been singled out for greatness, the youngest war-captain any could remember. The Manitous smiled on him; Saquasis, the great Sachem, would smile also. Or had Saquasis been playing with him in so readily agreeing to this war-band, comprised only of young men? Tidesso had jumped at the chance of having his dream fulfilled; and when Alaskana had shown up two days along the trail, he had felt resentment, but now he welcomed the older man's experience. Saquasis was a cunning old weasel, but a jealous weasel; all knew it. Did he perhaps secretly desire Tidesso's failure? Tidesso was beginning to see the full import of keeping the pale ones alive. The significance was far greater than the prospect of other plunder. What were more heads, scalps, wampum, or even other captives in comparison? No, he must hasten directly to the lodges of the people and deliver up these wondrous gifts.

"Give them back their strange peltries," Tidesso heard himself command, surprised at the brusqueness of his own words. He tempered the tone. "Let them cover their fishy limbs. I said that they had hidden powers. Now all have seen and know this to be so."

He stopped fingering his bowstring and watched, nodding approval as articles of clothing were reluctantly unknotted, unwound, tugged off and flung at the feet of the prisoners.

"If it is true that they have turned Wadawagwa into a Maquak, then they have the strongest of powers. They must be coaxed into making him a whole person again. Let them look upon the light side of our faces and I'm sure that they will smile back at us."

Tidesso unslung his otter skin quiver, withdrew the score or so arrows, then from the bottom pulled a piece of protective bone and a small, flat, membraneous bundle. He unwrapped it carefully, cries of wonderment greeting the dazzling shafts of reflected sunlight that rebounded like fire-flies off faces and limbs. It was the cracked looking-glass. All who gazed into it could not help but laugh and squeal with delight at what they saw.

"Hey, Matty, that be my lookin' glass they's all gorpin' into... 'ark at 'em pissin' theyselves wiv laughter. Anyone'd think they'd bin in the Turk's 'ead all night! 'Ere, 'ow did 'e get it then? I fought I'd left it on board."

As he spoke, Dodds was trying to untangle a grease-ridden blouse that had been used, turban fashion, to adorn the head of one of the savages.

"Phew! The stink off this! I fought two monfs of guttin' fish would be bad enough, but this grease they puts on everyfing turns me belly right over. 'Ere, 'ow you feelin' Matty? Finally got rid of the shits, 'ave you?"

Tyrell was slowly pulling on a pair of sail-cloth breeches, his face screwed tight like a man walking on thin ice.

"You know who these breeches belonged to... That tosser Pugh, God rest 'im, that's who. His blood's all over 'em! Anyway, I don't feel so bad now. Things have taken my mind off it."

"And me, too... Still, I wonder wha's gonna' 'appen to us? They di'nt look too 'appy about wha' we done to their mate, did 'em?"

"Yes, I thought our time had surely come, but they seem contented enough now, don't they? Here Sam, don't look now, but they're smiling."

"I knows...It do make my flesh crawl."

"No 'tis different, I think they're trying to be friendly."

"I knows... Tha's wha' I means!"

"It was your singing that did the trick."

"Talk abou' singing, Matt...I tell you one thing that gets on my wick though."

"What?"

"These bloody chirpin' bugs! They don' ever seem to stop."

For three more days they pushed on. Two of these days were taken following part of the inlet-riddled shoreline of a huge lake, wherein lay many wooded islands. In some places the slopes reared up from the surface in great, glittering slabs of micah-speckled granite that would have dwarfed the mightiest of man-made ramparts, and from crevices and fissures spewed great, frothy gouts of white water, as if the great Mother Earth herself was offering up her milk. And everywhere there were trees, wave upon crested wave of tall, silent trees.

As they skirted the water's edge, Tyrell and Dodds were not permitted to converse other than in the briefest of whispers, though on the passing of a huge flock of pigeons, Tyrell could not contain himself and he ran flapping his arms and squawking with delight along the shallows, his din reduced to nought in the drumming of a million pairs of wings.

Much to the relief of the Pennacooks, Wadawagwa stopped speaking in the tongue of the 'eaters of men's hearts'. Alaskana, with his fifteen years seniority over the others, suddenly recalled the hazy, childhood memory of warriors returning to one of the people's towns with Maquak captives, amongst them a child with big ears that bent forward. Of course none mentioned it to Wadawagwa. It would have been very bad manners to suggest that he was once not one of the true people.

Even though Wadawagwa maintained a mask of cold indifference towards the two Wobigen, the general mood of their captors had softened. So much so that words and short phrases were addressed to them and when, with much twisting of tongues and pulling of faces, they managed to approximate the sounds, wide smiles of childlike delight were the reward.

"Pennycooks, then. Tha's what these painted babbies do be called."

Dodds beamed, nodded his head at one of the tribesmen and rolled the word around his tongue once more. "Pennycooks. Yes, I got it right...Pennycooks."

The tribesman nodded and grunted approval.

"Just so long as you don't 'ave a mind to cook us, my babby. No, don't put us in no pot, we won't taste good. We're not Frogs are we, eh Matty? No, not Frenchies. English. Tha's wha' we be. Say English... English."

Dodds banged his chest for emphasis, then pointed to himself and Matt Tyrell. "Englishmen."

"Yingeesh.. Yingeesh.. mens." It was the turn of the savage to try to wrap his tongue around the strange sounds.

"That'll do, that'll do my babby. Thas' what we are a'right Yingeeshmens an' no mistake... We'll soon 'ave you speakin' Yingeesh. Jus' like King Dick 'iself."

It was the early afternoon of the eighth day of captivity. The tribesmen had not intended to stop, but a large, bony, snouted fish, the length of a man, had been skewered through the brain with a well-placed javelin, cast as it basked in the shallows. Not wanting to offend the fish's spirit by not partaking of its flesh, Tidesso allowed a small fire to be kindled; and like the fat dribbling into the flames, the melting cheer bubbled and spluttered inside each man's belly. Soon not a scrap remained and on a thin neck of beach they lay replete, dozing like dogs.

Suddenly a cry of pain and surprise erupted from amongst the gathering. There was much commotion, with shouts ringing out from the wooded slope that rose steeply behind them. The time for small talk and smiles vanished as Tyrell and Dodds were roughly grabbed and pushed down behind a large boulder. They had the sense not to protest, realizing that something very serious was afoot.

The unmistakable 'zip...zip' of arrows in flight followed. Heads down, they hugged the cold, damp sand of the shadows as overhead, shaft after shaft banged and clattered into the rock, showering them with splinters of bone and chert.

Around them they heard the comforting twang of twisted sinew as the Pennacooks began to return shaft for shaft. They heard also the jeering insults and whoops of triumph that swooped down between the trees, only to be reciprocated by like sounds from the Pennacooks. Only one, much repeated word, stayed with the two Englishmen - the word was 'Paquatuog'. They had heard it after the first volley, and the word had been accompanied with a sense of distaste and dread.

It was not until they were sprayed with blood belonging to Alaskana, that they began to grasp the full seriousness of the situation. The older tribesman had taken an arrow in the thigh, and by the amount of blood that gushed out, it appeared to have struck an artery. Alaskana sat in the sand beside them, just staring at the fountain of blood that spurted from him, not making any attempt to staunch the flow, just staring and singing in an eerie dissonance that set the already taught nerves of the two captives jangling like frayed tipple strings.

Dodds and Tyrell looked on in horror.

"The bugger's blood is drainin' away faster 'n a ship wiv an 'ole, an' all 'e can do is sing like a witch wiv a besom stuck up 'er arse... 'ere Matt, your good wiv' a bo'n'arrow. Use 'is while I throttle 'is leg."

Dodds wrapped his shirt around the wounded man's thigh, then breaking the arrow shaft, he used it to twist and tighten the fabric. Tyrell, meanwhile, was scanning the lay of the land. Immediately ahead was a slope of ferns and between fifty to a hundred paces up the slope began the trees. He loosed three shafts. The first was inept and made him cringe, the second was clumsily sent too high, but the third was well placed, keeping to his chosen course. Though he glimpsed the fleeting shapes of human figures way up the slope, he concentrated on aiming at a single tree and seeing how the strange bow reacted to his handling. It was a little shorter than the yew bows he was used to, but wider and flatter too, with a slight recurve towards the tips of the limbs and a greater kick. He had noted that none of the savages pulled their shafts all the way back to the ear as English archers were wont to do, but rather seemed to snatch it to their lips - with the bow canted almost horizontally - letting fly with the briefest of aims. He saw why. They drew their arrows between thumb and forefinger with only the middle finger hooked on the string, much like a child's grip, yet it seemed to serve them well enough. Although not even half the draw weight of an English yew bow, nonetheless the bow was more powerful than he had at first imagined. It was no child's plaything. It vibrated like a wild serpent in his hand, the string marking his wrist with its powerful lash. It confirmed his earlier doubt that if these savages had had a mind to slay himself and Dodds as they ran by the seashore, nothing could have stopped them.

None of the shafts struck the tree, but the third one came within a hair's breadth. Despite hardly holding a bow for over a year, his aim was returning, even though the fingertips of his right hand were throbbing with pain. It became obvious to Tyrell that the attackers, whoever they might be, had by far the best advantage. They had gravity on their side, allowing their arrows greater range, the trees to hide behind, and as time wore on, the sun would prove to be an even greater ally by dazzling those below.

He was no soldier, but he saw clearly that they were skilfully trapped. Cursing with frustration more than fear, he loosed another shaft up the slope, but not waiting to mark the arrow's flight, he immediately ducked down behind the bank, sucked the red weal on his arm and smiled with perverse satisfaction as an answering missile cleft the space that his head had just vacated. Part of him quaked, but the greater part of him was beginning to enjoy this fight more than he imagined possible. He began to hum softly to himself.

"Paquatuogs!" spat Tidesso. Mateguas had not been mistaken. What were the Destroyers doing this far north?

He retrieved another of the hawk-fletched missiles from the sand at his feet. Its shaft, though heavier and shorter by a finger's length than those of the Pennacooks, was nevertheless nocked and sent in a high arc to clatter among the distant branches.

"Why are you here?... Are you lost? You Paquatuog fish shits make arrows fit for children. Come nearer. We'll show you what a real arrow looks like."

He knew that his words would not be understood by the Paquatuogs, as the Pennacooks in turn did not understand the insults that were shrieked down at them. Though the two tribes had once long ago shared the same tongue, neither side was aware of it. The insults were done more for his own benefit and for that of his followers. He had made a grave error in stopping to build a fire in this place when there had been signs of others spotted. He should have pressed on till dusk, but the fish spirit had demanded that its flesh be eaten. Some, Managnon included, had mumbled dissent, whilst he in his mantle of confidence had brushed it aside. Now the Manitous mocked him for his careless assumptions.

"Do not lurk in the trees like sparrows, Paquatuogs. Come out into the sunshine and fight."

Tidesso knew full well that if the roles were reversed and it was he that commanded the high ground, he would not budge, certainly not until the sun had moved sufficiently for them to rush down, aided by its dazzle. But staying put in his present position was more than he could bear. He had to do something, or by the time the Paquatuog rush came, his band would have already sung their death songs. He signalled Managnon to his side.

"The Destroyers... They are a long way from their own hearths. Do they smoke with the Nipmuck, now? Or are they on a raid like ourselves?

Managnon shrugged his shoulders and loosed an arrow.

"How many do we face?" Tidesso asked, without taking his eyes off the slope.

"It's hard to say, they are well hidden, but I have counted no more than three hands full of arrows in a flock - that is when they want to impress us."

"Yes, I have counted also... There could be fewer of them than our people."

"Yes, but they have the high ground and they must have a lot of shafts in their quivers, I think they are but a few, keeping us here until others join them, then they will come sweeping down ."

"It is bad for us if they have made allegiance with the Nipmuck."

They heard the angry hum and dived for cover. From the bank they counted the volley that sprouted like reeds in the wet sand.

"The same number...We could send some of our people up there and round the back of them." Tidesso pointed to the steep, rocky crags that rose either side of the wooded slope. He shook his head, however, when the true logistics began to unfold.

"No, it would take a long while to get them in position and if, in the meanwhile, the Paquatuogs came down on us or more of their warriors arrived, we would be split in two, with one half unable to help the other."

"We could become like the big fish we caught and swim to one of the islands," sneered Managnon.

"Becoming a fish was not part of my dream."

"Was stopping to eat one?"

Sensing the others' irritation, Tidesso knew he must act. Spurning the use of the Paquatuog arrows, he withdrew one of his own. He kissed the duck feather flights, whispered to the chert tip and nocked it. Then scrambling onto a boulder, he started to ascend the slope of ferns. Immediately arrows began to spit from the trees across the fifty or so paces of open ground. Jumping high, twisting then bobbing low like a Commoco spirit-dancer, he dodged the angry missiles and from amongst the ferns hooted like a loon. From the trees furious insults echoed, but even so the voices were slowly withdrawing. Onto the slope sprang a handful of the Pennacooks and with them a surprised-looking Matthew Tyrell - once again his legs had dictated his actions.

Upwards they scrambled, whooping, weaving, spurred on by the example of their leader, who had by now reached the first line of trees. Tyrell brought up the rear, clambering and cursing like a drunken sailor on a rolling deck, a wisp of smoke marking his upward progress.

"Light , damn you, light."

In his right hand he held a smouldering fire-brand. Cradled diagonally across his left arm was one of the cumbersome matchlocks. He paid no heed to the arrows that zipped around him, but puffed on the brand and fumbled furiously with the serpentine. If the taper refused to light, he would have no option other than to open the pan, thus exposing the priming, and when the moment came, apply the smouldering stick and hope that the powder had not also been spoiled.

It had been Dodds' idea. He had known exactly who had the guns and where to locate the brass powder flask. Unfortunately he had not been able to find the lead balls - some of which had been beaten flat into ear pendants - and instead had rammed home a handful of small pebbles. Tyrell was unaware of the ammunition's shortcomings when the gun was thrust in his hands, and he found himself being borne along by the general enthusiasm. He was also unaware that Dodds had poured a more than generous portion of black powder down the barrel.

"Did you ram her tight, Sam?" was all Tyrell had asked.

"Tighter 'n a mermaid's twat, Matt," was the chuckled reply, and up the bank he'd clambered.

Tidesso and the rest of the Pennacook advance party had by now disappeared into the trees, where their shrieks and taunts marked the progress of their apparently advantageous assault. Tyrell finally reached the trees. Suddenly all was deathly quiet.

"Hold on, lads, I'll be right wi' you," Tyrell had called.

"I think it's gonna' be alri..."

Hurtling past him, in a shrieking blur, came Tidesso and the others.

"Hey, wait a mom...ent."

A deafening roar like a tidal wave rose above him, and down between the trees poured a whooping swarm of Paquatuogs.

Struggling like a man trying to land a huge fish, Tyrell raised the long barrel, lodged it on the charred stump of a tree, and flicking open the priming pan, rammed home the smouldering stick.

It seemed to take a lifetime from the initial puff of smoke and the shower of yellow-blue sparks that rose like a genie from the priming pan to the thunder crack of the main charge.

There was a time gap where it seemed the wayward priming, like some prodigal infant's return, had somehow lost its way into the touch hole and in that slip, a horrified Tyrell saw the look of uncertainty flash across a dozen or more grotesquely tattooed faces. Then came the blast and the hammer blow to the shoulder and two of the screaming faces completely disintegrated in a froth of blood, flesh and bone. Tyrell had only the faintest knowledge of this as he flew backwards down the slope and tumbled like a rag doll in the bludgeoning recoil.

CHAPTER 4
A Broken Gun

Mathew Tyrell tried to sit up, but the pain in his right shoulder sent him sprawling backwards with a curse. He could hear blood-chilling screams echoing in the woods above, but he could not fathom their meaning, or his part, if any, in their significance. It was a piece of still-smouldering wadding that started the chain of recollection whirring in his brain, and in a flash, despite the bruised shoulder, he sprang to his feet. Where on God's earth was Dodds? What the devil did he put down the barrel of that firepiece to make it kick so? 'Oh no! Damn it to hell!' In the grass, ten paces from him, he spied the gun. He saw, too, the end of the barrel, the fingers of jagged metal splayed out like the petals of a 'piss-a-bed' dandelion. Lurching towards it his legs buckled, sending him sprawling. In horror he turned over on his back and with the left hand began exploring his own body for any hurts that his befuddled brain could have overlooked. He had witnessed handguns explode before, twice resulting in the death of the shootist. At the very least it meant disablement of some kind, but here he was, by all accounts, whole but for a badly bruised shoulder. It took a painful effort, but he managed to bless himself with his right hand and give thanks unto Christ for his deliverance.

From up in the woods urgent whoops of fury alerted him to the fact that danger still lurked. Once more he found his feet and peered all around.

"Come on, Sam Dodds, where the Devil are you?" he hissed with impatience and pounded a fist into an open palm.

Down the slope at the water's edge he could see the prone figure of the wounded Alaskana. The man lay still as death. A large, crimson blossom stained the sand beneath his tourniquet-bound leg. He felt a twinge of panic. Had they all gone off, leaving him for dead? No, Sam Dodds wouldn't do such a thing, not unless he had no choice in the matter. A sharp report, way up amongst the trees, startled him. He stood frozen, and then from above came cries of both triumph and pain. 'So, Sam, you be up there somewhere, showing them painted devils the sting of hellfire and brimstone. I only hope you put less of a clout in your piece than you did in mine.'

Rubbing his shoulder, Tyrell began to trace his earlier steps up the slope to the trees, picking up the broken gun as he went. The stock had also split in two. The pieces of exposed wood lay white like freshly-splintered bone. It was a miracle he had not been badly maimed. Breathing in deeply the mix of sulphur and pine resin, he stood amongst the first line of trees in the same spot where he had finally managed to ignite the powder. The blast had sent him back nigh twenty paces. In disgust he flung the ruined gun at a tree stump, but realising that he had no weapon, and that even a disabled gun would serve as a club, he strode to retrieve it.

It took a handful of seconds before Tyrell realized that the fly-blown bundle of sticks nearby was the faceless body of a Paquatuog warrior. The man's torso was wrapped in an armour of wooden rods, bound by strips of rawhide. Even so, the body was pierced by at least a dozen Pennacook arrows. Not far away lay a similar, armoured figure - half this man's head was missing. Tyrell looked at the tattooed half-face, turned away, then looked back again. It all came back to him then - the charging savages, the flash, the boom, the faces that were screaming one moment, then the next had disintegrated. He had done this thing, snuffed out the life of two human beings. He prodded one of the bodies, as if disbelieving any action he was capable of could result in such a finality. He had never slain a human creature before, yet here lay two men, as dead as any fish, their spark snuffed out by a brimstone spark of his making. He found himself mouthing a prayer, but before the prayer was ended, he felt a surge of exhilaration. He had survived. He had won. These savage heathens would have cut him to pieces had their stride been swifter than his reluctant priming, but he had slain them first. In truth they were not his enemies. If any should be considered enemy it would have to be his captors, the killers of his shipmates, who deserved that particular epithet. But in these lost days since the massacre, he had witnessed many things. He had seen behind the painted masks; the bonds from his wrists had been cut, he had been smiled upon and smiled back with a full heart and his belly had been filled no less full than their own. The memory of the sweet, smoky flesh of the giant fish still graced his palate. Try as he might, he could no longer look upon them as just enemies. The decision to fight and kill for his captors was an act of self preservation, pure and simple, though he preferred to see it as the will of God - his pathway to deliverance. Yes, it was a victory for Christ over the powers of darkness, no less.

Making no attempt to stifle the cry of triumph that roared beast-like from his own throat, he bounded between the pines, swiping at each trunk with the gun, revelling in the musical ring that emanated. Suddenly seeing movement, he lunged towards the nearest tree, standing shoulder-on so that the slim trunk afforded a semblance of concealment. The feeling of carefree jubilation evaporated, leaving him shaking, his mind racing furiously. How had he let himself become so careless, so foolish? If these were the Paquatuogs approaching, the enemies of his captors, what were the choices? He could run back down the slope and maybe lurk in the reedy shallows, but then what? It would only prolong the inevitable. He had seen how well these savages followed the slightest spoor. There was no other choice. It would have to be a dash or certain death.

A dry stick snapped to the right - closer than he expected. He tried to mould himself to the tree. Voices whispered. He braced himself for the run, but a clink of metal against metal held him back. That sound could only come from the other gun. A throaty chuckle confirmed that whoever they were, Dodds was amongst them and, by the sound of it, in excellent humour.

Grinning wide, Tyrell jumped from behind the tree. He realised his mistake too late as an arrow hummed and clattered into the broken gun barrel, knocking it from his grasp.

"Steady there, Matty! These buggers be right jumpy. They got the taste for blood on 'em."

Wadawagwa rushed forward, brushing past him as if he were part of the undergrowth. It had been his shaft that had hit the gun. He growled and shook the retrieved arrow under Tyrell's nose, as if he held Tyrell responsible for its shattered point. Tyrell braced himself for a jab, but it did not come. Instead, muttering something under his breath, Wadawagwa strode off down the slope. Tyrell noticed that his body bore many bloody lacerations. In fact, as his eyes swept the others, all seemed to have wounds of some degree or other, though none seemed disabled or unduly concerned by them.

Dodds chuckled and spoke, "Don't turn your back on 'im for a while. 'E be right pissed off tha' 'e ain't taken no 'air. I be alright mind," Dodds patted his bald pate, "but I seen 'im lookin' at your top-not afore an' lickin' 'is lips, so I 'ave."

"What happened up there? Did we win? I heard your piece goin' off... Not as loud as this'n though!"

Tyrell held up the broken gun and before Dodds had a chance to reply, the Pennacooks had surged forward to probe and examine the damaged weapon.

"What did you put down the barrel to make it blossom so? It's a wonder my head wasn't blown off like them other two."

Dodds just grinned and watched from the side as Tyrell was playfully jostled and patted by the tribesmen. Tyrell felt great relief and was soon laughing and singing with the others as the broken gun, like a sacred relic, was passed from one to the other. It was not until they had returned to the beach, and the mood had become sombre as the Pennacooks gathered around their dying comrade, that he became aware of the sticky offering that had been pushed into his open shirt. As he opened his mouth wide, it was Dodds' firm grip on his arm that stopped the shriek from spilling forth.

"'Tis hair! Hair and skin... Why? What?"

Tyrell pulled the bloody scalp lock from his shirt. Dodds grabbed it from him before it fell to the ground.

"Don't you see, Matt? 'Tis an 'onour. This be the top-not of one o' they Peapods you killed. Don't let 'em see you chuck it away. 'Specially Wadawada... Big-Ears... whatever 'is name is. 'E be mad enough as 't is."

"But I don't care to have it. Don't you understand? Have you forgotten already that they have the hair of our shipmates stretched on hoops."

His voice rose. Dodds looked down at the water's edge and, grinning at the staring Pennacooks, spoke from the corner of his mouth. "If you don't take the friggin thing, Mathew Tyrell, I swear I shall box you so 'ard tha' you sleeps through to the next sabbath - whenever that may be! There be no place 'ere for any fancy ways. I can't write my name like you, but I knows 'ow to read faces and them there faces

73

need to be kept smiling at us, 'cause I just seen what they done up there to the poor bugger they caught alive."

"What do you mean? Did they torture one of them to death?"

"Not exactly. 'E be still breavin' like, an' walkin around up there." Dodds turned, grinned and waved to the tribesmen.

"Well, what then?"

"Well most of the Peapods disappeared. Got away... Seems tha' your little thunderclap knocked the fight out of 'em. Anyway tha' head fella friend of yours, the one wiv my lookin' glass, 'e got a couple, bewtful shots they wus too, one got 'it right frew the neck... Oh, and a couple more got some, about five dead... 'course I din't 'it any, though I makes a gurt noise an' lots a' smoke, an' clips off a branch or two, right onto the 'ead of a scamperin' savage. Anyway this 'ere babby was pretendin' to be dead, makin' a good job of it to, 'e 'ad I fooled, standin' on top o' the bugger I was - but not our Pennycooks. Oh no, by jove! They coaxes 'im up like, an' they asks 'im one or two questions like... Don' ask me what, though... And 'e were answering 'em, right cheerful too it seemed, then they starts to cut off all his fingers, one by one, 'til all 'e 'as left is stumps. They be joshin' an jokin wiv 'im, an' 'e be singin' an' larfin' mind whilst this be goin' on, tha' is until they cuts out 'is tongue and pops 'is eyeballs! They left 'im 'is ears though, no doubt out of the kindness of their 'eathen 'earts."

Tyrell shook his head with disbelief.

"What! His eyes! All his fingers! Dear God!"

"Oh, I forgot, they cut off the end of 'is pizzen! 'es most likely bled to deaf now... Like you said yourself, Matt, God holds no dominion over this land."

"Sweet Jesus! What next?"

"Come on, lad, pull yourself together. I seen worse things 'appen on Saint Michael's Hill. Do you mean to tell me tha' you ain't never seen a burnin' or an 'angin, drawin' an' quarterin' afore! Pha! They only lets you dangle for a moment or two, then down you comes an' they slits you up the belly like a pollock 'Ere you don't mean to tell me tha' tha' don't 'urt? D'you think they waits for you to die first, do you?"

"Yes, but that's different, they be heretics, traitors, murderers, witches and the suchlike."

"Yes, well, I seen what our own boys done to they Hanse bastards. They drove us from the waters of Iceland, but not wivout a fight, mind. One o' they ships, a gurt big three master, don't forget, this be only ten year ago, an' we still be sloppin about in a cog, no match for their fancy thing. Anyways, up out o' the fog comes this gurt biggun and rams us full on. Well, I never seen men move so friggin' fast - warmest I was all friggin' trip! Well, in a flash we be all over tha' gurt ship like bluebottles on a piemakers turd! They just weren't hexpectin' tha, they must 'ave fought that we'd just slip to the bottom nice an' peaceful like." Tyrell looked impatiently at Dodds. "Anyways, tha' ship now be's a Bristol ship, the Matildal. 'Course, along wiv 'er name, she's changed 'er appearance a little. Anyways, wha' I be sayin' is tha' not one o' they Hansards lived, an' their passin' din't go easy eiver. We be usin' they fingertips as bait for a week."

"Get away with you, the Matilda...? Fingers...? I don't believe that," said Tyrell, the beginnings of a smile tugging at the corners of his mouth.

"'Tis God's 'onest truth... 'course we 'ad to pull the fingernails out first, on account of it not bein' to the fishes' likin'.

"Yes, yes, yes... I know. Alright, give me the accursed thing."

Dodds smiled and handed Tyrell the hair.

"Give 'em a whoop an' a wave, Matt. They don't look to be too 'appy now."

"Call them down, Managnon!" Tidesso spoke, a hint of desperation in his voice. "There might be something they can do for Alaskana. He has lost much blood, but maybe it is possible to save him yet, although I think he joined this warband to die."

All knew that ever since his wife and son were taken by the Pasmaquoddy two summers ago, Alaskana had clamoured to be included in every raiding party. Not all would take him, saying he was getting too old for the long, hard travel, but until the arrow struck him, his pace had never once wavered on this journey.

Managnon climbed the bank and beckoned Tyrell and Dodds down.

"They come now, Tidesso. You know that we must leave this place. Now that the Destroyers and those of The-Great-Blue-Hill have exchanged the black wampum belts, we are squeezed in the middle. We must get back and warn our people."

"I hear the truth in your words before they leave your tongue, but what would you have me do - leave Alaskana here?"

"No, but if we do not leave this place now, we may never leave, and our bones will be picked clean by the fishes. I do not wish to greet the spirits of my ancestors as a fish! Even though my given name is that of a fish."

"Some fish are very intelligent. They speak to me sometimes in my dreams"

"Yes, they know when to seek the shadows at the approach of death."

"Managnon! All of you! If there is nothing to be done for Alaskana, then so be it. We are gone from this place, but we take him with us if there is a chance he might live. The two Wobigen - it is possible that they have the power to make him live. I do not have to remind you of the power of their thunder weapons and I think you know now that if it were not for these things making the fear grow in the hearts of our enemies, then we could all be strewn around here, like fallen ears of maize."

To everyone's astonishment, Wadawagwa cleared his throat and spoke, the first time he had properly addressed the band since he and Dodds had fought. All listened intensely, expecting him to break into the abrasive, Maquak speech at any moment.

"All that you say is true, Tidesso, but the memory of fear is short and our enemies are many. They will come for us now as long as we dawdle in these lands, even unto the palisades of our town they will come. Do not forget that one of these thunder sticks lies broken, as useless as a bow without a string. I say they are wizards and if Alaskana dies, they should die too." There was a murmur of assent from some of those present.

Tidesso held up his hand. "No! I say no! Your eyes are clouded with hatred and sorrow. The great Saquasis will decide what shall be done with them when we return."

With a look of disgust, Wadawagwa pushed through the throng and proceeded to noisily empty his bladder into the lake.

Tyrell and Dodds came rushing down in a cloud of debris. Guessing why they had been summoned, both crouched over the fallen man. Much to Dodds' surprise, the tourniquet appeared to have been loosened by the injured man himself.

"T'aint no use. Why did 'e do such a thing? Might 'ave stood a chance if 'e'd left it alone, but not now... No, 'e 'ave less blood 'n a fimble in 'im."

Dodds shook his head in disbelief. "This 'un's gone an' killed 'isself plain an' simple," he added.

Standing up, he shook his head. "There be nuffin' I can do... not one earfly thing... Shame, just when I were gettin' to know 'im an all."

Guessing by the tone of his words and the language of his hands, the group of savages seemed to slump as one; and when, a few minutes later, Alaskana finally died, they all commenced a great wailing that sent Tyrell and Dodds to the shade of a boulder to watch and wait.

Each tribesman added further to the lacerations that already criss-crossed their bodies, then all submerged themselves and the dead man in the shallows. Finally, they bound the washed body of Alaskana in his skin sleeping robe and once more struck up an eerie chanting. It was during this obeisance that Tyrell committed an act of stupidity that very nearly cost him his life. Without thinking, he flung the broken matchlock out into the lake. At first, the loud splash did nothing to halt the dirge. Tyrell had turned his back to the water and was walking back up the beach, when he noticed the look of dread in Dodds' eyes. He realised then that the chanting had stopped and in its place a single cry of rage resounded, but before he could look round, a heavy pain between his shoulders sent him sprawling. He was conscious then of a man's weight astride his back, forcing all the breath from his body. Grit and sand were in his mouth and eyes, a hand grabbed his hair and tugged his head back, until he felt that his neck would snap.

"Godamn...! What?"

The two words were all he managed to spit out before the look of horror in Dodds' eyes silenced him. And then, from somewhere behind, came a barked command, the hand made one last, angry twist, then let go of the hair, causing his head to fall forward. The weight was lifted from his back, but he remained clutching the sand, shivering with fear. Later, when he had the opportunity, Dodds told him what had happened.

"No lad, twern't tha' Big-Ears, but the one called Managnon tha' near done for thee. It were Tidesso, the leader fella, tha' stopped 'im though... I think we stays as close to 'im as we can. Don' you?"

To the two captives - for captives they felt themselves to be once more - fell the hapless task of portering the corpse. Bound to a sapling, they took wretched, retching turns holding the rear, where the swarms of bloated flies and the stench of putrefaction was greatest. Upwards they climbed into hill country. For two days it was berries and maize-mush again that was the sustenance of all, pushing on even faster than before without stopping to hunt, even though deer and moose were spied within bow shot. To their further torment, Wadawagwa had reassumed the guise of persecutor, but even he no longer prodded them with arrow tips, relying instead on his bony forefinger to chivvy them along.

On the morning of the tenth day of captivity as they descended into a wide gorge, Wadawagwa contemptuously shoved Tyrell, who in turn pushed Dodds forward, and down they skidded, dropping their foul-smelling burden in the process. The seemingly bad-tempered tribesmen surrounded them, pulling, pushing, waving clubs in their faces. Both captives sat down exhausted, resolved to go no further, even if it meant having their skulls caved in. Wadawagwa pranced and shrieked above Dodds, his club cleaving the air inches above his sun-peeled scalp. Dodds yawned, smiling weakly; then, closing his eyes, burst suddenly into song.

Softly at first as if unsure of the words and melody, but when Tyrell joined him in a haphazard harmony of third and fifth intervals combined, the tribesmen fell silent, and some, despite themselves, giggled with a strange mixture of pleasure and embarrassment.

All for the shoals of Poor-Jack
I venture the Ocean Sea .
Take this tassel from my hat
And set it in yon tree.

"Tha's right Matt, try it again... 's nice an sweet... Keep it sweet, we aint serenading seagulls."

Western winds when wilt thou blow.
The salt rain down can rain.
Christ, if my love were in my arms
And I in my bed again.

"Ere Matt, what wouldn't I give for a taste o' salt... Never mind a bed!"

CHAPTER 5
The Thunderbird

They sang many times that day, giving thanks unto their God who once again had delivered them from harm at the capricious whims of their captors. It was the two voices joined in harmony that enchanted the tribesmen, even to the point where they would take turns standing in between Tyrell and Dodds, holding their mouths lest they whooped with amazement at the wondrous effect. One of the warriors could not stop himself from joining in with a high-pitched dissonance and had to be restrained from spoiling the magic. Even the ears of Wadawagwa twitched and reddened a little as he took his turn, though his face remained impassive.

The tribesmen appreciated full well the importance of song. They had songs for every occasion; laughing songs and magical songs, secret songs they would use on waking to call back Cowwewonck (their souls) from their dream wanderings; but these strange sounds that seemed to transport the very being into another new dreamscape were truly magical.

It was a riffle of cool air blowing down off the mountains and the dull rumble of thunder way off in the distant peaks that drew a halt to the music; and soon they were splashing across the stream in the gorge bottom and up the wooded slope opposite, to come to a sticky halt beneath a large overhang of rock. Even though they appeared agitated at the inevitable approach of 'Wuchowsen', the thunderbird who flaps its great wings at the edge of the sky, something in their captors' easier manner and general deportment - the way they had allowed, even encouraged Tyrell and Dodds to sing at the top of their voices, and their obvious foreknowledge as to the whereabouts of the overhang - indicated their arrival in familiar, if not friendly territory.

Like a serpent's tongue, the lightning lashed the slate-heavy skies with silver light and above them the wings of the angry thunderbird flapped as if to crack the very rock asunder. All began chanting, pleading for deliverance, and the roof of granite moaned with their cries. Then suddenly the cacophony ceased, and each held their breath in the heavy moments of stillness before the deluge began.

When the flash and fury had moved to anoint some other valley, the spirits rose with the steam from their bodies and Tyrell and Dodds were made to sing once more to the accompanying tattoo of the rain.

For most of that day, into the mid afternoon, the rain kept up a solid downpour; and when they had exhausted their songs and it became apparent that the tribesmen had had sufficient exposure to two-part harmony, and were displaying signs of becoming inured to its spell, Dodds attempted a little conjuring - just simple sleights of hand, yet another skill that most seamen were, by tradition, expected to acquire on their long voyages, along with the dancing of hornpipes and throwing knives. The effect was startling. The tribesmen practically clambered over each other to get a better view of his palming of pebbles, groaning with a mixture of pain and delight as he seemingly rammed them in his ear, only to spit them forth from his mouth after patting the back of his neck.

It was Wadawagwa who, ever jealous of the attention afforded the two captives, pushed himself forward and grabbed the egg-sized pebble from Dodds' hand, shouting at the top of his voice to the amusement of many.

"Hi-Yi! See it now... See it! Now I too will make it disappear!"

He said it several times, sniffed the pebble, then, after putting it in his own mouth, spat it out down the slope, slapping his sides with laughter. The conjuring show curtailed, the two captives were for the time being ignored as the tribesmen talked amongst themselves, examined arrows, moccasins and plucked at unwanted hair growth with mussel-shell tweezers. Dodds begged the use of his own knife and hacked at his beard. Afterwards Tyrell tried, but deciding his wispy growth was not worth the effort, returned the blade to its new owner. Looking up, he caught Wadawagwa grinning. He grinned back, but felt a fool as it dawned on him that the other's expression, rather than conveying friendliness, was laden with mischief and contempt.

"Ha! For a moment I thought the ugly devil was going to clear the foul growth from his face... Too much to expect, though... Hi yi! See, he smiles like a simpleton... So much for one with great powers!"

"Wadawagwa, would I be correct in thinking that you don't think much of our new friends?" Tidesso enquired sarcastically.

"Friends? Hi-yi! Tidesso my brother, I do not understand the attraction. They are ugly, they smell, they are creatures of small intelligence. If we abandoned them in the woods, they would walk round and round in circles until they made a hole in the earth, that they would be too weak to climb out of! And if they make that vile singing noise again, I will rip out their tongues."

"The thing they do with their voices is pleasing to me. It gives a strange lightness to my heart. Even you thought so, I saw your ears move... maybe it was not real singing and not equal to the songs of our people, but was it not interesting? And what about the pebble, did that not impress you?"

Wadawagwa scoffed, shrugged his shoulders and recommenced the fingertip search for the errant hairs that had so far eluded his tweezers.

"Am I to be blinded by such small magic when we have amongst our own people Mateoulins who can transform themselves into bears and birds?"

Tidesso nodded as if conceding the point, then in the dust at his feet, absent-mindedly drew a crude representation of a man pointing a gun.

"What about the hollow lance that roars fire? That certainly impressed the Paquatuogs." Tidesso chuckled at the memory, then obliterated the picture with the sweep of his hand. "They saw their warchief still charging down the slope, without a head on his shoulders. Never have I seen the like, or seen such confusion in the eyes of men! And good for us that it was so... Don't tell me that that did not impress you."

Again Wadawagwa shrugged and continued to search and pluck at his scalp.

Tidesso shook his head, sighed with exasperation, then, on retrieving the looking glass from his quiver, he commenced denuding his own head and chin of the unwanted hair growth. Staring at the reflection of his scalp, he caught the look of determination on his face, the tip of his tongue clamped between teeth, the bulge of his eyes, like a man shitting a jagged rock. He tried hard not to break into laughter, but found it impossible to halt the burst of giggles. Hi yi, if this was not the strongest laughing magic - then what was? The surface of the mirror tilted this way and that. He noticed all, including Wadawagwa, were intently watching his every move.

"Here, Wadawagwa, try this. Look deeply into this Looks-Back, as you would a still pool of water, I wager that it will make even your belly ache with laughter."

Wadawagwa peered down his long nose as if he were being addressed by a persistent child and sighed. "Oh, and what will you wager? What will be mine if it doesn't have the power to make me laugh?"

Tidesso thought for a moment. He shifted weight from one leg to the other and his bearclaw necklace rattled with the movement. Ah, the necklace, why not? he thought. There would always be plenty of bears to stir from their winter sleep and slay with a spear thrust whilst they still yawned in their earth lodges. Lifting the string of claws over his shoulder, he placed it solemnly at the feet of Wadawagwa. He let his fingertips lightly dance across the claws before pushing it back towards Tidesso.

"No, I could not possibly take such a valuable token of your own bravery from you. It would not be a good thing to do."

Tidesso looked at the Looks-Back in the hands of the other and reached out to touch it. Was that what he desired? he wondered.

"No, forget the wager! Forget I mentioned it," Tidesso exclaimed, speedily withdrawing the mirror, flustered at the thought of losing the cherished object. Others in the band immediately signified their disappointment by jeering, stamping feet and shaking quivers so that the arrow shafts rattled angrily. There would be no backing down without losing face. He realized now the wager would have to stand, even if it meant losing the looking-glass.

"Ha, you misunderstand. I do not want that Looks-Back. No, what I want is a small thing, a thing of little or no importance," exclaimed Wadawagwa with a shrug of indifference.

Tidesso smiled, relieved that the looking-glass was not to be the forfeit of its own possible failure, but nonetheless he sensed a trick.

"Name it then... What is it to be?" He looked equally unconcerned, but his mouth was as dry as the earth floor on which he sat. The others called for Wadawagwa to name his prize should he win. Even the two captives joined in, carried along with the mounting excitement - though they had not an inkling what was happening.

"Very well, can you not guess what I want?" Wadawagwa was smiling with smug satisfaction, like a hunter witnessing the prey sniffing at the bait of a deadfall; and when he saw the two captives calling along with the others, he could contain himself no longer and rushed out into the rain to shuffle and sing out his cruel laughter. He returned, still leering, dripping wet, and shook himself like a dog, taking great delight in the groans of displeasure from those around him. Then, sitting on his haunches and fully composed, he stared hard at Tidesso.

"Hi-yi! I have laughed enough. Now pass me this Looks-Back."

At that moment Tidesso guessed that Wadawagwa's prize somehow concerned the two captives. He nodded his head in their direction.

"Ah yes, now I do know what you want. It is their blood, is it not?"

"No, no!" He laughed and held up his index finger. "Not both, just the blood of the older one will do... Now pass me the thing."

For a few brief moments, all was silent. The two captives, sensing something serious was afoot, gazed longingly across the distant ranks of blue trees, wishing they were white-capped waves, rolling in to carry them home. Outside, the rain had ceased and as the sun blazed through once more, steam was beginning to rise between the glistening boughs. Somewhere in the vicinity, ravens began cackling to one another and the silence was ended.

"Wait!" called Tidesso, making no attempt at concealing his anger. "You have spoken, now be silent and I will name my prize."

"Name it!" sneered Wadawagwa, feigning complete indifference as he played with the stretched loops of his right ear. With his mind racing in desperation, trying to focus on something that would cost his opponent dear, Tidesso's eyes darted around all those present, and, as if inspiration lay somehow in the rock ceiling, probed every crevice, every fissure, before finally coming to rest on the snake eyes of Wadawagwa.

"I would have Attitash," he whispered, then spoke the name of his opponent's wife again, though louder so that all present could hear. "Attitash! I would have her."

A sharp hiss escaped Wadawagwa's lips. He was powerless to halt the escape of a nervous snigger, then with eyes that smouldered like twin coals, he glared back at Tidesso, searching for a clue as to the reason behind such a provocative choice. A murmur rose from the other Pennacooks. Some chuckled and slapped their thighs with delight. Others sucked in huge draughts of breath and blew hard like basking whales. The stakes had risen dramatically. This was no longer an idle game to while away the boredom, but a deadly contest - one of the captives would live or die by the success or failure of their magic and a woman might be called to stir the 'sutsgutahash', and warm the sleeping place of a new man.

Tidesso was equally perplexed by his own choice. Attitash was no beauty - the women of the Etechemin seldom were - but Wadawagwa had taken her captive three summers past and though she still spoke the language of the people in a harsh northern way, and grew fatter with each passing moon, Wadawagwa doted on her. No, the only reason to choose her was to wound him for his presumption in demanding the blood of one of the captives - Tidesso's captives. It had been his idea alone not to slay them at the side of the great salt water, to bring them back whole to the lodges of the people. He had seen the picture of his triumphant homecoming spread before his dream-eyes many times. The major part of that triumph depended on the impression made by the two captives and the display of their magical skills, especially the hollow lance that spits fire and thunder, and the container of the black seeds that they used to fuel its deadly bark. From these few, black seeds he would grow more, plant a whole field full to be harvested and ground into the magic powder.

He saw them all lined before him, all the great men of his people, the Sachems, the Mateoulins, the war-captains. He saw too the young women who would rush naked through the gateway, to take up the enemy scalps and mark their homecoming with the victory dance of the exposed parts - a vision sweeter than the sap of the sugar tree. Saquasis, the great Sachem, would learn to speak his name with respect, maybe even bestow one of his own daughters or a new name on him. Wadawagwa knew how important this was to him. Tidesso had made no secret of his desire to wipe away the stain of his brother's failure and now Wadawagwa in his bitterness and envy was trying to undo his dream. But maybe he, Tidesso, would be his own undoing? Attitash? Now that was a foolish mistake. Why had he chosen her as a prize? She could not be forced against her will to leave her place in the lodge, or to welcome a new man into it, even through a wager. It could only happen if she was dissatisfied with her present marriage to Wadawagwa and he with her, and if there was fire between her and another. Tidesso and Attitash had never shared more than a few perfunctory pleasantries together. There was certainly no spark or even damp smoke between them, but now Wadawagwa would think there was, and there was nothing he could do or say to make him think otherwise. He thought again and the stupidity of it was compounded. Blinded by a thirst for blood and now tormented by a worm of jealousy, Wadawagwa might have received from him the very power he required to withstand the magic of the Looks-Back. His heart would now be firmly closed to laughter. Tidesso glanced at his opponent as he seethed before him; and he saw a stranger, he saw one born as a Maquak, an eater of the flesh of men; he saw no kinsman but an enemy intent on undoing his dream.

"Sam! Pssst Sam! What do you think they be doin? They've gone all stern."

Mathew Tyrell lightly touched Dodds' arm. His companion jumped with the shock, so tense had the atmosphere become.

"D'you think I an't noticed? Look at the face of ol' Sailcloth ears. I think there be a storm brewin' 'ere that'll make the one we just 'ad appear like plum stones fallin' in a bucket o' spit."

"Tis the looking-glass again. Look! What's'is face is giving it to our ugly friend."

"My lookin'-glass if you don't mind, Mathew Tyrell. I an't forgot you took it wivout askin'... God 'elp us... 'e be just starin' at it... 'e'll crack it to pieces wiv 'is gurt ugly mug."

Wadawagwa changed his position from resting on haunches to sitting cross-legged, never once taking his eyes from the mirror in his hand. Opposite him sat Tidesso, an exaggerated look of unconcern on his face. All eyes were on the pair of them and on Managnon, who with both hands filled with dust, was letting a thin trickle spill from the left.

"It be a contest of sorts... I an't quite worked it out, but that's what it looks like... I'd stake my life on it!"

"I think you're right... It's got something to do with the glass, he's not ceased gorping at it,... an' look, look at that other one - he's marking the time of it... I tell you what."

"What?"

"I don't like it... I don't care for the way they're looking at us either... Just like a ship's cat wiv a cornered rat."

"Ere Matty, you don't think they be goin' t' eat us, do you?"

Tyrell laughed nervously. "No that aint it, they like our singing too much for that... My throat's red raw mind, I'd give anything for a cup of ale... I wish I knew what's going on, though."

"We'll find out soon enough...look, the dirt's run out o' bofe 'is mits."

Managnon held up his empty hands for all to see, the agreed period had elapsed and Wadawagwa had demonstrated his own power to be stronger than that of the Looks-Back. Silently he placed the looking glass face down in the dust, breathed deeply, then sprang to his feet with a nerve-jangling shriek; he did not even glance at Tidesso, but faced the throng, his arms held wide in triumph.

"Now I choose to laugh."

Wadawagwa began to chuckle, slowly at first, like a small earth-tremor. His body began to vibrate. It grew in intensity until, unable to contain it any longer, the laughter erupted, carrying all along with it. Even Tidesso was not immune to the hilarity and began to chuckle along with the others. At least he was not obliged to go through the pretence of wanting Attitash; and even though one of the captive's lives was now forfeit, the other would still live to impress the Mateoulins and Saquasis. Yes, Saquasis. He would make a gift of the

Looks-Back to the great one and if the old Sachem did not also laugh, then he, Tidesso, would slay the other captive himself.

"Wadawagwa, your power is strong." Tidesso knew that he would have to be seen to demonstrate magnanimity and also, as leader of the war-band, he had to appear to be in control of the situation. He had seen in Wadawagwa a challenge to his position. If he did not act decisively now, what little authority he possessed would evaporate like the last drops of the downpour. Already the late summer sun was burning again. It was time to leave this place and if the blood of one of the white captives was destined to be spilled, then let it be a gift to Cautantowit the creator.

"Your power is stronger than that of the white captives."

All became quiet, but for a few final sniggers. Wadawagwa lowered his arms, and from the waistband of his breech-clout withdrew his knife. Running his thumb along the blade he tested the finely-chipped edge, let a brief smile of satisfaction flicker in his eyes, and raising his smug face, waited for the eulogy that he assumed was his due.

"But...!" continued Tidesso, raising his voice, "but the power of Cautantowit is greater than that of all the people and he has shown through Wadawagwa that he thirsts for a blood sacrifice... Our brother was correct in making us aware of this... We all of us thank him."

Wadawagwa, sensing that he was about to be cheated in some way, made a move towards Dodds.

"When we reach the lodges of our people, then it shall become the honour of Wadawagwa to torment the older of the two captives, but let it be before all the people, so that all can derive strength from it."

Stopped in his tracks, flustered by the murmurings of agreement, Wadawagwa turned and snarled at Tidesso, who, pretending not to notice, continued his speech.

"He has won the honour to demonstrate his skill before all of our people. I, Tidesso of the bear clan, chosen leader of this warband, have spoken."

The further grunts of appreciation at the wisdom of his words made his breast swell. This was good. Most of those present were also of the bear clan. Along with just three others, Wadawagwa was of the marten clan. There were also two wolves, but Tidesso felt sure that none would gainsay his decision. The more he thought about it, this was far better than winning the wager in the first place. Providing, of course, that Wadawagwa was not moved to stick his blade between his ribs, this had turned out well. Wadawagwa pushed his way towards him, glaring with anger and frustration. He stopped at arm's length, his mouth opening, closing, unable to form the feelings into words.

"You have won the right to sacrifice the captive. Are you not pleased Wadawagwa? Is that not what you wanted?"

Although his words were aimed at Wadawagwa, they were uttered aloud for the benefit of all. Again Wadawagwa opened his mouth to speak, but again he was confounded by his own anger. With a snarl he pointed his knife at Dodds, miming the cuts and slashes he would make, leaving little doubt as to the older captive's ultimate fate. Then, quitting the shadows of the overhang, he made his mud-splattered way down the slope. One by one the others followed until only Tidesso and Managnon remained.

"I did not think that you would find the words to release yourself from that snare you were in, but find them you did. You have learned the cunning of a wolverine, my friend, but I fear you have made an enemy in Wadawagwa. You will need someone to watch your back. The Maquak blood flows strong in him like the venom of a snake... I will be the one to watch your back."

Tidesso clasped Managnon to his breast. The warmth in his heart banished all feeling of unease.

"I thank you, Managnon. It makes my heart swell to know that you stand with me. I have felt that there have been times when a torrent has flown between us, and I did not know the way to get across to you, but now I look and the torrent has receded."

He strung his bow, emptied the arrows from his quiver and stooping down to retrieve the looking-glass from the sandy floor, carefully examined it. Then, replacing the arrows, he continued.

"So, you saw it also? You saw the the face of a Maquak? Now, whenever I behold him, since he babbled in their tongue, I feel my shadow shiver. When we first trod on this path, I counted him as a brother, but not now... Ah well, though his hatred rattles within him like a snake, like a snake it sends a warning when he is about to strike."

Managnon chuckled and nodded as they started down the slope.

"I detest Maquaks above all others, even more than Paquatuogs. At least Paquatuogs speak in a manner close to our own, they make lodges almost like ours, even their wampum is acceptable. But these Maquaks, all those of the Hodenasaunee are very different. All their lodges are long. Each one is ruled by a woman. Can you believe it? Is it no wonder that their menfolk are an ill-tempered lot? No, I detest them more than all our enemies combined, for in a way they have already supped on my own blood."

Tidesso looked momentarily baffled.

"How is this thing so?"

"My father told me how they had cut the heart from his own father when we fought with them and the Onondaga at the foot of Agiocochook, the Cloud-Splitter mountain. They cut out my grandfather's heart, stuck it on a lance for all to see, then ate it and fed the rest of him to their menstruating women."

He shuddered as he spoke and flexed his bow in anger.

"It has been a long time since we have fought against them. I hear that they have grown in numbers. It is good that they have other enemies to train their attentions on."

Tidesso laughed and lightly touched the arm of Managnon. "Is it not good that we have the Paquatuogs and Mahicans in the way to protect us?"

Managnon chuckled.

"I had not thought on the Destroyers as our protectors before. Ha! yes, you are right! Are they aware of the great service they perform for our benefit? Maybe we should pay them tribute instead of fighting them."

A silence followed as they entered the still dripping woods, then at the side of the newly swollen stream, as they waited their turn to cross, Managnon turned and whispered to Tidesso.

"Think on this. A warband, led into the lands of the Maquaks, would - were it successful - live in the stories of our people for many winters. Long after the spirits of those brave enough to undertake such a journey had risen through the smoke holes in the sky."

He agitated two fingers as if they were both spirits of warriors and tongues of flame, then letting his arm rise, they became wisps of smoke.

Tidesso nodded as if only half listening, displaying a mix of irritation and amusement at the ungainly attempts of the two captives' crossing of the stream.

"First, we get these two clumsy noise-makers back; then when our bellies are swollen with sagamite and our hearts strong with bear meat, and the people are growing restless with the exploits of this journey, then come to me and we'll talk again. I do like the sound of your words, but if we stir the hornet's nest, they will look to return the attention."

"We are nearly home. Already we have entered the lands of our allies the Squakheag. Soon we will see their rows of corn bidding us enter their lodges and pass a while with them."

Tidesso frowned as he braced himself for the leap to the first boulder. "I have a feeling that it would not be good to show them our captives and their thunder-stick."

"They will be insulted if they know we have crossed their lands without accepting their hospitality! We have no choice. They will know we are here by now... the pale-skins' singing may have reached them already!"

Tidesso did not answer, but leapt from rock to slippery rock. Managnon followed.

"Tell me one last thing," he whispered, on reaching the other bank. "Did you truly desire his woman for your own?"

Tidesso screwed his face with mock terror.

"There is only one thing I dislike more than a Maquak, and that is an Etechemin woman. They are well suited... I would not want to come between such a union."

CHAPTER 6
Breathing Smoke through a Tube

On the twentieth day of captivity they made camp at the head of a pass that snaked between two mountains. Three members of the band who had been sent to scout ahead returned jubilant, with the body of a young deer dangling from a spear-shaft. They were also accompanied by two others - a youth of roughly fifteen, with his scalp freshly tonsured in the manner of a warrior, his cheeks bearing the purple swirls and scabs of fresh tattoos - and an older man in his late middle years. This older man was a Mateoulin, with hair grown long but for a denuded forehead that in the eyes of the captives bestowed on him the balding appearance of an almost comforting familiarity - as if by some spell he had been magically transported from the cluttered counter of an apothecarist's shop to this wilderness. This illusion was short-lived when they caught the malevolent glance that was flashed their way and when the rest of his apparel registered. He wore a long, hide shirt, decorated with human hair and a necklace of human finger-bones that rattled as he hobbled into the circle, chanting and holding high a wide belt of white shells. After formal greetings these two newcomers sat in silence, gently swaying on their haunches as the deer was broiled before them. The guests were served first. Only after their platters of birch bark were heaped high a second time, did the others descend on the meat. Soon not a scrap remained, other than the animal's hide and paunch.

The paunch was filled with water, suspended from an apex of poles and into it placed the bones and several handfuls of pounded, dried maize. Stones were heated in the glowing ashes of hardwood and then one by one retrieved and dropped, to sizzle and splutter in the water. Each spitting stone helped transform the thin liquid into a bubbling broth and soon two steaming, horn ladles were being slurped clean, passed, then replenished, until the bland broth was no more. Finally, following a glance from the older of the two newcomers, the other dutifully took the paunch and left the hearth-side to go and secrete the bones in the forest. His nervous chants and supplications wafted back from the darkness. All present nodded and grunted with satisfaction at the correctness of the ritual.

The youth returned, trying hard to conceal his obvious relief at leaving the dark shadows, but unable to halt his haste in resuming the vacated place at the circle. It was noticed, but with amusement rather than any sense of reproach, and when he sat down, the warrior next to him playfully nudged his arm with an elbow and offered the briefest flicker of a smile.

His older companion paid the youth not the slightest attention, but concentrated on cutting and rubbing together a mixture of bark and dried leaves. All eyes were on him. The two white captives watched with fascination as the mixture was placed in the stone bowl-end of a long thin wooden tube, caused to glow with fire, pointed to the four cardinal directions, and then inhaled deeply as if the man was about to play a flourish on a sackbut. But there was no music forthcoming, even though the man appeared to be enraptured. Instead, taking the tube from his mouth, he blew out a succession of smoke rings, grunted with satisfaction, cleared his throat and began to speak slowly and deliberately.

"Ah,good! Good! I am glad that the deer offered himself up to your arrows - I bade him do so."

Once more he inhaled deeply, "So, I see you tread the warrior's path... I observe that one of you will tread the path no more."

He nodded respectfully at the bundle wherein lay the body of the slain Alaskana.

"It is good that you bear his bones back to your own lodges... a warrior could ask no more of his brothers."

All grunted in appreciation. Inhaling the smoke deeply once more, he passed the pipe to the next man in the circle, then continued speaking.

"We are honoured that brave warriors of our friends the Pennacook have chosen to enter the lands of the Squakheag. We are but a small people. However, blessed with the protection of the mighty Pennacooks, we multiply and grow prosperous. Already our women pound the corn and paint vermillion in their hair in readiness at your arrival in our town... When the new sun rises, you will allow me the great honour of leading the way."

"Let it be so, Grandfather." Betraying none of his impatience to press on, Tidesso solemnly thanked the old man, indicating nothing would give him greater pleasure.

"Good, it fills my heart, I am an old man, but my legs are still sturdy. You will not have to take smaller strides, believe me."

The young companion nodded in confirmation and the others chuckled. The Mateoulin turned his attention to Tyrell and Dodds.

"I see you have wandered far in your exploits. Tell me, where did you find ones such as these? I confess I have never seen the like before. Are they of the same tribe? I have observed them conversing in the same hideous tongue, but they look very different. That one is very ugly." He pointed a long finger at Dodds. "His skin is as pale as a fish! Did you pull him from the waters of a lake?"

Dodds leaned forward, aware that it was he who was being discussed. The confused look on his face turned to anger when the old man spoke again and all laughed, pointing at him with their greasy fingers.

"I would have thrown him back... Or do you intend to fatten then eat him, as the Maquaks do?

Before the laughter subsided, Wadawagwa intervened, much to the annoyance of Tidesso, but Wadawagwa now held the pipe and it was his right to speak if he so wished.

"He is mine to caress when we reach our town, Grandfather... I won this right," he bragged. "All witnessed it."

Passing the pipe, he stuck out his chin and turning his head, examined each face, as if daring any to challenge him.

A long silence followed. Only the crackle of the fire and the draw of the smoke through the pipe sounded. Again it was passed on, this time to Managnon.

"This older captive we talk of fought with Wadawagwa here and beat him, Grandfather. That is why this one would slay him - to wash away the taste of defeat that must spoil the flavour of the finest deer flesh and," he paused to take in another draw of smoke, "this fine Pooke."

A rumble of excitement passed through the gathering. Wadawagwa hissed his displeasure at Managnon, but the impatient expression of the Mateoulin silenced any protest.

"And what of this other one, the young one? He has an altogether more pleasing countenance. I have never seen such hair before. It curls like a vine. Is it truly as pale as it appears in this fireglow?"

"We have trophy hair we can show you. Some of it is paler still, but none curls like this one's."

Tidesso spoke, his words trailing clouds of exhaled smoke. Before passing the pipe on he turned to the Mateoulin. "Tell me, Grandfather. Have you had many dealings with the Nipmuck people recently?"

A longer silence than before followed. The Mateoulin remained impassive, whilst his fingers busily worked at shredding more dried leaves. His younger companion stared straight at the fire.

"Why do you ask? They have moved two of their towns further south and pushed back the Patuxet... I understand some of our young men make the longer journey to trade. Why?"

Tidesso picked up a piece of wood and standing up, laid it on the fire. "It seems that now they have fallen for the blandishments of the Paquatuogs and run with them in war... You did not know, Grandfather? It is indeed fortunate that our paths have crossed, for now you can warn your own people."

"It is indeed fortunate...Tell me, did your departed brother meet his death at the hands of these entwined snakes?"

A further flurry of interest made all the heads turn elsewhere. The pipe had finally reached a nervous Dodds and Tyrell. On its journey round the circle, the bowl had been replenished twice. It fell to Dodds to try the smoking tube first. Hand shaking, he gave three short sucks then followed with a deeper one that scalloped his cheeks and bulged his eyes. He sat as if waiting to explode, and then out came the choking blast of smoke, followed by a raw, gasping tongue, that looked to detach itself at any moment. Only Tyrell laughed, slapping his thighs with delight. Laughing, that was, until the pipe passed to him. In an exact duplication of Dodds' actions, he gave three tentative sucks, then the hot smoke seared his throat and he committed the gravest sin possible. Instead of sucking, he blew, and out of the pipe shot the burning wad of pooke, coming to land on the shoulder of none other than Wadawagwa. The savage turned his head almost nonchalantly, and staring at the wad as if it were some owl turd dropped from the heavens, he contemptuously attempted to blow it off, but the faggot glowed fiercer in the blast of his breath and refused to budge, adhered as it now became to his greasy, melting flesh. With a yelp of agony he sprang up, brushing furiously at his shoulder, covering everyone with showers of sparks and ash. It was not the sparks, however, that brought most of the circle to its feet, but the screeched, foreign babble pouring from his mouth that all now recognised as the hated speech of the Maquak, returned to haunt them.

"What is this, a Maquak in our midst?"

The Mateoulin shrieked and rattled his necklace, as if to ward off any evil spirits.

Yet again, the war-club of Wadawagwa was brandished and raised in anger. Tyrell was on his feet, with the long pipe held ready in a feeble attempt at parrying the threatened blow. At his side Dodds was furiously fumbling with the folds of his shirt. Tyrell briefly turned, giving him a look of helpless resignation. But the club did not descend to pulverize his skull. Frozen in mid-swipe, Wadawagwa appeared as surprised as anyone at the foreign sounds issuing from his own mouth. From the corner of his eye Tyrell saw something fly from Dodds' hands. The next thing he knew, there was a mighty, flashing roar from the fire, and billowing upwards grew a mushroom of smoke. Momentarily illuminated in a confusion of limbs, flashing eyes and teeth, all scattered into the blackness of the forest, wailing like demons as they careered into the trunks of trees and each other. Only the two captives, along with Tidesso and the old man, remained peering at one another across the scattered embers dimly glowing in the murk.

"In God's name, what was that, black powder?" hissed Tyrell from the corner of his mouth.

"Fire n' Brimstone... It done the trick a'right dinnit? Shame it weren't packed tight though, with an 'andful of stones, now tha' would've been a bang!"

Dodds could barely contain his pleasure at the effect he had caused.

"Where did you get it? They took the powder flasks back, didn't they?"

"Yeh', I thought they'd do tha', an' tha's why I filled one o' they mussel shells... just in case like."

"Manitlowock?.. Manitlowock!... Musquantum Manit... Manitlowock?"

"What be 'e jabberin' on about?"

The Mateoulin had found his tongue, and pointing a finger at Dodds and Tyrell, he began to shout and shake - the fingerbone necklace rattling in angry accompaniment.

"Are they Demons? They are Demons... Angry Demons... They are Demons!"

Tyrell gazed at Tidesso. He felt in some way guilty, as if he had let the leader down.

"He's not happy... Now what have you done?"

"Me?... What 'ave I done?... Tha' be very nice Mathew Tyrell... Thankee very much."

Tyrell strode over towards the Mateoulin and grinning nervously, he held out the pipe as an offering. The explosion had scattered the fire, cutting visibility down to an acrid, smoky blur, so it was only when he had approached within arms length that he realised the old man was quaking - petrified with fear. The Mateoulin would not take the pipe at first, so, whilst babbling nonsense in a soothing tone, Tyrell placed it on the ground before him and withdrew. The Mateoulin did not move. Finally, Tidesso picked up the pipe and on addressing the Mateoulin, managed to make him take it. Then he set about re-assembling the fire.

One by one the tribesmen crept back into the clearing. Some, trying to channel their fear into aggression, had arrows nocked and rattling against their bows, making as if to pierce Dodds through. Others came in visibly shaken, to sit in the dim light, pick tiny, bloodied shards of mussel shell from their skins, and sway back and forth as if in a trance. One of the last to appear was Wadawagwa. He skulked in empty-handed, taking his place silently, displaying neither anger nor fear, but shaken nonetheless.

With the returning of the flames the chill of fear was slowly thawed, though the gaps between Tyrell and Dodds and those either side had grown noticeably greater. Over the other side of the fire Tidesso and the Mateoulin were huddled in conversation. Slowly the others pulled their sleeping robes around them and with feet almost in the embers proceeded to fall asleep.

"I wonder what they're talking about," Tyrell nodded towards Tidesso and the Mateoulin.

"Us o' course!"

"I know that, but do you think they'll kill us... I mean, that old man is obviously somebody important, er, a priest or a Mayor or something."

"Wha', 'im a Mayor? Ha! Witch more like. Fine chain of office 'e do 'ave! Look Matty, these beggars are murderin', smoke-suckin' savages. I ask you, whatever next? Look lad, they don' 'ave Mayors. Why, they don' even talk proper, I means, Frenchies and Dagoes jabber, but tis a proper kind of jabber, not like these beggers, they be like unruly children, imps is wha'! Look, our lives 'ave been in the balance ever since they took us - one moment they be all smiles an' pettin', the next they be about to bash our 'eads in, 'specially ol' sail cloth ears! 'Ow many times as 'e dangled 'is gurt 'ead crusher above us? Go on, 'ow many times?"

"I know! I know, but your fire-show just then... It was different... They won't let it pass."

"Well, maybe you be right... I 'ad to do sum'ing, din't I? Anyway they won' do nuf'ing now, so best thing is get some sleep, an' say your prayers - all of 'em." As an afterthought, as if talking to himself, Dodds quietly added, "It be my blood they be thinkin' o' spillin anyways, not yourn... So do like I say, Matty lad... Go t' sleep."

Retrieving half-burned nuggets of hardwood from the fire's periphery, Dodds consigned them once again to the still glowing centre. He sat for a long time staring into the revived embers, watching the occasional courageous spark's bid for freedom as it eddied upwards in the invisible column of hot air. Some he thought he could trace until they rose almost level with the tree-tops, but their glimmer was extinguished or lost in the greater sparkle of the stars. He fantasized about slipping away whilst all around him slept, but how far would he get before they found him? Somehow he felt the mark of death had descended upon his head. He could not put his finger on it, or begin to fathom the change, but the change had surely come when they sheltered beneath the overhang. It had something to do with the looking-glass and of course the savage with the big ears; and it was intended for him alone. He felt it, saw it in their eyes, the same look a crowd gives a condemned man as he is borne along to the scaffold.

Up until this moment he had stowed away - as all mariners must learn to do - his thoughts of home, knowing that if he once tampered with the clasp, it would weaken his resolve, but now a deep yearning for things familiar opened before him. It was no longer a convenient cask to take out when it pleased, and after choosing a memory, slam tight the lid. No, now it was all there, demanding attention, glowing, crackling in the fire. He sat, gently swaying, staring at the bright fire glow, and the harder he looked, the more colours were revealed. Blues and greens of the sea danced and writhed amongst the yellows and reds of a wheat field studded with poppies. He saw a multitude of faces, friend and foe, the living and the dead, all mingled together, laughing, crying, loving, dancing, eating, drinking and chattering. What wouldn't he give to sit on a stool at a trestle, to chatter like a tipsy sparrow, to drink and dribble cider and eat a chunk of bread, even stale, black bread? And salt. Salt, the one taste a seaman above all other could not deny. Yet here he was in the midst of a forest as vast as any sea with not a pinch to be had. What wouldn't he give to be on the rolling deck of a storm-tossed ship, or in a rain-sodden skiff bailing out with one hand, pulling up the Poor-Jack with the other? The fish-gut stench of creaking oak was as much home as the piss-splattered alleys of Bristol. He would gladly settle for either - billeted beneath leaking timbers, or dodging piss-pails in the gutter.

He gasped with the pain of yet another image, as he beheld the mound of earth marking the common grave wherein lay the bodies of his wife and children, side by side with others, strangers who had succumbed to the dread pestilence. It had struck whilst he had been at sea. He had returned to nothing, an emptiness greater than the Ocean-sea itself. And now they too lived again for him. He felt the soft breath of a child on his cheek and the dew-sweet kiss of a loving wife - the image so tangible that he gasped for breath as if a blade had been forced between his short-ribs and slowly twisted. The pain so great caused the chasm to close, the faces to vanish beneath a vale of anguish, and the keepsake tears puthered down his face onto his hand as it rose, shaking, to clamp his sobbing mouth tight. His first thoughts were of sea spray; here was the first salt – the taste of tears. He wanted so much to take the hand away and blubber out loud, but he wouldn't, couldn't, not only for fear of waking the savages, but for fear of waking the helpless boychild that lies curled, sleeping deep within the breast of every man.

And what of these slumbering shapes, these savages, who one moment could be quaking with fear over a mere brimstone bang and the next happily asleep? They held no such inhibitions about weeping. Even Big-Ears had mewled like a babe over the loss of their older brother at the lakeside fight. He had seen the child within each of them then. None of them could be much older than twenty years. For all their cruel posturing and paint and trophies of human remains they were boys - dangerous, deadly boys and he wanted to be far away and have done with them.

But how could he abandon Mathew, this other sleeping boy? They would surely vent their spite on him. Or would they? In the last few days he'd noticed a subtle change in the way some of the captors treated his young friend. An easiness from which he was excluded. He felt the creak of age and a pang of jealousy for the youthfulness that was perhaps beginning to bond them. All the same he wondered how far he could get, if he were to just up and go, just keep running. The stars would tell him which way the Ocean-sea lay, but the in-between, the eternal wilderness, the enormity of it deadened the soul. And what would he do if and when he reached the salt water? He fantasized about having the power to keep running and running, with the heroic strides of a giant, leaping from ridge to ridge. And for a moment the eternal forest, the stinking swampland, the blood-sucking insects, the tangles, the thorns, the grey, broken tree stumps, the wide, treacherous waters, the snakes, the bears and the cruel savages were brushed aside. In his mind's eye he already stood at the lip of the ocean, but the great expanse was empty. Try as hard as he might, he could conjure no ship to appear on it.

He had left the circle initially to empty his bladder, not trying to be particularly quiet, and no one had stirred; but then that was their way, they never posted guards. Were they that sure that he would not run off, or that others would not creep in and slay them as they slept? He relieved himself noisily against the leaves of a fern, whilst at the same time peering over his shoulder at the humped shapes and the dull glow of the dying fire. Still no one stirred. He cleared his smoke-singed throat and spat – nothing moved. The resinous fragrance of the trees beckoned. He was powerless to stop himself going forward.

"Just a little way, my babby, just a tiny taste of freedom and then back, with none the wiser."

He whispered and stole another glance backwards as his toes poised to feel the way forward. Just a few moments as a free man again would be a triumph to give him strength and succour - knowing that he had walked 'willy-nilly', without savage, black eyes watching his every move.

It seemed that only a handful of paces were needed to slip the halter. Just a handful of steps before he was engulfed in thick darkness, with little moonlight to penetrate the branches and, of course, no stars to guide him. Earlier he had succumbed to the shame of tears. He would not allow himself the taste of panic.

The absolute blackness relented a little as he knew it would, the slender trunks of white birch standing out like funnels of light. One who had poached in the woods of Henbury as a boy, one who had tasted the flesh of badgers - sweeter than any hog - knew what to expect. Yes, and one who had felt the clamp of their jaws - stronger than any keeper's trap - knew that the pair of yellow eyes in front of him belonged to no witch or demon, but maybe one of those sharp, spiked creatures that the savages avoided, because of their eye-watering stench. He found himself chuckling, wondering if the stink would penetrate the savage's slumbers. Kneeling down, he searched the immediate ground for a stone or stick to throw. His fingers found a brace of pine cones, but the yellow eyes had vanished when he looked again. He threw the cones anyway - one hit the trunk of a tree, the other made no sound, simply disappearing in the dark void. He sniffed the air, waiting for the stink. It did not come. Again he moved forward. Now he could see more clearly, see the dark, sentinel shapes of the individual trees. Slowly he moved around a waist-high boulder and stopped, knowing that the ground sloped away somewhere near. His toes brushed against a smooth stick, a polished piece of wood with no rasp of bark to its touch. He knew immediately that the finish bore the design of man. Nudging it aside, his toes registered a peculiar, weighted feel to one end; and on stooping down his fingers firmly clasped the haft of a club. Raising it above his head, he revelled in the lethal beauty of the balance, the power contained in this the basest of weapons. With this deadly extension to his arm he experienced a surge of power and confidence, wanting to charge, bellowing through the woods, smashing at the tree trunks. He cupped the brutal ball end in the palm of his left hand, feeling the pointed spur of stone that protruded - a small touch of head-cracking refinement. It was all of a piece, some heavy hardwood, carved and smoothed to perfection. Obviously it had been dropped when the exploding mussel shell had sent his captors skittering away from the fire. Although there was no way of being positive before daylight, he suspected straightaway that it was the weapon of Big-Ears; the one that had so often been brandished above his own and Tyrell's skulls. Now it would be his, at least until daylight.

At the foot of the slope lay a swift, running stream. He thought he could just hear its gurgle beneath the breeze-stroked creak of the treetops, but could not be sure. Earlier, around dusk, he and Tyrell had been sent the short distance to fill water bladders. They had dawdled, trying to entice trout with their fingertips and would have succeeded, had not an irritated tribesman insisted they return to the campsite. But now it was not the fat, mountain trout that interested him - his belly being still full of half-chewed elk meat - it was the cool water itself. He needed to assuage the burning rasp of the necromancer's smoke. What had been the purpose behind it? Had he and Tyrell undergone some diabolic initiation? Had they unwittingly taken into their lungs some mind-poisoning potion? He shuddered on recalling the images in the flames. They had been so vivid, too vivid. Witchcraft! That is what it was. He crossed himself and swung the club around his head. Never had he known his throat to burn so. He would drink the stream dry and then he would bathe his aching feet. Although he was becoming inured to the constant trudging, day in day out - indeed he took satisfaction in matching the steps of the younger men - the thought of immersing his face and feet in the icy mountain water was becoming a focal point of great significance. The icy caress of the water on his tongue would compensate for the suppressed sorrow and wretchedness that had threatened to undermine him.

The picture of the downward path was still fresh in his memory, as if he had already rehearsed this midnight ramble and knew the exact place where each foot would fall. In truth, since the first day of captivity, he had rehearsed a thousand escape routes, from rolling down ravines, to hurling himself into churning waters. They were all nothing more than fancy, brought on by the knife edge of fear and the rattle of a half-empty belly, the grapes and berries fermenting along with the ever present dollop of mush. Now here he was alone for the first time in days and days, with a full belly, and a mind for the time being purged of helplessness. Not that this was an attempt at escape - he endeavoured to remind himself - he would not leave Matty, could not leave him, it was unthinkable. He accepted that, as the older man, it was his duty to protect his young friend, at least to give him the impression that things were not hopeless, but it was a strain, constantly having to appear cheerful, with answers to events, the outcome of which he really had not the slightest inkling about. And now he felt duty bound to return, even though he believed his life was ultimately forfeit.

The hoot of an owl caused his heart to jump; and in a reflex action the club was raised above his shoulder.

"Steady on there, Samuel my babby, you be as jumpy as Bastard Big-Ears."

Feeling a little foolish, he lowered it once more and began the slow descent to the creek. His night eyes had fully returned, assisted by a three-quarter moon that penetrated the large patches of the slope where storm-ripped trees had fallen to reveal an open swath. He had to constantly check his speed, hold himself back lest he stumbled, twisting an ankle or worse. The rush of the water was now perfectly audible. Its silver sparkle tantalizingly beckoned between the waterside branches. A different, furry creature startled him and again the club was raised. He delighted in seeing it scurry along the length of a fallen trunk before disappearing in the shadows. 'I knows you be good eatin'. As sweet as badger. You be lucky my belly's full'... The owl called again, this time from further away. He quelled the desire to mimic it. That would surely penetrate the sleep of the savages. They, the masters of copying animal calls, would know immediately that it issued from the throat of a Bristolman.

The trail down eased itself onto a grassy plateau that ended abruptly in a face of vertical granite as tall as a merchant's house. Whilst filling the bladders, he had earlier marvelled at the tenacity of the trees that had taken root in the rock's fissures, their trunks curving skyward with all the grace of swans' necks. He was aware that the last part of the descent would be the hardest, the path becoming a steep,rocky scramble, but as he approached he saw the reflected light off the water helping to illuminate the way. Sticking the club down his breeches, face to face with the granite, he swiftly made it to the grassy bank below.

"Well, Doddsy my babby, you done it, no bover."

He permitted himself a whisper and a low chuckle. Although still only less than a high longbow shot from the campground, with the walls of rock behind him he felt a free man. He had escaped, admittedly only for a short time, but he had escaped nonetheless.

Cupping his hands, he drank his fill, swishing the sweet water round and round his parched mouth. The reality of bathing his feet did not match the fantasy. The mountain water was colder than he remembered even the North Sea being, and relief only came after he had withdrawn and rubbed them dry. The air too was cooler. Earlier he had welcomed it, but now his teeth began to chatter and his hide prickled like the skin of a plucked capon. He danced on the spot, as was his habit when on night watch, rubbing his arms and thighs. He would be damned if he returned yet awhile. He was meant to be here in this beautiful place. If only that impatient savage had given him a few more moments when they filled the water bladders, he would have tossed a startled trout at his feet. Yes, he would have liked to catch a fish, to have been a fisherman once again; even though there was not the slightest hint of salt to their flesh.

An overwhelming need to pray commanded him to kneel. Had something greater than a desire to bathe his feet brought him to this place? Did not the act of bathing feet itself have some deep spiritual significance? Resting his head on an altar of rock, he thought suddenly of Christ in the garden of Gethsemane and began to silently anoint the boulder with his wretched, pent-up tears, convinced, now more than ever, that if he returned to the savages, he was a dead man. However, the will to live was not diminished. If anything, it had grown stronger. His body also screamed with a desire to run and run, to outdistance the savages and the guilt.

"Forgive me, Jesus, but I aint goin' back! I knows you will look after your servant Mathew Tyrell, for 'e be a good, God fearin' lad - even if he don't be much of a seaman. I knows too that you will find a way to soothe the hurt an' the cruel anger o' they savages. For tis my belief that they look kindly on 'im and will preserve 'im. I fear tha' if I goes back Lord, tha' they will put me to a cruel 'ard death. I'm ready to take my chances in the wilderness, like you done. So I aint goin' back, Lord... It be tha' simple."

It was whispered, but it was said nonetheless, as true as if he had shouted it from a crow's nest or pulpit. Had this been his intention all along, he wondered? Partly in shame, he suspected it had.

Yet again an owl's hoot had him reaching for the club. Something about it was different. It had come from above, but had sounded closer to the ground than the usual tree-top call... Damnation! Had he left it too late? Had they noticed his absence already and were coming to drag him back? Leaving the waterside he made for the shadows, pressing himself against the cold, hard rock-face. He was shivering again, this time with fear. He would give roughly the equivalent of a turn of a sandglass and then cross the creek whatever. It seemed somehow significant to put water between him and them.

He judged the imaginary grains of sand had run their course, and on leaving the shadows, was just about to enter the water when another owl-call came from somewhere high up the slope opposite. Lurching back to the rock-face, he made the sanctuary of the shadows in time to hear the answer come from almost directly above, at the cleft in the rock where the downward path began. The club was shaking in his hand, gripped so hard that the finger nails bruised the flesh of his palm. For an age he waited, until his hand steadied, and fear was replaced with self ridicule. "It be only an owl an' its mate goin' about their nightly business, Doddsy, get a grip o' yoursel'!" The strange, strangulated gobble of a different kind of bird rang out, only to be mimicked moments later from the other side - this time closer to the water. So there was his answer. His initial circumspection had not been foolish. He was now convinced human savages were definitely on the prowl. Had they crossed the stream some place further up, then swung round to trap him? He had not been absent from the campsite all that long. Did they really possess the skill to cover such a distance, and in the darkness too? He felt like a helpless fool.

No longer standing, his body having retreated into a shivering crouch, he sensed that someone was starting the rocky descent. He became momentarily aware that his eyeballs felt as if they had swollen to the size of crab-apples and the hair at the back of his neck had risen in anticipation of the scalping blade. What should he do? Cower in the shadows, hoping that they would somehow miss him? Step boldly out playing the innocent, acting as if nothing was amiss, humming a tune even; or pounce on the one coming down, pounding his head to a pulp? He decided that acting the innocent fool was the best course to take - providing that it was not Big-Ears. If it was that son of a whore, he promised himself, he would take a swing with the head-crusher, and hope that whoever was closing in on the far side would put enough arrows into his own hide to finish the job swiftly.

There was a soft thud as the intruding figure leapt to the ground. Dodds was somewhat relieved to see that it was not one of his captors at all, but the same youth who, along with the older, wizard-like character, had joined them earlier on. 'Why, the poor babby 'ad seemed right frit o' the darkness when 'e were made to go an' bury them bones. Wha's 'e doin' down 'ere then? Why, we can go back together.' Dodds wondered, grinning broadly, and was about to reveal himself, when the youth stood upright and facing the stream, began signalling with wide sweeps of both arms.

The grin on Dodds' face froze. A somewhat peculiar sound turned his attention to the opposite slope. It seemed strangely out of place, reminding him of a sound not unlike the faint creaking a rustic cot made, when a man and his wife were keeping themselves warm and trying not to wake the children. There it was again, almost comforting in its incongruity - he stifled the nervous laughter that threatened to escape. Then he saw them, the perpetrators of the noise, as they slowly filtered through the trees like wicker ghosts; and he knew from the fantastical shape of them, the rod armour, the oblong shields of slats, that they were the Paquatuogs come to claim blood recompense for their earlier defeat by the lake.

PART TWO

CHAPTER 7
Long Live The Tudor

Thomas Croft dismissed his manservant Roberts, and raising a brim-filled goblet to his lips, let the malmsey wine flood into his mouth. He swallowed hard. Then, taking another smaller draught, he strode towards the window, swishing and swirling the strong, sweet liquid twixt tongue and tooth as he went.

The rhombic glass in the large window-frame was not of the finest quality. True, it allowed scales of light to flood in sufficiently and kept the wind and rain at bay, but it did not afford what, in the opinion of Thomas Croft, was its primary function - a clear view of the waterfront. A Customs House denied a clear view due to inferior glass was not what the port of Bristow - the second town in the land - demanded. He wrestled one-handed with the window catch and raised the goblet to his lips with the other. There was stubborn resistance in the leaden frame. Wrenching again, harder, it opened with a jolt. The rim of the goblet, striking a tooth in the process, sent dribbles of wine down the front of his green doublet.

"Rudkin! Rudkin! Here man, here! At once, if you please!" he bellowed like a bull.

From the waterfront below came hoots of drunken laughter.

"Rudkin, Rudkin, 'ere man, 'ere!"

His command echoed back at him in extempore song.

"At once, if you please," a voice attempted to mock his haughty accent.

"Who's supped all the beer?" came the rhymed reply, followed by a self-congratulatory guffaw, and the sound of feet shuffling in the street below.

Croft's eyes bulged, his face reddened with outrage. Shaking with pent-up fury, he waited until the group of seamen and their doxies had passed by. Then he exploded.

"Ruddddkkkiiiinnnn!!!!"

Grumbling, panting, the sound of the Customshouse keeper shuffling up the final flight of stairs reached his ears. Croft counted off each of the dozen steps and watched the door's iron ring handle twitch like a fishing float, then slowly turn.

The door opened to reveal the stooped figure of the wheezing man, Rudkin. Croft, who was also in the process of catching his own breath, opened his mouth to speak, but before his tongue had time to tease forth the first word of the prepared tirade, the ensuing draught caused by the gaping door and window set the room in a swirl of dusty rushes. Croft's eyes narrowed in disgust, then his body jumped as the window banged shut behind him.

"Yes, Sir, Master Thomas. You summoned I?"

Rudkin had shut the door behind him and was now stooped over, laying the disturbed rushes back on the exposed floor.

"Once a week, I commanded you," he barked down at the keeper, who in the eyes of the mighty Thomas Croft, Collector of Customs for Bristow, once Member of Parliament for Leominster, was little more than a menial - and a saucy one at that.

"Once a week what, master?"

"The rushes, man! The rushes! I said have them changed once a week top and bottom. Look at the dust. Just... look... at... the... dust. Why, tis like some desert storm."

Croft coughed and reached again for the window.

"Do I appear unto you as some Blackamoor perhaps, one who derives his very sustenance from the sand, that I should suffer so?"

With the pointed toe of his kid bootee, he flicked aside a patch of the floor covering.

"Did I, or did I not say, have them changed weekly?"

There was a long silence whilst Rudkin began picking up the same matted rushes he had just laid down. "T'aint my job," he mumbled under his breath.

"Not now. Not now, you fool. What's more, I don't expect you to do it personally. Get one of your boys to do it. You are supposed to be the Customshouse keeper. Don't you know anything, man?"

Again there was a silence whilst the rushes were put back in place. The resentful keeper sneezed and stood to attention. In his hand he held an imaginary ballock knife. He imagined himself ripping the blade up through Croft's ample belly and the man's greasy guts spilling out over the rushes.

"I derst know one thing, Mast' Croft," he said, barely attempting to hide his indignation.

"Ha," scoffed the Collector, shuffling towards the table and reaching for the jug of wine. "And what, pray, can that be? Curing of warts perhaps, or maybe that the Turks of Constantinople have become Christians?"

Croft chuckled to himself, tipping the jug until the ruby liquid formed a shimmering meniscus on the rim of the silver goblet.

"Come on then man, out with it! What is this one thing you know? This one pearl of petty intrigue."

He gingerly raised the vessel to his mouth, and like an overgrown, rosy-cheeked cherub, puckered his lips in readiness at quaffing the contents.

Rudkin cleared his throat, and standing easy, began speaking, "It appears, master, that we 'as another 'Enry... 'Enry the seventh if I'm not mistaken."

A loud gulp, followed by a choking sound, issued from Croft. Rudkin took a step forward, offering assistance, barely flinching in the fine spray of wine that greeted him. Croft, motioning for him to halt, struggled to regain a semblance of composure.

"What did you say man?" Again he coughed. "Tell me all you know. Tell me! Tell me!"

"The King is dead. Long live the King, whoever 'e might be, is what I says," said Rudkin, with a hint of barely concealed sarcasm.

"Henry Tudor, Earl of Richmond... You mean the Tudor is now our King?" Croft drained the goblet.

"And how, pray, are you privy to this information before I myself have heard a whisper of it? I who have supped with kings. I who have known the very friendship of kings!"

Croft knew full well that having had the good fortune to be a childhood companion to Edward the 1Vth had more than a little to do with his position as Customs Collector. However, holding onto the position these past two years since Edward's death had been a source of wonderment to himself and the cause of not a few sleepless nights.

"How do you know this to be true, eh? Come man, out with it!"

Croft took a pace nearer to Rudkin but stopped short by a sword's length, and sniffing the air with exaggerated distaste, half turned his head. In lesser circumstances the deeply ingrained sense of superiority would have allowed him to carry off this newly assumed pretence of indifference. But not this time. The man Rudkin had information that was of the greatest import, and the insolent knave knew it.

"Rudkin...! If you are jesting, it will go ill with you. I could have you in the stocks at the flick of a finger, aye and a spike driven through that wagging tongue too. At the very least I could turn you out of here with a handful of stripes across your back."

'Yes Crofty, an' I could slit that fine tunic an' the gurt belly 'neath it in a twinkling,' thought Rudkin.

"Mast' Croft, I wun't jest 'bout such a thing."

A hurt expression spread on the bony, grey-stubbled face of the keeper.

"Well, out with it! ... Tell me all you know."

Croft abandoned the pretence of indifference and was visibly shaking with anticipation. He had lately changed allegiance from Richard of Gloucester to Henry Tudor. The outcome meant everything to him. Was Rudkin aware of this too?

Rudkin cleared his throat, opened his mouth to speak, then coughed again, this time massaging his larynx, as if some blockage hindered him from talking further.

"Here man here!" Croft took Rudkin's meaning.

Without hesitation he filled his goblet one more time and handed it to the man. If Rudkin derived much satisfaction in having the great man waiting on him - the lowly keeper supping from the great man's own silver goblet - he had the good grace not to show it. He did, however, on draining the fine vessel, hand it back to Croft rather than placing it on the table himself.

"Bos'orth, I think it was... Yes, a place called Bos'orth somewhere up mid-country. A big, bloody battle by all accounts. 'Eads, legs, n' arms 'acked off, 'n entrails everywhere, all over the place, horses, men tripping over, getting tangled up in it, see."

"Yes, yes, but what of Richard? How did he er...?"

"They say that cannon were fired from the hills, and horses and men were ripped asunder by lead shot and blinded by the flashes of the arquebuses and culverins that crashed and shrieked like the Devil's own legions."

"Yes, but what of Richard? How ...?"

"They do say tha' 'e fought like a lion. Could 'ave fled the field, lived to fight another day like, an' kept 'is crown. But they says tha' 'e charged into the enemy, an' got cut t' pieces!"

"Good God, man!"

"And some say that he took an arrow in the eye like Harold before him, while others say he threw his helmet aside to rally his side and a Welshman sneaked up from the flank and fired molten lead-shot through his head."

Croft began to look a little pale. For Rudkin, the warmth of the wine and Croft's discomfort was near bliss.

"Beggin' your pardon, Master. I was forgettin' that maybe you han't 'ad the pleasure of being stuck in the middle of a battlefield with arrowls whistlin all about, and don't somehow understand what i's like to look the Grim Reaper in the face. Me, well, Towton, up in Yorkshire it were, over twenty year past, just a lad an' all... My feet was raw with marchin'... Snowin' too. Us boys from Bristol we showed 'em though. We showed 'em a'right, shooted our arrowls out of the blizzard, then running back out o' range whilst they Lancastrians returned volley! Let the bastards use up all their shafts, then we let em 'ave it good n' proper."

As he spoke, Rudkin gazed upwards, a pious expression adorning his face. He guessed that he had tweaked the raw nerve sufficiently and quickly blessed himself, as much to ward off immediate chastisement from Croft as to give thanks for divine deliverance from the field of that long-ago battle.

"It is no concern of yours what I may or may not comprehend. I will say in warning, however, that Towton was a Yorkist victory. It would behove you well not to brag of it now, even though a score years have passed. Now proceed. How did this information seek out your ears? Am I perhaps the last man in Bristow to hear of it?"

"Well now, your honour..," The false piety fled from his features, and having derived sufficient satisfaction from the point scored, Rudkin adopted a more obsequious tone, "I am sure you knows this to be true, Mast' Croft, that th'aint nothing that travels swifter than the tale of battles won or lost, not even one of those roundshots. Why, sir, a mounted man could gallop fresh from the field and afore he reined in 'is 'orse and rapped at the Alderman's door, the word would 'ave spread an' been well talked out in the tavern. Aye, and tossed out with the night's dregs."

Despite himself, Croft found he was nodding in agreement.

"So, as I first thought, I am the last man in Bristol... Er.. I mean Bristow to know." Croft deliberately emphasised the 'W' ending in the town's name. He could never get used to the way the local inhabitants insisted on placing an 'L' sound at the end of so many words, in particular the very name of the city; and now here he was doing it himself! How long had it been since leaving Leominster?

"Am I the last to know?

Rudkin shook his head.

"Last night there was not a whisper about, but 'smorning when I goes in the Moon to get me draught, every tongue is at it - natterin' about the battle and the new King, God save 'im. 'Enry, yes, that's it. It'll be the seventh Enry we've 'ad. But the first Welshman, so they says... Well I 'opes 'e keeps 'is wits about 'im."

Rudkin held up a hand and began counting his fingers.

"Tha' be four Kings we've 'ad in two years. I carn' keep apace with it myself."

"Ha! Then 'tis true. You are right, man. Saints be praised! These are good tidings. Merciful Heavens! Good tidings indeed!"

Croft's feet tattooed a jig on the floor. He then commenced skipping around the room, clapping and rubbing his hands together with unconcealed joy. Rudkin's shoulders relaxed, the earlier resentment forgotten. A wide grin transformed his face and like a weather-cock he turned to mark Croft's progress.

"Good, good, good tidings Rudkin... Yes, indeed they are."

Croft, abruptly ceasing his perambulations, grabbed the table and caught his breath.

"Good man Rudkin," he gulped. "Good man!"

After a short while, he dispensed with the table's support and plunged the freed hand into his purse. The chink of coins forced the grin on Rudkin's face to spread even wider. Inside the leather pouch the merchant's fingers deftly turned over each coin, sifting the alloy from the gold.

"Here man, here," he whispered, and beckoning Rudkin over to him, placed two light groats in the man's outstretched, bony hand.

"Go now, back to your tasks, leave me to my own. Oh, and Rudkin..."

"Yes, Mast' Croft?"

"Should it be your good fortune to hear other tidings of great import... Do I have it that you will not dawdle or show a moment's reticence in informing me?"

Rudkin touched the side of his nose with his index finger and sniffed.

"You shall 'ave it, Mast' Croft. Straight away after the tidbit

126

in question 'as teased my ear, then the first wag of my tongue will be in your own good ear...So's t' speak."

"Very good, very good. Now back to your duty."

Rudkin made a small bow and left the room. No sooner had the door closed than Croft, letting the palmed golden noble slip back into the purse, withdrew his hand and reached for the wine jug. Chortling to himself, he tipped the jug above the goblet. Then, just before the wine flowed, he thought better of it and up-ending the goblet, drank deeply from the jug itself.

"Long live the King! Aye and long live Thomas Croft!"

The faint, finger-roll rap at the door startled Croft again, and again the wine dribbled down his doublet. There had been no warning footfall. It sent a shiver of fear through his body that in a twinkling banished the tipsy rapture. Four Kings in two years, these were indeed troubled times, capricious times that changed by the hour - seemingly at the whim of the wind, or the colour of a rose. Where the devil was his manservant, Roberts?

Croft tugged the belt around his swollen girth until the sheathed dagger appeared from under the folds of his gown and likewise the purse was shifted into concealment.

"Who knocks?" he said gruffly, purposely pitching his voice lower. His fingers nervously played with the pommel of the dagger. "State your name and business."

"'Tis I again Mast' Croft. I, I err...

"Rudkin! Rudkin! You again. What the devil, man? I thought I'd dismissed you?"

Furiously he strode to the door and pulled it open. The keeper stood there, smiling sheepishly. Croft noticed the man's shifty eyes alight on the absence of the purse and the sudden appearance of the sheathed weapon. Croft saw the man's smile depart, though the ghost of it remained etched in the lines at the corner of his thin-lipped mouth. He knew, too, that Rudkin sensed his fear. Croft's features hardened. He would not be intimidated - however slightly - by the likes of Reginald Rudkin.

"Well... What is it man? I have many pressing tasks. Speak up now! What is it?"

Rudkin shuffled his weight from one foot to the next and back again, then sniffing deeply, he rubbed the side of his nose with a grime-stained forefinger.

"Beggin' your pardon, Mast' Croft, but I forgot. There be not one thing, but two things that I do know... and I did not tell but the 'arf of it... But I can see that you are occupied with your weapon," he nodded down towards Croft's midriff, "and besides, what I 'as to tell will reveal itself in due course, for better or for worse, now the tide 'as turned."

Rudkin turned to go. An awkward Croft tugged at the belt until once more the purse showed itself.

"Speak man!"

'Got you, you old bastard!' thought Rudkin. Again the clink of the coins in the purse sounded.

"Why Mast' Croft. 'Tis the Cornucopial returned from 'ibernial."

Rudkin stressed the word Hibernia and once again with knowing looks stroked the side of his nose.

"The Cornucopia. Where is she?"

"I 'eard she were wi' the barges comin' through Horseshoe bend. She should be in the Gorge by now."

"And what of the Swallow...? Any word?"

Rudkin scratched then shook his balding head.

"Why Rudkin, you disappoint me, only word of one of my ships?"

Rudkin, looking a little crestfallen, nonetheless took the single proffered coin. Thomas Croft made a show of dropping a similar coin back into the purse. It nestled amongst the others with a chink. Rudkin swallowed hard. Croft tightened the drawstring and, patting the closed purse, remarked... "And there the 'tother one shall lie 'til you bring word of the Swallow waiting at Kingroad... or better yet," he added with a sneer,"a sighting off Porlock would make it yours much the sooner. Ha, but of course, even your eyes and ears do not stretch that far?"

Without waiting on a reply, or even dismissing the keeper, Croft pushed Rudkin backward with the index finger of his left hand, hooked his pointed toe around the door and slammed it shut in the man's face. Then, with ear pressed hard against the door, he marked the disgruntled descent, the cursed accompaniment to each step. When he was certain that the man had gone, and making no attempt to suppress his delight, Croft began to fill the chamber with roars of laughter. This laughter grew fit to engulf him, then, with some imperceptible internal signal, the laughter changed to tearful lamentation. Falling back into a chair, he stifled the sobbing until, near exhaustion, he sat breathing deeply until a semblance of composure was regained. These last two years had been in many ways purgatory. Four Kings in two year! He sighed and shook his head in disbelief. How long will this Welshman's head stay atop his shoulders? Is this to be the end of these bloody wars? This had been a near-run thing. All could so easily have been lost. But it hadn't been lost. For the foreseeable future he, Thomas Croft, was still the Customs Collector, by God! He banged the table, sniffled one last time, grabbed the wine jug, and, after draining the dregs, lowered it to reveal a grin.

"Well, Thomas," he addressed himself. "You've done it again, my good fellow. The gamble has paid off, and what a gamble! You could have lost everything, including your poor head." He paused to stroke his neck, then continued, "Still, man, the wise choice made with the Tudor, and the safe return of the Cornucopia. And loaded down with stock-fish, I'll be bound."

A look of exaggerated distaste momentarily clouded his round, ruddy face. He pinched his nose and spoke with an exaggerated nasal twang.

"Cannot abide the stuff myself. Give me a jellied pike or bream stuffed with mushrooms and barley anyday."

How he loathed Fridays. It seemed that the whole town reeked of the smell of the Poor-Jack boiling, steaming, bubbling away in its foul liquor - the very cauldrons of hell. Why, in the summer, it seemed the fishy vapours combined with the town's other foul delights to hang, visible in the streets like the angel of death. Even his own sumptuous dwelling in Redcliffe Street could not escape the pestilence.

"'Tis a Peche-tilence."

He tipsily slurred the word and the pun slithered forth. Self-congratulatory delight sparkled in his eyes, and denying to himself the possibility of any accidental intervention, he revelled in his self-perceived, ingenious wit and rolled the word around his mouth again and again.

"Pechetilence... Peche...tilence."

There was yet another jest contained therein. Maybe the Almighty had a sense of humour after all? Was it not in 'His' name that, every Friday, Cod fish was partaken of? And was it not within the portals of His holy house - Saint Mary Redcliffe - amidst the clouds of incense, that was found the only place of refuge from the wretched stench.

Notwithstanding, the stench meant profit for him and his partners. Considerable profit with small risk. Now that, way across the Ocean Sea , the most abundant fishing grounds had been discovered, there was no better way to make it.

In truth, once safely landed at the Redcliffe Back, nutmeg,

cloves, cinnamon and pepper made a more handsome return, but the initial outlay and the risks incurred were far greater. Nothing could get past the sharp eyes and curved scimitars of the Mohammedans without them extracting a huge impost. And was not the whole Mediterranean awash with Venetians and Genoese? They were worse than pirates. The thought of being robbed or having throats cut was bad enough, but being subjected to pious justifications whilst it happened was too much to bear.

Now all a man had to do was load a ship or two with a small crew, a score or so bushels of salt, wave them off across the Ocean Sea and wait. There were no Icelanders to barter with for the privilege of shivering in their dreary waters and no sausage-eaters from Cologne and Danzig to be civil to. Even better than all this, for a man in his own position, who, in his capacity as Collector of Customs was not supposed to dabble in trade, it was exploration, plain and simple. Had not a Royal Commission pronounced as much four years past? So what if the ships returned full to bursting with stockfish? Ordinary catches of fish were not liable to customs duty nor was there any requirement to keep records. So it was not trade at all. Who was there to trade with? No sovereign nation. Nought but a bunch of wild savages clad in skins and paint. No, they sailed not with the intention of trading, but of finding a certain Isle of Hy-Brasil.

Of course, it didn't do to blather about the fact that in actuality they had already found the 'New Land'. It amazed Croft that all in Bristow, from the wealthiest merchant down to the humblest drab, kept the secret close to their chests. It was as if the whole city was bound together in the keeping of the great, sly jest.

In London the men of Cologne and Danzig had ears everywhere, but a jest always seemed to slip through one ear and out the other, leaving a look of puzzlement on their moon faces. In fact, if any outsider, be he Londoner, Hansard or the King himself thought to ask, they were all told the same tale.

"From the waters to the west of Hibernia are the Stock-Fish taken."

Mouth agape, Thomas Croft opened the window once again. He knew better than to subject his delicate nose to the waterfront's pungent essence without the aid of a clove-pierced orange. But he needed to observe - observation was, after all, his official occupation.

It was late August. The sun was hot, but a light spray of rain served to temper the rising vapours of the day's fresh ordure. He ventured his head further out until a satisfactory view of the River Frome was gained. The broad daylight and the fine droplets of rain on his face caused him momentarily to blink. To the left was the place of the ship builders, with its rope, its barrels of tar, the ankle-deep wood shavings and incessant rasp and tap of mallet and saw. Croft loved the place, so much so that from time to time he would abandon his fine raiment for more humble trappings and go wandering, unrecognised he supposed, amidst the resinous maze of blossoming boats.

Just beyond the shipyard the smaller Frome flowed into the larger Avon - a union between Mother and Child that spread its arms in wide protection of the town. It was here that the Avon curved round Channon's Marsh and the incoming and outgoing ships, from the colossal Mary and John, of 900 tons, to the smallest, single master, were spied and recorded.

If Rudkin was correct in his sightings, the Cornucopia should have reached Saint Vincent's Rock or thereabouts, and would soon be stealing into view. Croft always felt excited at the prospect of one of the flock in which he had an interest returning to the nest. It gave him great pleasure to see a voyage into what were still uncharted waters being brought to a successful conclusion. It was not a question of profit alone. Officially he was not allowed to trade for profit. No, for him, an equal feeling of satisfaction was held in the wealth of knowledge gleaned.

A gift of a printed book had lain gathering dust until a fever had confined him to bed. He had called for that book, 'Mandeville's Travels', and had read it from cover to cover, staying abed for an extra day to complete the task when in truth he had been able to rise all along.

All the knowledge contained therein had transfixed him, not least the confirmation that the world was indeed a globe. Most men now knew this to be true, believed it with their heads, but somewhere in their hearts still they feared the world was as flat as a bread trencher. It was the hardest thing to cast off the prejudices of the cradle. For his mother, up until her dying day, the world was flat and that was that. Sir John Mandeville, the writer and great traveller, knew otherwise, and the precision of the printed word spoke in such a way that it banished all doubt for Croft and many others. It occurred to Croft that there was an authority in the black, ink characters that surpassed even the stone-etched edicts of Kings. But the secret knowledge pertaining to the New Land, however, would have to bide its time before trumpeting out from the printed page for all to hear.

The renowned fellow merchant, John Jay, was one of these others fascinated by the possibilities of 'New Lands'. He, along with Croft, William Spencer, Robert Strange and William de la Fount had commanded Thomas Lloyd, the most competent seaman in the whole of England, to venture westward into the Ocean Sea to search and find the Island of 'Hy Brasil,' and its reputed, endless supply of red-dye-wood. With it, the famed red cloth of Bristow would gain even greater renown, and the purses of the Genoese would be that much the lighter. For nine weeks Lloyd had roamed until forced back by storms. In the fog-bound waters he had spied no land, but he had felt the shift of the tides and smelt it; and that was good enough for them. 'If the nose of Lloyd believed there to be land, then land there was.'

The following year of our Lord, 1481, confirmed it. The two ships, the Trinity and the George, found land, not the 'Hy Brasil' where the red-dye-wood grows, but in a way almost as beneficial; a rocky shore, a 'Newland,' enshrouded within swirling fogs and with stockfish in such abundance that if a basket were lowered over the side it would need four pairs of hands to pull it back aboard. Of course, both ships just happened to be laden with salt enough to fill their holds to bursting. The nose of Lloyd be praised!

How it had all grown in four short years! So many salt-laden ships back and forth, back and forth. Croft wondered how much longer they could keep the secret. Ultimately, the most jealously guarded of treasures demanded display.

And with every ship returned, laden down with stockfish from that Western Sea, came a greater bounty of fantastical stories. There was no doubt in the mind of Thomas Croft that Antilia, the Isle of the Seven Cities, would soon reveal itself and its gold. Maybe even another route to Cathay or Cipangu lay to the west. 'Had not those pushy Genoese brothers, one a mapmaker... now what were their names?... Eight or ten years back... bored everyone rigid... can't for the life of me remember. Colon, Columbo? No. Anyway, that was their belief. Now, that would be the greatest prize,' he mused, 'greater even than the Isle of Hy-Brasil.'

At the present, though, he thought he would settle for word of the Swallow. She was by far the smaller of the two carracks, only eighty tons compared to the Cornucopia's hundred and fifty, but she was a beauty. Croft had lovingly watched her grow from lead-lined conception to spokeshave finish. And on her maiden voyage to Lundy Isle he had not once left the deck, other than to climb the lower rungs of rigging, laughing and jollying with the hands, halloing to the sea birds, even pissing over the leeward side like a common seaman. But that was not all of it. He shuddered at the memory. That nimble-footed young seaman deserved better thanks than those he had received.

He had been on their territory and had known it. Even though his gelt had caused the boat's very existence, the barefoot men who ran, spat, cursed and climbed like Barbary apes were the true guardians of his roving mistress. At the onset he had felt the sting of jealousy like a spurned suitor and had stood, stone-faced in the false armour of dignity, whilst the barefoot boys ran rings round him. All through the Gorge he stood, a wind-whipped statue, ignored by all, especially Ross the Master. He was dutifully occupied, barking gruff commands that rebounded off the cliff walls at the river pilots below.

It had not been until they were well out in the channel that events conspired to change Croft's demeanour. An irreverent herring-gull had taken upon itself the task of anointing his robes of office. He had turned in a red-faced fluster, not sure of what action to take, cursing himself for not having brought his manservant Roberts aboard, when a young lad in a red, woollen hat had boldly stepped up to him and voiced his opinion.

"A fine parcel o' good luck bees tha' bird's doins, your honour."

Taken aback, Croft had been unable to keep a straight face and had exploded like a falconet, surprising himself, not sure which emotion would erupt, laughter or rage. He was relieved it was laughter that boomed round the deck. Lurching for the main-mast, he steadied himself until the tears ran; and when he finally summoned enough strength to wipe his eyes, he noticed that all the seamen were laughing too. Checking his balance, rubbing his eyes again, he stared at the faces, not sure at first whether they laughed with him or were sneering at his awkwardness.

"Give the lad the robe, Master Croft. He'll do his best to clean it for you."

A well-mannered voice that betrayed a smattering of learning had spoken out from amongst the crew, and Croft watched as a young mariner of barely twenty years shuffled forward to join the lad. He could tell at a glance that they were brothers, with about five years' difference in age. Something about the pair of them was most pleasing. The older of the two was a good hand taller than the other, his head a mass of tight, flaxen curls that would have not looked amiss atop the pate of a fine young lady. Thankfully, the fellow had a beard, albeit a sparse one, and attired in blouse and breeches like his fellows, appeared manly enough. The younger one shared the same fine features of the older although his darker hair, once he had doffed the red woollen cap, was straight as straw.

"Cider or salt water, Master Croft? That's all we've got, but my brother'll do a good job... You'll do a good job for the Master, won't you Sim?"

"Salt water for the robe, but cider for me," answered Croft, and the men had all guffawed. How eager to please they had all seemed at the mention of drink! He had tipped them a knowing wink, then performed a sideways glance in the direction of Ross, signifying that the captain was the ultimate authority and he a mere mortal like themselves. The boy had taken the cloak and the other had made movement to return to his duties, but something had made Croft bid him stay and converse. The fellow had smiled awkwardly, but complied nonetheless.

"I see that you are brothers. Strange. I thought the custom was to avoid serving on board the same ship?"

"Yes sir. We be brothers, though it's just this once, this being the Swallow's first time out."

Croft nodded, as if in acceptance of the reply, but he was more interested in the way the young man was now attempting to mask the refined edge of his tongue.

"What do you think of her?"

"She be a beauty."

"Isn't she just. Almost as costly as my wife, mark you."

The comely-looking fellow had laughed awkwardly at the jest. Croft sensed that, having already singled himself out for whatever reason, he desired now to return to the anonymity of his duties. But Croft was intrigued and could not resist learning more. However, his probings were now directed in a more circumspect manner; he lowered his voice and the young man was forced to take a step closer.

"You are dressed like a common mariner, barefoot too, yet your speech, even though you have just made a half-hearted attempt at concealing the fact, reveals learning. On the other hand, your brother shows none of it. How is your hand? You write and read, do you not? Let me guess now. You have received instruction from the Franciscans?"

There had been an awkward silence. The young man had looked around to see if any of his shipmates listened and was just about to answer when the ship had dipped, and he had taken the opportunity to escape towards the aft tower railing. His place had been straightaway taken up by the younger brother. He had proudly thrust towards Croft a full cup of cider, hardly a drop of which had been spilled. Croft took the cup and even though his stomach churned, quaffed it dry. The boy up-ended the cup and held it above his head, sticking out his tongue to catch the last drops. Croft playfully boxed his ear and the cheeky lad scampered off. A spontaneous cheer had erupted and Croft, feeling the warmth spread in his belly, had grinned broadly and, with a flourish, saluted the ship's company one and all. Even the gruff Ross was seen to crack a smile. Moments later, when the Swallow again lurched, he had lost his footing and was sent careering towards the side. He had been unable to halt his momentum and the prospect of going overboard seemed inevitable. At the last possible moment, with his girth already poised over the edge, the lad had appeared from nowhere, and managed to hold him back until the older brother was able to lend a hand. Although Croft had laughed it off at the time, it had been the subject of several subsequent nightmares. Always the same tipping away of the deck, but each time the angle growing steeper, and his momentum growing faster until finally the deck had become a greased chute, and the choppy waters of the channel the very fires of hell. Then, merciful heavens, the dreams had ceased.

Despite this near-tragedy, the draining of the cup and the ripping off of the soiled robe had been like the peeling away of a callused, outer skin. From that moment on until the Swallow edged back into the Frome, he was, despite the obvious discomfort of ship's captain Ross, as one with the crew, turning the windlass, even pulling on a hawser to raise the 'fukke' sail, and blistering his hands in the process.

Croft allowed himself a smile at the recollection. The smile vanished. The unforgiving hardness of dry land demanded his re-assumption of the trappings of office once he and it were reunited.

He recalled with a faint twinge of guilt how, barely a month later, the same young sailor had impishly hailed him in Marsh

Street. He had purposely looked straight through the lad's puzzled face, not even halting his stride or intervening when the manservant brushed the boy aside like a worthless fribble, knocking his red cap in the gutter.

Croft patted his purse. The coins chattered inside the soft doe-skin. Yes, when the Swallow returns to the nest, I'll have Roberts make it up to the lad, him and his older brother. Now what was their name? Had he ever known it? It was getting harder than ever remembering names, but something about the pair of them intrigued. What it was he could not be sure, but he made a note to ask Rudkin to look up the name in the log. 'Yes, I'll remember to do that... Yes I must not forget.' In the corner of his memory slate he scribed the shape of a woollen hat, momentarily wincing at the bite of the hard, stone point. The thought of a good deed to be performed sometime in the abstract future added to his inner glow - a credit taken now for payment that in all probability would be forgotten.

The light shower had ceased. It had been the first touch of rain for many a long day - already the tease of its sparkle was beginning to fade. Croft's attention was drawn to the view from the right hand window, where, over the river, the sun-browned slopes of Brandon's hill rose. Way below the shrine atop the summit he could make out a large group of figures milling like flies on a dead dog. What was their purpose? What occupied them, virtue or villainy?

"Villainy, I'll be bound... Yes, villainy, most definitely."

"Now, where is that insufferable manservant Roberts?" he muttered. "He should have returned with the mutton pie by now."

CHAPTER 8
A Bladder Filled With Peas

On the lower slopes of Brandon Hill a crop-haired youth of seventeen lay drowning in his own blood, a lung punctured by a broken rib. Neither of the teams in the friendly game of football paid him any heed or, for that matter, the other two casualties who rolled and moaned in the dry grass. They were more fortunate, with but a broken arm apiece.   At least they could give vent to their suffering with wails of anguish, whilst through the tears still watch the progress of the game. All the drowning lad could do was slowly splay, then clench his fingers, whilst in his throat the faintest of rattles sounded.

"Three all... Three all!" came a shout and a cheer from the apprentices' team. The pig's bladder filled with dried peas had just rattled between the two piles of ragged smocks that marked the goal of the seamen's side.

"You calls tha' a goal, do you? Well, we agreed 'ands only in dribblin', 'tis feet an' kicks for scorin'. That ball was chucked!"

A young, bandy-legged seaman with a barely broken voice screeched above the murmurings of dissent. It had been his misfortune to have been guarding the goal and he had just suffered the double indignity of having the ball not only slip between the bundles of shirts, but between his legs.

"Or 'eads," another voice chipped in.

"Yes, or 'eads, but not 'ands... 'ands only for dribblin'," the screeching voice tried to continue.

"And whacking 'eads!" the same voice chortled. There was a thud as a fist slammed into the side of an apprentice's cropped head.

"Play on! Play on!" squealed one of the apprentices in a falsetto of desperation. Play on they did, but the game had ceased to bear any resemblance to football. Instead it took on the appearance of a skirmish; and then, as knives and belaying pins were drawn, more the appearance of a full-scale battle.

By the time authority, in the guise of the Common Sergeant and four wheezing guards with rusty pikes and a bolt-less crossbow, burst on the scene, most of the players had fled - the criss-cross trails of crimson marking their bloody flight. All that remained were five sprawled figures: four that were dead or dying, their short, cropped heads denoting them as apprentices; and the other, a bandy-legged sailor, lying unconscious beside a punctured ball.

"Pssst, this'n still breathes. Come over 'ere quick afore 'e ups an' legs it," the Common Sergeant hissed to his men.

They paid no heed, but simply carried on rifling through the belongings of the four dead youths.

"I said, you lot come over 'ere now, at the flamin' double. And you, Wilson, see that blade over there in that clump of grass?"

His voice rose and his leather-mittened finger wagged furiously.

"Not there, you flamin' dolt, behind you."

The heavy-set figure of Wilson twisted and turned in vain to see the blade. The others laughed and banged their pikestaffs on the ground. Wilson growled and thrashed around, then, letting out a squeal like a stuck porker, retrieved the knife with his bloodied paw.

"God's 'oly bollocks, Wilson, you're always muckin' about.

Now 'urry up an' bring it with 'ee. Quick! 'E'll be comin' round in a trice."

The Common Sergeant took the long knife and holding the tip of the blade between thumb and forefinger, let it swing to and fro like a pendulum.

"What do we 'ave 'ere then?... A mariner's knife if I'm not mistaken, as wot is used for disgorging 'ooks from fishes' froats, poppin' pearls from oyster shells, rings out of Dago's hear'oles. Pha! Rings from ladies fingers more like. And well, well, lads, look at this!"

He steadied the knife and pointed at the blade with the forefinger of his free hand.

"Blood is what we 'ave 'ere," he answered his own question. "Fresh, red blood that ain't set yet an' I wager it don't be fish's blood."

"No, Sergeant, it don't be fish's blood," squealed Wilson. "It be my blood! Just look at my 'and, 'tis a miracle that a finger ain't bin sliced clean off."

"Wilson!.. Shut that gurtt fat gob, will you? 'Tis a miracle I an't sliced your 'ead off afore."

Common Sergeant White knelt down beside the unconscious youth and prizing his fingers open, lay the handle on the opened palm.

"Why d'you do that, Sarge? When 'e comes around an' finds a gurt sticker in 'is 'and, ain't 'e gonna want t' use 'im? They all be handy knife boys, do seamen."

"Yes, you gurt 'airy quim, but we'll be ready for 'im, see. Won't us?"

An expression of pained exasperation covered the Sergeant's face.

"Evidence... Tha's what t'is. Hevidence fit for an 'angin. Now get round 'im an' get ready. I'm gonna wake the sleepin' babby up... An' Wilson, if you gets in the way, I'll 'ave your bloody guts! I aint forgotten about them bolts you lost."

Sergeant White stared hard, snarling with curled lip at the useless crossbow in Wilson's possession, then stooping low, he eased the young sailor's return into consciousness with a brace of gentle pike prods to the groin.

"Ow!... Kicks is for scorin'... 'ands is for dribblin'."

The youth's eyes sprang wide open. They did not focus, but flitted hither and thither with fear and confusion. From his mouth poured another jumble of words.

"It were agreed! Kicks only for scorin, 'ands for passin' an' dribblin."

"'Ere Sarge wha's 'e mean all this dribblin' stuff?"

"Shut it!"

The sergeant took a step backwards, pike held at the ready. The youth raised his head.

"Did us win?"

"Ha! Did you 'ear that lads?" White scoffed and moved back another step. "Yes, sailor-boy, you won a'right. An' wha's more you gets the prize. Thing is, see, you 'ave to come along with us to collect it."

"Wha' d'you mean?... 'ere, wha's goin' on?"

The young seaman sat up, went to rub his head then noticing the bloody knife in his hand, let out a gasp and cast it aside.

"'Ere wha's 'is then?. A gurt sticker!. How's 'e get in my 'and?"

"Don't ask us, sailor-boy."

Sergeant White, feigning a puzzled expression, turned his eyes over where the four crumpled bodies lay.

"No, don't ask us... Ask they poor buggers you cut up over there."

The youth turned his head, his mouth dropped open and a look of fear dilated his eyes.

"Wha' you talkin 'bout?"

The four pikes and the unloaded crossbow were raised to the height of the youth's head.

"Murder is what we're talkin' 'bout. Murder plain an' simple like... so up you gets, my jolly sailor lad and come with us to the castle, where we knows just the one to take the greatest delight in your salty, savoury company. Dursn't we, eh lads?"

White turned, smirking to his men who guffawed and nodded.

"But I ain't killed no one! Cross my 'eart an 'ope to die!"

The young sailor began to slowly rise. The pike points rose with him, marking his fearful eye-level.

"D'you 'ear tha' lads? E 'opes t' die."

All five guards were beside themselves with mirth, the pike points wobbling with the laughter.

"I reckons 'ow we knows the right pair of 'ands to accommodate you on tha' particular score, my salty-babby."

Suddenly the frightened expression on the young sailor's face vanished and a look of sheer child's delight took its place. Sergeant White appeared perplexed, his authority momentarily undermined by the youth's distracted attention.

"She be back!" the youth shrieked. "Look, 'tis the Cornucopial back from the Ocean Sea . The Swallow won't be far behin'. Ain't she a beauty? Just look at 'er rig, 'as to be 'er."

He thrust his arm out and pointed down the slope towards the distant River Avon where, sure enough, a three-masted carrack edged along the water. Resisting the impulse to turn, Sergeant White smirked like a man who knew all the ruses and was certainly not about to fall for this, the oldest of them all.

"The young bastard's right, Sarge, it do look like the Cornucopial," said Wilson, waving the crossbow.

To all in the port of Bristow, the return of one of the ships from the Ocean Sea was an event of some significance. Though most would have no stake in the event, other than a flake of Poor-Jack to lay atop a trencher next Friday, to many it was a matter of civic pride. For others it was a time to pay out or collect wagers. One such was Sergeant White. If the observation was correct, he was down a half Rial to Rudkin, the Customshouse keeper.

"It's 'er a'right, Sarge... Look at 'er rig."

"Oh, look at 'er rig is it, Widowson? An 'ow long 'ave you been an expert on marine matters?"

"I gets sick on water... overwise..."

White sneered. His resolve not to turn was beginning to waver, but still he kept one eye on the miscreant. The order had come down from above, loud and clear, that these bloody games of football would have to cease. An example would have to be made, and he was fortunate to have a candidate for that particular pleasure within his grasp. What a feather in his cap this would be! 'Steady now!' he told himself. He knew that it was his first duty to restrain - with bonds or chain - one that he had placed under arrest, not letting his eye wander for an instant. Even the promise of a hundred gold nobels would not have served to keep his head from ultimately turning.

"Yeh.I sees 'er." White cleared his throat and spat. "So wha, of it!"

The young sailor had not intended to make a bid for freedom. He had not begun to fully appreciate the danger he was in. The germ of the possibility of escape had not begun to form in his still addled brain. The opportunity, however, simply presented itself when all present had taken an involuntary step forwards to gain a better view of the homecoming ship, and in so doing, the hooked pike-points became ensnared above his head. At that same moment he noticed that the cross-bow in the fat guard's bloody hand, although cocked, was bereft of any missile. Before they, or even he himself knew it, he had shouldered Wilson out of the way, sending the porcine dolt careering down the slope, and then had taken off like a greyhound in heat, up and over the top of Brandon Hill.

"Come back or 'e shoots!" White bellowed.

"Wilson, where the frig are you? Why, the lit... You stupid bastards! God's bollocks! Quick, a'ter 'im!"

The four pikemen, like dancers round a maypole, tried to untangle their weapons, but White, in his rage, made matters worse, tugging, twisting, spitting incandescent fury. Wilson, meanwhile, was still charging down the slope, his drawn-out screech rising in pitch and volume as he gained momentum, until finally the cry stopped and a metallic clatter resounded, as rusty breast-plate and gnarled trunk of hawthorn made violent contact. He lay in a leg-kicking heap, whimpering, helpless as an overturned woodlouse.

Sergeant White left his men to untangle the pikes and took off up the hill. Purple in the face and spitting globules of yellow-green phlegm, he finally reached the top where the remains of the shrine to the Irish monk, Saint Brendan, stood. Clutching the side of the crumbling wall, he cursed through his teeth as the distant, running figure of the escapee crossed the track in the valley bottom and scrambled up the steep, wooded slopes of the opposite side. White cupped his hands and bellowed across the valley.

"I'll 'ave yoooouuu... You be gallow's bait so 'elp me!" He coughed and spat again. "I'lllll 'ave youuuuu!"

The scampering figure briefly stopped to urinate, turned and waved nonchalantly across the distance then, just before disappearing beneath the canopy of leaves, he raised two fingers high in the 'Agincourt salute'.

White turned, seething. To an old archer this was the worst possible insult. He scanned the slopes for his men, in particular

Wilson. As ever, Wilson was destined to bear the brunt of his fury, and to make matters worse, instead of following their sergeant up the slope, the others had wandered down to assist the hapless oaf.

Looking over his shoulder once more, White marked which way the youth was heading. He caught a last good glimpse of him, seemingly meandering without a care in the world, climbing up to Clifton Wood. The youth turned and waved once again, then he was lost from sight.

"'otwells... 'otwells, yes, 'as to be." He mouthed the place name 'Hotwells' over and over in time with his downward stride.

They did not hear Sergeant White's return. All four, including a dazed Wilson, were intent on the progress of the Cornucopia.

"It's 'er a'right, you can tell for certain like by the rig."

"Oh yes, Widowson, an what's 'at then?"

"I don't know, do I? But tha's wha' the sailor babby sez, din 'em."

"Yoooouuuu worthless bunch o' steamin' hog turds!"

At the sound of the Sergeant's booming voice they froze, none daring to look round.

"Look at me! Goddamn! Look at me, you scabby sons of 'ores! At Towton with the other Bristol boys I slew 'undreds of the Lancastrians. Me an' Reginald Rudkin, yes I mean that Rudkin, the Customshouse keeper. Wun't think it t' look at 'im now, but he were one of us. Well, after we'd let loose all our arrows, we slew ten apiece, slashin' an' stabbin' in the snow 'til we cus'nt slash no more, an' a couple o' they were knights on 'orses an all."

White paced up and down, his breast-plate heaving. Slowly, with heads bowed, his men turned round.

"An' what 'ave you done, eh? Tell me 'ow many mortal men you 'ave sent to their maker? Come on now... I don't means escortin' felons to the 'angman, or poor Lollards an' 'eretics to the stake! Armed is wha' I mean... I mean armed men. How many?"

There was no answer. The leather-helmeted heads were lowered even further, until chins almost rested on chests.

"Just wha' I fort, not a flamin' one... An' to top it all you can't even 'old onto one young sailor-boy. Well, you may be hinterested to know tha' 'e's off over Clifton Wood. Now my nose sez 'e's gonna' come down by the 'otwells... Eiver tha' or 'e'll cross the Gorge somewhere over by the Downs."

White's harsh demeanour eased somewhat as he regained his breath. The tone of his words no longer seemed to carry the same sting of bile.   Slowly the heads were raised.

"Course if 'e slips across the river an' gets into Stokeleigh woods, well we lost 'im good an' proper. Give 'im a few nights in them woods an' 'e'll eiver be off 'is 'ead, or playin' at bein' Robin 'ood wiv they other thieves an' cut-throats out there."

The men laughed nervously, nudging each other, elbows flapping like fledglings attempting to fly - relieved that his humour had appeared to improve. Finally, growing bolder, Wilson plucked up the courage to ask a question.

"Sarge, can we get some pies? My belly do thinks my froat's been cut, it bees rumblin' sumut awful?"

It was the wrong question. White, speechless with fury, strode up to Wilson with fist raised and struck him down to the ground.

"Get up! Get up I said!"

A bloody-nosed Wilson cowered in a ball as White stood over him, his fist ready to strike again.

"Get up!"

The pounding of a horse's hooves stayed his hand.

"Well, Sergeant Wright. What seems to be the trouble?" enquired a voice, heavily laced with sarcasm and affected tedium. "There appears to be a lot of apprentices and ruffians lying about. 'Tis the wrong time of year entirely to leave dead bodies lying around, don't you think?"

Taking two paces forward, in order to hear above the horse's panting, White glanced up at the mounted man, saluted, then lowered his face. The sunlight glared from behind the man's head, bouncing dazzling rays off his helmet straight down into the Common Sergeant's eyes.

"Beggin' your hindulgence, Captain but 'tis not Wright. Tis Whi..."

"What! Not right?" The horseman let out an exasperated sigh. "My dear fellow, I know 'tis not right. Didn't I just say such a thing, Sergeant?

The horse shook its head, whinnied, then snapped at the sergeant, who sprawled backwards into the arms of his men. The Captain of the Guard signalled him to advance with the wiggle of a finger.

"We'll try again, Sergeant." Again, another sigh of exasperation emanated. "Why are those dead bodies lying around? And what is more, why are they dead in the first place?" The captain's voice became firmer.

White nervously approached the mounted man, his eyes never leaving the horse's head.

"Well Captain, sir, they wus playin' football."

"Playing now? Play? T'would seem that they had been more than a touch serious... Deadly serious!" The captain's tone became cold and brittle.

"That be so Captain. And what's more sir, we had happrehended the main villain, the murderer of they poor unfortunates."

"And where is he now? I don't see him."

"Well, Captain, 'e 'ad 'idden habout 'is person a most wicked blade. And we wus jus' about to halter 'im an' bring 'im in for justice when out 'e whips it, an' wha's more he cruelly cuts poor Wilson on the 'and... hold it up, Wilson. Hold it up! Show the Captain your 'and. Look sir, the 'eartless devil nearly slashed 'is poor finger off."

Wilson winced in mock agony and held out the bloody hand. There was a sympathetic murmur from his comrades. The Captain let a sigh of indifference escape, then at the onset of a thud of excrement from the horse's backside, he gracefully rose in the stirrups, waiting for the motion and the accompanying torrent of urine to cease. White stood to attention, with captive breath, nose a' twitching in the aromatic cloud of steam.

"So you let him go. How long? Which way? Describe this villain."

The Captain, still erect in the stirrups, instinctively scanned the direction of the seaman's flight. Both he and the horse were plainly irritated, the animal snapping at the bit and the Captain snapping out the questions like a volley of gunshots.

"Three turns of a sand-glass at most, sir. Down, then up over they woods."

Sergeant White side-stepped the horse and pointed out the path of flight.

"And?"

"Seaman. Lanky, about twenty years and fierce as a fox wiv it," White lied, adding at least five years to the youth's age.

"Right then, you er, men, follow me!"

And with that, the Captain withdrew a long sword from its scabbard, whirled it around his head and cantered off, leaving the pile of steaming manure as a seal of his authority.

"It were done wi' the Devil's 'elp, sir. I fought at Towton, he wun't get past me wivout the Devil's 'elp!"

The words were lost in the dull pounding of hooves.

Sergeant White turned to the four men, his face in a snarl. He shook his fist in Wilson's face, grabbed a pike and off they went, groaning at each laboured plod.

CHAPTER 9
A Blood Pudding

How unutterably pleasurable life was, thought Thomas Croft, as he scooped up the last drop of mutton gravy with the final morsel of white bread. He knew full well that his manservant, Roberts, had helped himself to part of the loaf's heel as the repast had made its journey from the kitchens of his Redcliffe home to the Customs House.

"Beggin' your pardon, sir? It appears tha' in my haste to get the tasty morsel to you while it was still pipin' 'ot sir, I must 'ave caught the end of the loaf somewhere."

Croft had dismissed the man, deciding to let it pass for the time being, but a menial with a taste for fine, white bread could not be tolerated. Why, next the man would be demanding flesh twice a week! Nonetheless, he had brushed the matter aside. Nothing could be allowed to spoil what was becoming the most perfect of days, what with the succession of the Tudor to the throne and the safe return of the Cornucopia.

He transported the final mouthful to the open window and, still chewing, watched the progress of the Cornucopia's mast tops as it glided past the opening of the Frome. If he hurried now, he could be at the Saint Nicholas Back in time to greet her. No doubt Strange, De La Fount and the others would be there all a buzz, not least because of the new King. Why, the whole of Bristow would know of the ship's return from the Ocean Sea and would be congregating, hoping to glimpse a Dragon's foot or at least a mermaid's tail brought up from the hold.

He strode to the door, opened it, and bellowed down the stairwell.

"Roberts, have my horse ready and tell Rudkin to accompany me. He can hold on to the stirrup and run alongside."

"Did you 'ear his magnificence, Mister Rudkin? Best not eat all that blood pudden' or you'll give yourself a seizure. You know what it's like runnin' alongside the high an' mighty Thomath Croft when he's got a mind to gallop, Why, 'e don't stop for no one, chargin' through the streets like Sir friggin' Lanthelot. Why, I swear by almighty God tha' 'alf the time my feet don't touch the ground when 'e's in a hurry. And does 'e give a fig? Not on your life."

The manservant stood with hand on hip and quietly hissed, showering Rudkin with random gobbets of spittle.

"Don't you never mind me, Roberts." Rudkin wiped his face in disgust. "Look to your own business. Go on now... Go an' get 'is charger ready... He won't go too fast for I. Me an' ol' Crofty 'ave an arrangement see..."

Rudkin cut another slice from the blood pudding and lifting the knife to his mouth, ate from the blade. Not once did he take his eyes off Roberts. He was willing the servant's disappearance; something the man seemed most reluctant to comply with.

"G'warn wiv you now Roberts, you mincing Catamite, get a move on. If you think I'm leavin' 'ere wiv 'arf a blood pudden' on the table, an you on the loose, well you must 'ave worms for brains! I'd rarver give it the 'orse."

"Oh thank you very much, Mister Rudkin." He stressed the word 'Mister'. "I wouldn't touch your pudden if it were all that lay between me an' starvation."

Roberts spun on his heels and flounced out of the room. Rudkin sighed with relief and cut another chunk of pudding, but before he could lift the morsel to his tongue, he heard the clump, clump of Croft's riding boots on the stairs. Clearing his throat, he reluctantly laid down the knife and standing approximately to attention, awaited the manifestation of the great presence.

"Ah, Rudkin, I see you are eager for a chance of exercise. Good, good, you have long legs fit for a lope, I've no doubt you'll keep apace with the nag."

As if in league with sundry black arts, Roberts had silently materialized in the room. His face suddenly appeared over Croft's shoulder and leered at Rudkin. Despite himself, Rudkin's lip curled with distaste. Croft looked on, unaware of the malign presence behind him.

"Upon my soul, Rudkin, you are becoming a very surly fellow. You pull faces that would make a gargoyle crumble. If you care to leave the employ of this Customshouse, just maintain that crabbed countenance and you will find yourself out of here in a trice... and by way of the stocks, mark you."

"Ah hem... sir, your horse awaits you."

Roberts announced his presence with a bow and a sickly grin, then the moment Croft's back was turned, he lolled his head to one side, fixed his eyes on the blood pudding, and like a cat waiting to pounce on a wounded mouse, licked his lips.

"No offence hintended Mast' Croft," Rudkin flustered. "I 'as this ter'bul pain in me 'ead on account of when I was battered thereabouts at the Battle o' Towton. Sometimes it do creep up on me and cause me to curl my lip an' all."

"Towton again, is it? You make too much of it."

Croft looked Rudkin up and down, the beginnings of a sarcastic grin playing with the corner of his mouth. "Leeches, man, that's what you require. You need to lose blood, not to take onboard more of it." He pointed down at the blood pudding. "Get rid of it, man, cast it out! Roberts, get rid of this foul thing the moment we are gone."

"Consider it done, sir."

Roberts bowed his head. Croft made for the side door where his horse awaited.

"Come along, Rudkin. A quick dash to Redcliffe Back will stir those sluggish humours. Oh, and bring the ledger, man. It all must be entered."

He smiled knowingly and rubbed the side of his nose with a forefinger in imitation of Rudkin's own habit. Rudkin managed a weak flicker of a smile

"Certainly don't let my horse see you with such a sour face, Rudkin. It would not go well with you should the beast bolt in terror."

Roberts dashed ahead to open the door and together he and Rudkin eased Thomas Croft up into the saddle. Rudkin glared, Roberts smirked, then as they moved off, a livid Rudkin turned once more and shook his fist at Roberts. The smirk on the servant's face broadened as he mockingly blew a kiss goodbye.

CHAPTER 10
The light across the Gorge

Simon, the young fugitive seaman, had changed his mind about a descent to the river by way of the Hotwells. Instead, he had kept to the woods that crowned the hills and gorge around the hamlet of Clifton. There were many pathways leading downwards; some terminated in mid-air with a drop sheer enough to freeze the soul of Icarus. Only a handful led safely to the bottom.

He had once ventured this far with Matty, his older brother, who had bragged all the way of his knowledge of the pathways, but when it had come to it, had nearly broken both their necks. After several abortive attempts they had made it down to the muddy Avon, but neither of them had dared ford across and climb up into the woods of Stokeleigh. Over there were Boggarts and Greenmen.

Where was Matty? If only he was around he would know what to do, but then he had not been around much for a good while and Simon hardly recognised his brother when fortune allowed them to be on dry land together. True, the five year difference in their ages seemed less of a chasm physically, but in other respects the gap had widened. Matty could read and use an astrolabe; soon he would be a helmsman and after that maybe even a Master. Already it seemed that he spoke like one. Three years with the Franciscans had left their mark. Soon though, Matty would be back and would know how to help. Somehow he must stay at large and God willing get to his brother. They had promised their mother not to crew aboard the same ship. He would have given anything to have been aboard the Swallow with Matty and crossing the Ocean Sea instead of stuck onboard the usual deckless landhugger. He knew where they were bound. Didn't everyone? The size of some of that Poor-Jack they brought back! What fun it must be hoisting them up! Hard, backbreaking work, but all the same, not like hauling stinking cow hides and tin. 'Gurt fishy Monsters!' he exclaimed aloud. None had seen the like before.

But this splitting the two of them up, where was the sense in it? In case of accidents, was it? This accident would not have occurred were he aboard the Swallow, would it? And what of that promise now? Were they still held to it now that their mother had passed away? Matty did not know this. How could he? He had already been gone two weeks when she died. Simon felt sick remembering her passing. He also felt a sharp pang of jealousy. It was Matty she called out for as the dreadful, sweating sickness took hold. Only Matty, yet he had been the one to help nurse her. Yes, her curly Matty, with hardly a word for himself, but then it had always been that way. He filled his lungs with air, held his breath for a count of ten, then exhaled. The jealousy passed.

"It were only right after all, 'e were the eldest."

He loved his brother. Who else was there left to love? His pisshead uncle? There was no more family left. His father had died long ago and was not even a memory. Yes, he loved his brother, ached for him. 'Come on Matt!, 'urry up 'ome, will you?'

Maybe the Swallow was passing through the gorge this very moment. He wondered, but knew in his heart that if so, the cries of the river pilots below would be audible even at this distance. He let out a frustrated growl, sniffled, then, picking up a rock the size of a hen's egg, hurled it into the woods.

"Bastards... Goddamn Bastards!"

He sent another rock hurtling down the wooded slope. It slammed against a tree trunk and from the tangled top branches a drum-roll clattered. He jumped, his own heart fluttering wildly, as two plump pigeons rose into the sky. Standing on tiptoes, he watched with a deep yearning as they made a wide sweep out over the gorge. He could not resist tracing their flight, with his outstretched forefinger an imaginary gun.

"Bang! Bang! Pigeon pie for supper. Why did my mates leave I behind for they guards to capture...? Goddamn bastards!"

He muttered, sniffled again and screwed his eyes tight, fighting back the tears. No, he would not cry. He was fifteen years old and cursed 'Goddamn' like a seaman was supposed to. He had ridden a five day storm on his first time out and not puked once. On the return he had quaffed the fiery grog of the Irishmen at the harbour of Kinsale, taken a full swig to quench a child's thirst, thinking that nothing could be stronger than cider. His eyes had watered fit to pop from their sockets, but he had not cried, he was a real seaman. Goddamn!

"Goddamn bastards! I never kilt no bugger. Four dead 'e said, an' me wha' s'posed t' 'ave done it. Can't be right, 's not right."

Again he screwed his eyes, but the tears breached the closed lids to well and drip in great, single droplets onto the cracked clay earth of the pathway.

What was he going to do? Where was he going to go? Sanctuary in a house of God? Priests disturbed him as much as Common Sergeants and Boggarts. He had a vague idea of crossing into Stokeleigh woods and hiding out until the commotion had died down and maybe then stealing back to the waterfront. There were plenty of places to hide out there before secreting himself onboard a boat. But what of his mates? Would they hide him or turn him in? They would know he hadn't killed anyone, but would they be able to hold their tongues as they slaked their thirst in the Moon? Four dead, though, over a game of football. He could not believe it. Most of them had appeared to be crop-head apprentices. There would be more fuss made over them than for seamen, and the seamen would be blamed. It was very serious and would be a long time dying down. Even if he managed to get on board a boat, the boat would return soon enough. He sent another stone crashing through the branches. Goddamn! Would things have been different if he had saved the goal? He squirmed and felt a sharp pang of shame at the memory of the ball rolling between his legs. That had been his greatest crime. They would never forgive him, and he would never forgive himself.

"Bastards 'ould give I up to the guards, an' no mistake. Come on Matty, 'urry up 'ome."

His empty stomach rumbled like voices in the distance. He rubbed it until it settled down. Then he did hear voices, real voices and they were not that distant at all. Instinctively he knew whose they were.

"Oh no! Not they friggin' guards wi' their gurt big pikes again. Goddamn guards..."

Another wave of guilt engulfed him, this time for his continued blasphemy. He had never felt so alone, so wretched before. He thought about giving himself up but remembered the twitching body of another young seaman two years back, about the same age that he was now, hoisted up on the waterfront gibbet for the thieving of a bolt of red cloth. He swallowed hard, rubbed his throat, and then, quickly blessing himself, darted down the wooded slope.

"No, Goddamn they shall not 'ave I to string up an' gawp at whilst I be a twitchin' an' pissin'. I'd rarver go over the friggin' gorge!"

He followed the pathway down, heedless of the clawing brambles. Faster and faster he ran until forced to grasp at branches to slow his pace. Breathless, he came to a halt, bloodied arms entwined around the trunk of a smooth barked beech, hugging the tree to him and sobbing once more.

"Oh Mam, Mam, why me, Mam! Why me? You knows I din't do no killin' don't you?"

A twig snapped somewhere above. He froze, and releasing his embrace, peered up the slope. He could see nothing. The tree marked the division of the pathway. Choosing the right hand fork, he began to run. For about a hundred paces he scampered until the pathway abruptly turned upwards. In breathless panic he swerved round and retraced his steps again at full tilt. Racing past the tree he had just embraced, he noticed a smear of his blood on the bark and thought about rubbing at the tell-tale sign, but a cough and a curse from above sent him careering, crashing downwards.

There were voices shouting and growling close by; loudest of all he recognised that of the Sergeant.

"Some babby's crashin' about down there an' it ain't no coney. I reckons it be 'im, our sailor boy! Wha' a stroke of luck! I think we do 'ave 'im in us grasp. Come on... An' watch they friggin' pikes!"

In a flood of light the fugitive was out of the trees and amongst the bushes and the sunswept crags of grey and orange stone. Still going fast, too fast, he looked back, hearing but not yet seeing his pursuers. Leaping forward with only a cursory glance ahead, more concerned about what lay behind and seemingly unaware of the void that loomed ahead. Suddenly, scraping to an abrupt halt amidst a welter of rubble he grasped at a crag, hugging it harder than he had earlier hugged the tree, and stared wide-eyed, petrified as the dusty shower of rock shards tumbled into emptiness. The crag halted what would have been a spectacular launch into thin air. Again, his stomach screamed out as if it were some separate entity desirous of terminating their association there and then, and once more it heralded the approach of the guards.

"Down there, look!. See 'is 'ands on tha' rock over there... Come on, quick afore 'e flies away."

"He ain't gonna fly away, Sarge, only angels and witches can flllyyyyyy!!!!"

From above the fugitive came a metallic clatter, accompanied by terrified cries and clouds of dust and rubble.

"Wilson, I swear I'll 'ave your flamin' 'ide..."

Sergeant White extricated himself from the human tangle, briefly brandished a fist before thinking better of it and grabbed another hand-hold of rock instead.

"Look, 'e's bloody well gone over the edge! Quick go down there... see if you can see 'im."

"I ain't movin'!" squealed Wilson.

"Wilson, Widowson, Smith! I'm orderin' one o' you to go down an' 'ave a look."

"I ain't a movin' eiver."

"Nor I."

Down below, the young seaman was galvanized into a spider-like activity. He descended a fifteen foot face with relative ease, his toes and fingers instinctively finding the holds. At the foot of the face he stood on a wide ledge and looked over the edge. Beneath him a sheer drop of over a hundred and fifty feet swooped down onto a jagged jumble of rock that sloped steeply for an equal distance down to the grassy banks of the muddy Avon. He steadied himself, attempted to turn, but made himself stare down until the dizziness passed. After all, he was a seaman. It may have been a long drop, but, unlike being aloft on a ship, the cliff face was not moving. He watched the white specks of gulls as they skimmed above the river's surface, their own shadows like dark hawks mimicking every turn. One way or another he would soon be down there beneath them. There was no going back, that was certain.

The flash of a falling pike startled him into glancing upwards. It sped past his shoulder, clipped the ledge, then, turning lazy somersaults, clattered and smashed on the rocks below. He looked up again in time to see the rotten-toothed face of the Sergeant leering over the edge.

"You 'ave to be careful down there, my babby, you could 'ave a haccident. Tell you what... Why don't you clamber back up 'ere? We could 'ave a bit of a chat about fings... Get 'em straightened out like."

"Leave I be." he shouted back. "I never killed no one! You ain't stretching my neck! I'd frow myself off 'ere first!"

The face above retreated, there was the sound of grunting and scraping of rock being manoeuvred against rock, and then over the edge tumbled a large stone the same size as the sergeant's head. Again the ledge was struck, this time with a loud dull thud, the vibrations of which he felt in both toe and fingertips. The leering Sergeant peered over once more and Simon Tyrell shuddered. There was now no doubt in his mind that the man wanted him dead one way or another.

"Hello, down there, 'tis I again. Ere, where be you? 'Ave you gone over? Say somefing will you?"

The fugitive did not answer. He knew that, if he were to survive, he would have to block out all distractions. From this moment on he was up aloft in a storm-tossed sea and below, awaiting a slip, were the gaping jaws of the fiercest of stone serpents.

He knew better than to attempt the vertical face that lay directly beneath the ledge. Instead, he commenced inching along a wide crack that ran horizontally to the left for about fifteen feet. The crack accommodated his toes; his fingers stretched and found sufficient holds, but half way along it became apparent that the outward curve of the face would compel him to lean backwards with only his fingertips to save him.

There was no sound from above. Had they seriously thought he had gone over the edge and given up their chase? He moved further along until the projecting part of the rock curved out beside him. With his right hand he quickly blessed himself then rubbed the sweating palm in his shaggy hair. The left hand followed. In turn both hands were rubbed in the dusty crevices. Breathing deeply, he launched himself along and outwards. It seemed that at that same exposed moment the wind chose to come blasting, mocking, along the gorge. It was not a cool refreshing wind to bring strength and succour, but a hot sultry gust to crackle and cackle, leaving an unwanted gift of gritty dust in his eyes.

"Ah now! There 'e be! Di'nt I say tha' 'e wun't leave us again lads?...'least not wivout sayin' goodbye."

Blinking furiously, the fugitive turned his head to see his leering pursuer standing on the same ledge that only moments before he had vacated.

"Tha' do look difficult... 'ere, let me give you some hassistance."

The young seaman saw with horror that one of the other guards had leaned right over and was passing a pike down to the Sergeant.

"Let me 'elp you in your moment of difficulty."

The Sergeant passed the pike through his hands and then, chuckling to himself, began to jab at the youth.

Simon felt the sweat flooding his palms once more. The rock face above was virtually unblemished; there appeared to be nothing for his fingers to grasp. The tip of the rusty, iron point rudely prodded his thigh - once, twice, three times it jabbed like the beak of a blackbird attempting to smash a snail's shell. The fugitive stole a glance. It appeared that the Sergeant had extended the pike to the maximum his strength dare allow. Any further and the heavy point would overbalance and wrest itself from the man's hands. The Sergeant no longer smiled, but scowled and spat with the effort. Instead of jabbing with the point, he began to swing it wide like a scythe. Out it swung, then in it came, smashing into the rock beside the fugitive's thigh.

It had occurred to Simon then that it was impossible to carry through the manoeuvre he had committed himself to, but if he could somehow get his fingers into the horizontal crevice now occupied by his toes, he could dangle from there and hopefully reach another toehold below. At least he would be out of reach of the thrashing pike. The only problem was in executing the move. But how to move his hands down to the crevice when their tenuous grasp was all that stopped him from falling backwards into oblivion? The only possible way was to go back, and that meant moving into range of the pike.

"Wait, stop clatterin' that gurt rusty thing. You nearly knocked I off... I'm comin' back," he called out, purposely exaggerating the quiver of terror in his voice

"Eh, wha' you say?"

The Sergeant checked himself and lifting the pike up to a vertical position spoke again, his tone one of bewilderment tinged with disappointment.

"Wha', you mean you're givin' yourself up to my custody? An' just when I was beginnin' to henjoy myself too."

"Yes, I'm comin' over."

"Right, come on then. No tricks mind."

"Tricks? Wha' tricks? I carn 'old on much longer."

He pretended to quake with fear as he moved back along the crevice.

"Ooouucchh!!!"

"Wha' is it now? Get a move on."

"I can't, sominks bit my toe! Felt like a viper."

He moved one hand down to the crevice and made a great show of rubbing his foot.

"D'you 'ear tha' lads? Serpent's got 'im. Must be the bite o' the Devil hisself for bein' such a hevil little fellow."

From above there was a chorus of guffaws. Then the Sergeant's jaw dropped open, speechless. Suddenly, in a single agile movement, the young seaman moved his other hand down to the crevice and swung his body below so that he was now suspended by his fingertips. Then before the astounded Sergeant had time to protest, he had swung himself back along the rock, below the overhang that had earlier confounded him, and out of sight.

"Wha'?... Why you little lyin' bastard! I'll see they burns you wiv 'ot faggots afore they do string you up! Come back 'ere or I'll..."

"Where's 'e gone, Sarge? 'Ave you lost 'im?"

"No, Wilson, we hain't lost 'im, 'cause you an' Smiffy are gonna go back along an' down by 'otwells an' then you're gonna find the 'igh an' mighty Captain 'and, an' tell 'im we got the little bastard trapped up 'ere."

Simon would have given anything to see the look on the Sergeant's face, but the sounds of the man's foul bluster was music enough to his ears. The gamble had paid off. Not only were there toe holds in profusion, but they led to a veritable stone staircase that it seemed the hand of God had fashioned for this very purpose. Within the time it takes a thirsty man to quaff a yard of ale, fugitive and pursuers were separated by a diagonal distance of over a hundred feet. He could no longer hear the Sergeant's curses, and the pieces of rock that the man threw fell far short.

It was moments later, as he was about to hurl himself across a fissure onto a bushy ledge, that something on the opposite side of the Gorge caught his eye. There was a flash, a fleeting glint of light amongst the foliage, like the sparkle of a fish's flank in a dark pool. It happened again, amongst the trees at the top of the magnificent escarpment of sheer rock that rose to span the whole height of the Gorge. Somebody was trying to attract his attention with the sun's reflection on a mirror. He did not know why, but something about the glimmer of light gave him hope. Relief in some shape or form lay on the other side of the river. It was no longer a question of just escaping the guards, there was a prize to aim for and he was determined to hold tightly to its promise.

Vaulting the gap, he began to thread his way from bush to bush down the last fifty feet. It was easy. He hummed as he made the final part of the descent. All that remained was a ten foot drop down onto a grassy slope. He turned, chuckled, and holding onto a bush, let his legs dangle ready for the final drop.

For an agonising moment he thought he was imagining things and that the firm prod in the square of his back was his memory of the sergeant's pike returned, but as he tried to let himself down, the prod did not go away, staying firmly pressed in his back. Behind him a horse snorted. For the young seaman it was nothing less than a dragon breathing fire. In terror he tried to clamber back up, but the prod pinioned him firmly to the rock face.

"Well now, Lady Rowena, we appear to have our miscreant. What, pray, shall we do with it? Let it up or let it down?"

A haughty, authoritative voice spoke. Again the horse snorted and pounded the earth with a hoof.

"Please sir, your honourl, sir. Who ever you be. Can I come down? My arms be killin I..."

The unforgiving prod was twisted and pressed further into the youth's back.

"Did you hear that, M'lady? The wretch speaks before it's spoken to. Shall we let it down? Shall we let it down, so that in due course justice may be obliged to hoist it aloft again on a gibbet, eh? Or shall we run it through and save justice the expense?"

"Please M'lady, bid 'im take it away afore I's spitted on it... I carn 'old on any longer."

He was pleading now. The child that skulked in the still breaking voice once again rushed to the fore and squealed for mercy. And then, mid-cry, the prod was suddenly removed and down into a ragged, puling heap the young seaman tumbled. Through tear-filled eyes he stared up in horror at the horse and rider, and backed off to cower against the rock. The horse took a step nearer. Simon sniffled, and wiping his nose on his torn shirt sleeve, attempted a nervous smile.

"Who be you? Where be this Lady Rowenal then? All I can see is a' gurt 'orse."

He coughed and spoke from the rear of his throat, trying to purge the child's tone from his speech. The horse snorted once more, right in his face, and the mounted man in shining cuirass and helmet roared with anger. With the same long sword that had tormented him so, he smote the rock face, raining debris and sparks down on his shaggy head.

"Get up on your feet, wretch. Do not utter a single word unless I bid you speak."

Quaking with fear, Simon shot up, trying not to let his knees knock. The sword point urged him around in front of the horse.

"Halt there!" He stood dejected, head hung low like an already condemned man. "Very well, we shall proceed along by the river. Halt when I command, and move when I command... Oh, and if you even look as if you are contemplating another of your little bids for freedom, then I shall run you down and smite your head from your body... Now move on!"

In unison with the last command the horse lowered its head and nudged the terrified seaman forward. Taking his cue from the beast, Simon started at a trot. He had not covered thirty paces, however, before sensing something strange had happened. He moved forward alone, not daring to look round. 'Bling!' There came a distinctly metallic sound from behind - not unlike a blacksmith striking an anvil - followed by a smack like wet leather against cobble stones. The horse screamed like a poleaxed pig and its hooves thundered into a full gallop. Still Simon did not turn round. Instead he closed his eyes, hunched his shoulders and prayed as the rush of air from the charging Lady Rowena sent him reeling. Thankful that he had narrowly escaped being trampled, he blessed himself and opened his eyes. The animal was charging and rearing as if possessed by Satan, and the armoured rider was reeling in the saddle as if possessed by strong liquor.

Simon heard laughter and jeering from the opposite bank and turned in time to see two hooded figures whirl and loose a brace of egg-sized pebbles from long leather slings. 'Slap!' 'Bling!' The two same sounds again. He had seen it happen, witnessed the twin missiles spit across the muddy banks and cheered, smiting the air with his fist when contact was made. There was cheering from the opposite bank too, but it became lost in the maddened screams of the horse. Rearing again and sending the rider backwards with arms flailing, the animal retraced its raging steps to once more brush past the young seaman, then, abruptly, it swerved and headed for the river, still with the backward-bent rider aboard.

Down the grey, glistening slope, in a halo of mud the horse bucked, buckled and skidded to an ungainly halt barely a yard from the water's edge. Picking up the fallen sword, Simon rushed to the edge in time to see the somewhat revived rider trying to disembark from his sinking steed. 'Bling'- he did not see the missile but there was that same sound again. The man raised a gloved hand to his helmet, then off the horse he toppled, to lie face up in the mud, limbs moving slowly like an upturned crab.

"Get 'is armour. You can come over if you gets it," one of the two hooded men called across through cupped hands.

"Ay, an' 't sword, get that 'n'all," called the other. Simon noted that this one spoke in a half-familiar accent. Not quite a foreigner, maybe a North countryman.

"Well, 'ow am I gonna' get it? I'll get stuck like 'im an' 'is 'orse... 'ere what d'you take me for?" He twirled the sword above his head. "I got the sword already, see. 'Ere, do you be Boggarts then?"

Without answering, the two hooded men turned to each other and conferred. Then one of them bolted for the trees.

"Wait reet theeyer," called the remaining man.

"Oh yeh, an' wha' if I chooses not to?"

"Ha! Wheeyer y' off t' then lad? Ownt bloody 'angin that's wheeyer! Y'aint gorra choice in t'matter. Just wait theeyer ant don't sod about."

The other hooded man raced from the trees. Simon could plainly hear him panting. Over his shoulder he carried a coiled rope of plaited leather, and in one of his hands a longbow.

"What you gonna' do 'ey? 'Ow you gonna get 'at across?"

"Look 'ere lad, No more soddin' questions! Just shut yer gob and do like we sez, and then everybody's 'appy."

"Don't mind 'im, my babby," called the one with the rope. "He be's a bit grumpy cause 'e ain't et nuffing for 'alf a 'our."

Simon deliberated for a few moments, took a swipe at a clump of grass with the sword and called back.

"I ent et all friggin day. Wha' you wan' I t' do then?"

"We got a 'og all trussed up for roastin' wiv an apple in 'is gob up in they woods... 'e'll soon be cracklin' away. So, get tha' bastard's armour an anyfink else tha' sparkles. I bet 'e's got a full purse on 'im too."

"Then what'd I do?"

"I'm gonna send a fishin' line over on this 'ere arrowl. You gives it a tug an' pulls over this rope. Then bundle all the stuff up in your shirt, tie it to the rope, you're a sailor boy so you should know some good fancy knots..."

"Tell 'im not too soddin' firm... we 'as t' get bluddy things untdone," growled the other one.

"Yes right, not too firm knots mind... we'll pull the stuff over an' then send this 'ere uvver arrowl over to you, an' then over comes you. A little bit wet an' muddy granted, but we'll see you right... Just think o' tha' little piggy-wig all drippin' an' a cracklin' away up there."

The young seaman's head was whispering caution, but his belly was screaming 'Yes, do it, do it'. He gazed down at the horse and rider. The man was still on his back and no longer moved, but Lady Rowena had managed to clamber up the muddy bank and was nibbling nonchalantly at the clumps of grass, as if nothing was amiss with the world.

He stared down at the grey slick of water that oozed itself like a giant rat's tail between the sloping mud banks and shuddered. The tide had long turned but not yet reached its lowest ebb. Even so, in its sluggish withdrawal lurked more treachery than a hundred rock faces; he could climb like an ape, but like most seamen he was unable to swim more than a stroke or two.

"Right then, shoot the arrowl, but don' you let go of I."

He stood back in amazement as the two hooded men attempted to shoot the arrow in a combined effort. He had not noticed before, but under their raiment, both seemed to be minus a hand. One of them held the bow whilst the other gripped and aimed the arrow.

"Up a bit... bit more... nay, down a bit... left... tha's it... Now draw it back nice an' slow... Now loose!"

The young seaman closed his eyes and hugged the firm ground at the crest of the bank, waiting.

"Get it then, lad! 'Urry up... tug t' soddin' thing ovver," came the impatient call from across the river.

He opened his eyes to see the shaft barely a foot from his nose.

"Hey, Goddamn! Wha's 'is then? This could 'ave friggin skewered I!"

Indignantly Simon snatched the arrow and began to reel in the fine twine, followed by the slimy leather rope. Next came the bit he was dreading even more than being pulled across the water - the journey down to the fallen rider. But he had a plan to make it a little easier.

"Now what's t' little sod doin'?"

Simon was scampering along the edge of the mud and reeds. He returned with an armful of driftwood and reeds.

"Thee's not meckin' a soddin' fire, is thee?"

He did not bother to answer. Instead, holding his nose in the air and the rope between his teeth, he proceeded to make a pathway with the reeds and driftwood planking. At first it did not reach the stranded man. Like a furious rodent he scampered off again returning with more of the reeds and flotsam. This time it reached. Nervously he approached the fallen figure.

"God's Holy arse, get a bluddy move on! If thee can't undo straps... get 'is short blade an' cut um... Sod's bound to 'ave one!"

The man was still, his whisker-framed mouth gaped wide; the breast plate, dented by the sling stone, betrayed no movement. The equally dented helmet was pushed forward and obscured the eyes. Simon was relieved that this was so; he had no wish to see the man's face, particularly his eyes. Whilst he stripped him of his armour, the helmet would remain in place until all else was removed.

He tried to unbuckle the straps, but the mud on his fumbling fingers made it impossible.

"Cut it!"

He was beginning to dislike the Northerner intensely and had half a mind to get up and walk away, but where to? He thought of the spitted pig turning over a fire, the fat spluttering in the flames, and before he knew it he had withdrawn the man's long dagger from its sheath and was slitting open the straps.

"What about t' purse? A can see it bulgin' from 'ere... Chuck it ovver."

Obediently he cut the purse strings, and taking the pouch in his hands, tossed it from one muddy paw to the other. The clinks it made brought excited murmurings from across the water.

"You be right, tis full t' burstin'."

"Well, chuck it ovver then."

He stood up and made as if to lob it over, but suddenly thinking better of it, stuffed it down the front of his breeches instead, and demurely knelt down in the mud to finish prising off the armour.

"Come on then, stop pissin' about, chuck it ovver! What's thee think thee's playin' at?... T'aint a soddin' cod piece, lad!"

"If I chucks it over it might break, or not make it. No, it comes over wiv I... That way I be sure of gettin' acrosst, don't I?"

Like the opening of a lid to a treasure casket, he carefully pulled off the breastplate and was horrified to see a slight movement in the man's jerkin. The dry crackle in the throat sent him reeling back onto his makeshift causeway of driftwood, which by now was becoming firmly embedded in the mud.

"Goddamn!... Goddamn! He be movin'... I ain't touchin' the bastard! 'E be still breevin'!" He blurted out the words whilst negotiating a backwards retreat.

"Oh aye, thee are if'n thee wants t' come ovver 'ere ant find sanctuary in t' greenwood."

"Go on lad, you can do it, s'easy," called the friendlier of the two hooded men. The familiarity of the accent was enticing, a counterbalance to the repugnance he felt towards the other fellow.

"Aye, s'reet simple like yer sen... Just tek soddin knife an' stick 'im wi' it! Aye an' then we can all get back up t' suppin' on't 'og."

The young seaman looked down at the long-bladed dagger in his shaking hand.

"But.. but.. I carn't kill 'im just like tha', can I?" he blurted out, horrified.

"Mek thee mind up. T'is you an all if I af'ter come ovver theeyer."

"Cyril, shush... don' bees too 'ard on 'im... Don't you listen to this'n my babby... If you 'urries up you can 'ave all tha' stuff off afore Captain Hand there wakes."

"He'll 'ave a reet soddin' 'eadache if 'e does wek up."

"Goddamn it!" squealed the young seaman up at the walls of the Gorge as he made his muddy way back to the body. He retrieved the half-submerged sword and began to prod the ribs, lightly at first, but then, recalling the way the man had earlier pinioned him against the rock face, he jabbed harder. There was no movement other than that caused by his own frustrated actions.

"That's it lad... Stick 'im!... T'sod's stuck enough of our folk in't past."

He did not answer, but convinced now that the body laying before him was devoid of spark and that the throat rattle that had startled him so was the trapped breath escaping, he positioned a piece of wood and, kneeling down, cursing to himself, began tugging off the gloves. He noticed how white, almost delicate the fingers were before they flopped in the mud like dead sprats. But he did not see them resurrect eel-like from the slime, with the speed of a striking conger, to curl and rasp tight around his throat. All he saw was the flash of the upturned sky, the snarling, whiskered face, followed by the thick, black wetness flooding into his head. A crushing weight held him under. In roared the water, in gaping mouth, nostrils, bulging eyes, and deep into the ears it swashed like icy bodkins. He hit out at the man, striking the helmet, trying to gouge at the eyes, but the strength was slipping from him and his fingers simply brushed the man's face like strands of seaweed. He was being throttled after all, he thought, as the judicial grip of authority tightened. It was his inevitable punishment. It was as if, resignedly, he was accepting his fate.

There was a sudden jolt. The grip relaxed and into his throat flooded the river's foul emulsion. The weight was gone. Strength and anger returned to his fingers, and by furiously grabbing handfuls of mud and long-submerged pieces of stick, he was able to right himself in time to glimpse, through the blur, the glistening figure staggering towards the grazing horse.

"Rowena!... Rooowena!" came the anguished cry. The horse neighed and backed off, then recognising its master beneath the slime, it returned to its position on the edge of the slope.

"Up a bit... Nay, down a touch... Tha's it. Loose!"

The words rang out clearly across the water. Simon, who by this time had cleared his eyes and was beginning to focus, saw the captain tottering along the makeshift causeway. He saw too the streak of the arrow that slammed into the man's shoulder. Standing up he wanted to scream... 'Stop him from getting away!'... But no words would come. All he could manage before slithering over was an open-mouthed screech and an outstretched hand that trembled and pointed the direction. The captain reached the horse, and leaning his head against the saddle, breathed deeply, thankfully, in the manner of a shipwrecked mariner cast safely upon dry land. Then, after raising a foot to a stirrup, he swung himself aboard, bellowing with pain at the effort. Like a fishing float the shoulder-piercing arrow rose and fell with each breath. It would soon be too late to strike.

"Don't let 'im get awa..." shrieked Simon.

The horse lurched forward. A stout fishing line and rope of plaited leather rose from the mud as taut as a harp string. The Captain screamed again and tumbled backwards off the horse.

"Got 'im! Reel 'im in."

"That Captain Hand 'as a reet lorra trouble stayin on 't back of 'orse."

Paying no heed to the comments from the other side, the young seaman wrenched the sword from the mud once more and bounding up the causeway like a blood-crazed berserker, he began to stab and slash at the prone figure.

Later, after the two hooded men had pulled him safely across, counted the coins and patted his back, he puked and rubbed the dead man's blood from his face, a wretched murderer after all. And later still, in a secret camp above the gorge, with a belly full of pork and strong cider, he laughed and boasted whilst miming the heroic thrusts and slashes he had made.

CHAPTER 11
Pigs and Cider

Sunset, and with the peal of the Tun bell still ringing in his ears, Reginald Rudkin leaned against the doorway of the Full Moon Inn, and with a stick, scraped the pig excrement from the wooden soles of his galoches. He could not decide who he loathed more - Croft, his servant Roberts, or any one of the hundred or so pigs that freely roamed the Bristol streets. Though Croft had not, as Roberts suggested, charged like a knight at a joust, he had nonetheless taken the horse down the maze of alleyways where even a trot was a risk to life and limb, so close were the houses. A pot of piss flung from a second storey window had narrowly missed him as he jogged behind the horse, and when Croft had stopped at St Nicholas Street to remonstrate with a wine porter for daring to bring his sled into the town without a permit, it was Rudkin's rump that the livid man had taken a passing kick at.

But Thomas Croft was maybe not so bad, not when compared with some of the other 'High and Mightys' and 'Tuftaffeties' who rode through the streets with their faces pressed into nosegays, and acting as if anyone beneath the rank of councillor was invisible, or should willingly retreat, forelock between thumb and forefinger, to stand ankle-deep in the open sewer as they passed. Not that Thomas Croft was beyond playing the high and mighty, but there was some earthy fibre to the man, especially when 'toped up', and that seemed to be a more frequent occurrence in the last couple of years. 'Mind you,' thought Rudkin, 'the pace tha' England's used up Kings these past two years, 's' wonder the whole Realm ain't reelin' blind drunk.' He scraped at the green-black excrement and swallowed hard. It occurred to him that before the curfew bell tolled, he too would be reeling blind drunk; what with the groats from the purse of Thomas Croft, not to mention the half rial prize from Sergeant Bill White, collectable on the Cornucopia's safe return.

He stamped his foot and examined the undersole. It was clean enough not to pick up too much straw from the tavern floor. No, it would have to be Roberts who earned the true focus of his hatred. Roberts, who was always tampering with his ledgers and quills. Roberts, who would have doubtless consumed the remainder of his blood pudding. At least a pig could be killed and eaten, turned into puddings and pies, that was if the owner did not step forward within two days with fourpence in his mitt to claim the carcass. Killed, providing of course the pig did not have a little bell strung around its precious neck. Then, of course, it was a privileged swine and, like its human counterpart, was free to roam at will - usually with its snout in the air. But Roberts was not privileged in any eyes other than those of underlings and beggars.Rudkin wondered why Croft had employed him for so many years. The man was a thief plain and simple and deserved a letter 'T' branding on his forehead... "Yes an' an 'S' for Sodomite on each cheek of his gurt fat arse."

"Wha' was tha' you said, Reg?... Did I hear you a'right?... An 'S' for what?"

"Oh don't you start, George. I've 'ad it up to 'ere." He sat down at a rough trestle and raised a hand up to his eyes.

"What'll it be then, the usual?" enquired the burly landlord.

"No, give I cider, your best, mind. Ale just ain't the same drink no more, not now. Well, ever since they brings in these foreigners from the Low Countries with their fancy beer stuff, wiv all they bitter 'ops in it. 'Ave you seen they 'ops? No, well 'ard little green fings they be, like sheep turds. Anyway ever since they come in with their fancy lace for all the ladies at court, and ever since King wha's 'is face, decides tha' 'e likes this 'ere beer drink... din't do 'im much good, mind... well ever since then, tha' was the day good ol' English Ale died! Nowadays if you asks for ale, all you gets is gnat's piss beer."

"Alright, keep your 'air on! What was tha', a large 'n?"

"George, 'ave you ever known me say otherwise? What? The day I asks for a tot is the day they carries me out of town on a 'urdle wiv a 'alter round me neck."

"Phew, it don't 'alf whiff all of a sudden. 'Ere, wha' 'ave you brought in wiv you?"

Ignoring the question, Rudkin threw a half groat on the bar, and raising the black, glazed beaker to his lips, paused neither for breath nor answer until it was drained. Letting out a long sigh of satisfaction, punctuated by a single resonant belch, he slid the vessel towards the landlord and smiled contentedly at the sound of its replenishment.

"Tha's better, George. Yes tha' be better by 'alf. Just keep 'em comin til it be all used up." Rudkin stared round the empty tavern. "Not many in tonight then, George?"

"You could say that. It'll fill up later. I ain't complainin' mind, this be the first time I've had a few quiet moments."

"Course, they all be down at the Back a' gorpin at the Cornucopial, 'opin' t' catch a glimpse of that there painted salvage they got in the 'old."

"Salvage! What Salvage be tha', then?"

Rudkin put down the tankard and stroked the side of his nose.

"Come on, Reg... Come on, you can tell I."

The landlord took the half-empty tankard, and filling it to the brim, placed it before Rudkin. Rudkin stared down as the last remaining bubbles vanished from the surface of the golden liquid. He waited until it was still, then into the cider he plunged a finger and withdrew a tiny gnat.

"A gurt biggun!"

"What, that little flea?"

"No, the friggin' salvage. 'Ere I fought you were interested in 'im?"

"I am! Go on...please."

"Oh please is it? Oh very well then. How can I refuse?" Rudkin's sarcasm escaped unnoticed.

"He be in the Cornucopial's 'old. 'E's got a gurt long, skin jerkin an' long, black locks all down 'is back."

"Be 'e black an' all? Do 'e 'ave a tail like Lucifer's own?"

"Nah, 'e aint no blacker 'n a Portugee sailor. Got markings mind, swirly whirly fings on 'is face an' all over, I expect. I din't see no tail mind."

"They got 'im in irons, then?"

"No, they an't. Don't ask me why. No, 'e be stood there babblin' away, Kwa! Kwa! Kwa! like a friggin' gurt crow, a gurt big bow o' red wood in 'is 'and. Wiv Old Crofty, Spencer, Strange and a few uvers gorpin' on an' babblin' back in bits o' Hunn, Frog, Dagol an' uvver such foreign chatter. Tryin' to communicate wiv 'im, see. Why, there was even talk of fetchin' a priest to try a bit o' cassock chat. That be when I sez - make sure 'e brings some communion wine wiv 'im, that'll loosen 'is tongue."

"What, you said tha' to Thomas Croft an' all they others? G'warn wiv you!"

"I did too. They fought it were a good idea."

"Then what?"

"Nuffing, this big salvage man turns 'is back on 'em an' starts a singin' or wailin' like 'e's got toofache or sum'ink, an' tha's when I left. Not before I 'ad a good nose around, mind. After all, that be my job, 'avin' a good nose around, ain' it?"

"What else did you see, then?"

"Oh I seen lots. Smells more like. Full to burstin' she be wiv' the Poor-Jack, gurt big flakes of it, but 'taint what I sees tha' counts mind, no, it be what I 'ears tha' matter most."

Rudkin stroked the lobe of his ear. The landlord took the half-empty tankard and again filled it with cider.

"And wha' be that then, Reginald?"

Rudkin hastily snatched the tankard, clumsily spilling some of the contents as he raised it to his lips. The landlord impatiently drummed the counter top with his fingers and watched the man's stubbly Adam's apple rise and fall half a dozen times, signalling the draining of the contents.

"Phew!... That bees a gurt fine drop o' ciderl, George. Now, where were we?"

"'Tis a wicked thirst you 'ave on you tonight, Reg. Anyway, you were saying tha' you 'eard summ'ing. Wha' be tha', then?"

"Oh yes, so I did! Well, for a start it do look like the Swallow won't ever see these shores again."

There was a long silence. The landlord's jaw dropped open; his eyes took on the pitiful set of a man who has just had sentence of death pronounced upon him.

"Wha's tha'? Tell me, tell me please!" He whispered the words first like a felon's last request, a throat drained of moisture, then repeated them louder, more like an inquisitor's demand.

"The Swallow! Wha's tha' you say? You mean tha' newun they made barely a year past? Tell me!"

His hand shot across the bar and, grabbing Rudkin by the

upper arm, pulled him closer. A somewhat affronted Rudkin looked first at the large mitt that firmly squeezed his arm and then up at the man's pained face.

"Wha's this then, George? Joined the night watch, 'ave you? Talkin' of which, 'ave you seen Sergeant Bill Whitey? 'E owes me a penny or two."

"Wha's 'at? Wha' you say?" The momentary pugnacity left the landlord's face. "No, no I ain't. Forgive me Reg, I, I... I don't know wha'... 'ere 'ave another." He released his grip on Rudkin's arm and again grabbed the beaker. His hand shook as he placed the vessel under the barrel tap.

"It be my late sister's boy, Matt, Mathew Tyrell... 'e be on the Swallow... You won't know 'im but you'd know Sam Dodds a'right, 'e be on 'er too, an' Johnny Whaite, an' Langleg, an' Pugh. This is terrible, a disaster! Be you sure, Reginald Rudkin? Be you sure 'tis the Swallow? Would you swear to it?"

The barkeeper slammed down the beaker, shook his head and rubbed at his eyes. A still dazed Rudkin, ignoring the splash of cider down his jerkin, took a quaff and commenced massaging his bruised arm. Then, after once more scanning the empty room, he answered.

"You're forgettin' tha' Martin Spycer be the master of the Cornucopial, an' next to Lloyd there ain't none better. If 'e says tha' the Swallow's wrecked, then wrecked she be!"

"Why? How?" the landlord implored, his voice almost howling the questions.

"Doin' their duty, tha's 'ow! You don't think tha' it just be the Poor-Jack tha' they crosses the Ocean Sea for, do you? No George, tha' ain't the 'alf of it. There's some tha' says the New-found-land be the Isle of Brasil and some tha' says she still be out there waitin' for our boys to 'appen across 'er. Hexploration tha's wha' it be. Crofty and they others 'ave got the bug worse than a parsel o' Portugee. Between you an me, they talks of nothin' else. And so once their 'olds is full t' burstin wiv the dried fishes, off they goes hexplorating for the Isle of Brasil. If they finds it, an' the red dye wood, well then, just fink wha' it means for the red cloth o' Bristol. We don' 'ave to pay through the nose to no Ayrabs or Genoese, tha's wha'!"

"But... but... but Matty an' all them lads lost... An' Doddsy... I can't 'ardly believe it."

A long silence followed whilst the landlord filled and drained a beaker himself. Both knew it was a cruel fact of life that a good proportion of men who took to the open sea invariably ended up at the bottom of it; and that hardly a week would pass by without word of souls and boats gone down. It was also not unknown for men thought of as long dead to walk through the doorway of the Full Moon and demand the whereabouts of their wives and the names of the ones they had taken to husband in their absence. The ensuing fights were considered great entertainment by the regulars, equal to the tales of shipwreck, piracy, abandonment, or whatever else had kept the 'lost soul' from his place at the bar.

"What did for 'em then? Tempest?"

"Well, see, after they'd taken on board fish t' burstin, they followed the coast for many leagues, with the Swallow nearest the shore on account of she bein' the smaller, the best at manoeuvring. Anyway they got separated in a storm... tempest or whatever."

"If they be separated then, 'ow do this Spycer know she ain't still out there somewhere?"

"'Cause he spent best part of a week combing the coastline for 'er afore the westerlies blew 'em back in a trice... eighteen days were all it took. Incredible to think, all that distance in a little over two weeks."

Rudkin heard the landlord swallow hard.

"And?"

"Don' ask me 'ow, but by the grace of God they found 'er wiv 'er back broken on a sand bank."

"What about the lads?"

Rudkin shook his head, took a single sip and continued,

"No one alive on board the poor ship. A skiff went onto the beach and found 'em. Well, found what was left after the sea birds 'ad pecked at 'em. Nasty, vicious beaks they do 'ave an all."

"Wha' all of 'em?... Did they count 'em?"

"Wha' count 'em? They was all jumbled up, bits an' pieces wiv arrowls stickin' out of 'em."

"Wha', you mean salvages got 'old of 'em?"

"Yes, George, painted salvages. Look, I'm sorry about your nephew."

"Well, they got one of they salvages a'nt 'em. Are they gonna 'oist 'im up?"

"No, George, 'e be a different kind of salvage. The one they brought back is from somewhere to the north of all these goins on... Different 'eathen babbies hentirely."

"Well, he still be a salvage pagan all the same. I says 'oist 'im up... Wha's my poor wife Tilly gonna say? Wha' am I gonna say to 'er? 'Ow on earf am I gonna tell 'er? Tha' boy Matty was so dear to 'er an' to me too. I bet you didn't know 'e could read an' write! 'Ad schoolin'... I said to 'is muvver she should put 'er foot down an' not let 'im go to sea like 'is no good father! But 'e wun't 'ave it. And now look wha's 'appened. It be a tragedy wha' wiv 'er passin' away like not more 'n a month past and now our dearly beloved Mathew kilt by salvages."

The landlord broke down then, alternately snarling, sobbing, and all the while pounding the bar with his great fist. Rudkin took another swallow of the cider. His head was

186

beginning to spin. The liquid was beginning to taste sour and flat. He thought his belly was sloshing full of sea water. Tossing a coin on the bar, he bolted from the tavern without saying another word.

Toying with the idea of heading for the Saracen, where he would be more or less guaranteed convivial company, he made towards Marsh Street. All the while the sound of a great fist pounded in his head, like a battering ram at the city doors. Though the night was still young, already it lay in ruins. The pounding became replaced with a twitting cackle. He knew at once who the cackle belonged to. It was that foul catamite, Roberts, who now occupied his thoughts. Rudkin stamped his right foot on the cobblestones. Once again, a slimy cushion of pig's droppings covered his galoches. The cackle inside his head rose higher in pitch. Rudkin knew then that he would have to rid himself of Roberts, once and for all. Now, where would Billy White be? Maybe he would not take his half rial from the Sergeant after all. Maybe there was some arrangement that could be made to the mutual satisfaction of both parties.

CHAPTER 12
A Little Night Talk

Three, stout raps at the front door. Thomas Croft listened out for the ungainly shuffle of Roberts in the hallway and the lifting of the heavy latch. With a sigh, he laboriously manoeuvred himself out of his favourite chair and stood to receive his expected guest. De La Fount was invariably good company, almost a friend, but now Croft was beginning to wish he had not extended an invitation to visit. The day had been exhausting, with dizzy peaks and troughs, the like of which he had not experienced before. So much had transpired that the past morning seemed an age away. He could not get the sight of the skin-clad savage out of his mind. In fact his supper of cold cuts had been somewhat tainted by the remembered, gamey smell - Rudkin was a posey by comparison. The heathen's caterwauling had driven him to distraction. Spycer had had him on display in the helmsman's castle and Croft and his partners had tried in vain to conjure up some mutually intelligible tongue, but to no avail. It had become apparent, however, that the savage had a taste for strong waters and soon he had set to shuffling and chanting in an outlandish fashion fit to wake the dead, and the small aft cabin had set to vibrating like a tabor. The eerie monotone haunted Croft still and he feared disturbed dreams would be his lot. Maybe it was good to have company after all.

"Ah William, welcome. Come in... sit you down... That will be all, Roberts... Now, away to your bed. 'Tis a big day tomorrow and I want you up with the Angelus bell."

Roberts sighed heavily, bowed, and left the room. Croft waited until the door clicked and the sound of the man's footfall receded before continuing.

"It seems I am fated to spend my days in the company of saucy fellows. All of my servants, from scullery to chamber, well, 'tis hard to describe, 'tis not what they say or do, but the insolence lurks there beneath the surface. And if you twit them about it, well, who looks the fool? Of course, my good lady wife looks at me as if I were a mad man. For her 'tis nought but smiles and sweetness... Tell me, do you have this trouble, William?"

"Yes Thomas, I do. I fear 'tis the character of the natives of Bristow. Yes, and before you ask, my wife takes me for a madman too."

"With luck Roberts will have his throat slit by Rudkin and Rudkin will be hanged for it. A glass of sack, perhaps...? Can I tempt you, William?"

"You most certainly can, Thomas. Why not do as Robert Strange has done? He has a man and wife from Iceland in charge of his whole household. Swears by them... Apparently, a good number have taken residence in this fair city since our boats no longer fish their waters and they are only too happy to work for meat and a roof, oh, and fish on Fridays! Of course you would know all this already, Thomas. Thank you, most welcome."

Croft handed De La Fount a fine cut glass filled with the pale liquor.

"Indeed, I was aware. Ahem, I suppose a toast is in order. To Henry the seventh, King of England. Long may he reign!"

"Yes, quite. God bless him. Long may he reign... 'pon my soul Thomas, this is a very fine drop... Canaries? I missed out there, didn't I? Still, next time, do let me know if more of the same comes in."

Croft nodded and reached for the crystal decanter.

"Of course... Strange, a younger man than ourselves could cope with the foreign tongue, but alas for us I fear 'tis... 'tis too late... It takes me long enough to understand what these beggars say, and as for Roberts with his incessant sibilance, it seems I'm stuck with him, leastways until Rudkin murders him! 'Nother drop, William?

"Splendid! Here's to Rudkin then!"

"Yes, here's to Reginald Rudkin. He has his uses, mind. Joking apart, not much passes through this port without Rudkin's knowledge. Why, this very morning first thing, there he is knocking on my office door... 'Scuse me Master Croft, but the Cornucopial she be sighted off Kingroad. Oh, and by the way sir, we 'as a new King.'" Croft imitated the city's pronounced glottal accent. De La Fount slapped his thighs.

"What more could you ask for from a keeper?"

Both men guffawed loudly. Croft refilled the glasses. A brief silence reigned, broken ultimately by De La Fount.

"Bad luck about the Swallow though, Thomas. A fine ship, very fine ship. And the men of course, God rest them! Savage shores, Thomas. Unknown savage shores."

Croft's face clouded. He drained the glass and poured himself another, spilling droplets of the wine onto the polished table top. With his forefinger he drew the outline of a ship and beside it another shape. De La Fount left his seat and stood beside him.

"Ah yes, the Swallow, but what is this, some kind of cap Thomas?"

"Yes... 'tis nothing. I don't know what possessed me to draw

191

its likeness. Tis naught but a silly woollen cap, a red woollen cap, 'twere better suited to a scarecrow than a seaman."

"It's one of the objects Spycer brought back isn't it, Thomas? I noticed you appeared ill at ease when he showed us. How so, Thomas?"

"Tis nothing, nothing. Another drop, Walter?"

Croft, attempting to shake away the melancholy, smiled briefly and replenished De La Fount's glass.

"Do you know, William, this had the makings of a perfect day."

He swayed slightly as he spoke, his voice trailing off to a whisper. De La Fount sat forward in the chair, his head cocked to one side like a cockatoo.

"Why so pothered, Thomas? There are golden days aplenty in the offing. No more accursed war with father fighting son, brother slaying brother, God willing! I know it appears we have lost the Swallow, but the Cornucopia has returned safely, laden full of stockfish; a handsome profit for us all. But equally interesting, you saw our savage guest's bow. Well, what colour wood was it fashioned from?"

"Red of course. Red, red, red - the reddest of red wood. By Jove! William, perhaps we have found the Isle of Brasil after all?"

Croft, his humour regained, paced the room chuckling to himself, then sat down in the opposite chair.

"What is it, Thomas? What tickles you so?"

"Well, he would not let us examine his rude, red bow, nor even suffer us to lay a finger on it, even though we plied him with wine. I was just musing... There we were in the musty hold of a ship, trying to relieve a savage of his simple bow, whilst so many leagues across the western sea, on his own shore, a savage kinsman could be trying to fathom the workings of an arquebus. That's if they got them ashore."

"I'm sorry Thomas, I don't quite follow."

"Ah, William, forgive me, how could you follow my meanderings?" Croft drained the glass, belched, begged pardon, then continued, "You know that included in the Swallow's ordnance was a brace of matchlocks. I...er... wanted them to make a fine show, you understand."

De La Fount politely nodded as Croft spoke in deliberately laboured tones, as if his tongue, weighing each single word, was reluctant to let go of it.

"You know that... er... Knowles the, bell maker is now turning out the finest cannon in England? Yes, well, he expressed an interest in developing... er... handguns and when that Hansard carrack was taken off... Pem, Pem Pembroke last year, a marvellous piece... came into my possession - wonderful craftsmanship. You know they're all making better guns than us, Frenchies even. Pistoia's the place though, so I understand." Croft paused again and stared at the empty glass in his hand. "Of course we all know it's the longbow that both makes us great,yet holds us back, that's why. 'Tis cheaper, but look how long it takes to train an archer? Now archers, don't get me started, they really are saucy fellows.See how they strut? And there were guns won Henry's battle. Yes, guns! Yes, Pistoia's the place. Where was I?"

"Hansard carrack? One of their handguns? Knowles?"

"Ah yes, William. Forgive me, the liquor makes me ramble. Yes, this fine piece, I let Knowles look at it and now he fashions a like deshign, even improved the... er... firing mechanism, though not quite so elegant to behold... Well, alas, they're either in uncomprehendin', unfathomable shavage hands or at the bottom of the sea. That was the point I was making."

"I see... I think," said De La Fount, still unsure of the connection, but not wanting the conversation to stall should Croft reveal hitherto unknown delicious secrets, as was sometimes the case when in one of his inebriated states. Of course, he already knew about the handguns, even had one of Knowles' finest in his own possession, liked nothing better than firing it off. Had not the finest, corned gunpowder from Seville proved a good, steady source of profit for them all these last seven years?

"Getting back to our pagan friend, Thomas. We could arrange an archery tournament, longbows, crossbows, even handguns, why not? A competition... Or maybe a hunt. Yes, a hunt would better suit a savage. Their eye is more attuned to the spring of game than the stationary target... What say you, Thomas?"

Croft opened an eye, smiled and nodded.

"Somehow, during the course of the hunt, we could contrive a way of relieving the fellow of his bow. Why, we could make him a present of a stout English yew bow - after we have demonstrated its superiority, of course - the very moment he felt the cast of it I'm sure he would be only too pleased to offer up his own rude stave. He has only one pair of hands after all said and done."

Another long silence ensued. Croft's eyes were closed though he sat upright in the chair, gently wafting from side to side. Suddenly both eyes sprang open, taking De La Fount by surprise.

"I must confess... I like the shound of that, William. A hunt, yes, over by Ashton, the woods run thick with game, deer... and... er... boar, yes boar. Have you spied those big ugly shnorters with tusksh like a Blackamoor's shcimitar, William? Of course you have."

Letting out a hoot, Croft lurched from the chair towards the table and carelessly slopped the remainder of the sack into his glass, catching the rim with a musical 'chink'.

"I wonder how... er... our shavage guest deports himself in

the path of... er... a charging hog? Will thoshe black hawk'sh eyes search and find the shpot to put a shaft, eh William? Will hish... inshtinc know?"

"Forgive me, Thomas. Will his what?"

Yet another silence followed.

"Hish inshtinct!" purred Croft from his slumped position in the chair. His head lolled forwards.

"Ah yes, of course, his savage instinct."

William De La Fount sat in silence for what seemed an age, watching a large spider climb the gilded edge of a tapestry depicting the resurrection of Christ, waiting for a sign of life to emanate from the stupefied Croft. Finally, a loud snort heralded a rhythm of alternate snores and whistles as his ample stomach rose and fell. De La Fount prized open the stubby fingers that clutched the glass.

"I bid you a goodnight, Thomas," he whispered. "I'll see myself out."

CHAPTER 13

In the Belly of the Beast

Keskooskwa, the bearstalker, had never before known such confusion and anguish, for he now believed his soul to have become lost from the moment he had boarded the great, floating lodge. Over the walls, the hairy-faced demons with the broken teeth had dangled gifts that glittered brighter than the flanks of fishes; and their fingers like seaweed had entangled and hauled him up as he reached out. He knew now what it was to be a fish, to be tugged from one world into another. Had he suffered a kind of death and slipped into this strange, foreign world without being aware of his passing? Surely it were possible. Had he not witnessed many of the people leave life within the midst of speaking their thoughts? Leaving an unfilled space for the still unspoken words? He must have done the very same; maybe back in the lodges the people had sat staring into his death face, waiting for him to finish speaking.

Commencing what had become a daily ritual, Keskooskwa tugged up his hunter's shirt and examined every part of his body. There were no wounds. No arrow or spear thrust had snuffed out his life-spark. He raised his hands, aware of the slight tremor and began to feel his hair. It was all still there. No scalping blade or warclub had consigned him to this nether world. There must be another reason. Somewhere inside, he secretly suspected that a half-forgotten display of cowardice in the face of enemies when he was a young man had marked him out; and all the succeeding acts of daring and courage had not absolved him.

Slumping against the oak walls of the ship's cabin, he began to softly sing into the wood and beat time with his bare fist. It had truly been an awesome journey to this nether world. The enormity of the expanse of water made him shudder. At first they had travelled still within sight of land, and at one point taken him past the broken bones of another great canoe and onto a beach where he had seen the signs of a fight where many had died. And straightaway there had been much anger directed at him. The hairy-mouths with the broken teeth had not smiled for many days afterwards; he had tried to tell them that it was not his people but the southern ones, but they had shook their fists in his face.

They had kept him captive in the stinking belly of this creaking, bucking beast for many days - though he had no idea how many as no daylight penetrated the darkness. Then eventually they had brought him back into the world, laughing, singing, stroking him as the sunlight screamed into his eyes. They had even given him back his bow, though its spirit had been offended; and bade him shoot at the single sea bird that roosted in one of the tall, naked tree trunks. At first he had refused, but after they had given him a burning drink, he had wasted a handful of good arrows before the great bird flew off unharmed. The shame of it cut him still. He had missed, and to add to his humiliation, one of the hair-mouths had taken up a bow of his own, and had embedded three shafts in the topmost part of the tree where the bird had been. Keskooskwa shook his own weapon at the thought of it. Garr! If the chance came again, he would show them.

He thought on the four laughing wizards who had confronted him today in this very lodge and shouted spells at him. One even tried to take away his bow. They had given him the fire-drink and he had nearly succumbed; only his songs had saved him. He must not let this happen.

They might be demons, but they bleed and die like any man. This puzzled him greatly. If, indeed, he had passed into a nether world, and was in the company of Booninack, was there yet another spirit world to pass into beyond this? Had he not seen one of the hair-mouths fall from the straight branches that held the great, white wings? The dead one was stiff as a two day fish when they cast his body over the side. This was nothing like the spirit world he had expected. Where were his own people? Those who passed before. There must be the spirits of others of the 'Niqumac' around? Even a spirit place populated with enemy warriors would be better than these innumerable hair-faces.

When they had brought him up from the stinking belly to their land, though they had covered his body, still he had managed to look around him; and the teeming sights that lacerated his eyeballs had filled him with such dread. Never had he seen so many two-legged beings, buzzing, milling, like the blackflies in the swampland.

Though he had been left in darkness, the fires from the waterside taverns had sent sufficient light through the cabin windows, but as curfew came around, one by one they died out, leaving just the teeming ripples of the reflected water dancing on the ceiling. On the other side of the wall that sometimes swung open he could hear the voices of two of his captors. Their ill-tempered words were heavy with slumber and slurred from the strong drink. Even though he did not understand the words, he had learned to marry the faces to the tongues; and had on occasions mimicked the strange sounds 'Goddam! Goddam!- much to the delight of the hair-mouthed ones. But it was his calls of birds and animals that had delighted them most and they had smiled on him, called him and given him much food. These ones did not want for food. In the belly of the floating lodge he had seen more dried fish than all his people could eat in a year.

He gently tried the catch on the cabin door. It would not open. Keskooskwa began to experience the dread once more. For many days he had been given the freedom to roam at will. All over the floating lodge he had sniffed and crept. His favourite place had become the tops of the smooth trees, easily matching the agility of the hair-mouths, marvelling at the ease with which the giant, white wings were made to become small or great at the tug of a rope. Delighting at the surge forward when the wings made a captive of the wind. Yes, he had grown to love the tree tops, to drink deeply of the sweet breezes. Even the harsh gales had pleased him, helping to blow a little of the heartache away. Was it not he, Keskooskwa, who had first spied land? He had called and pointed it out to the boy, the one whose eyes should have been the keenest. The boy had looked but not seen, until it seemed the shoreline was racing forward to meet them. Yes, they were indeed strange demons. None seemed stronger than the warriors of his own people. He would not think twice about fighting them.

He tried the door once more. It was fastened from the outside. Now he was truly a captive. Were they eaters of human flesh? Is this why they had kept his belly filled, so that they could fatten, then eat him, after first torturing him? He kicked the door and wailed, half in anger, half in anguish. A harsh voice from the other side barked at him. He kicked and wailed again. The hair-mouth voice spat and growled once more. Keskooskwa recognised the perpetrator. It was good. It was one of the ones he detested. He would have no compunction in slaying him if needs be. Suddenly he sprang back. Something hard hit the door and clattered on the floor. Singing his war song, Keskooskwa strung up his bow, took out an arrow and began to methodically kick the door as if it were a great drum. Even though his song was loud, he sensed their approach in the faint give of the floor planks. Pah! These demons could not even be silent. He nocked the arrow and waited.

CHAPTER 14
Round in a Circle

Simon ventured his head past the entrance flap of the wattle hut. The daylight bludgeoned him back into immediate retreat, there to cower and moan in the darkness.

"Jesus! my 'ead, my poor 'ead. Feels like a gurt 'orse kicked it."

"Keep the noise down, friend," came a sinister voice from what appeared to be a bundle of blankets at the rear of the shelter. The creak of a cot made him wince.

"The cup has a stronger kick than the horse. 'Specially when taken in the quantity that you did last night, my friend."

"Who be that talking? Ouch! Who be there? I carn't see a Goddam' thing."

"No curses, friend, I'll have no curses in my castle."

"Oh yes, an' where be your castle, then?"

"Why friend... you are a guest in it now."

"Not for long, I don't be!"

The seaman brushed aside the sack cloth door flap, winced momentarily at the flood of light, and without a backward glance flounced out of the hut.

"Pha! Call tha' a friggin' castle?"

He staggered around the hut-ringed clearing, even stamped barefoot through the still warm embers of last night's fire, searching for water or weak ale to slake his thirst. Nothing stirred. Even the flea-ridden dogs deemed his foul-tempered progress unworthy of opening both eyes; and on the high, stony bank that enclosed one side of the camp, the slumped figures of the armed lookouts slumbered on.

"Anybody awake?"

He called and clutched his ringing head. Nothing stirred. Emboldened by thirst, he crept towards the nearest hut and despite the indifferent growl of a dog, lifted the stiff, hide curtain. It took a while for his eyes to grow accustomed to the darkness. The foetid mixture of sour cider-breath, stale clothing, unwashed skin, caused him to both gag and experience a twinge of nostalgic regret. The slumped bodies could have been sleeping seamen - all that was lacking was the creak of oak timbers. But they were not seamen - indeed they were not all men. Within the tangled limbs and sleep-ridden garments he glimpsed breasts, thighs and the soft curve of female buttocks.

The front of his breeches twitched. Smouldering with embarrassment and faint through lack of fresh air, he withdrew, letting the hide curtain fall back, censuring his befuddled rapture. Had he imagined it? Was there really an uninhibited display of female nudity behind the thin screen? The tales of old mariners and even the drunken boastings of younger ones always included the juiciest reference to willing wenches, preferably scantily clad on a sun-bleached shore, and simple-minded enough to bestow their favours on the plainest of scurvy-ridden seamen. Along with sea serpents, mermaids, fire-breathing dragons and unicorns, he believed this revelation was his birthright and with each distant voyage undertaken, each salt water baptism, one or all of the wonders would, in due course, become realized. Indeed, had he not crossed over water to get here? This was no sun-drenched shore, but the light flooding his battered brain tempted him to believe it might be so. Nothing could stop his trembling hand from pulling aside the curtain and lapping at the scene once more. His thirst for water had receded. All he could think of was bare, curvaceous skin. His grubby hand fluttered towards the curtain, and pinching the greasy hide, began to slowly raise it. His eyes were ready to alight on the swells and curves. Their exact location was tattooed on his mind.

"An' what do you think you're gawping at?"

The voice, though not unpleasant, lashed him like a whip. He stood in the doorway, one hand holding up the curtain, unable to take his eyes off the half-naked young woman who confronted him.

"Well...? Got your eye full,'ave you?"

Finally he found his own voice.

"I..I...I..er...Water...I need water."

"What? Who's 'at?"

Another harsher, older female voice called out from the hut's dark recess. He glimpsed the flash and quiver of a more pendulous nudity, and accordingly began to glow a deeper red.

"He wants water. Tis that young lad they brought up last night... Simon, whatever 'is name is."

Disappointed, he watched the first girl struggle back into a loose smock, then as his aching arm let the curtain fall back to immerse the hut in darkness once more, a man's voice coughed and spoke.

"Oh tis thee, eh? Simon t' seaman... Simple Simon, might 'ave soddin' well known! Wait reet theyer."

He heard a hand slap against bare skin, a yelp and a giggle followed.

"Get thee arse outta me face, woman, 't sailor boy's dyin' a thirst."

"You din't mind it bein in your face las' night, Cyril Hardwyke."

"Shussshhhh!!!... Careless bitch, no real names!"

He caught the menace within the whisper and strained to hear what else was hissed beyond the skin curtain.

"Til we knaw wun way or t'other that 'e is what 'e sez 'e 'is. Reet?"

"Awright Cyril... leggo my arm awright."

The curtain was flung aside; the young seaman quickly took a step backwards.

"Reet, Simon, in't it?"

"Sybald... Simon Sybald... I ain't simple."

Instead of the surname Tyrell, the young seaman blurted his dead mother's maiden name, blinking furiously at the leering, red-eyed face that thrust out towards him. It was half way to being a false name. Yesterday, dusk had descended before he had been finally dragged across the river, and in the half light he had not fully seen the Northerner's face. Last night they had poured cider and half-burnt, half-pink, fatty pork down him. In truth, he had been drunk with relief at his deliverance, even before the first drop or morsel touched his tongue, and he had not wanted to admit to the possibility that all was not how it first appeared. But now, even through the pain of a drunkard's retribution, he thought he saw the truth - the missing hands, limbs, bloated faces, red-rimmed eyes and the hoods that all seemed to wear, even though the night had been warm and the fire had nearly singed his hair with its heat. It could only mean one thing - he was in the company of lepers.

He felt his legs go faint and all strength drain from his arms as Cyril pushed past him. In a delayed reaction he flounced backwards and watched speechless as the gruff Northerner disappeared behind another hut, only to return moments later, staggering, his head tipped backwards, drinking from a leather flask.

"Don't worry thee sen... Theeyer's plenty left."

Cyril shook the pear-shaped flask to demonstrate that it still contained ample liquid, wiped his mouth with the swathed stump of his left hand and tossed the vessel to the young seaman. Simon's hands weakly clasped thin air; the flask bounced off his chest spraying water in his face. It fell to the ground between his feet, emptying itself into the dry earth.

"Gerrit then! Clumsy oaf."

He could not move. The water drained away, leaving a damp stain around his toes. Gazing up, he caught the look of amazement on Cyril's face turn to thunder beneath the ragged hood.

"Wha' thee playin' at? That's sweet spring watter."

"Lepers!... You be all Lepers."

Simon found his voice, and with it his arm rose to wag an accusing finger. Moments later he was cuffed to the dirt. He lay there in horror, feeling his skin crawl, as from the ring of huts and lean-tos shambled forth those he had taken the night before to be merry men of the greenwood. Last night there had been much laughter and mirth, lifting his spirits higher than a mast top sighting of land. Now, in the harsh sunlight that swept the clearing, there was no place for merriment. Uttering no sound, the menacing figures closed in. Only the shuffle of their feet betrayed their connection with living beings. All about them was the sight and stench of disease.

"Get away from I... I don't wanna catch it!"

He backed against the hut with the leather curtain and scrambled through the opening.

"Don't let 'em get I... Don't let 'em get I."

At first all was black, but eventually the darkness of the interior gave way to gloom. In it he could make out the shapes of the two women. His fingers reached out and grasped the hem of a smock.

"Don't let 'em ge'..."

"Will you stop blatherin' like a milk-sop kid! Rise up now! Up with you!"

The garment was brusquely snatched from his grasp. At the same moment a small drape was tugged aside from a window opening, filling the single-roomed cabin with light. The younger of the two women giggled at his fear and discomfort. Blushing at the sight of her apparent unblemished beauty and laughing mockery, he fought to regain a semblance of composure, but a sinister voice from outside made him sag and quake once again.

"If you'd be so kind as to step back out into the daylight, friend."

Simon turned to the older woman, his eyes imploring her to intercede on his behalf. Recognising her as one who had shown him kindness the night before, pushing bits of pork crackling into his hand and smoothing down the mud-spiked hair of his head, he tried his best to smile. Her features softened, he saw the imprint of beauty still clung to them. Raising a hand to brush aside a snatch of hair that tumbled across her forehead, he noticed that only the thumb and forefinger remained on an otherwise scarred stump. He felt the smile on his face freeze. A look of hurt, then resignation, then anger, flickered in her eyes.

"You could try apologising. It don't go well to abuse folks you 'ave freely supped with... Din't your Mother teach you any manners?

"Ain't got a mother no more, 'ave I?"

"We are waiting, friend... Don't make me come and get you!"

The voice the other side of the curtain was barely above a whisper and all the more terrifying because of it. He froze like a fieldmouse in the shadow of a plunging hawk, but a warm, sweet breath at the nape of his neck served to thaw him.

"Go on, apologise. I won't let them hurt a hair of your head."

A gentle, but firm push from the girl sent him on his way. Through the hide curtain he strode, imbued with a new found courage, feeling better protected than had he been encased in a suit of the finest armour.

"I most 'umbly beg yourrrr..."

Firm hands grabbed him. Over his head a sack was thrown and a drawstring pulled, pinioning his arms helplessly to his side, his protestations and beseechings becoming muffled like the squeals of an unwanted puppy dog destined for the mill pond. In anger more than terror he writhed and kicked. Someone or something kicked him back and over he tumbled. Round and round he thrashed. Then above his impotent roars, he heard the girl's laughter. In utter confusion and exhaustion, he ceased all movement and lay in the dust. Caught in a silence more unnerving than a thousand angry voices, he sensed someone approaching and though he bit his lip, a whimper escaped. A hand began to gently stroke his thigh. Someone in the crowd sniggered as he began to tremble. The fingers moved higher and the same sweet breath, accompanying a moan that served to pluck at his deepest centre, penetrated the rough fabric of the sack.

"Wha's goin' on?...Wha's 'apnin'?"

He tried to speak, but no one paid any heed to the muffled croaks and mumblings. The preying fingers brushed against his genitals. He bucked in terror and embarrassment, thankful at least that the sack hid his burning blushes.

"Come off it. 'Ere, wha's your game then?"

In vain he tried to will away the inevitable outcome, but nothing short of castration could impede his ensuing tumescence. From the females among the gathering came random cries of mock appreciation at his endowment. He panted, almost choking on the dusty fibres of the sack. The sultry moan close against his ear was repeated, laying his soul bare once more. His member grew harder still, pushing like a barber's pole against the front of his breeches. The moan gave way to a giggle that in its turn gave way to the braying mockery of an ass. The rough hands grabbed him once more, lifting him to his feet as all present chorused a deafening "Ee haw!... Ee haw!... Ee haw!"

His breeches were pulled down to his ankles and a coarse object inserted between the cheeks of his buttocks. A cheer rose, and round and round he was led by his stiff member. The same deft fingers continued coaxing him into maintaining his hardness, then all was silent as the fingers played back and forth. He could feel the surge from within and fought against the outcome, but the tormentor's fingers sensed it too and quickened the pace. No power on earth could hold back his spurting forth. The ensuing cheer and applause were deafening. Then all was again silent, save for the sound of his breath. The drawstring to the sack was loosened, he was given one last turn, and left alone to pant and suck in the dusty centre of the leprous mob. Immediately on their release, both his hands dived to his ankles and hitched up his breeches. This time groans of mock disappointment came from the mouths of the women as his nakedness was concealed. From his backside he extracted the switch of horsehair that had been forced there and threw it at the crowd - again to the howls of much laughter. He struggled with the sack, almost reluctant to leave its sanctuary, but relieved to taste fresh air nonetheless. Another round of deafening applause greeted his emergence. The grinning, leering faces were all chattering at once through scabrous lips and broken, blackened teeth. He searched in vain for the girl, but only her older female companion stood close at hand. He smiled bashfully, hoping for a glimmer of something approaching maternal concern. Instead she winked brazenly back at him and with her thumb and only remaining finger made a slow, milking motion. The crowd roared with laughter at his reddening discomfort, and as it obviously began to dawn on him that the true perpetrator of his ordeal had been the older woman all along. The following events confirmed it. A shrill, bone whistle was blown and in the ensuing silence the crowd parted to let a tall, leather-jerkined figure stride forward. Before the man opened his mouth, Simon knew him to be the owner of the voice that had unsettled him from his first, waking moments.

"Ah, friend... your initiation is complete. Welcome to our merry band. It would be true to say that you have been worked like an ass, if I may make so bold."

Glancing down at the sack, Simon saw that it had been crudely fashioned into the head of an ass, with the corners bound as ears, and a stupid, grinning face daubed on the front.

"Truly, friend, now you know all is not what it seems."

Raising his hand to silence the guffaws of the audience, he continued, "We have many failings true, some... er... God-given advantages have maybe been mislaid, dropped off as it were, but we have many strengths - indeed, many accomplishments. Witness your own obvious delight at the hands... er... excuse me, at the finger and thumb of Mistress Susan here."

With a flourish he bowed to the one called Susan, who curtsied demurely in return.

"But to continue, as I said before, all is not as it seems. Indeed there are amongst us unfortunate lazars - those who have the curse of leprosy upon them. Did not God himself, in his infinite mercy, command that every leper be put out of the host?"

He looked around. No one moved or spoke.

"Well my friend, put out, cast adrift they surely were. Now they are here, as are you, and as am I. There are others who, for the sake of a mark here, a blemish there, have also suffered the pain of banishment, plucked from the bosom of their loved ones. But when the disease did not ultimately manifest itself, were they allowed back within the portals of the town to reclaim that which was once their own? Not a bit of it, friend. Not a bit of it. For they had become lost souls."

Stopping to quaff at a flask proffered by one of the onlookers, he paused, shook his head and exhaled, paying melodramatic homage to the strong liquor contained therein. There was another momentary pause where he looked as if he might pass the leather flask to Simon, but, thinking better of it, he returned it to another's grasping hand and continued his speech.

"There are those who should rightly be here to take their place amongst us."

A loud murmur grew from the crowd. Names were shouted and heads nodded in assent. Raising his hand, the murmur abruptly ceased, and the speaker continued.

"Some are very highly placed indeed, who through birth or the cloth, or some such, manage to maintain the outward display of rude health; those who, through their influence or gelt, escape the pain of banishment. Of course, one way or another, some of the glitter finds its way to us... because for the most part, we know who they are."

The man laughed. For the first time Simon looked into the face of the speaker. It was a bony, pallid face, bordered by close-cropped hair and beard of wiry texture that revealed ample flecks of grey amongst the black. The nose had been broken and re-set at an angle, giving the man a somewhat brutish appearance, but the fierce cunning of the blue-grey eyes belied this; and the educated tone of his voice, laced as it was with a scrivener's exactitude and a lawyer's derision, held the young seaman entranced in a welter of inhibition and shame.

"I din't mean to offend no one's feelin's... 'onest I din't, cross my 'eart!"

Simon heard himself blurting out the words and felt foolish when the man held up his hand.

"Friend, for the most part our hides are grown thick and horny, and some amongst us have lost all feelings - some never having had any in the first place - but we thank you anyway. Now young friend, are you with us? Do you wish to become one of our merry band? Or do you take the fast way out of here?"

He rolled his eyes, turning his face to the edge of the gorge, so that Simon was left in no doubt as to the meaning of the term 'fast way out'. He shuffled his feet, confused in his wretchedness. His throat was so dry. Had the clutches of the foul disease already taken hold? Suddenly a burst of light played in the earth at his feet and slowly it rose up his leg, to dance like a wood sprite at his crotch. He looked up and the light hit his face, dazzling him. The girl laughed and waved the looking-glass in her hand. He rubbed his eyes and opened them in time to see her smile and skip away between the huts. Of course, he thought, that was the light that had given him strength the previous afternoon as he clung to the rock face on the opposite side of the gorge.

"I think I stays," he said.

CHAPTER 15
A hot, soothing cup

"He has done what?... There's no need to shout, man... Now, begin again."

Thomas Croft shook his head, winced and tried not to focus on Rudkin's spittle-filled mouth. However, a piece of seeded bread trapped in a tooth crevice drew his attention. His stomach churned with the acidity of the previous night's wine.

"As I sez, your honour...the bird 'as flown the coop. Tha' gurt, swirly-faced savage 'as jumped ship after maliciously woundin' one of our lads wiv an arrowl, an' scarin' the ballocks off of another."

As if sensing the whereabouts of Croft's attention, Rudkin's tongue curled and slithered along his rotting teeth until, discovering the offending seed, it stopped. Then, in an effort to dislodge the morsel, it began an obscene, agitated motion, accompanied by a vile, sucking sound. In desperation, Thomas Croft rapped the table surface with his riding gloves, wincing again at the effort. Rudkin stopped, closing his mouth firmly.

"D'you mean the Cornucopia, man?"

"Tis the only one I knows 'ad a 'eaven savage honboard, sir."

"Well, where? When did he go? Last night obviously... Did anyone see him... What about the watch?"

Rudkin shrugged. Answering his own questions, Croft continued.

"Ha! the watch. A more useless bunch of laggards you would have to travel the length of Christendom to find."

Rudkin nodded and coughed.

"Beggin' your pardon sir, but 'avin' caught a glimpse of the savage, it be my thinkin' tha' 'e aint gonna' get lost in a crowd so's t' speak. I means we got some right 'orrible lookin' pieces o' work out there, but tha' there savage is gonna stick out like a wart on a nun's nose."

Croft nodded, and allowing himself a pained smile, sank backwards onto a chair. The leatherwork creaked and squealed in protest; Croft covered his ears and sighed.

"Yes, Rudkin. Yes, yes, yes, and I suppose a well-placed fellow like yourself, with eyes and ears everywhere, would be in the best position to track him down?"

Rudkin smirked, sniffed, then rubbed the side of his nose. Croft's fingers busied themselves inside his purse.

"I know, man. I know. Don't say a word."

He cast a small, silver coin on the table, winced again at the metallic clatter. Swifter than a striking viper, Rudkin scooped up the coin, imprisoning it in a clenched fist. Croft chuckled to himself.

"Rudkin, before you run off to alert your friends, be so kind as to instruct Roberts to fetch me a cup of hot galangal water."

"Beggin' your pardon, Mast' Croft, but Roberts 'ave popped out."

"Popped out! On whose authority?"

"I don't rightly know sir. Maybe 'e's gone for your victuals - a nice pie or such like."

"No more! Stop!... I'll thank you not to speak of food... Never mind, Rudkin, you will make my beverage, won't you?

I trust you can boil water? By the by, where did you get those stripes, man? They look nasty. Whore's gentle touch I presume?"

Rudkin's hand lightly brushed his cheek. He seemed momentarily flustered, his face turning almost as livid as the three parallel scratches that ran from his left eye to jawline.

"Err... would that be with a spoon of honey, Mast' Croft?"

"But of course, man."

Rudkin bowed low and swiftly left the room.

"A big spoon of honey, mind, and I mean hot water! I want to see steam rising!... Oh, and report back the moment you hear anything."

Rudkin stopped on the stairs.

"Right you are sir, steamin' 'ot it shall be."

Thomas Croft rubbed his eyes. The previous night's excess had tangled his normally alert mind with cobwebs of doubt. Flashes of anger and regret tried to make inroads, but all he could focus on was the desired hot beverage. His instinct was to bawl out for it, chivvy Rudkin on, even though the poor dolt was probably moving as swiftly as possible. If he were to call out, he knew that retribution would follow. Even the faint cackle of the gulls outside was driving him to distraction.

Eventually the drink arrived and, alone once more, he inhaled, then sipped the aromatic cup, letting its peppery, sweet infusion seep into his being.

"Why, the ungrateful heathen! We were to take him hunting boar. Give him a yew bow... Damnation! I wanted that red wood bow! Must get him back... Must bring him back! Now where has that scoundrel Roberts disappeared to?"

CHAPTER 16
Ancient Rubble

It gradually became apparent to young Simon that fewer than half the company of vagabonds and fugitives were truly leprous. These unfortunates, it seemed, operated their own system of segregation, keeping themselves mainly to five of the huts. They were, however, treated equally, with far more kindness than anything they could hope to gain from those in the towns. Some who had not contracted the disease were the wives and husbands of those who had; and rather than be parted, had opted to run the risk and stay with their loved ones. These were watched carefully, as the disease was only contagious in the early stages, a fact that was continuously ignored and overlooked almost universally. But the outlaws were content with this particular state of ignorance. All were aware that the lepers' presence was a safeguard, a front - the main reason why the camp had not been overrun by the authorities long before now. As far as the good Aldermen of Bristow were concerned, there was a camp of vagabonds and lepers somewhere in the woods on the far side of the Avon Gorge and as long as it remained there without causing too much nuisance, then lighter would be the demands on the town coffers to set up another hospice.

Simon was greatly relieved to find out that neither the young girl, nor even Cyril and the woman who had helped in his humiliating initiation, had been contaminated. The woman, Susan, had worked as a drab in the city stews, and had lost her fingers when her pimp had suspected her of thievery. He was right, she was a thief, but she was supposed to steal from the customers not him. She had, in return, managed to talk Cyril into bludgeoning the pimp, and together they had fled to the sanctuary of the woods. The girl, Sarah, had fled with them. It caused Simon much anguish, however, to find out that despite being little older than himself, she too had worked the stews for over a year. He tried hard to backtrack, not to think of her in the mooncalf way that had begun to take such a hold of him - itself a kind of sickness. But it was too late. He found himself being helplessly drawn towards her every move, though he tried his best to conceal it, and always when she passed by, he looked up, unable to halt the scalding blush that would inevitably follow. In sleep, he dreamed of her; not even the swish of the salt sea intruded. He had become bewitched. No one had warned him what it would be like, or offered any advice as to what could be done for this malaise. Once, she had called him into a thicket, lifted her dress to display her nudity, only to run off laughing as he ambled towards her.

Everyone referred to the leader as 'King Arthur'. His short-sighted second in command, who was reputedly the worst bowman in the company, was affectionately called 'Robin Hood'. These two men organised the workings of the camp, designating who should go out hunting, who should beg outside the city walls, and who should prowl the highways in search of plunder. They maintained themselves by thievery and brigandage, though the worst excesses were carried out far from the camp and the city boundaries.

Though none were aware of it, the camp itself was the remains of an ancient Iron-Age fort. Of course there were those that guessed that the overgrown ramparts of limestone rubble were not a natural feature, but as to the original builders and inhabitants, none had a clue, or a desire to dig too deep - lest dark, supernatural forces be unearthed. This semicircular wall rose from the bottom of the outlying ditch to a height of thirty feet, and commanded the main approach to the camp. There were two other sides to the perimeter, both of them precipitous slopes, the lesser of the two being crowned by a haphazard fence of brambles and wattle. The camp itself consisted of a score of huts. There had been no attempt to fell the ancient ash and beeches that stood where once a large clearing had been. Instead, the hovels of mud and sticks nestled beneath the boughs like overgrown bee-hives. A natural break in the trees served as the central clearing, and in this space most of the inhabitants gathered - along with assorted dogs, goats, chickens and pigs - to discuss the forthcoming business, to sniff at and stir the great, black cauldron of thick pottage.

Within the five days he had stayed at the camp, Simon Tyrell, now Simon Sybald, had learned the names - or rather the assumed names - of most of the inhabitants; and though he still maintained a more than discreet distance between himself and the unfortunates, he was encouraged by the kindness and civility that most showed to each other to feel 'at home' for the first time in a long while. Even Cyril Hardwyke or 'Yorkie' - as he preferred to be called - proved kinder than he himself hoped his hard exterior revealed, although he liked nothing better than to brag about the ones he had 'dispatched'.

"Well, as thee asked like, 'appen I'll tell thee. It's reet 'ard to put an exact number on't on account of a great many were smote in battle."

Adjusting himself on a log set against one of the beeches, Yorkie slashed and parried with an imaginary sword.

"Aye, I done a reet lot o' me smitin' in the 'eat o' battle like, when I weren't much older than thee sen... Aye an' 'appen there's bin more than a couple since. But mind, I've never 'armed a soul who weren't askin' ferrit in t' first place... An' anyone whose daft enough to travel alone wi' a full purse, is askin' ferrit. En't they, eh? He! He!"

Amused by his own jest, he started to cackle with laughter, which caused him to cough up and spit a wad of phlegm, accidentally hitting the snout of a wandering piglet.

"Ha! Ha! did yer see that... right on't snout o' porker." He laughed, coughed and shook fit to burst. Simon waited for him to settle.

"Be tha' 'ow you lost your 'and then?... In the 'eat of battle?" asked the young seaman. "Who werr it against then?.. They bleddy Frenchies?"

A long, heavy silence followed, where Yorkie stopped his imaginary parrying and looked the young seaman up and down.

"Nay, it soddin' wun't, Simple Simon."

He looked away, his grizzled features becoming lost in the shadows of his hood. In his eager naivety Simon Tyrell pressed the matter further.

"Well then, Cyril, 'ow'd it 'appen then? Y'ain't got the rot, 'ave you."

"Less o' thee Cyril... Yorkie t' you... 'ow many soddin times... No real names... What thee soddin' 'ead don't know, thee tongue can't tell... Y'understand?... No, I aint got the soddin' rot!"

"Well then, Yorkie... Now tell I, 'ow did it 'appen?"

Simon hung on like a terrier, thankful for the distraction in not having to brood about the girl.

"Yes Yorkie, tell us?"

Both turned around to see 'King Arthur', leaning against the tree.

"That ain't very nice, Arthur, creepin up on folk like that... Not nice at all."

"I do beg your most humble pardon."

The leader swept the ground in an exaggerated bow. Cyril, either genuinely satisfied, or choosing not to notice the glaring mockery, cleared his throat, spat again and continued.

"Well alright then, but I'll brook nay sniggerin' from t' young un... It were bit off by a greet big 'ound on't moors near Steeton in t'blessed county o' Yorkshire. I'd just killed me an 'ogget. On t' site of what once were me own village, if yer please. That were 'til Lord friggin' Fairfax decides 'e wants t' knock village down ant mek room f't parkland. Just turned all t' folk into beggars... Just like that!"

He clicked his fingers and spat once more. Tears filled his eyes, and with clenched fist he began to pound his own leg.

"Where were I? Oh, aye right. Well, I reckoned as how Fairfax at least owed me this little sheep, so I 'ad 'im. An' I were just about to gut 'im when I 'ears soddin' keeper's 'orn, an' up lopes this great big 'ound... Course, if I 'ad gutted 'ogget, then I coulda tossed this 'ere 'ound a tasty distraction like, something' it wun't bin able t' resist... Well I 'adn't, so it were me arm that were tastiest distraction like, an't 'ound bit reet int' bone, wun't let go, even after I'd 'acked its ugly 'ead 'alf off its body."

"So wha' you do then Cyr...er, Yorkie?"

"What d'you soddin think? I 'ad to 'ack off me own 'and, wi' nowt but a rusty short blade, afore I were captured and strung up."

A reverential silence followed, broken finally by Simon.

"Did it 'urt?"

"Did it what? Did it soddin what? What d' thee soddin' think?"

Simon was butted off the log into the dust. His face was a picture of confusion, uncertain whether to 'laugh it off', apologise, or to display anger. A roar of laughter from 'King Arthur' settled the matter and a grin, more from relief than humour, settled on the lad's face.

"Did it hurt? Ha! I like it!" Arthur exclaimed. "Come on, Yorkie, don't be too hard on our new friend."

Cyril growled under his hood. The leader offered his hand to Simon, and pulling him up, gave the lad a wink.

"Now then, Yorkie, I need your advice. Do you think our young friend here is ready?"

"Ready f' what?... Aye, ready fer a good duckin' int' river."

"Listen, I'm being serious now... Is he ready to go on a little jaunt with you? Since Harry and young Davey got stretched, we've been short of help. What do you think? He has to start earning his bread sometime soon."

Yorkie stood up, and without saying a word walked around the young seaman. Simon, conscious of the fact that he was being sized up - as if he were a beast at market - breathed in and stuck out his chest. Yorkie hovered close. His sour ale and onion breath blew hot on Simon's left ear.

"Can thee use t' longbow?" His mocking tone was barely above a whisper. "I'm talkin' about a man's bow, one that can pierce through t' links o' chain mail... Norra kiddies toy fer knockin' squabs off 't perch."

Simon slumped a little and did not answer.

"I don't know! Young'uns today!... D'yer mean t' say that a big lad like yersen can't draw back a man-killin' arrer?... What is the world comin' t'?... Seamen, they're all t' same, stockfish ant sodomy."

Yorkie spat with disgust, and looking at the leader, rolled his eyes.

"There be many a seaman who can draw a full yard, and

shoot from up aloft an' all," answered Simon, his voice rising with indignation.

"Oh aye! Wharra bout thee sen then?"

"Well, I can use a sling, better n' you... And I can chuck a knife for three turns an' 'ave it stick in more times than not." Simon blurted out the words, half convinced himself that it was true, when in actual fact he had not long learned to perfect a single blade spin.

"Ha! Good three turns?... Well said, young friend... We don't have any knife throwers in our company, or fire eaters for that matter... but we can use as many diverse talents as the good Lord sees fit to send us... Don't you agree, Cyril... er Yorkie?"

"Garn! Fire-eaters? Soddin' seamen, all t' same."

"And I can shoot a matchlock gun."

Simon was unable to halt another half-truth escaping his lips, but it was swiftly followed by a crimson blush. A faint whistle escaped King Arthur's lips. Yorkie sniggered.

"Oh, gun is it? Thee can shoot a soddin' gun, can thee? Would that be a covey, culverin, or crapaud?"

"It were a gurt 'andgun."

Sensing the lad was lying or at the very least embroidering the truth, Yorkie pressed the matter, intent on ridicule.

"Since when 'ave the port of Bristow been armin' their sailors wi' 'andguns? Why, not even the nightwatch 'ave a gun t' muck about wi', norra' 'andgun leastways."

"Well we 'ad one, gurt big long 'un, this big."

He held his hand a few inches above his own head, then proceeded to backtrack a little.

"Well I ain't sayin' I 'eld it, but I 'elped load it, and I put the match to the touch hole."

"Blagh! 'appen 'e's a soddin' fire eater after all."

"Tis the same thing, I could fire one up if I wanted."

"Listen lad! Thee can meck as much noise an' smoke as thee wants... Whar' I'm talkin about is a grown man's weapon, norra device for scarin' the drizzlin' shite outta' 'orses an' soddin' seagulls."

"Well then, wha' about yourself then? You can't shoot a longbow on your own wivout someone else 'oldin' it, can you eh?"

Yorkie made a lunge at Simon. King Arthur stepped in-between.

"Thee little bleeder! Thee din't complain when me an' Alf shot t' rope over t' yer."

"That's enough! Stop, both of you... Right, tomorrow you, Simon, will accompany Cyril on a little jaunt to Shepton Mallet. In the meantime, go to my hut and get yourself a longbow, one with a gentle cast to it, we don't want you pulling your finger joints out, do we? And Cyril here will instruct you... Won't you, Yorkie?"

Cyril shuffled, spat and mumbled sarcastically.

"Garn!... If it pleases thee, lordship... I do 'ave things to do mind. I promised t' woman I'd meck 'er a new stool fer milkin' 'er goats... Anyway, why can't soddin Robin 'ood show 'im? They can practise together."

"Because, Cyril, I want you to... Our very own Robin is beyond help, and well you know it. Tis not his fault that his eyes are failing him, but he has other talents... So come along now, be a fine fellow and pass some of your skill on to our young sailor boy."

"Alright, but it can't be learned in a day, as well thee knows... I'll show 'im, if thee 'as a word wi' t' woman. She 'as a fearsome temper if she don't get what she wants."

"That I'll do, now take him away, I have some further plans to make for the morrow's little jaunt."

Without further ado, King Arthur turned and made

towards the weed-covered ramparts, then like a proper monarch ascending a castle stairway, he daintily mounted the ancient ramparts; and once atop, nose in the air, hands clasped behind him, commenced his daily, regal inspection.

"Just teck a look at 'im struttin' around like sparrow on t' shite 'eap," growled Cyril. "T' look at 'im you'd think 'e were next King of England, norra common felon like t' rest of us."

"Wha' did 'e do then, Yorkie?"

Cyril peered from under his hood at the young seaman. His scowl softened a little. Simon guessed that maybe it was being addressed once again as 'Yorkie' that helped.

"Well now, Simon, from what I gather, 'e were in the employ of some Lord up in't London, 'is personal physician ant barber. A trusted position, but 'e got greedy, 'e kept 'elpin' 'imself t' silver spoons, til there weren't a one left, ant lord dungface, worever 'is name was, 'ad to slurp 'is mess o' pottage direct from t' bowl, like rest of us ruffians. Needless to say, 'e weren't right 'appy, but by that time our leader up there 'ad legged it all the way to these parts."

"Well 'ow come 'e got to be leader then, if all 'e did were nick some spoons like?"

"Simple," Cyril chuckled, "Broke t' neck of the last'un we 'ad... Great big ugly bugger 'e were an' all, more like a jailer than leader.   Anyway, norr only is Arthur good at mendin bones,'e's right smart at brekkin' 'em. It were in a fair fight mind... Anyway, Black Parker, t' last 'un were a right soddin' prick, scuse me language but 'e were, what with demandin' 'is way with all t' women, ant keepin all the best bits o' plunder for his sen... So, King Arthur - t' spoon thief - is everybody's 'ero... Specially since 'e seems t' 'ave some magic touch wi' lepers... Cobwebs ant mouldy bread 'e uses as ointment like. I don't know, mebbe it's wi' Devil's 'elp, but thee must admit, thee wun't find a bonnier bunch o' lepers anywhere... As thee

227

can see everyone's content to do anything 'e says."

"Even you, Yorkie?"

"Why certainly, sailor boy... I may 'ave a little grumble now an' again, but someone 'as t' give t' orders, an our King Arthur is good at doin' it. I tell thee, there's more order in this camp 'ere than any army. Why 'appen we've only lost five men this year, two t' 'angman, an three lost in the course of duty."

"Wha' d'you mean lost... dead like?"

"What does thee think? I'm beginnin' to wonder. I mean, does thee think?"

Freely exhibiting the returned signs of his customary irritability, Cyril tapped his head, looking at the young lad as if he were addressing an imbecile.

"Two 'oisted up, and three cut down, all in their prime. All fer bein' careless like, an not listenin' t' orders. So, Simple Simon lad!" He slapped his hand hard on the lad's shoulder and clamping his fingers firmly, steered him to the wattle fence at the edge of camp. "Thee'll be a good lad, won't thee, ant list t' all that yer uncle Yorkie tells thee?"

Simon nodded and grinned sheepishly, letting himself be steered. Then all of a sudden he stopped dead in his tracks. Yorkie pushed him, but he stood his ground, even though inside his heart was fluttering. Over by the ancient ramparts King Arthur, the spoon thief and the girl Sarah were entwined in each others arms. Simon gasped for breath as if struck by a thunderbolt.

"Thee gonna stand theer with thee greet gob open catchin' flies, or are we gonna shoot some arrers?"

CHAPTER 17
The Parting

Finally, after crouching frozen in the shadows, watching the foremost of the assailants approach the far bank, Dodds had overcome his dread paralysis and taken a rush at the betrayer. He resisted the urge to roar out an accusation. Instead, moving close against the shadowy rockface - keeping behind the young traitor - he swung the club in an almost casual manner. The weapon's lethal balance did the rest, staving in the side of the smooth skull as if it were an egg. The youth had been so preoccupied with the gathering host that although he had ultimately sensed the danger, it was too late to turn and see his attacker. Dodds was thankful for that. He too did not wish to turn, but had nonetheless felt the sickening crack, then thud, of his fallen victim as he mounted the rocks.

He had expected a chorus of blood-chilling warcries from the Paquatuogs, but there was nothing - only his own heavy panting - as he climbed. Then as he neared the top and the moonlight transformed him into an irresistible silhouette, he heard the many sinew twangs, like a thumb's busy strum across the bass strings of a lute, and twist and turn as he might, he was caught in the midst of the deadly hail.

A heavy jolt somewhere in his back sent him reeling, though not quite falling. On regaining his stride, he felt a second thud of searing pain in his left shoulder. Both legs were still moving swiftly, heroically. He wanted to call out a warning to Tyrell and the sleeping Pennacooks, but all he could manage was a strangled rasp. Breath would not translate itself into the luxury of a shout. Glancing down at his shoulder, he noticed how a stone-point protruded clear of his shirt, and how his blood glistened wine purple in the moonlight. Strangely, the violation of his flesh did not frighten him. The spreading numbness in his back somehow served to assuage the horrifying reality that somewhere deep within his vitals a similar, barbed grub nestled - slicing, severing, burrowing deeper with every breath and bound.

Despite this physical numbness, his mind was imbued with a crystal clarity, perhaps too much, so that the awareness itself became a distraction. He had heard the hissed commands, the splashing of many legs wading the stream and knew that it would not be long before they mounted the cliff; and once again his back would irresistibly draw their shafts. If he could only reach the trees in time, then his crashing through the lower boughs would surely alert the others.

But it was a false clarity. In a sudden darkening of the senses it deserted him. As a last parting gesture he was made aware that, in time to each footfall, he had been silently mouthing the 'Lord's Prayer', but any comfort he hoped to glean from it was dashed when the words became lost, as if somewhere deep inside a slate was wiped clean. The club slipped from his fingers. He was ten paces further on before he felt the loss. Retrieving it took precedence over all else. This break in the momentum snapped the will, allowing an opening for the pain to speak to him. There was no choice now, other than to listen to its stubborn command. He was conscious of yelling, but in place of sound came only blood. Turning and lurching forward, he somehow found himself sitting, staring at the cliff edge and the murky shape of the first approaching enemy warrior. The club was again in his hand. He had managed to retrieve it and derived a small crumb of comfort from having the haft in his grasp. Though his grip was weaker than that of a newborn babe, he attempted to raise himself with its aid, but after the first failed attempt the desire disappeared, and there he was condemned to sit, mumbling and twitching, tasting blood salt again, waiting for the shapes to rush forward.

When he had first seen the hated captive rise from the cliff edge, Wadawagwa was tempted to send an arrow into his belly. Earlier, on waking to find that Dodds was missing, he had begun following the trail that led to the stream and had resolved to claim the already forfeit life. None could reproach him for slaying one who was attempting to flee, one who had displayed all the signs of being an evil sorcerer in their midst. It was an ideal opportunity to have done with the foul creature who had continued to humiliate and reduce his standing among the band. The thunder-roar at the camp ground had been the final indignity. It had taken him a long time to stop shaking.

Delighting in the illuminated manifestation of the detested one, he raised his bow, but when he saw the agitated motions, he knew others had seen the man first. The insect flit of many arrows confirmed it; the moonlight was just sufficient to reveal the swarm, and the victim's double shudder at the impact was evidence that some had left their sting. His first feelings were of outrage that any should be bold enough to steal his prize, but when he saw the Wobigen's efforts to ascend the slope and his strangled attempts to call out in what appeared to be a warning, everything changed. Wadawagwa realized then that the Paquatuogs had - as he had predicted - followed them even this far north, and were mounting a surprise attack. They must have hoped to catch them all helpless, sleeping like babes. How could they have come so close and in darkness? They must have strong magic, or someone had shown them the way.

Somewhere in the shadows the captive had crumpled into a heap. Wadawagwa wasted no time trying to locate him, but rather concentrated on the cleft in the rock where the pursuers would appear. Even above the babble of the stream he heard the faint creak of the wooden armour. Pha! What fools! Did they not have enough bear grease to spare for the bindings? Had they filled their bellies instead? He heard faint whispers from just below the edge and knew that, at any moment, a human target would appear. Again he raised the heavy war bow, his lungs filling with air as the grooved arrow shaft was drawn towards his mouth. Motionless he waited, willing the prey to show. The first one came over slowly, crouched low, but unable to slither because of the slatted breastplate. Still Wadawagwa did not move, though the strain of the bow was starting to tell. He waited until the figure, on gaining confidence, rose and started approaching the spot where he guessed Dodds lay. Then he drew the shaft the last remaining distance to his lips and let it fly. The second arrow was nocked and drawn as the first still flew. It was this second shaft that hit the Paquatuog with an audible clack! The murky shape had gone down, toppled backwards with a grunt of pain. Delighting in the perfection of his accuracy, Wadawagwa shrieked out his warcry.

"Come on, you Paquatuog dogs, show your ugly faces! I have arrows enough to go around! Come now whilst I am one alone!" He ran to a fallen tree, letting fly another shaft. "You thought to slither in amongst us like serpents, but your game is spoilt. Come on, you cowards, do not run like women. I am but one alone!"

Wadawagwa shouted his insults in loud bursts so that the Pennacooks would waken and so that he could hear the inevitable flight of arrows. One of the Paquatuog bowmen had loosed his shaft moments before the others, and the hum of its downward flight alerted him to the approaching volley. From the safety of the fallen tree he hooted and derided them for poor marksmanship, though in truth the group of arrows had come unerringly close. Did they have with them a Mateoulin who could not only see as if night were day, but also through rock and wood? he wondered.

"Missed me, you eaters of skunk turds! You can do better than that... I'm over here!"

Where were the others? A hint of panic made him turn and call again, much louder.

"I'm over here!"

The ensuing whoosh of arrows above his head and the much flatter trajectory of their flight told him that he was in trouble. While he had bragged and sheltered, some of the Paquatuogs had climbed up another way. How many, one, two? It could not be more, but more would surely follow if he was not swift. More shafts zipped by, one so close that he felt the hiss of its breath on his shoulder.

"Hi-Yi! Tricked you!... You've missed your chance... I'm not alone any longer... See, my brothers come."

Where were they? he screamed inside. Wake up, you fools!

Springing from the fallen tree, he let fly two more arrows in the direction of the cliff edge. They flew wide, swallowed up in the murk. Drawing another from his quiver, he was shocked to discover that only five remained. There was no sign of the enemies who had mounted the shadowy landscape, and there was still no sign of the Pennacooks. If they did not come quickly, he would have no alternative but to retreat and stir them. Hi-Yi, if only they were to arrive soon, they would see him in his glory, single-handedly fending off the attack, and all the former humiliation would be wiped away. That would be something to brag about - keeping the enemy at bay whilst his brothers slept. Why, even Tidesso, and the curly-haired captive with the lance that spits fire, would be hard pressed to cause such a stir when they returned to the people. Bent low, he rushed to another fallen tree, let out his warcry and loosed one more arrow.

With relief, he had sensed movement in the trees behind. At last the others were coming, so drawing himself to his full height, he struck a nonchalant pose and hummed aloud.

Managnon was the first to signal his approach. A tossed pine cone struck the left buttock of Wadawagwa. He stiffened, then smugly spoke without bothering to turn.

"Ah, it is you, brother. There was no need for you to stir, I have them cowering under my deadly arrows."

Managnon crept closer, an arrow already nocked.

"How could I sleep with all the noise you are making?"

Wadawagwa let fly another of his shafts.

"What do you shoot at? Demons, night spirits, or is it squirrels?"

"Yes, squirrels... Paquatuog squirrels... Here give me some of your arrows, mine have nearly all gone."

"Ah, then it is fortunate that the others come to join us."

Wadawagwa turned to see a shadowy glimpse of the Pennacooks coming. Amongst them a single red glow, like a firefly, zig-zagged down the slope. He sniffed and caught the faint whiff of saltpetre, signifying the presence of the curly one and his foul-smelling weapon. A feeling of fear and revulsion rose in his gorge.

"Come on and fight like men, you Paquatuog shits! Come on!"

He called out again, then turned to mark the progress of the red fire glow. The clatter and the evil smell annoyed him.

"Are you sure they were real and not dream spirits?" enquired Managnon.

"Do you mock me? Go down to the edge. Should you reach

there without taking an arrow in your flesh, you will see the body of the older captive. He was trying to call to us, but he could only croak like a frog."

Managnon slowly lifted his head and scanned the foreground. He could make out the crumpled shape of Dodds.

"Is he dead? Tidesso will not be happy."

Wadawagwa shrugged. Inside, he was furious. They were more concerned about the death of an escaping captive than acknowledging his magnificent act of heroism.

"Look again. Nearby you will see the body of a Paquatuog," he hissed irritably.

"No, I see no other, only shadows. Perhaps it was a shadow you slew."

"It was no shadow," spat Wadawagwa "it was a..."

The air was rent by a deafening crash and a stab of fire; both tribesmen jumped, then ducked low. A clatter of many birds fleeing from the nearby trees followed; and then eerie silence, where bitter smoke drifted and curled all around.

Taking the dying echo of the gun's thunder-crack as a signal, the Pennacooks screamed, let fly a volley of arrows, and swept forward in a headlong dash, coming to a crouched halt two yards from the cliff edge. There had been no opposition to their charge. In tense silence they waited, whilst on his stomach Tidesso inched forward to peer into the gloom.

No angry whine of arrows came as greeting. There was no sign of the enemy whatsoever. But as the first hint of dawn breached the gaps in the highland, a voice bellowed out from way up on the opposite slope.

"Pennacooks... we will swallow you all!"

More was shouted, but apart from 'kill' and 'cut', most of the words were lost in the distance. All the Pennacooks jeered back, some turning to bare their buttocks, others climbing down the cliff, calling out as they went. There was a maddened roar when the body of the young Squakheag was found. It was assumed that he had been slain by the Paquatuogs. All thought it strange though, that he had not been scalped or mutilated in any way. Only Tyrell remained above, hugging the lifeless body of his friend, rocking and moaning with grief.

It was the hand of Tidesso laid gently on his shoulder that temporarily assuaged the pain. Tyrell had not heard him approach, but he could not fail to notice and appreciate the genuine show of solace and the look of concern in his eyes. Untangling his arms from the stiffened body of his friend, Tyrell pulled himself upright, wiped his nose on the back of his hand and lightly touched Tidesso's arm. Tidesso frowned and pulled Tyrell to him, Tyrell felt the wet run of the savage's tears on his own shoulder. Was this really happening? he asked himself. This savage is shedding tears for poor old Dodds.

"He was like an uncle to me... Like an uncle. No, not an uncle, more like a father... father," he blurted.

Tidesso nodded as if he understood, then, stooping down, began to gently sing to the dead man. Horrified, Tyrell realised that, in his grief, he had said no prayers for Dodds. It had taken the canting of a savage to remind him.

"No, wait! He be a Christian man. He needs the words of the one true God saying over him. And he's goin' to have a good Christian burial, if I have to dig his grave with my bare hands." Addressing the corpse, he continued, "D'you hear that, Sam, I'll see to it, don't you worry."

He was blubbering again, blubbering and praying. Beside him Tidesso had stopped singing and was busily engaged in examining the club that Dodds still gripped. Slowly withdrawing it from the dead man's fingers, he held it close, wiping the flakes of freshly dried blood from the stone spur, a look of puzzlement on his face. Then, laying his hand briefly on Tyrell's shoulder once again, he walked away, this time taking the club with him.

Dropping down to the stream, level where the rest of the band was congregated, Tidesso was in time to catch Wadawagwa's ranting account of events. In his hand Wadawagwa brandished a bundle of the enemy arrows and pointed out stains of fresh blood as proof of his bravery. Tidesso knew better than to interrupt, but biding his time, waited until the other had finished bragging before speaking himself.

"Wadawagwa, your power grows stronger. Let me be the first to say how well you have done. We all owe you our thanks. There are many things, though, that I do not yet understand."

Appearing at first not a little pleased with himself, Wadawagwa suddenly looked confused, then catching a glimpse of the club in Tidesso's hands, he smiled and pointed to it.

"You have my Tomahawk! I would wish it back. How did you come by it?"

Remembering then that he had dropped it in the trees where he had cowered, after fleeing from Dodds' explosion, Wadawagwa backed off and started to blare out about his bravery once more. This time Tidesso interrupted.

"Do you know how this, your tomahawk, came to be in the hands of the dead captive?"

Wadawagwa shrugged his shoulders.

"He must have stolen it. He was a thief... He was marked for death."

Not bothering to reply, Tidesso pushed his way through the others and went over to the body of the young Squakheag warrior.

"See here! Look! The wound in the head fits the stone spur of the tomahawk."

A growl of anger rose from the gathering, all crowded in to witness Tidesso fit the club to the wound.

"Where is the Squakheag, Mateoulin? He should witness this. Why is he not here? Will someone go and bring him? We have need of his wisdom."

"It is obvious," Wadawagwa spoke. "The dead captive slew him. He must have been trying to escape, but was seen by this brave, young warrior who got his head knocked in for his trouble."

Wadawagwa stood apart with arms folded like a wise Sachem, and made the pronouncement as if he had suddenly been imbued with the power of divination.

"You see, did I not maintain all along that he was evil, a demon? Well, now my words have fallen true. The other one is obviously evil also. Give me the tomahawk, I will go and finish him too. Listen, he whimpers like a child still. The sound of it is making me angry."

Tidesso was also becoming angry, but not with Tyrell. There was something in the words of Wadawagwa that on first hearing appeared to resound with truth, and if his dislike of the other had not begun to take such a hold, he would no doubt have let it go at that. But something troubled him. He was not sure what. The broken pieces, though, would be made to fit before he even began to contemplate the slaying of the curly one. Besides, he had within him a warm feeling towards the young captive, and strangest of all, felt a little sadness for the death of the older one.

"Wait, none shall harm the curly one. Do we not all weep when one that we love is taken?"

Wadawagwa snorted, shook the bundle of enemy arrows and turned towards the others, as if the words of Tidesso no longer held any weight.

"Wadawagwa, your own words to me when I first joined you up there, were of the dead captive's attempt to warn us."

It was Managnon who this time spoke softly and deliberately. Wadawagwa spun round to face him, snorting the air once more.

"Whenever the words of one of you reach my ears, the words of the other follow soon after." He pointed to both Managnon and Tidesso. "Is it your intention to go along hand in hand like lovers from now on?"

Tidesso merely laughed, but the insult was too much for Managnon, who jabbed hard at Wadawagwa with the end of his bow. Laughingly, Wadawagwa jumped back, throwing the arrows hard at Managnon; hitting him 'flat on' about the head and shoulders. Laughing no longer, Tidesso banged the earth with the club, and, snarling, leapt in between them.

"Stop this! You can fight each other when we get home... Not now, not when there are enemies lurking close by."

"Good! He will take the place of the dead captive," jeered Wadawagwa.

Raising a finger to touch the red weal that now decorated his cheek, Managnon spat out a reply and with the same finger stabbed the air.

"It is I who will slay you, and none will mourn you or come to me demanding payment for your death, for you are not of the people... you are the spawn of Maquaks! You are an enemy."

All present drew quick breath, then were silent. Even the sobbing of Tyrell had ceased. A look of surprise brushed the face of Wadawagwa. What was this? Enemy? Maquak?

"Ha! What do you mean? What words are these... I am no enemy of the people! A Maquak?"

Tidesso motioned to Managnon to hold his tongue, but the angry Managnon chose not to notice.

"Our brother who was slain by the lake-side was old enough to remember a child of the Maquaks being welcomed into our lodges... That child had big ears! Ha! Ears like the paddles of a canoe."

From those positioned behind Wadawagwa came a chorus of suppressed sniggering. A hand rising to touch an ear fumbled furiously with the shell pendant that dangled from the looped lobe. Somewhere in Wadawagwa's memory a snatch of a cradle song echoed. Managnon continued his mockery.

"I, for one, am surprised you do not remember. Ever since the dead captive caused you to kiss the tree, you have been turning our bellies with that foul tongue."

Wadawagwa could not deny that his tongue had been spilling forth strange sounds - strange tasting words, that sprang from an unused part of his mouth - sounds that nevertheless formed pictures in his head.

"There! Did I not say he was a Demon?" Wadawagwa looked around, laughing loudly, nervously. "He cast a spell... That is how come he got the better of me in the first place. I will go and cut off his head now so that his evil dies with him! I am no Maquak! I am of the true people!"

He laughed again, peering at each face, hoping for the cruel jest to be revealed for what it was. But something had changed. Those he had called brothers, those who only moments earlier were applauding him for his bravery, were now as strangers to him. Inside his head was a swirl of utter confusion. Was it true? No, not a Maquak, surely? He too detested them. They were eaters of human flesh. Inside him his stomach twisted and turned. He had no memory or knowledge of being adopted, but where had the words come from? The first mother and father he remembered had been swept away in a flood and since then another man and woman had called him son. Could there have been yet others? Those who had given him life - a life begun with different blood, amongst a different people? This in itself was not unusual. He knew others who had been adopted into the tribe as children and none spoke of them as being anything other than 'of the people'. Even if it were true, what had he done to deserve this treatment? At least they were not accusing him of having Paquatuog blood.

"Do you call me enemy? How swiftly you forget that it was my arrows that left you time to sleep. I hope you cherished the dreams? They could have been your last."

Suddenly a commotion was caused by the running return of the one who had gone to fetch the Squakheag Mateoulin.

"He's gone! Moving fast for an old one... Wide tracks like a running deer!"

"He said he could travel fast... But why did he go in such a hurry? He could not know that his companion is slain. Why did he not wait? There is a bad stink in my nose from somewhere."

Tidesso stepped to the water's edge, then kneeling low on a boulder, splashed his face and upper body, before cupping his hands to drink.

"There has been treachery here...I know the taste... Now I understand!"

Walking over to the slain youth, he rolled the stiff, cold body on to its back and peered into the lifeless eyes. Suddenly he drew a blade and stabbed into each socket, then, starting at the base of the ears, he began to methodically peel off the scalp. Disregarding the grunts of uneasiness that rose from behind, he slashed the torso, arms and thighs to the bone. The moment the grisly task was completed, he sprang up, cupped both bloody hands to his mouth and roared his warcry across the water and up into the high ground.

"Should they still watch us... I want them to know we have discovered their treachery. They have turned the Squakheag

241

against the Pennacook. I do not know how, but it is bad for us. This one was to lead them to us. The dead captive saw it and slew him with Wadawagwa's tomahawk. We must catch or kill the Mateoulin before he reaches his town, and we must warn our own people that all are turned against us."

Anger roared its way to the surface. One of the young men stood over the dead youth, lifted the breech-clout with the tip of his bow, screeched and shot an arrow into the exposed genitals. Taking this as a cue, each in turn put a shaft into the inert shape, until the body bristled like a porcupine.

"Wadawagwa, will you take three of our swiftest runners and capture this Mateoulin? Bring him to us at the painted rock. We will wait there a day for you. If you cannot bring him, but you have the chance, make him talk, then kill him. Be wary, he will know much magic."

Wadawagwa seemed taken aback, one moment treated as a hero, the next reviled and revealed to be of the blood of the most hated enemies, and now seemingly welcomed back to the fold. He could not help but laugh a little.

"Do you trust a Maquak? Surely not?... Might I not feel hunger and wish to tear out his heart to give me strength?"

"You said yourself that in your own heart you are a Pennacook."

Wadawagwa looked straight into the eyes of Tidesso and raised an open hand.

"I would have my tomahawk back. It belongs in the hand that made it."

Tidesso gave it back. Wadawagwa smiled, then shrieking with pleasure, whirled it around his head, the ball end coming within a hair's breadth of Tidesso's face. He did not blink or move a muscle, but appeared unconcerned as the whistling breeze caused his scalp lock to flutter. With a final chuckle, Wadawagwa lowered the weapon.

"See! It reveals pleasure at being reunited with the one that gave it life."

"Good. Then will you go with haste and capture the Mateoulin?"

Nodding his head, Wadawagwa strutted amongst the group, lightly tapping the shoulders of three. A startled Managnon was one of them. What was this? Managnon wondered. He cast a swift glance at Tidesso, as if questioning the wisdom of allowing the decision, but the leader remained impassive, knowing that if he objected, Wadawagwa would take it as a sign that he were not trusted. This way there would be a chance for him to regain his standing and Managnon would be along to witness everything, providing of course that they did not come to blows.

Without a single word or a backward glance, they clambered up the cliff. The others followed, then gathering around Tyrell and the slain Dodds, they watched the chosen four casually lope into the trees. Once hidden from view, the four would bound along the Mateoulin's trail and providing the Paquatuogs did not second guess them, they would overtake him before he reached the town of the Squakheag.

Suddenly, way up in the high ground, a turkey gobbled. The call was immediately answered in the trees near the opposite bank, and then again somewhere in the distance.

"They have grown in numbers. They no longer need to hide in the shadows of night... We must go!"

Apart from the occasional shudder, Tyrell had stopped his sobbing. With the heavy, cold barrel of the gun across his thighs, he sat next to Dodds' body, unable to move, mumbling half-understood prayers in a long-dead tongue, his drained face a tear-stained smear of dirt and gunpowder. Again Tidesso laid his hand on Tyrell's shoulder, and pointing at Dodds, softly spoke, whilst at the same time urging him to his feet.

The gun was taken from him. He made a feeble attempt at holding on to it, and found himself standing up in the process. Firm hands grabbed his shoulders and began steering him up the slope. The still, soft words of Tidesso washed over him, their tone helping to sooth his anguish. They had reached the trees before Tyrell realised that they were leaving the unburied corpse of his friend behind. The hands that held him were ready for his attempts at tearing free, digging deeply into his muscle. His yells of protest were also stifled as a piece of folded leather was stuffed into his mouth, a strip of rawhide tied tightly around his jaw and another bound his wrists. The soothing words ceased and he was dragged along, a mere captive once more.

CHAPTER 18
Blue Herons and Boats of Bark

The burning anger and grief that boiled in a mute frustration, finally subsided, becoming a smouldering resentment that only showed signs of dwindling when later that day, after much hard travelling, two of the band disappeared, taking with them the body-bundle containing the remains of Alaskana. Later, in the next valley, these two caught up with the main band. They were visibly exhausted, empty-handed, having hidden the remains. Slowly Tyrell began to appreciate that he was not alone in grief. To have carried their kinsmen's remains thus far, then to leave them, indicated the seriousness of the situation. All were sombre. Some wept openly, though silently, knowing that in all likelihood the body would be discovered and desecrated before the day was out.

With nought but a handful of the same cold mush mixed with maple sap to sustain them that day, they threaded their way well into dusk, only stopping when darkness finally made the trail too hazardous. Forsaking the more level ground, and a score of more desirable sleep-sites, they collapsed halfway up a steep, wooded hillside, each one curled tight against a tree trunk or boulder, lest he roll away in the night. Moments before succumbing to sleep, Tyrell thought he heard the faint rumble of thunder, like some giant, drunken ogre stumbling about in a distant valley, but he was too tired to care.

Too exhausted to dream, Tyrell woke with the dawn to find that the tree chosen as his nightly support had failed him, and that a hard, mossy boulder two yards below had been his ultimate resting place. Normally a light sleeper, he had been oblivious to his downward slide. He scratched furiously at his head and brushed away the cobwebs and forest debris that clung to him, before realising that his bonds had also disappeared without his knowledge. He was thankful, too, that Dodds' spirit had not chosen that night to appear to him. Almost equal to the pain of losing his friend was the enormity of guilt he felt at not being able to inter his remains. A shudder passed through him when his mind alighted on the image of what in all probability had befallen his friend's body.

Bloody butchers! Heathen scum! Every last one of 'em... He momentarily ceased the scratching to cross himself and pray.

Tidesso and another came down and helped him to his feet. The young leader smiled briefly and addressed Tyrell once more, and again the gentle tone of the unknown words acted as a salve for his sorrow. Fortified by the growing feeling of self-preservation that had returned with the new day, he forced himself to understand their actions, though part of him dearly wanted to see them all dead, wiped out of his life.

After a mouthful of the inevitable cold, stale mush, they moved on again. Tyrell was given the gun and powder pouch to carry. The significance of this gesture did not escape him, and even though it was cumbersome, he much appreciated it.

Even to his untutored eyes, it was plain that they were taking the more obvious trails, forsaking their usual convoluted course, pushing at a steady jog, only slowing their pace where it was known that two or more trails converged.

Later around midmorning, they came to a rocky bluff that

overlooked a wide, fast-flowing river. Runners who had been sent ahead returned breathless, but in good humour. This palpable lightness of spirit spread to all and added an extra spring to each step. Tyrell was soon to discover why. A convergence of several, well-travelled trails led to a long, shingle beach, at the far end of which was a cluster of rude, bark lodges and most important of all, on the beach - keels upturned - lay five large, bark canoes.

The Pennacooks spread out and walked nonchalantly down the beach, making no attempt to hide their approach, though all had an arrow nocked and another ready in their bowhands. With shaking hand, Tyrell attempted to pour powder and ball down the gun barrel and ram home the charge whilst walking, but Tidesso signalled to him not to bother.

Out in the shallows, perched on a rock, a lone blue heron watched their progress through its gimlet eye, only reluctantly making an ungainly ascent when one of the Pennacooks came within reach. The handful of round lodges were nestled at the forest's edge, and but for the thin fingers of smoke that rose amongst them, gave Tyrell the impression of being devoid of human habitation - their appearance more like the nests of hitherto unseen, giant rodents. The pack of yapping dogs that came hurtling down the beach disabused him of this notion, though their wolf-like demeanour made him wonder whether the hand of man was totally absent from this place. They halted within spitting distance, to snarl and bare fangs, with heads slung low and neck hair ruffled like the intruders' own scalp-locks. None of the Pennacooks relaxed their stride and the snarling dogs obligingly walked backwards, maintaining the same distance.

From out of nowhere, a loud, disembodied voice boomed. It was a voice with undeniable human qualities, but also bearing a supernatural timbre, as if emanating from somewhere below the earth. As one, the Pennacooks instinctively drew back their bowstrings, the dogs started, then reluctantly retreated, and from underneath one of the canoes a grinning man suddenly popped up. He was completely naked, without even a flap of leather to hide his semi-tumescent state. The light breeze off the river caused the long, coarse hair to whip his deeply-lined face, but the smile remained, as if carved from the clay banks. Beside him materialised an equally naked, younger woman with protruding belly and lop-sided breasts. She tried her best to smile, but as the Pennacooks came closer, one of the hands that she was using to shield her groin rose to cover her tattooed mouth. Eventually, following another barked command from the man, she turned and ran up the beach, to disappear squealing and giggling among the lodges.

The menfolk were next to issue forth, most from the lodges, but some crept from the forest. Tyrell counted fifteen in all, armed with short bows and long, fish spears. Like the older man, all had long, free-flowing hair that reached way down their backs. On closer inspection, he saw that only ten were men, the remainder being young women. All looked equally fierce in their fresh raiment of glistening red clay and grease daub. The naked old man pointed a grime-encrusted finger at the reception and shook with laughter, whilst his other hand absent-mindedly scratched at his genitals. Beside him the bark canoe groaned and rolled over to reveal yet another plump, naked female. As she too disappeared in a confusion of breasts, buttocks and shingle, the old man held out both hands, shrugging his shoulders as if he was equally surprised by her appearance. One of the Pennacooks started to chuckle. The old man, sensing he had a potentially appreciative audience, scratched his head, feigning disbelief, then ran around peering beneath the remaining canoes. All gave free reign to the laughter, as if discovering, for the very first time, something that was more important than food or air itself. Tyrell, in particular, grasped at the release, roaring and shaking louder than all the others. And the more he roared, the more the old man peered at him, this time his face a picture of true astonishment.

"What is this? Where did you find this one? I have never seen the like before... It has long been my belief that our brothers the Pennacooks have kept the strangest company... but this creature before me is the strangest yet! And what is this peculiar shining lance he carries... I can see that it is very heavy. What stone is it made from? What use is it?"

Tyrell's laughter became drowned in the heightened pleasure taken by the gathering at his expense. Then, just as quickly, theirs too began to fade as the memory of their situation re-asserted itself. Replacing the arrows in his quiver, Tidesso embraced the old man and began to explain the full course of events that had led them to this place. However, fearing the headman would demand a demonstration of the gun, and the ensuing boom announcing their whereabouts to all, he referred to it simply as a lance. Sensing that he was being talked about, Tyrell wiped aside the tears of laughter and watched intensely. So preoccupied did he become with the body gestures of both men that he did not notice the newly swelled ranks behind him, until a girl's round, painted face peered up into his own.

"Hello!.. I er.. I bid you good day!" he croaked, taken aback. The girl shrieked, but quickly covered her mouth with a hand and with big, laughing, black eyes, peered at him through her fingers. Tyrell cleared his throat, not having spoken hardly a word since he last saw Dodds alive. He swallowed and tried again.

"My name is Mathew Tyrell... I come from way over the Ocean Sea ... Where the sun rises... A town called Bristol in England is my home."

His lip trembled as he spoke. Just to curl his tongue once again round his own name and mention his homeland once more made his heart shudder with a desperate sadness. What was he doing here, attempting to make himself understood by a savage who was staring at him as if he were some dimwit? He, a mariner and an Englishman, no less! Why was God being so cruel to him? The young woman giggled, then, forcing two fingers in his mouth, ran them along his teeth and tongue. Nearly gagging, Tyrell resisted the desire to clamp his jaw shut on the foul intrusion and quietly succumbed to the ordeal. He was not unaware of the close proximity of the girl's breasts brushing against his ragged shirt as she stretched to peer into his mouth. Irresistibly, he raised a hand to stroke one, but stopped short.

"Well?" demanded the headman. "What kind of tongue produces a sound like Moose rutting?"

Again there was much laughter, though the taste of the woman's fingers had abruptly curtailed Tyrell's good humour, and he hobbled down to the waterside, to drink and immerse his battered brain.

"It is always a pleasure to see our friends and protectors the Pennacooks... You will smoke pooke with us and eat some fish?"

The first canoe woman appeared, no longer naked, but attired in a deerskin kilt that bore the mottled pattern of innumerable grease stains. In one hand she carried a bundle from which protruded a pipe stem and in the other was another bundle. This second object she threw at the leader. Sighing with exasperation, he bent down and retrieved what proved to be an equally greasy breech-clout, and giving his genitals one final scratch, proceeded to put it on. Taking the pipe bundle, he then steered the assembly towards the shade of an oak tree, the boughs of which spread out over the shingle.

Motioning for all to be seated, he ordered the woman to transport part of a fire to the centre of the gathering. She returned, grumbling, with a mound of hot embers on a sheet of bark, and making a great show of demonstrating her efficiency, blew a cloud of burning ash towards the headman. Ignoring the ill-tempered display and the coating of ash, he licked his fingers, and taking up a glowing ember, dropped it in the bowl of the pipe and commenced sucking.

"So Tidesso, my young friend, a big party of Paquatuogs, Mahican, and now Squakheag snap at your heels? I never cared for those Squakheag, I always thought of them as being a treacherous people. The Destroyers, though? They are a long way from their own lands... How is this so?"

Tidesso took the pipe, inhaled deeply, then blew dual channels of smoke from both nostrils. The first smoke was strong. It made his head spin and his bowels rumble. He took another draw and relished the tingle in his fingertips.

"That, I do not understand. It is a long while since we have fought with them. And as for the Squakheag, well, who knows? We have been away for many, many sleeps, maybe too many sleeps. Maybe something has happened during this period. Anyway, as you say, they are a treacherous people. Not at all like you of the Winnecowet. You have been our friends since the first salmon swam up these waters. Together we have stood at the cascades with our fish spears touching."

"With the Squakheag and the Pawtucket, too. At the cascades all are friends for as long as the salmon leap."

"This is true... Tell me, Magcoos, where are the rest of your people? I heard that you had moved your town to the other side of the big Ammonoosuc. What brings you here? Is it to pray at the painted rock?"

"Yes, you are correct in both your assumptions, though in each there is more to answer than just a simple nod of the head. My people have moved, but what at first sight appeared to be a good place with sweet breezes, has proved to be a cradle of evil. Not a few of our people have gone under with sickness. All the spells and ministrations of the Pawaws seem helpless to prevent it, so we move once more. We few are here to hunt and paint the rock. It was in a dream I had, over and over the same dream. I stood outside my body and beheld myself laughing and I knew then that I must come and provide a new skin of paint for the image that Cautantowit, the great Manitou, gave to us. It will return health and prosperity to our people. So whilst we perform this task we are safe. Even the Paquatuogs will know that they cannot harm us."

"I hope this is so, for they too are a treacherous people, almost the equal of the Maquaks. The Maquaks would certainly have no compunction in slaying you and eating your hearts."

Magcoos, the headman, sat stone-faced, gently swaying in the welcome breeze. After a time had elapsed where he made no move to speak, Tidesso cleared his throat and continued.

"We must also go to the rock and wait there for four of our brothers. They will have a fifth with them, though he will be dragged against his will, for he will realize that the long death awaits him."

The eyes of Magcoos widened and he sat bolt upright.

"Tell me, my young friend. Who might this be to have earned your wrath?"

"He is a powerful Mateoulin of the Squakheag. I did not ask his name and it was not given, but I think he is the one they call Warriksos. Two nights ago, he and a young warrior came into our camp and took meat with us. It was a trick, for they nearly led the Destroyers into our midst whilst we slept. The young one has already paid for his treachery. The Mateoulin will sing loudly before he dies."

"If he is a powerful Mateoulin like you say, might he not change himself into a bird and escape, or change your brothers into rocks?"

It was the turn of Tidesso to be lost for words. Magcoos scratched his head and swiped at the halo of flies, then talked further. A slight hint of irritation had entered his tone.

"Would it not be a mistake to bring him here, for he too would claim immunity?"

Embarrassed by his apparent lack of forethought, and made to feel like an impetuous child by the headman's tone, Tidesso sought to change the subject. There would be no immunity for that one.

"Tell me, have you completed painting the rock?"

"Not quite. As you see, our young men, and our young women are freshly painted though! When they heard strangers coming, they must have daubed their bodies with the magic paint, so that had you proved to be enemies, they would have been immune to your arrows. Alas, now we must make more."

Tidesso stood up, and without excusing himself, walked to the edge of the water, and shielding his eyes, stared up at the smooth face of rock that rose above the trees. Then, with his forefinger, he traced in the air the same serpent outline that was etched there. From where he stood he could not make out the whole shape. Somehow it looked different, as if something had been added. However, the treetops obscured the lower section of the pictograph from view. He returned to a silent gathering. Magcoos, feigning unconcern at the display of bad manners, lifted a leg and broke wind as the young leader took his place.

"Straightaway after eating I must go and see the rock. Many seasons have turned since I last viewed it. I see Askooke the serpent still writhes on the rockface? As a child I had many black dreams about him rising from the depths to pull me from my father's canoe."

"Then it is good that you come now whilst he is faded, for when I have completed giving him a fresh skin, he will be more fierce than ever before... And it will inspire you to paddle your canoe faster than ever before."

A long silence reigned, finally broken by Tidesso.

"You talk of canoes, and I see you have five good, strong ones... and light too... The craft of the Winnecowet are much renowned, and quite rightly so! I would ask that you take us up the water as far as the cascades. We could go with one of your own men in each, they could bring them back here before nightfall, and we also would be within a day of our own town, otherwise it is two more sleeps. It would be a good thing for you to do this, Magcoos... The great Saquasis would show his gratitude to your people. I, Tidesso, would see to it."

The mood changed abruptly. Even Tyrell - though not understanding a word - felt the change, and edging towards the fire surreptitiously played with a smouldering twig. Again Magcoos broke wind.

"As you well know, we are the true friends of the Pennacooks... If you were to come to our town, all that is ours would be yours to take. Do we not give you ample gifts every ripening as a sign of our gratitude for your protection? Are we not joined by much blood? Look around you. Some of these young people have mothers or fathers of your blood, as I know some of you must bear Winnecowet blood... But we are a small people, and the Pennacooks are many... What would be our fate if the nest of hornets you have stirred descends on this spot, and they discover that we have helped you flee? You yourself said that these Paquatuogs are a fearsome, treacherous people... There would be no escape for us if you take our canoes."

Tidesso was smouldering with suppressed anger and frustration, both at the leader's audacity in not straightaway offering the use of the canoes, and in hearing his own words used back at him. Magcoos was correct in his analysis of the situation, but the Winnecowet owed allegiance to the Pennacooks. Or had they, like the Squakheag, been lately poisoned in their opinions? Tidesso was unsure, but he knew he was anxious to move on.

Suddenly, four older women edged from the makeshift lodges, each one bearing a bark platter heaped with steaming food. The wonderful, savoury aroma of broiled fish, maize and maple sugar, momentarily caused the evaporation of any ill feeling, and straightaway fingers were swooping down to scoop up the welcome repast. After the empty platters were tossed aside, lookouts were dispatched to both the painted rock and the main trails. To aid the digestion, another pipe was lit and passed.

"It will not be long before the Paquatuogs come, I feel it. Why do you not come with us?... We could all cross the river. The canoes take half of us, then return for the other half. The Paquatuogs, if they decide to come further, will most probably follow the trails on this side then cross at the cascades - by which time, we will have alerted our people. You could return to this place when they have gone and then fulfil your dream prophecy... Cautantowit would be more than satisfied, I know it... And so would the great Saquasis."

Tidesso was thankful that the food had arrived when it did. Finished now, his belly was by no means full, but yet the strength taken from the food had aided his powers of persuasion. The nimble wisdom of the fish had transferred itself into words that teemed readily on his tongue. Sensing the initial reluctance of Magcoos to be easing a little, Tidesso reached for his quiver, and after withdrawing the arrows, retrieved the skin-wrapped looking glass.

"Permit me, Magcoos, to show you some of the strongest magic you have yet seen. It will help to unburden your heart."

He unwrapped the bundle, but before passing the mirror over to Magcoos he stole a glance at himself. The red-ringed eyes that stared back at him gave him a start. It surprised him how much he had aged. A cleft had appeared in his brow and even under the layer of bear grease, his face appeared drawn. This time he had not laughed. Was the Looks-Back losing its power? Or did it have the power to both bestow strength, then, on some mystical whim, steal it away.

With growing trepidation, he passed the looking glass to Magcoos, holding his breath as he waited for the reaction. At first Magcoos looked sick, like a man seeing the ghost of his dead mother-in-law returned to haunt him, then he exploded with a whoop of delight. In a flurry of disgust, once again the same blue heron flapped clumsily from its rock. The young Winnecowet men crowded round and chorused Magcoos's reaction, and from the lodges rushed the women and young girls, intent on sharing the wonderment.

"Hi-Yi!...Hi-Yi! This is it! This is my dream!"

He screamed at Tidesso and snatched it away from his woman's grasping fingers. Refusing to be put aside so easily, she kicked at his shins and demanded to be shown the magic.

"Woman! This is my magic! This young Pennacook leader has come specially to give it to me! It is as prophesied in my dream. All of you know this to be true. You women can clear off lest you take away the power. This is not for your eyes. If you want to admire yourselves, go down and look at the water."

The womenfolk set up such a wail of protest that straightaway Magcoos relented and the looking-glass was passed around, whilst he fretted and hovered, demanding that they be careful. Finally, it returned to his anxious custody and there, before the dazzling surface, he preened and beamed.

"But where did you get such a magical thing?"

"From this very curly one who walks amongst us." Tidesso indicated Tyrell, who was occupied, staring open-mouthed at the young women. Magcoos shook his head in disbelief.

"For this gift you shall be taken up the water... Yes, all the way to the cascades you shall go. But I warn you, last night I dreamed I heard the thunderbird flap her wings in the distance, the cascades could soon become very troublesome."

CHAPTER 19
Upriver

Tidesso was both angry and relieved: angry that Magcoos had assumed the Looks-Back was a gift, destined for his bony paws, but relieved that at last the canoes would be made available. He still had the curly one and his thunder lance to show off, and at last they could put water between themselves and the Paquatuogs. Once past the cascades, nothing could stop them reaching home. He wanted to be gone from this exposed place, but knew that they were bound to wait a little longer for Wadawagwa and the others.

After the pipe had passed round one more time, and the nausea born of watching Magcoos slavering over the cherished Looks-Back grew intolerable, Tidesso made it plain that he would visit the painted rock without further delay. He had decided to go to the rock, make a small offering, and, even if there were no sign of the others, embark up the river. The Winnecowet would relay his plan to them should they show up later.

After issuing instructions for the canoes to be made ready, Tidesso and two fellow tribesmen, Mateguas and Pulowech, started the steep climb to the rock. The twisting trail was well worn and as they approached the rock face, many of the bushes and branches bore the recent and tattered older remnants of offerings - feathers, beads, shells and withered bunches of pooke dancing and tinkling in the breeze. In his hand Tidesso had a strip of prized wampum as his token. Managnon and the others would recognise it, know that he had waited here, and understand the words of the Winnecowet to be true.

He felt nervous as the rock came into view, remembering all those dark dreams of long ago. It rose naked and unforgiving above the trees, a great smooth face of micah-sparkling granite. At the base, level with the spruce tops, was a narrow ledge where the lookout that he had earlier dispatched was dozing in the sun. After brusquely questioning him, he sent the young warrior back to the beach, and in silence stared at the painting.

The like of this painted Askooke he had never seen in the flesh, though the people's grandfathers said that they still inhabited the deeper lakes and were known to rise and take swimmers and lone canoeists. Suddenly he felt a bubbling of anger and outrage. The painting was different. It had been altered. Who had dared to desecrate the sacred picture? Beneath the writhing serpent's body had been added another painting of inferior quality. It was a series of human figures in obvious disarray, one being represented as having just fallen from the jaws of the great Askooke, droplets of vermillion blood all around it; and most sacrilegious of all, a lance pierced the serpent's side. Who had done this? No Pennacook would dare. Was it the Winnecowet? Had this also been in Magcoos's dream? Without daring to touch the pigment, he moved close. Although still bright, it was not fresh, but neither was it too old. Who had done it? He tried again to make out the full scene by moving back on the narrow ledge as far as he dared. The full glare of the sun did not help. He realised that only by growing wings, or from a canoe mid-stream, would the full picture be revealed.

"I think that it is a broken canoe with many men falling from it," whispered Mateguas.

Tidesso nodded, and kneeling over the ledge, with fumbling fingers tied the piece of black and white wampum to the uppermost branches of a tree. He was becoming greatly disturbed, feeling the need to be gone from this place growing stronger than ever.

The sudden boom of the thunder-lance resounding off the sacred rock caused his already taut muscles to jolt, nearly sending him toppling into the trees. What was happening? Had the Paquatuogs already come? He could hear screams from the beach... Was it the sound of fighting?

"Have the Destroyers come?" he hissed, and looking feverishly all around, began instinctively to withdraw an arrow from his quiver, then letting it slide back, slapped his chest and growled in frustration. What had possessed him to leave his bow behind? His companions had theirs, but all he had were the arrows, nothing to shoot them with. Such stupidity! He did not deserve to be a leader of a warband. Sensing the frustration of Tidesso, Pulowech handed him the long, sharp knife of the dead captive. A little relieved, Tidesso nodded thanks and respectfully took it. He straightaway resigned himself to fate, but had no desire to face it empty handed. Swiftly running a finger down the flat of the rusting blade, he felt the power in the touch of the hard, cold substance, the same unknown texture as the hollow lance; and with a snarl, down the trail he bounded.

The heron was blown from the rock. Only its stick-legs protruded from the water surface to twitch like rushes in the shallows. Tyrell saw the wide eyes and open mouths through the gun smoke. He also heard the screams and wails of the Winnecowet, but the gun's report had temporarily deafened him, causing him to view the scene with an air of detachment. He wanted to laugh at their cowering ignorance, and even though he squeezed up his face, he could not stop a snigger from escaping. Only the sight of the old man's bloody fingers snatched him from the daze. Shaking his head, he looked up to see one of the Pennacooks remonstrating with him, the others were occupied in trying to calm the Winnecowets down. At first he thought that somehow the old headman had also been struck by the ball, but when he saw the light catch the glittering slivers, he realized that the looking-glass had been smashed. Ignorant of the consequences, the old headman had attempted to pick up the glass and fit the pieces of the puzzle together - his expression one of bemused dread as the blood filled his palms and raced down his arms.

"Don't try to lay the blame on my head, Muminquash, whatever your name is!"

Tyrell pointed to the Pennacook who had shouted at him.

"You wanted me to fire it off! Why, you even gave to me the firebrand... nearly jabbed it in my eye too! Thank you very much! No, it weren't my idea... So stop tryin' to make out that it was."

Muminquash, the one in question, looked startled that he was being shouted at by Tyrell, then he looked embarrassed. Some of his fellow tribesmen sniggered and jeered at his discomfort, then embarrassment turned to anger, and the warrior snarled back.

Catching his breath, Tyrell blew down the barrel to clear the touch hole and commenced reloading the piece. He knew that none present could understand a single word of his tirade, but he was enjoying the sound of his own voice. It had certainly stopped the communal wail. All the Winnecowets sat open-mouthed, staring at him.

"Well, Master Headman, Master... Mad... cuss, Magcoosso you've got bloody fingers, 'ave you?"

This time, with the ramrod in his hands like a schoolmaster's cane, Tyrell waved it accusingly at the quaking headman.

262

"Serves you right for sticking 'em everywhere."

Suddenly he turned.

"What's that?"

A dog barked, and in a flurry the pack appeared scampering between the legs of the gathering, to snarl and snap at the edge of the woods. Tyrell pointed to the trees, crouched low and fumbled in a pouch for one of the handful of remaining leaden balls. He had been the first to see the movement, but he was last to realize that it came from approaching friend not foe. Leaping into the open came Tidesso and his two companions. The dogs were called off. All lowered their weapons, a communal sigh of relief escaped; though the tension in the atmosphere remained like a dark thunder cloud that had not yet passed. Tidesso saw the slivers of shattered glass and ground his teeth with fury.

"Why did the curly one make the thunder-lance talk? It has now told everything that breathes where we are."

Without waiting for a reply, Tidesso strode up to Tyrell, and as if he were but a troublesome child, wrenched the matchlock from his hands. Tyrell protested and pointed at the old Winnecowet and the Pennacook who had bade him shoot. But it was to no avail; a sharp rap on the shins with the gunstock silenced him. Mumbling insults, whilst rubbing at his leg, he spied the same young girl who had earlier pushed her fingers into his mouth, retrieving the torn remains of the heron from the shallows. She was both crying and kicking at the dogs. Tidesso jabbed towards him with Dodds' rusty knife. Lurching backwards with a nervous laugh, Tyrell saw in Tidesso that same savage he had first encountered by the sand-dunes and felt the fear rise in his throat. Was he to be killed over the death of a bird? What about the bond that had grown between them? Why, only yesterday Tidesso had shed tears for Dodds. Tyrell wanted to protest, if only to hear the words himself, but he remained silent and helpless. Tidesso turned and moved towards the main gathering, leaving a kneeling Tyrell to mumble a mixture of prayers and curses, like a condemned felon at the foot of a gibbet.

He paid little attention to the moans and gesticulations of the group, but was glad of the moment's respite and the brief time it allowed for him to prepare for the worst. The last time they had spoken, poor Dodds had talked of the feeling that his death was near and he had been proved correct. Now Tyrell had the same feeling.

They were pointing at him and shouting. The old leader took up the bloody heron, and prancing forward from the group, tossed the dead bird at Tyrell's knees. Tyrell saw that he retreated faster than he had advanced. The gun's power had obviously impressed him, but there was so little powder and shot left that soon it would impress no one. Maybe a dozen shots at the most. It would have to rely totally on the tall tales of these savages to impart the roar of power long-past into its empty muzzle.

Tyrell started to sing then, remembering how he and Dodds had beguiled them into lowering their clubs once before. But without the magic of his friend's rich harmony, his own voice felt shrill and exposed. Tidesso turned around glaring and the song stopped dead in his throat. Tyrell looked down to see the eye of the heron boring into his own. Flies hummed and crawled over the carcass and around his own head. He swiped them away, but back they came, increased in numbers. Shielding his eyes, he saw between his fingers that some of the savages had started towards him. His shoulders tensed as the many moccasined feet shuffled into view, and he braced himself for what he thought would be the inevitable blow.

Recognising the quill design of the moccasins and the shins directly in front of him as those of Tidesso, he could not stop himself from looking up as if wanting to bid his executioner farewell. He had seen this enacted before, in the last moments of many condemned men, an almost polite bond between themselves and their dispatchers, like a hurried, final business arrangement. He wondered if it were the same amongst savages.

"Let's do it then," he croaked. "Come on then, get it over with."

The shiny, copper faces above him revealed nothing. The sun's dazzle was of no assistance, causing him to squint and lower his wretched head once more. A hard, heavy weight was laid across his shoulder, and all the feet shuffled past. The heat of metal burned against his ear. Though his eyes opened, the confirmation was superfluous. He had known from the first that the heavy weight was the matchlock. It had been returned to him. They did not intend to kill him after all.

The delicious feeling of relief rushed through his body and up he sprang with a single chuckle. The girl rushed forward to snatch up the dead heron, and still sobbing, raced back to her own people - a white dog snapping at her heels. The hollow scrape of the canoes as they were turned and lifted into the water, filled him with even greater joy. At last, they would be leaving this camp of primitives and taking to water. He marvelled at how light, how graceful the craft appeared and wondered how such flimsy looking things could be expected to carry the fourteen Pennacooks, four Winnecowets and himself. He shouldered the matchlock and marched purposefully down to the water's edge. No one acknowledged him. Those not concerned with holding the craft steady were carefully laying their belongings inside, whilst Tidesso was examining each tribesman's stature, deciding who would take up what position. Still no one had acknowledged him. A new anxiety began to toy with Tyrell's mind. They did intend to take him too, didn't they? Surely they would not leave him on this shore?

One of the craft was more substantial than the other four. Equally fashioned from the bark of the white birch, ribbed and framed with cedar, it was broader and nearly twice the length and required two pairs of hands to hold it steady. Without looking at his face, Tidesso tapped Tyrell's shoulder and indicated that he take up position in the middle of this canoe. Treading gingerly on the cedar ribs, he took his position, kneeling like the other occupants. He was instructed to lay the gun lengthways down the centre of the canoe, each man to kneel astride it. A hardwood paddle was placed in his hands. He delighted in the smooth finish of the blade, the perfect balance of it, and could hardly wait to feel it slice the water. The canoes themselves were the most wonderful examples of balance and buoyancy, riding each eddy like frisky horses waiting to race. Had this group of naked beggars, whose huddle of rude, upturned nests lined the bank, really constructed such things of beauty? He could not believe it possible.

Tyrell noticed that the Winnecowets had moved nearer. They appeared sullen and somewhat resentful, like bewildered losers in a game of dice, silently waiting for some higher power to intercede on their behalf, relieving them at the last moment of their losers' obligations.

There were no fond farewells. Tidesso simply grunted something, raised his arm in half-hearted salute, leaped into the stern of the large boat and off they went upstream. Turning back once, Tyrell saw a group of the young men pacing them along the bank. He nodded in a brief farewell, then, facing forward, put them out of his mind.

It was not so easy finding the rhythm of the bark craft as he had first imagined. When fully laden, the water's surface skimmed by perilously close, and as he shifted to gain a semblance of comfort, the canoe lurched sidewards in response, earning a grunt and paddle-splash from the warrior in front. But by mimicking the actions of that man forward, he started to get the measure of it; and though his muscles soon began to ache fit to tear, he began to experience a light-headed feeling not far removed from pleasure. He sensed that he was not alone in experiencing this pleasure. No words or facial expressions from the others were needed. As for the Winnecowet in the prow, he could not be sure, but he somehow got the impression that they were less than enchanted about their undertaking.

Tyrell felt a great desire to accompany the metre of the paddle strokes with a song, but regretfully he resisted the urge – even though they were midstream and well out of bowshot. But sing is what he would surely do if he were in a skiff laden down with Poor-Jack and rowing back to a ship. That is what he and his dead shipmates - God rest them all - would be doing at the top of their voices. He thought it strange that even the image of Dodds did not puncture his mood. He did not even feel guilt over the fact that he was not required to dwell on it, but instead took pleasure in stabbing the surface with the paddle, tugging the river towards him.

And then, inexplicably, after what seemed an age of time and distance, they stopped paddling, or rather the others stopped and a firm grip from behind arrested the return motion of his arm. With slow, deep strokes the big canoe was held steady in the current, hanging there like a sun-basking trout. The lead craft had turned a bend in the river, but after a bird-like shriek from Tidesso, the other three stopped and the lead canoe drifted back into view. Tyrell knew better than to ask what was afoot, but simply contributed in holding the canoe steady and scanning the left bank along with the others.

The heavily-wooded bank revealed nothing. From aft, the same, piercing call issued again. Tyrell turned to see the leader kneeling, flexing an arrow on his bow, and the feeling of contentment vanished. Again he experienced complete helplessness and ignorance as to what was happening. The gun was loaded, but even though it was at his knees, it would have required the disembarkation of all the canoe's occupants before becoming retrievable and, even then, the match would need to be lit. Withdrawing the paddle, he held the wide blade in line with his exposed body as a form of meagre shield and slunk low in dread as the canoe moved inexorably towards the bank. What were they doing? They were like sitting ducks. A volley of arrows could come from the foliage without them ever glimpsing an assailant. They were not this stupid, surely?

This time four descending notes of a Yellowleg's whistle rang out clearly from somewhere amidst the trees. Tyrell thought he caught a glimpse of glistening, copper skin, but his attention was quickly drawn to the snags and half-submerged branches that waited like harpoons to pierce the thin, bark tegument. He heard Tidesso talking softly and looked up, thinking it was he that was being addressed, but saw that the leader's words were spoken to the inaccessible bank. He also noticed him pointing upriver. A short, husky reply came out to them. Tyrell glanced again at Tidesso, whose face swiftly changed from relief to anger. Sheathing the arrow and once again taking up his paddle, he spat out a single command and the canoe shot forward into mid channel with such force that Tyrell was nearly displaced.

Striking deep with the paddle, Tyrell gladly assisted the withdrawal from the bank, but even midstream all pretence of pleasure had been dispelled. The single thought that now occupied him was his helpless exposure to the bank. Eyes squinting against the spray, he stabbed and wrenched harder, again following the example of the man in front, thankful that it afforded him no opportunity to watch the banks. They had become towering, spruce-topped bulwarks of shadowy granite that pressed closer, and the river in consequence began to foam in turbulent protest. For how long he tore into the water he had no way of knowing, becoming naught but a beast of burden in the mind-numbing repetition of stroke after stroke, until, that is, his paddle struck against a submerged rock, jarring his brain into a semblance of awareness. The Winnecowet in the prow was gesticulating at Tidesso and again the canoe was allowed to slip backwards. Suddenly, in a deft turn, Tyrell was presented with a painted face staring impassively into his own, as with a single bodily swivel the man forward became the man aft. The warrior's laboured breath blasted directly into Tyrell's mouth. He made as if to attempt the same manoeuvre, but the looming face shook 'no', instructing him to remain still. Again they were heading towards the left bank. The four smaller canoes were following. He could see them quite clearly as he rode backwards to the bank. What had made them turn? He had seen for himself that the river was becoming more rocky, but it was not impassable, or maybe it was further on? Did the incessant rumble indicate falls, or was it the quake of fear roaring in his head? With a jarring scrape, the canoe was masterfully guided onto the top of a large, flat rock that lay just beneath the surface. Straightaway all leapt from the craft and assisted in dragging it onto the small, shingle beach, situated at the foot of the high, rocky banks. Brushing past Tyrell - who was busy extricating the gun - Tidesso waded back onto the flat rock and with silent gesticulations steered, one by one, all four smaller canoes into safety. The beach was barely large enough to accommodate all the party and canoes. The apex of rock face that rose from it was sheer above the height of two men and devoid of any apparent hand holds. It soon became plain to Tyrell that they did not intend to stay long. He watched in amazement as the large canoe was placed vertically against the most accessible face, and whilst two pairs of hands held the base, it was used as a ladder to reach the grassy summit. Tyrell matched their agility in climbing - the hours spent clambering to the tops of masts had given him a good head for heights - even motioning for the matchlock to be handed to him as he fearlessly leaned way out. It was offered up reverentially; he, in turn, passing it to those who had preceded him. Feeling confidence returning, he instructed them to hold on to his heels as the smaller crafts were raised one by one. After the last man was up, and Tyrell was hoisted back onto his dizzy feet, the hands that gripped him were firm with renewed camaraderie and he beamed as the blood ran from his head. Glancing up, Tyrell caught the wisp of a smile in the eyes of Tidesso. Their fingers touched briefly as the leader handed him the gun and powder flask. He wanted to withdraw the charge and reload - in all probability some water had entered through the touch hole or muzzle - but no sooner had he gathered his wits than they were off once more. Again, he marvelled at the versatility of the bark craft, so light yet so durable. The larger one was carried like a turtle shell on the backs of three men, but the smaller canoes were managed by a single man apiece. He had seen the men of Wales portering their own little, round coracles in a like manner, but they were naught but toys compared to the craft of these savages. Granted, toys from which they speared salmon and hung nets across rivers. Still, he thought, the Welsh were little more than savages themselves. Their dark, sing-song speech was more a mystery than the tongue of these Pennacooks. At least he was starting to recognise the meaning of some of the sounds. Tyrell shuddered then, as he remembered the ragged breeches that still clung to his loins had belonged to the Welshman Pugh. The dead man's blood still decorated the hole in the right thigh where the arrow of one of his new comrades had entered. The ambush at the beach had receded in his memory, so much so that he could no longer remember the men's faces, could only recall the bloody dismemberment. Even the horror of that event had all but evaporated.

Along a faint, rocky trail they passed, with the river swirling below. From the higher vantage point, Tyrell could now see that what he had assumed to be the opposite bank was, in actual fact, a long, ridge-backed island bristling with trees and sharp rocks. Although only about sixty paces away, the gap between was a fast-flowing channel of white water. Beyond was the main body of the river, running more slowly but studded with half-submerged rocks. Somewhere, hidden amidst the distant trees, lay the far bank. What was happening? Why had they stopped on this side? Why hadn't they crossed the river to comparative safety?

He did not grumble when, on a gentle, grassy slope with good access to the water, they made camp. The night shadows were still a good way off, but Tyrell guessed there were reasons for stopping, other than weariness. He had just finished reloading the gun and rubbing grease onto the barrel, when the same four note call as before turned every head towards the trees. Tidesso stood up and echoed the short sequence of descending notes. A murky, four-legged creature moved between the trunks. It was evident, in its shambolic gait and the limp in one of its legs, that it was wounded and near exhaustion. As the strange beast staggered from the trees, Tyrell saw that in reality it was not a single creature at all, but two human beings entwined in a pained mutual assistance. Tyrell found himself rushing up the slope with the others. As he got closer, he recognised Managnon as the owner of the limp. He knew the other by sight alone - paying more attention to the finger-bone necklace the savage wore than his drawn face. Both were streaked in blood and dirt. Managnon had tied around his shoulders the scalp-strewn cape of the old man who had visited their campsite the night that Dodds was slain. What did it mean? he wondered, and tried to trace the obvious connection, but to no avail. His frustration was ameliorated by the realization that his usual tormentor was not with them. But where was that nasty, leering bastard with the big lugs? Tyrell found himself gladdened that he had not returned and hoped in his heart that the tormentor had met his end. He stepped forwards to scour the woods for sign of Wadawagwa, but when he saw that the others were returning to the campsite, he took it as a sign that the evil-tempered savage was not expected to return.

Even though he had a gun primed and loaded in his hands, the twisted punk in the serpent was still not alight. He felt exposed and withdrew swiftly to be amongst the others. Without flint and steel the cursed thing was a liability, always dependent on a taper from a savage's fire. He could not even make fire himself any longer. The patient friction of wood against wood eluded him, giving him naught but blisters for his effort.

When he joined the company, Tyrell took his place cross-legged amidst the group, and though all but a smattering of Managnon's words washed over him like the babble of the river, he began intently watching every gesture, hoping desperately for the essence of the story to be revealed. From time to time, his eyes would be irresistibly drawn from the speaker to stare into the woods. The half-glimpsed movement of a branch, the flutter of a bird, all served to tune his nerves to breaking point. His eyes too began to ache in the constant shifting of focus. Somewhere out there, if he understood it right enough, somewhere in that vast expanse of forest, maybe just beyond the ridge, an ever growing horde of enemy savages was closing in.

"As you can see by this mantle that sits on my shoulders, and likewise with the finger-bones of men that adorns the throat of Anadabijou here... we had the Mateoulin in our grasp. He did not lie. He could travel fast for an old one, but even so we overtook him within sight of his people's maize fields. He slew Sadanis with his lance... I will speak his name only once more, to say that Sadanis was brave, he was the first to rush in, even though he was warned against it. In sorrow I have to say that we were forced to leave his body behind as some Squakheag boys had seen us and gave the alarm. We had the old wolf in our grasp and we dragged him away with us, even though the land was swarming with mixed bands of enemies and their new allies."

He stopped and looked around.

"I see that we have a handful of the Winnecowet with us, and some of their fine canoes. It's good that not all of our friends are tempted by such treachery."

He nodded towards each Winnecowet, accepted a swallow of water and took long, laboured breaths. None interrupted the account. Tyrell glanced at Tidesso, whose face gave not a hint of the impatience his restless fingers betrayed. Each man was given his say without fear of interruption. If this was a group of Bristol seamen, he mused, all would be shooting off a battery of questions, not letting up until each was hoarse with the effort and in all probability none the wiser.

Having composed himself once more, Managnon continued.

"We managed to avoid these enemies, but it was only a matter of time before they overtook us. So, we found a good place and made the Mateoulin sing of his treachery. He threatened to turn us into lizards, and himself into an eagle that would swoop down from high and eat us up. In answer to this, the one who was once a Maquak - for neither will I soil my tongue with his name - broke both the Pawaw's arms, so that if he did become an eagle his wings would be of no use. He was not like a brave old warrior then, but shed tears like a child and pleaded for his life. The Once-Was-a-Maquak said that he would eat no coward's heart and offered him his life if he sang of his treachery. It is as we thought - the Destroyers have been talking to all the ones we protect and consider allies. They have grown jealous of our strength and feed lies to our friends of how we will offer them up as sacrifice to the five tribes from the west and the Pasmaquoddy from the north! Hi-Yi! As if we would even think of such a thing! The Mateoulin said that if his warriors were to help them against us, then when we are vanquished, the Paquatuogs will ask no tribute for their protection, but all would be equal, a confederacy."

Even though an interruption was considered bad manners, Tidesso could contain himself no longer.

"You do not mention Wadawagwa by name? Do we understand that he is also slain?"

"No! He is not slain! For that matter neither is the Mateoulin, though he most probably wishes that it were so, for he can no longer scratch when he itches, see or hear if friend or foe approaches, call for help, or whisper curses. And when he must piss, it will be crouched down as a woman."

The group rattled their arrows, signifying much pleasure in the revenge taken.

"As to the one who was once a Maquak - well, he deserted us whilst we slept."

An angry communal growl erupted.

"He has either gone over to the Paquatuogs or back to the ones who gave him life. Him, I hate above all others! I shall kill him if ever it is my misfortune to see his ugly face again."

Managnon sat down then, and closing his eyes, began to massage his twisted ankle. Tidesso shuffled to his side.

"I must ask you some questions. It is good to see you again. You have done well. It is true that I would have liked to question the Mateoulin, but I understand he will have a long time to dwell on the foolishness of his treachery. You had no choice in what you did. Our brother who went under knew the risks. It is sad, though, that he has no children to mourn him. Tell me brother, how near are the enemies? Do they mean to follow us even unto the palisades of our town?"

"They know that they must try to stop us before we warn the people. But even if they fail, there are many aligned against us. As many as the ears of corn in a harvest, but they come in different bands. There is a meeting place where they will all gather before they attempt to destroy the people."

"Where is this meeting place?"

"It was to be the painted rock where we were to gather. The very same rock!"

Managnon laughed at the irony, then, despite his efforts, winced at the effort it cost.

"It is indeed fortunate that you did not wait too long for us."

"Yes, and it's very fortunate that you were watching the river."

"We made straight towards it, then walked downstream towards the rock. But when the thunder-lance spoke, we were confused, not knowing whether or not you were fighting. But at least we knew you had made it that far."

"It was the curly one. He slew Kasko, the spirit bird, with it. I nearly took his own life in return."

"It is this thunder-lance that both draws our enemies on, but yet holds them back – word has spread wide of fearful destruction. Sometimes I think it would be best to have cast it in the lake with the other... Before we cut out his tongue, the Squakheag Pawaw begged me to tell him about it. I said he was better off in ignorance."

Tidesso sniffed the air, scanned the woods and the sky. Maybe the thunderbird dream of Magcoos would come to pass and the river would turn very angry. The cleft in his brow betrayed his troubled mind. He then turned and looked at the island. Managnon interrupted his thoughts.

"I know what you are thinking. Whether there is enough light left for us to make it to the island? I feel there is, but we will have to go now, strike up and across to make the only landing place that I can see."

Tidesso nodded, allowing the merest hint of a smile to grace his features.

"We will collect sufficient stout saplings to aid us. It is too late to cross the river to the far bank, but I think if we start now, we'll make the island."

"Yes, my friend, I think that would be the wise thing to do. Remember, they have tried to take us in the night once before. At least on the far side of the island we can build a small fire and smoke some of the Mateoulin's pooke and then at first light cross over."

Tidesso's face lit up at the mention of the superior smoking mixture and slapping his thighs with delight, he sprang to his feet and began to give instructions for the crossing.

All were relieved to be relinquishing the present location. It was not an easy place to defend should it come to it and all had the dread feeling that the breath of the enemy was but a whisper away.

The saplings were gathered and taken up, two men fore and aft in each canoe to stand and pole them across. Each man regained his previous position, although Tyrell was sent to one of the smaller canoes whilst Managnon was assigned his previous place in the larger craft.

Tyrell experienced apprehension this time. Although much relieved to be leaving the bank, the smaller canoe's lurching in the frothy torrent left him feeling exposed, expecting that any moment one of the polesmen would fail to find a purchase, or the green wood would snap and over they would spill. He held the paddle poised like a dagger above the surface, ready - however ineffectual it might be - to stab like a mad man. The sight of the muscle-wrenching strain that the lead polesman was undergoing and the grunts from behind added to his helplessness. He was conscious then of the wooded, rocky banks looming nearer, aware also that the lead canoe had made it safely to the small beach. Ahead the flash of glistening figures clambering up the rocks filled him with faith. The tense strain in his own muscles vanished sufficiently to allow him a backward glance. The big canoe was approaching mid-channel, where the slick, white current was swiftest. His thoughts briefly dwelt on the cargo that had taken precedence over himself - the gun had maintained its position of prime importance. He was secondary.

There was a buffeting against rocks that, for a moment, jolted the tension back in his body, but the scrape of the canoe's nose over pebbles and the frantic gesticulations of the lead polesman sent him readily scrambling over the side to tug thigh-deep at the cedar thwart. The action was more of a temporary anchoring, until the first tribesman joined him, and then together with the man in the stern still poling, the canoe was slid out of the water.

It was as they were caught in the action of tugging it over the pebbles and into the muddy trough behind, that Tyrell saw what, at first glance, filled him with anguish. It appeared that the flesh-tearing beak of a huge raptor had reared up from the waters to gobble up the crew of the big canoe. Shaking the water from his eyes and being faced with the reality did not lessen the horror. The snapping monster's beak was in actuality the curved prows of the big canoe. Somehow its back had been broken, and from the now vertical jaws spilled the occupants.

He found himself foolishly rushing over the pebbles and out waist deep into the water. However, but for a smoothed rock against which he was buffeted, he too would have been swept away. One of the polesmen roughly pulled him back and knocking him aside, clambered onto the half-submerged boulder, and long sapling in hand, vaulted to a distant rock and from there to another. Tyrell could see that he was trying to get himself level with the canoe in order to assist the floundering tribesmen. He grabbed the other pole and without thinking of the consequences should he slip, followed the first man in vaulting from rock to rock. The roughness of the sapling tore at his hands, but the urgency in his movement relegated the pain to the back of his mind. Somewhere near the forefront, however, was the sickening realisation that the gun had also gone to the bottom.

The one who had preceded him had moved further on. The prints of his wet moccasin still marked the top of the rock. Tyrell could see that he was busy hauling one tribesman from the water and another lay safely sprawled behind him - the man's rib-cage heaving up and down in tortuous gasps. No sooner had Tyrell held the pole out than a hand reached out and grabbed it. The jolt was so sudden that it nearly toppled him from his perch. He fell back onto his buttocks and from that position was able to tug the tribesman up beside him. It was one of the Winnecowets. The young warrior made no thanks, instead glowered at Tyrell as if he would like nothing better than to topple him into the water. Despite the scowl, together they hauled another man up. Tyrell was relieved to see it was Mateguas, who despite his exhaustion, came up onto the rock grinning and grunting with gratitude.

The two remaining canoes had also managed to pick up some of the spilled tribesmen. The foremost, now bearing five in all, had nearly reached the island, but for some reason the other was turning back. And then Tyrell realised why. In the fury of events his eyes had become accustomed to the creeping gloom, paying it no heed as his body reacted to the dramatic circumstances. But now, as he rubbed his eyes and watched the retreating canoe merge with the shadows, he knew that nightfall was about to win the race.

In the all-pervading gloom Tyrell and the two rescued tribesmen began picking their way back up stream to the landing place. Behind them they could hear others working their way along the rocks that lay at the foot of the bank. They halted to catch their breath and to guide a straggler to their side. Even though still shrouded in darkness, some sixth-sense told him the looming figure was Tidesso. Tyrell could hardly contain his joy, smiling and holding out his hand to the bedraggled leader. Though Tidesso did not smile back, Tyrell discerned in the other's hand-clasp a feeling of gratitude. He also sensed the man was hurt, but knew better than to draw attention to the fact.

They made it to the shingle bank where two canoes were now beached - the first one across having been already portered up the slope. A handful of dripping tribesmen were waiting by the canoes; others had gone ahead to see the lie of the land. One of these came back to the head of the slope and hissed down instructions. Tyrell was dumbfounded to see that they intended taking up the two canoes, but he made no protest, just silently scrambling along behind, weighed down with various waterlogged quivers and pouches - the wet fur like a litter of drowned kittens prickling against his skin.

At the top of the slope, much to Tyrell's relief, the canoes were laid side by side and most of the baggage taken from him. They left the canoes where they lay and in single file followed the guide up through a wooded slope. Over the ridge they clambered and then down onto the far side of the island. As they made their way towards a faint glow of firelight, they were joined by two other stragglers - the squelch of their moccasins announcing their sorry presence. Tyrell became aware that his teeth were chattering. The fireglow, however, had caused the pace to quicken. The rush to bask in its warmth became the prime consideration above all else.

As they approached and each converging face reflected the orange glow, Tyrell was gladdened to see that it was a substantial blaze, one that crackled. A blaze where a man could hold out his hand and be forced to withdraw it lest his fingers be singed; not one of their usual parsimonious kindlings that a soul had to virtually sit on top of before it satisfied. Of course, he understood their usual caution, but now to feel the bright blast on his forehead as he took his place in the solemn gathering filled his breast with more than a little cheer.

Clutching his bruised side, Tidesso paced the ring, counting and examining the faces. Hardly a word was spoken. Each tribesman was physically sound enough to assume responsibility for their own affairs, and though it was obvious that many bore hurts, each seemed more concerned about the bruised limbs of their weapons than their own bodies. Tyrell guessed then that the fire had been made large to afford ample light to examine the trueness of the arrow-shafts, and warm enough to dry and alter the cast should it be required. He shivered and thought about the lost gun. The nausea returned. His fate had been inexorably bound with that implement of the devil and now he was released from it; but he felt anything but relief. He thought of it lying buckled and broken somewhere on the river bed. Had the loss of it sealed his own fate? The looking-glass was gone also. What use was he to them now? He felt too weary to care.

By the awkward way he moved and the laboured manner with which he breathed, Tyrell guessed that Tidesso had either cracked or badly bruised his ribs. When he finally chose to speak, it was barely above a whisper - vying unsuccessfully with the crackle of the flames. Tyrell was reminded of Managnon, who barely more than an hour ago had addressed the group, and despite his best endeavours to play down his hurt, had also winced at the effort. The face of Managnon was not amongst this solemn group. Tyrell had already checked. Maybe he had been amongst those who had been forced by the darkness to return to the other side? Or maybe he too lay buckled and broken on the river bed.

Tyrell was suddenly shaken from his weary musings by the loud interruption of one of the Winnecowets who, having taken up a smouldering brand from the fire, limped towards him, and with a sneer proceeded to jab at his face with it. It was the same savage he had earlier pulled from the water. In outrage, all weariness brushed aside, Tyrell reacted by knocking the stick away with the back of his hand, sending a shower of sparks back in the face of the Winnecowet. Tidesso hissed a command. One of the Pennacooks stepped forward, and with a sneer of disgust the Winnecowet cast the brand in a high whirling arc and returned to his place amongst his own tribesmen. Shaking with anger and pain, Tyrell licked the back of his hand and cursed aloud.

"Goddamn! God's hooks, flamin' Savage...Goddamn!"

He saw an amused Tidesso step towards him, then felt a small pang of rejection as the leader, seeming to change his mind mid-stride, turned instead to converse with the four Winnecowets. The angry one who had jabbed the brand looked with disgust at Tyrell and stabbed the air with his forefinger. Tyrell knew that they were somehow laying the blame for the catalogue of misfortune at his feet. He knew also that there was a rage growing within his own breast - there would be no more cowering. Stepping nearer the fire, he turned his back to the heat, and lowering his ragged breeches, made a great show of warming his arse. Behind himself he could hear the Winnecowet rail and fume at the insult, and guessed that at any moment even the smooth words of Tidesso would be unable to hold him back. In his hand Tyrell clasped the shot pouch and braced himself to lash out.

"Am I to swallow this insult? If my bow were not lost, I would shoot an arrow through the flames into his crack."

"Look away. He does not know what he does... He is like a child. He means no insult."

Tidesso suspected otherwise, but he was determined to hold on to the captive at all costs. To return without the thunder-lance was failure enough. At least this captive with the curly hair would help redress the balance. But was his appearance sufficiently strange that it could turn the people's faces away from the sorrow for those who would not be with them? Besides, he could not help the thought grow, that when the sun rose, the curly one would have some magic way of being reunited with the thunder-lance.

"Why do you protect him so, when you know that his slaying of the long-legged spirit-bird has caused all this misfortune for your people and for mine? You were going to finish him yourself at the painted rock, but you did not. Well I, Mikshish, as the one who made the big canoe that broke in two, demand the right!"

There was some truth in the words of the Winnecowet, Tidesso could not deny it. The ache in his side also stayed his tongue. At that moment the flames proved too much for Tyrell, who, pulling up his breeches, withdrew into the shadows. The young Winnecowet meanwhile had turned to his fellow tribesmen and was trying to demand the use of a club. Fortunately, its owner seemed reluctant to release it. Another brief argument flared up amongst the Winnecowet, during which time Tidesso announced that he wanted to sleep, and asked them to be quiet. Mikshish had finally got his hands on the club, but when he turned around, he did not see Tyrell, just a ring of huddled bodies, with their feet almost in the fire. The frustration contorted his features yet further. He writhed, hissing like a snake, when one of his companions lightly tapped his shoulder. This older Winnecowet beckoned him closer and whispered in his ear. The anger left the features of Mikshish, and instead his mouth widened into a broad grin.

CHAPTER 20
To the Walls of the City

How they managed to sleep he could not fathom, but dead to the world they certainly appeared. Either side of him the two lookouts were huddled around their spear shafts, the rusty iron points catching the beams of moonlight, gently wafting like fishing floats as the owners purred on. The other two lookouts, who were positioned twenty paces further on, one in each direction, appeared to be in the same state of unconsciousness. He wanted to share in their complacency. After all, if they felt sufficiently confident to slumber, why couldn't he? Hadn't they said there was nothing to it when he had met them earlier in the afternoon?

"Everyone, even Kin' Arfur takes a turn on watch. Just get a belly full of cider, and when you need t' piss, well then, just dangle your dicken over the edge. You don' even 'ave to wake up!"

"But wha' if sumutt comes?" he had asked earlier that day. "What if the city guards decide to come an' get us?"

They had roared with laughter and mimicked his cracked voice. He had held his breath in vain, to stop the spread of the crimson blush that had announced its arrival with an unmistakable burning at the base of his neck. Of course, the girl Sarah had chosen that exact moment to come chasing an errant piglet.

"Catch it then, Simon Spindleshanks!" she had commanded.

But the piglet had shot between his legs, just like the pea-filled bladder in that fateful game of football that had cost him so dear. He had blushed so hard and side-stepped so clumsily, splattering mud on her dress, that she had stopped to scold him. In vain he had searched her face for a hint of humour; felt himself wilt like a snowman as she stood before him, hands on hips, and harangued him for being a worthless dolt. The other chosen lookouts had sniggered behind her, only to explode in an orgy of ribald mirth the moment she had flounced out of sight.

"Don't you listen to a word that 'un sez, lad. Ever since she 'ooked up wiv Kin' Arfur, she finks she be the Queen of Shebal... Anyway I'm surprised she ant 'ad 'er claws into you by now. She seemed to be 'avin' a good time of it, leadin' you around like an ass!"

"Wha' you mean?... It weren't 'er that led I... It were Mistress Susan... Weren't it?"

"Susan did the coaxing of you into readiness. Tha' be 'er speciality like. But Queen Shebal did the leadin' aroun'. Din't she lads? 'Ere, I'm surprised you couldn't tell the difference... Thatun's got all 'er claws! 'Ere, did she shine 'er lookin' glass in your face? Yes, well, she be workin' 'er way roun' to you. Don' you worry Spindleshanks, lad, she"ll get to you sooner or later! Mind you, don' let King Arfur catch you wiv 'er. Your voice'll go up a notch 'igher than it already do be. Won' it lads?"

With their cackle still ringing in his ears, he had turned his back on them then and stamped off to send a sheaf of angry arrows deep into the heartwood of innocent beech trees; and then been forced to miss supper whilst Yorkie had made him cut each one free and repair those that had sustained damage.

That was why his belly now twisted and rumbled louder

than the snores of his companions. 'Goddamn!' he hissed under the folds of his cloak. His fellow watch had even brought chunks of bread and cheese with them. Of course they had not mentioned anything about that to him. And when he had begged a piece, it had been purposely cast short of his reach, the crust rolling into the ditch and the knob of cheese falling into a crevice in the limestone rubble of the ramparts. Of course, they had found that hilarious beyond measure, so much so that he had stubbornly made no move to retrieve either bread or cheese - even though he was well aware of the exact whereabouts of both.

In truth, life in the camp had lost most of its sweetness. The football match killings and the slaying of Captain Hand seemed an age past and to the best of his knowledge no 'hue and cry' had been raised. Had it all been forgotten? And what of Matty, surely he would be back by now? He half expected Matty to somehow turn up in the camp and claim him. How had Matty taken the death of their mother? He was her favourite, no doubt about it. Yes, Matty would take it bad, maybe do something stupid in his rage; nonetheless, Simon longed to see him again.

He longed, too, to be back at the city wharves, or better still onboard a ship. There was no escaping the pull of the sea. The rhythm of it was so near, embodied in the slippery river below, the incoming and outgoing of the tide like the blood-pump of a huge heart. When he was not being forced to do menial tasks around the camp, he would climb over the thorny, wattle fence and pick his way out to a vantage point at the edge of the gorge and hope that a lumbering old cog, or, better still, a sleek, three-masted carrack would be passing below. But they would not let him out of their sight for long, especially after his miserable failure as an outlaw. He felt more like a prisoner everyday. What had made matters worse was the latest detestable nickname 'Simon Spindleshanks'. There was no escaping it now. He loathed it more than 'Simple Simon'.

It always seemed to be the girl, Sarah, who was sent to retrieve him. She could not resist announcing her presence with a dazzle of light from her looking-glass - a ritual that had lately begun to annoy him beyond belief. Even so, the sight of a returning ship, laden down with some mystery cargo, being hauled along by the river pilots and the rebound of their voices on the rock face below, was worth any indignity at the hands of a girl. Only two days past he had recognised some of his former shipmates on board a returning cog, and despite warnings of dire consequences, would have halloed them there and then if only the girl had not been breathing down his neck. However, if he was honest with himself, part of him still welcomed the nearness of the girl almost as much as the sight of a boat. But why? Now he knew that she dallied with King Arthur, his view of her had undergone a dramatic change, but despite it all he still felt helplessly bound to her. This mixture of feelings perplexed him to distraction. He wanted, above all, to be rid of it.

He tried not to dwell on the memory of his first excursion into banditry. His part had been such a lamentable failure, that on the first day of his humiliating return, he had nearly thrown himself headlong into the chasm. Unbeknown to Sarah, it was her appearance that had stopped him. He had returned the next day and swayed over the edge, but by then the humiliating jibes and insults had lost some of their sting. In the two weeks that had passed, his skin had grown an extra horny layer and a cold, sullen anger had started to grow within. But what still cut him deep was the fact that, in all that time, King Arthur had completely ignored him, to the point of not answering any of his questions and looking right through him as if he no longer existed. Only the lepers seemed to treat him at all kindly. though they too seemed to delight in calling him Spindleshanks like all the others.

'No one said tha' I 'ad to cut a throat to belong 'ere... Goddamn it!'

He silently mouthed the words and ground his teeth with anger, then looking at the moon, he crossed himself.

'Though shalt not bleddy well kill... Tha's wha' it sez...the Bible like.'

He remembered his part in the death of Captain Hand and shuddered at the thought of the man's bloodstained body disappearing under the muddy waters. Looking up at the moon again, Simon began to whisper in a beseeching tone.

'I din't kill 'im though, Lord. Did I now? I chopped at 'im like, I admit tha', but 'e were dead already. I aint killt no one, 'ave I Lord... Please don' forsake me, Jesus... I don' wanna be no Boggart man, killin' an' thievin' in the woods like, all I wants is to be a mariner again.'

He froze suddenly, then slowly turned his head. There had been a sound like purring somewhere behind him. To his relief a goat chomped grass in the shadows and from the nearest hut the sound of snoring rose to assuage his fears. Yes that would be it, thought Simon.

'Get a hold of yoursel', Simon Tyrell,' he mumbled.

That journey to Wells had begun at the first hint of daylight. His belly had rumbled right enough that morning, from fear and excitement mostly, but also from lack of food. That had been his own fault; there was greasy porridge a plenty, puckering and popping in a big, blackened pipkin, but all he could bring himself to eat was bread dipped in goat's milk. If he had known how fast Yorkie was to push them, he would have forced the lumpen mess down his throat and been glad of it.

By midday they had reached the edge of the Mendip hills near the little hamlet of Stanton Drew before Yorkie had begrudgingly distributed bread and curds. There were two others in the small company, both called John: Onejohn and Twojohn. Onejohn, the larger of the pair, with a shock of red hair, was a natural jester. His own best audience, he never ceased making himself laugh and never seemed to stop chattering. It was plain to Simon that Yorkie cared for Onejohn even less than he cared for him, especially since he had incurred a stiff neck turning round to 'shush' the babbler again and again. By the time they had reached their destination at the Wells-Shepton Mallet fork roads, Simon was willing Yorkie to turn and hack off the garrulous fool's tongue.

The other John was the exact opposite, a different kettle of fish entirely. Nobody knew where he hailed from, though it was obvious from his speech that it was the farthest of foreign parts. That was when he chose to speak. Most of the time he remained silent, responding only to hand signs and single word commands. He had simply appeared in the camp one morning, about a week after Simon's own introduction, almost naked, swaying on his haunches with a young buck spread on the earth before him. Some said he was like an Egyptian man adept in sorcery, pointing to the strange blue lines and squiggles on his skin as proof. It was true that not a single dog had yelped at his approach. It was also true that he conversed with the dogs. He even spoke to the trees more often than to other human beings. He received the name Twojohn, because one of the few utterances he made was to bang his chest and repeat the word Ji'nm, Ji'nm. This sounded close to John, and straightaway he would respond whenever it was used. But only King Arthur seemed capable of real communication with this strange man, once making him laugh nonstop for nigh on an hour. And, another time, the whole group had gathered in gasping silence outside Arthur's cabin as the strange one danced and howled his blood-curdling incantations. It was agreed by all that he was indeed a savage man.

This Twojohn, as he became known, had the blackest of hair and eyes. Squat and swarthy, almost as dark as a Saracen, he hardly ever smiled. But what a bowman he was. Never deigning to pull that thick-limbed red bow of his in competition with another archer, but never known to miss any animal he chose to kill. He soon became the camp's main huntsman. Always going alone, sometimes for several days on end, but always returning with meat. He received a lot of favours, especially from the women. Susan, much to Yorkie's discomfort, personally measuring Twojohn and making breeches and smock of green weave for him.

Simon was more than a little wary of Twojohn. He moved so silently, seemingly everywhere at once, and often Simon would feel those foreign, black eyes boring deep into his soul. He was also more than a little jealous of Twojohn's elevated standing amongst the group, particularly in the eyes of King Arthur, and particularly since Simon himself had been a member for longer, albeit a week. Also, nobody had led Twojohn round by his privates, dressed up like an Ass. When he had mentioned this to Yorkie, Yorkie had called him a 'crack-pot,' and bade him try it himself if he dared. Simon realised that it was a foolish thing to ask, and even more of a foolish thing to try.

Whether or not it was to escape Onejohn's incessant jabber, Twojohn would, much to Yorkie's consternation, simply disappear from the group only to reappear somewhere further along the trail. The strangest of bird calls would announce his presence. Though he grumbled, no rebuke was uttered, and Yorkie grudgingly acknowledged Twojohn's bow-skill when he sent a blunt, speeding arrow skywards to collide with a pigeon.

Of course Yorkie had then regaled them all with his past feats of bowmanship before he was cruelly robbed of his hand.

Simon remembered that it had been the sight of the gibbeted corpse that had so unsettled him. It had not been made any easier when Yorkie had pointed out that the rotting remains had once been young Martin Gittings, and although he had been taken to Bristol Castle for execution, the body had been transported back to the scene of the crime, to dangle in chains as a warning until it rotted away.

Whilst Yorkie had revealed the intended plan of laying in wait until what he deemed to be the right prize happened along, Onejohn could not resist 'acting the goat' behind his back. When Simon could see the corpse being gradually turned, his first reaction was one of sickening distaste, but when the prankster had let go and the grinning cadaver had whirled around like a spinning top - catching Yorkie a clout in the process - Simon had dissolved in a fit of laughter, and had only managed to stop when he realised the greasy, white object Yorkie was threatening to bludgeon him with was the leg-bone of poor Martin Gittings.

No traveller who could be remotely described of as 'possessing wealth', or thievables, passed by in the downpour that followed. It had been threatening to descend all afternoon and when it did, it rained well into the night, soaking them to the skin. Even though they had huddled where the leaves were densest, nonetheless the rain managed to insinuate its way between the coarse weave, making each man shudder as it reached the skin.

After much grumbling, Yorkie had permitted them to start a fire, but all they succeeded in doing was make a lot of smoke and blacken Twojohn's pigeon. They had attempted to eat it nonetheless, but the still-pink flesh and the thought of the hanged man had turned his stomach. He had offered his portion to Twojohn and it had been consumed in a twinkling.

He would gladly eat his share now, Simon told himself, and briefly squinted along the ramparts in the direction of where Onejohn sat slumped around his spear. That red-headed oaf had taken his portion of the bird in one mouthful and made a show of spitting out the singed quills of feathers. Despite himself, Simon chuckled at that memory. What followed though had given him nothing to smile about.

He remembered that following morning well enough. The sun had brightly shone, giving everything a dazzling emerald shimmer. Vapour had risen wraith-like from the grassy clearings and from the coarse, green cloth of their garments. And as they peered through the bushes that lined the road, it curled up from the puddles and water-filled horse tracks. Yorkie had angrily steered him away from the corpse, but Onejohn had taken delight in telling him how some acrobatic foxes had managed to get at it during the night.

They had re-strung their bows, the hempen bowstrings having been kept safe from the rain, and with the smooth, wet mud from the roadway daubed their faces and crowned each other's heads with bonnets of glistening leaves. At first he had squealed like a child, especially when the raindrops ran down his neck, expecting Onejohn to join him in his irreverence, but instead Onejohn and the other two had - once the mantle was assumed - been transformed into Boggarts - true men of the woods. Not that Twojohn needed much transforming. He expected as such, but Onejohn's transformation unnerved him. The fool had stared at Simon, hissed and bared his teeth. He had thought to laugh, waited for Onejohn's hard, mud mask to crack or dissolve into a smile; but it had not happened and he had felt the fool instead.

They had nocked arrows then and taken positions along

the roadside. The obvious choice as lookout, Twojohn vanished, only to reappear in the uppermost branches of a tall oak, then, from time to time, he would descend and come running back to report to Yorkie with guttural utterances and signs. These were the only words spoken for most of the day, until the signal that riders were approaching was given. Up to that point, he had all but convinced himself that he too had undergone the transformation into a fierce Wolf's-head. The lack of sleep and food had certainly made him mean-tempered, but the moment he heard the dull plod of horse hooves, his knees had begun to knock, and the arrow's tip had shaken so much that he had had to keep drawing the shaft to stop its woodpecker clatter against the bow stave.

A group of three, mud-splattered horsemen had jogged into view. One, a portly figure, dressed markedly better than the two flankers, and by his 'eyes straight ahead, nose in the air', deportment, a man of importance and wealth. The two flankers, swords drawn, scoured the leafy margins of the roadway. Each made occasional swipes at the overhangs. He remembered hearing the clink of coins in saddlebags, or maybe he had imagined it and it had simply been the sound of tooth clamped on bit. But in the confusion that followed, it was hard to catalogue the true course of events. There had been no warning, no call to halt, of that he was sure. He remembered seeing one of the flankers go down bellowing with an arrow through his middle. At the same time, Yorkie and Twojohn had run into the pathway screaming and waving branches in such a demonic manner that his own skin had crawled. The horses had reared up in fright, but neither man had been dislodged. He had remembered to loose his own arrow then and felt sickened when it lodged firmly in the neck of the rich man's mount. The stricken horse had bellowed louder than all the frantic humans put together, and turning, had charged -

with rider still clinging - straight past him and on into the woods. Yorkie had screamed for him to stop playing with himself 'like a whore's cat' and give chase. He had done just that, thankful to be away from the murder, hoping that both horse and rider would get away. But he had barely run two bowshots when he saw them both collapsed beneath the spread of a gnarled, old oak. He remembered the bellow-like sound of the wounded animal's lungs and the small fountain of blood from where the broken arrow protruded. His actions had caused the pain and he felt shame. The horse had raised its head as he approached, whinnied and snorted weakly. He avoided looking into the frightened eyes, instead concentrating on the unconscious rider who lay bloodstained, trapped beneath his mount.

"Cyril!... Cyril Hardwyke!... I means Yorkie... Yorkie, over 'ere... Over 'ere!"

He had shrieked at the top of his voice, then turned to look at the man once again. The man's pink, piggy eyes were wide open with terror. The pink tongue and mouth too were gaping in anticipation of a scream, but all that issued was a phlegm-filled rattling, like a wind-whipped pennant. It had dawned on Simon then that the man was in terror of his wild appearance, and before he thought better of it, he had found himself trying to calm the man's fears.

"I aint no Boggart man really... These just be bits of ol' mud n' leaves like... So don' you be a frettin' now, I can 'ear the others comin'. We'll get you out from under there in a trice. O' course, you'll 'ave to cross our palms with some of your gelt... for the trouble like."

He had laughed nervously. The man had moaned and frantically tried to pull himself free.

"Ere, wha's tha' smell then? Why, you've shat yoursel', ant you."

He had not heard Yorkie's and Twojohn's approach. The first he knew of it had been the hard cuff to the side of his head that sent him staggering onto the blood-smeared horse.

"Thee useless little turd! I said no real names... Now thee'll 'ave t' kill 'im... an' tis thee own stupid fault."

He did not know who had protested loudest, the man for his life, or himself for the prospect of taking it. Yorkie had thrust a long ballock knife in his shaking hand - the blade mottled with lard and rust - and pushed him towards the man. The man had kept shouting. "Mercy! Mercy...Please no! Please!...Please!" He had clumsily thrust towards the man, wanting to shut him up, but the man had grabbed the blade with his bare hands; and when it had been slowly withdrawn, the blade had turned crimson, like a magician's trick. In the end Yorkie had contemptuously grabbed the knife and dispatched the man, with the same air of detachment he assumed when sticking one of the camp porkers.

But what followed then had made even Yorkie turn pale. With the most hideous sound Simon had heard coming from a human throat, Twojohn had rushed at the dead man and taking a handful of hair, had, with a knife in the other hand, cut the stretched skin of the scalp free. It had made a sickening suction sound. Onejohn, who had just arrived on the scene, brayed like a donkey in foal and proceeded to retch. Simon had crouched behind the tree and his stomach had also done its best to turn itself inside out. And though none witnessed it, Yorkie had crossed himself and prayed.

However, to Simon's failure to kill was attached the greatest shame. The whole journey back to the camp was a wretched torment for him. All shunned him, unless it were to chafe and scold him and every step added further to his misery. As they neared the limestone ramparts, Yorkie had told him that it was only the weight of the man's purse that had stopped them from stringing him up next to the corpse of Gittings. As it was, he received a dozen strokes of a birch switch on his bare backside in front of the assembled camp. The humiliation of it seared him still. A flogging on the back was a seaman's due, to be taken standing, so that even should his legs buckle beneath him, some dignity was maintained. Most carried and proudly displayed the criss-cross of the lash as readily as they would a battle scar, but to be bent over, whipped on the arse like a naughty boy, was in a way a crueler punishment than being stretched. How they had all laughed when he had pissed himself! Not one of them could he now call friend.

"No one sez I 'ad to cut no froats! Oh Matty, come an get I out o' this shite 'ole."

The piece of bread, stale now and no doubt hard as shale, was still visible halfway down the slope, and though he could no longer see the chunk of cheese, he knew where to plunge his hand, providing the mice had not gotten there before him. His belly complained loudly again and he resolved to waste no more time, but to get the morsels straightaway. Making sure that nothing stirred in the woods beyond the outer bank, he began to shuffle down into the fosse. Despite his best endeavours he tripped back onto his arse, sending a clatter of weeds and rubble downwards. Still nothing stirred, so further down into the shadows he went and snatched the noggin. He filled his mouth with a chunk and clambered up to his place at the top of the embankment. As expected, the bread was stale, but he took great delight in reducing the gobbet to a paste with the press of his tongue against the roof of his mouth.

Whilst fumbling for the cheese, he made no attempt at being silent and noisily lifted aside the limestone rocks, openly chuckling with sly delight when his fingers found the lump. He wanted to see them stir. What right had they got to slumber on and leave him awake? Why, a whole army could come and go without them knowing. Yes, and put everyone to the sword. What was the point in having lookouts? he wondered.

The wedge of cheese glowed pale yellow as he held it up in the moonlight. Brushing off the revealed specks of dirt, he bit into it and then crammed the remaining mouth space with bread. Nothing had ever tasted so good before.

"You be a lazy load of pig turds."

He spoke aloud after half the mouthful had gone down, and giggling at his boldness, repeated it.

"Did you 'ear wha' I said? I said you be a lazy load of drunken pig's arse 'oles."

"Shush!... Shush!"

The horror of a whispered command, barely inches from the nape of his neck, turned him rigid. The masticated ball of bread and cheese rolled from his gaping mouth to splatter on the rubble. A light touch on his shoulder gently but firmly steered him round. His senses all tuned to breaking pitch, he knew before he fully turned, and by the unmistakeable fragrance, that it would be Sarah who confronted him. There was barely time to rub the crumbs and spittle on his sleeve before her mouth had rammed against his own. Over as one they slowly toppled, her giggling lips still pressed against his, her feline eyes boring deep into his soul. He tried to speak, to ask of King Arthur, but she would have none of it; and when he feebly tried to halt her predatory fingers from untying the thongs to his breeches, they raked at the back of his hands; and she alternately hissed and purred above him. He clenched his fist, ready to strike out at her should this be yet another of her games.

It took a few moments of disbelief before he fully realised that he had entered her, it was all happening so fast. He tried to talk once more, as if hearing the sound of his own voice was of paramount importance - a confirmation that this was really happening. Again, the press of her wet mouth silenced him and as he thrust upwards to meet her, the pound and twist of her hips fought to nail him down in another more silky wetness. Why couldn't she be more silent? he asked himself. She was enjoying making a noise. Was her intention to wake Arthur and the others? Yes, she was playing one of her games, toying with him. A rage grew within him and with it a great strength. He bucked his hips, she laughed aloud and tried to force him back down, but he was stronger and the laughter became stifled behind clamped lips and the eyes registered surprise as he began to force her over. She fought against the manoeuvre, hissing curses, trying to pull herself away. He held tighter, grinding his hips into hers, trying to turn her onto her back. And then the rage began to empty from him and his fingers release their grasp. She needed no further assistance, but sprang from him with a snarl, and with dress still gathered around her wax-white thighs, dashed down the bank to become lost in the shadows. He lay there gasping and leaking into the ground, his glistening prick twitching like a freshly-landed fish. And still the lookouts slept on regardless.

Had this really happened? Her smell was everywhere. Yes, it was true all right. His heart still pounded with fear, frustration, and longing for her. He wanted to scream out her name. What was he to do? If Arthur found out, at the very least his ballocks would be hacked off.

Simon's mind raced, but with a new-found clarity. It occurred to him that he would slip away from the camp there and then. There might never be a better time than this. All the other lookouts slumbered so soundly that it seemed nothing short of a cannon's roar would stir them, and the moon was sufficiently full to aid his progress. All he had to do was get to the bottom of the nearby combe known as the 'valley of the nightingales', and at first light cross the secret ford that lay close by. He had been watching the tides. It being a day after the full moon, the ebb tide should not be long after first light, but even if it were low, the ford still remained treacherous enough - the ledge of rock only reducing the water to knee-soaking depth at best. There was, however, an alternative that occurred to him. If the river was still too high - as he guessed it was bound to be - he could follow its course and eventually approach the town by the wall at Redcliffe. Should he lose his nerve about attempting to enter by the Redcliffe Gate, he could at the last resort claim sanctuary in Saint Mary's church.

There was, however, yet another alternative that he dare not address, one that was too big to contemplate, and that was to simply up and leave the whole area - start anew in a different part of the country. But that was too great an upheaval. He would gladly board a ship bound for 'God knows where', but it had to be a Bristol craft, one that would return to the mouth of the mother Avon.

He suspected that once it was discovered that he had deserted this place, they would follow him, and if caught, they would have no compunction in silencing him for good. But what choice had he? He guessed that Sarah, if questioned, would not think twice about accusing him of molesting her. No, there was no choice, he had to go and go now.

He was also aware that by returning to the town, he could in all probability be walking into the jaws of death. Indeed, if he managed to get safely inside the walls, he had only the flimsiest of plans regarding his survival, but that did not seem to matter as much as going now.

"No, they'd catch I an' kill I, t' keep I from blabbin' about this place... But, even if I gets in, I'd allus be peekin' over my shoulder, case tha' friggin' Sergeant were about."

A low, angry voice sounded in one of the huts below. Simon thought he recognised it as King Arthur's, but he was not sure. Not waiting to find out, he simply put one foot in front of the other, clambered down the bank, into and out of the ditch below, and with shoulders hunched, tiptoed into the welcoming blackness of the trees. He expected an alarm to be raised at any time, but none came. He had severed the halter, but wondered was he about to put his neck into another?

The pathway down the combe snaked brightly in the moonlight. The downward hurtling was foolish, he knew well enough, but his elation held no place for circumspection. Barely a quarter of an hour before as he had mounted the outer rampart of the camp, a nasty thought occurred to him that nearly turned him to stone. Had this all been a ruse? Did they intend for him to attempt escape, only to have Twojohn send a stone-tipped arrow into his back? He had expected at any moment to hear the tell-tale rush of air, feel the agonising thud, then go toppling back into the ditch. But it had not happened.

At the top he had stolen one last glance at the crumpled shapes, smirked at the deception of his own spear, jammed upright between the rocks and the tent-like shape of his vacant cloak, even taking a moment to stick out his tongue; and then he was off like a whippet.

Before he reached the river, he had made up his mind not to take the ford, as they would expect him to. It was nonetheless gratifying to see the water was getting very low, just a silver-grey trickle between the glistening mud banks of purple. He took further delight in going down to the ford, making deliberately deep tracks in the moist earth, and then walking backwards in the same prints. There was a chance that the others would be fooled, at least for a while, but he knew Twojohn would never fall for it. That was if they could rouse him from his drunken stupor and he could see straight. Simon had never seen anyone so affected by strong drink as Twojohn.

The dawning of the new day was still a way off. If he made good progress, he could make the edge of the marshland that lay this side of the village of Bedminster, but he would need the sunlight before venturing through the marsh. Once he reached Bedminster, then he could find somewhere to rest up before going on to the Redcliffe Gate. Mid-afternoon was the best time to attempt it. The guards were at their most careless around then - waiting to be relieved by the next shift and dreaming of fatty bacon and the first pot of cider.

Later, as he plodded through the marsh, it was the startled reaction of a reedcutter to his appearance that made him realise his garb singled him out as a man of the woods. Not stopping to think, he cast off the coarse green, hooded smock, delighting in the release from the sweaty garment. His sailcloth breeches would not cause a second glance. If the day remained fair, his bare torso would not draw undue attention, but should it decide to turn grey, or to rain, he knew he would be more conspicuous.

As he approached the village of Bedminster, he passed two foot-travellers going the opposite way. Lowering his face he started to hum a tune, hoping to appear casual, hoping that they would ignore him.

"You be in a 'urry lad. Wha's up then? Boggarts 'ad the shirt off your back?... 'ere, you can't go to church lookin like no savage... Hey! an where'd you get them scratches from? Bears? Or lady Boggarts was it?"

They guffawed and nudged each other, smirking with delight as, speechless, he blushed before them. No sooner had they finished laughing than the village church bells began to peel and from the distant city came the echoing chime of a multitude of brass-born praises. Sunday, Sunday. Oh no it was Sunday! He began to panic. Now more than ever he would appear out of place. Most of the townsfolk, even the humblest, would make an attempt to smarten their appearance, but he would be as a naked heathen in their midst.

Tongue-tied and blushing, he bolted off, his ears cocked for the second helping of laughter he felt was inevitably bound to follow. But there was no laughter and it worried him more not less. It unsettled him enough to make him take a last minute detour of the village, entering yet more marshland that threw him wide of his original destination, the Redcliffe Gate.

He was now inexorably set on course for the Temple Gate. Something about that entrance with its foreboding square tower built over it had never been to his liking. As a child he had seen a man hanged from it and he had only used it a handful of times since. But he would study it nonetheless, and if it were still not to his taste he would work his way along the wall through the cluster of dwellings back to the Redcliffe side. At least this roundabout route would delay his confrontation with the guards and the eyes of the townsfolk, something that he was beginning to dread more with every step.

He heard the strange, hooting sounds as he passed where the coarse, marsh reeds reached the height of his chest. The main causeway was firm enough, being fashioned of well-trodden earth on a lattice of compacted sticks, but the occasional paths that led off either side appeared water-logged and treacherous. Something made him stop and listen instead of pressing on. At first he thought it was a distressed waterfowl and to his mind sprang half-formed thoughts - with less substance than plucked feather down - of catching and cooking the unfortunate bird, even though he had no method of making fire. The combined image of cracked egg shells, golden yolks slithering down his throat, also flashed before him, with no account of the fact that any eggs had either long hatched or been taken by more successful predators.

Even before the images had faded, he knew full well the sound was human; and before he had gone a dozen paces off the main track, he knew the sound was not one of distress, but of pleasure. The salve for his curiosity outweighed any disappointment felt over the loss of potential sustenance, however uncertain. All his previous misgivings and fears disappeared in an instant, and forward like an ass he was again led, this time his stirring member divining its own course.

Through the reeds he glimpsed the rise and fall of the 'twin backed beast'. Had all humanity gone rutting mad? he wondered, caring not for the soaking of his breeches as his knees slowly submerged in the wet marsh earth, wiping away the cascade of sweat from his swollen eyes, following the course of a man's blackened fingertips. Stroking, with his own eyes, the girl's soft, white flank, he remembered his own coupling with Sarah and was envious of the obvious affection he now witnessed in the Sunday sun. This was a far more joyous celebration of life than any worship in a dusty church - listening to some dried-up old priest in smelly, black cassock drone on in the dried-up tongue of men long turned to dust. The envy turned to jealousy, that it was not him lying with the girl. Although he could see neither face, the raven-haired girl could have been Sarah, and the man - though obviously a good ten years older - could have been him. It was like watching his own glistening back rise up and his arms lock to take the strain. Here before him was an enactment of what he had imagined time and time again would be his rightful prize with the girl, Sarah. It had not happened like this. There had been no time to savour, no time for sweet talk, no sweetness. All he had received by way of affection at the hand of the girl Sarah, had been the dazzle from the looking-glass. And all the time he had been made aware of others attaining pleasure. Even the constant couplings through the thin, wattle walls and in the murky shadows of the shared hovels seemed joyous compared to what he had received. Had it really happened like he remembered, only a couple of hours ago? The scent of her had either gone or been masked by his own gamey stink.

Was he forever condemned to be a skulking observer, always peeking from the bushes at the enjoyment of others? He felt uncomfortable as his conscience pricked him and he remembered. Affection had been offered and sought in return-it was he who he had spurned the advances. One of the young leper girls had come near to him as he had watched the river, stroking his hair, making it plain what she wanted, even pulling aside her shift to let him examine every inch of her body. He had spluttered and pronounced it blemish free, not wanting to look at the poor girl's ravaged face, only daring to let her take his hand and place it between her thighs. He had wrenched it back in terror of the silky wetness, thinking it the disease's seeping poison. For two days and nights he had held a spider's web and a cross in his fist, not daring to tell a soul. What a green fool he had been in the greenwood.

"Simple Simon"... "Spindleshanks!"... "Spindleshanks!"... "Good for nothing!"... The imagined mockery stung him.

Just then the man loudly grunted, and back still arched, thrust deeply again and again, as if ploughing through an obstinate, root-tangled furrow. Then neighing and snorting like a heavy horse, the arms unlocked and down he collapsed onto the squirming girl. Simon crouched low in the reeds, burning with frustration, hardly daring to breathe. He wanted to collapse forward, spent like the man. What was he to do? He felt foolish, felt a danger that could not allow him release.

This man was strong, far stronger than he. The ripple of the man's back muscles had straightway alerted him to this much, but he had not stirred yet. Was he dozing so soon? Simon readied himself for a sprint. Then the girl spoke and once again curiosity bound him to the spot.

"That were nice Alfred. 'Ere Alf, wake up you gurt lump... you be dribblin' an' snorin right in my 'ear'ole, so you be... 'Ere get off me, the wet's comin' up frough your apron... Alfred, can you 'ear me?"

The man grunted, but did not stir. Feeling either more courageous or foolhardy - he was not sure which - Simon slowly raised his head and stared hard. The girl's face was hidden from view. Both her legs, like an up- turned beetle, wildly trod the air either side of the man's arse. He felt secure in the knowledge that he too was unseen and took his time poring over the scene. It seemed that they had made a bed of reeds and over this spread a huge, leather apron, the sides of which had curled up as the apron had been compressed by their pounding. Both were naked and pale, but for the tangled leather breeches around the man's ankles; and strewn around on top of the reeds were other articles of clothing. The girl spoke again and just as he retracted his head, Simon caught a glimpse of bright, white fabric almost within arm's reach.

"Alfred Tring!"

"Wha'?"

"You be squashing I into the muck... Alf! Get off I! I carn' 'ardly breave!"

There was a grunt and a shuffle from the other side of the reeds.

"Phew! Tha's better. Well then, Mister Blacksmiff... You've made I miss the service, I 'ope you goin' t' give I the price of my fine. I be bound t' get one after all this. You knows tha' old sour priest never misses a face."

"Wha's 'at?"

The man finally spoke, or rather, grunted, displaying a touch of irritation at being disturbed.

"You 'eard... 'Ere, you enjoyed yoursel' right enough... Din't you?"

"Well, din't you an all?" growled the man. "Ere, you never said nuffin' about no church fine?"

Simon saw the back of the man's head lift.

"Oh! You be awake now all of a sudden, do you be? I fort as much. Mention gelt an' it allus' 'appens... 'Ere, wha's tha' stirrin' about down there... feels like a gurt slippery serpent."

"Well now girl, if I'm t' pay for it, then I may as well 'ave my money's worth, din't I?"

A flurry of giggles was followed by the same sound that had originally drawn Simon Tyrell to this spot. Knowing that once again the couple were occupied with each other, he rose to his full height and reached out for the white garment. As his fingertips made contact, he remembered looking down, his eyes being drawn firstly to the wobble of a candle-white breast, then by the equally agitated dangling of the man's hairy bollocks - but it was the wide, staring eyes of the girl that froze his heart. Over the man's shoulder, the slash of her red mouth gaped open. The hair-raising scream that followed turned his heart from ice to fire and sent him haring off through the reeds, the white garment trailing from his hand like a captured banner.

Her screaming stayed with him long after he had raced out of earshot, unsettling him more than the angry bellowing of the man. Something heavy had thudded in the ground behind him, he knew not what, only that it had been flung over a large distance by a much stronger arm than his own. It served to add further impetus to his stride, carrying him over half a mile before stopping for breath and to examine his trophy. He saw then why the girl had screamed so hysterically. He had in his hands a woman's linen blouse, a clean, Sunday best, church-going garment, with fine, white, embroidered filigree along the breast and collar. At first he began to gnash his teeth with anger and frustration, wondering what good a female garment was going to do him, but when he thought of the girl trying to hide her nakedness on her return to the village, he could not help hooting with guilty laughter.

The distant bark of a dog cut his mirth dead and sent him hurtling down the causeway once more, but much of the spring had gone from his gait, as if his thievery and irreverent laughter on the Lord's Day had betrayed him and a leaden weariness descended upon his shoulders.

The dog barked again, and taking up a heavy, wet stick for a cudgel, he forced himself on, all the while looking over his shoulder, listening out for the patter and yap of approaching hound. When he finally heard the animal again, it was no nearer, but further off in the distance, so faint as to be hardly noticeable. He exhaled a deep sigh of relief, and staggering down a side path, flung himself face down across a large clump of the coarse reeds. Though he only intended to catch his breath, he fell fast asleep with his legs trailing in the mire.

When he finally dragged himself from the slumber, his back stung red from the rasp of the sun and his head felt as if it had been left in a baker's oven. It was late, well into the afternoon - he knew that much - and he was straightaway up and running towards the high ground before even giving his addled brain time to take stock. The sun was still sufficiently strong to worry his back as he jogged along, so he wet the girl's blouse and hung it over his shoulders, tying the arms around his neck. Further on still, his feet once more on firm ground and the edge of the city in view, he slipped the blouse on.

The scent of the girl had vacated the fabric's folds the moment he left the marsh, the dirt and sweat from his own body transforming the fine, Sunday blouse into little more than a work shirt. Some inexplicable foolhardiness within made him determined to test the reaction of the next person he should chance to meet. He made towards the first habitation he saw - a rude hovel set at the foot of a hill. Shielding his eyes, he looked up and nodded to a man who was repairing the thatch of the roof, even daring to ask for a sup of weak ale to slake his thirst. The man ignored him but called for his wife, who came out smiling with a half filled cup of tepid ale. She seemed pleased enough to see another human being and rambled on nervously, not once noticing anything strange about the blouse; instead letting slip that she was not happy about her husband labouring on the Sabbath for all to see. This was encouraging. She was too wrapped up in her own problems to notice his. Simon looked around. As far as he could tell, no one else was in sight, the nearest cluster of hovels being well over a bow shot away. Emboldened, Simon asked for a morsel to eat. The man growled down from aloft, but nonetheless instructed his wife to send him packing with a noggin of yesterday's bread.

Instead of taking the more direct path that led to the 'Temple Gate' road, something made him climb the outlying hill. A mouthful of bread and ale had given him vigour enough to stride to the summit, promising himself the remainder of the bread as a reward when he got there. With arms outstretched like birds wings, and mouth open wide, he gulped the welcome breeze and bounded forth. On reaching the top, the view kept his mouth agape. Only after a full minute had passed did he absent-mindedly begin to stuff it with bread.

The town of Bristol was larger than he had remembered, or imagined. Never having witnessed it from this aspect before, he felt a surge of pride as it shimmered before him - so many towers, so many church steeples. Before, as an inhabitant, he had simply accepted it all, hardly ever bothering to look up at the stone splendour, intent instead on running the gauntlet of the shit-infested streets. The pride vanished with the swallow of bread, to be replaced by a nervousness that threatened to make him puke. He wanted so much to be transported back into the centre, the familiarity of it all, and knew that whatever the cost, even if it meant ultimately being dragged in chains to the castle dungeon, he would take the risk.

The spread of the Port Wall drew his main attention, in particular the tower of the Temple Gate under which he was bound to pass. The girdle of wall stretched across the loop of the Avon, marking the old channel where, two centuries before, the whole river had been diverted. He found it hard to believe that in those olden times they had actually managed to change the course of the Avon, but there was the famed Bristow bridge as proof. The wall ran for a third of a mile, from riverside to riverside. The Avon swung round in an arc. The area thus encompassed was known as Redcliffe. Here lived the rich merchants in their tall, fine, waterfront houses and behind them the growing class of tradesmen - the tuckers, the weavers, glass blowers, soap boilers and dyers. It was an unknown world to him. Once through the gate, there would be no dallying in Redcliffe; the likes of him were not meant to tarry there, No, a plague on 'high and mighty' Redcliffe! But the bridge was different; the bridge was a marvel he would never tire of. It was a whole, dark, bustling street of shop after shop with even a chapel to the Blessed Virgin Mary across the centre. And if that was not wondrous enough, above the shops rose another four storeys and the marvel was, the buildings were all of wood. He smiled when he remembered the tale of a ship's mast crashing its way through a milliner's shop, and just a year later an ox had crashed its way into the same shop. Through the windows behind and into the river it had charged, a fine velvet hat on its horns. There had been talk of banning larger animals, but the bridge being the main thoroughfare from the south into the town, it was, of course, impossible.

Bounding and skidding down the hill he went. Pausing for breath and rubbing the stitch in his side, he stepped onto the road in the tracks of a cart, measuring his stride to the turn of the wheels so that he stayed an even twenty paces behind the lumbering vehicle. Something about keeping the cart in front of him made him feel better. He was not sure why, but he resolved to maintain the pace, even though it cost more effort to slow his stride than to overtake. For a long, dusty half mile he plodded on, and then a problem presented itself. From the back of the two-wheeled cart an object tipped into the road. Not being able to see at first what the object was aroused his curiosity, but the fact that the driver had not noticed left him in a quandary. Was he to alert the man, or was he to ignore it, simply carrying on minding his own business? When he did see what the object was, he knew that he had no choice other than to pick it up and run ahead.

"Wait!...Hey there wait a mo', will you?"

The cart stopped. Simon stroked the object in his hand, marvelling at the beauty of the craftsmanship. It was a carving of Christ on the cross, fashioned from mulberry wood or some suchlike.

"You there! How did you get that?" an angry voice harangued him.

"It fell off your wagon."

Jogging up to the driver, Simon smiled and held out the crucifix. He could see that the man nervously fingered a thick staff.

"Well, d'you wants it or not?... I aint comin' no closer if you're gonna give I a clout wiv tha' there gurt stick."

The man's grey beard parted to reveal a worn-toothed smile. The wrinkle-ringed eyes, though pink-veined and parchment-coloured, twinkled with relief and good humour.

"Forgive me, young man. I can see now, by your honest face, that you are intent on doing me a good turn and mean no mischief."

"Yes, well, it just dropped off your cart, like."

The man took the proffered carving, steadying the ass with his other hand.

"Yes, yes... I should have secured it better than I did, but in my haste to get away from the two villains who stopped me but an hour back I was careless, thinking only to put as great a distance between myself and them."

"Wha' villains?... Tell me wha' villains?... D'you mean... Greenmen?"

Not waiting for the reply, Simon bounded to the far side of the road and on tiptoes amidst the ferns peered back down it. He returned to the cart much agitated.

"Steady there! Steady now!"

Simon was unsure whether the old man was instructing him or the nervous donkey.

"Tell me please. Did one of 'em 'ave only one 'and?"

"Calm down... Why yes, that's it, one hand and the nigh incomprehensible tongue of a Northern man... er Yorkshire I think... Why? I do hope they aren't friends of yours."

The man's bony fingers again tightened around the stave.

"Cyril Hardwyke! Gotta be. No, they don't be no friends o' mine. They 'eld I captive in the woods, tryin' to turn I into one of 'em, but I run away, din' I?"

"Yes they did ask if I'd seen a youth... You are obviously he, but they said something about your mother ailing and needing to return you to her side."

"Ha! Our Mum's been gone for a few monfs now. Carried off by the sweating sickness, she were."

"Yes, they didn't strike me as the kind of fellows who would put themselves out on account of an ailing mother. They didn't rob me though, I must say, but the other one, a short, silent, foreign looking fellow, unlaced the back and ran his grubby paws over my carvings,"

"Oh God's wounds! Tha' be Twojohn. They must 'ave sobered 'im up some 'ow."

The old man continued, "I must say he showed great appreciation of my handiwork. Of course, I couldn't understand a single word he said, but somehow it was as if the spiritual significance of these humble carvings bridged that gulf. So I gave him a Madonna and child. You should have seen the reaction. I have never seen the like of it before. The poor fellow seemed quite overcome, whether with pleasure or grief I can't be sure. But he set up this dancing and caterwauling the like of which I have never seen before, nor care to witness again! Of course, all the while, this grubby Northerner babbled on. I knew he was spinning me a yarn."

"Lies all the time so 'e does... But 'e aint very good at it."

Simon ran to the far side of the road and stared nervously back down the track once more. "How far? How far behin' d'you reckon they be?... I can't see 'em."

"Easy now, don't fret so. I watched them walk back the other way. Or rather the foreigner danced and chanted, while the other one hobbled behind cursing at the top of his voice. Made sure they didn't double back too. Forget about them, we'll soon be safe inside the town... I presume that is where you intend to go."

Simon nodded.

"Good, then you can walk with me if you wish... I'm going with these carvings to the Franciscan friary in Pipe Lane. They

313

will feed me and give me a cot for the night. You appear as if you are in need of both these requirements yourself? It can be easily arranged. I'll just say you are my assistant."

The relief was immediately apparent on the youth's face.

"But you must do me a service in return."

Suspicion returned to Simon's features.

"Ha! Come now. Don't look so perplexed. All you have to do is stop those Mendicants from seeing the carvings. If they find out what they are, they'll be down on us like a flock of gulls on a dead mackerel, and they'll have them away, hidden in the folds of their cassocks. If that happens, then I might as well turn around and go back to Blagdon and live off nettle soup, for there is not one thing I could do about it."

Simon had forgotten about the Eremites, the begging friars, those crow-black, hooded figures who menaced the Temple Gate traffic - alms or damnation. He detested them, but was fearful of them too.

"Well then, what do I do?"

"The moment we get through the Port wall, you take this staff and guard the rear, rap any fingers that come too close. Break 'em if you have to."

"Wha' about the guards then? I can 'ardly go knocking' they about now, can I?"

The old man laughed, then from his tunic he drew forth two other carvings and with a crooked finger beckoned the youth closer. Simon whistled when he saw, in the old man's hands, the representation of a human male in one and female in the other, she with ample breasts and thighs, he with exaggerated phallus. The old man sighed and brought both hands together, then with palms apart he displayed the interlocking piece. Again he sighed resignedly.

"'Tis a sad state of affairs I know, but a handful of these little figures open more doors for me than a cart full of crucified

Messiahs. Talking of which, there's a double hangin' in the morning."

He crossed himself twice.

"If I'd known in time I'd have turned out some little gibbets an' jiggers. They go like hot cakes, so they do. Still, as it is I should be able to shift a few Christs. I won't let the Franciscans have 'em all. There's always the odd one or two in a crowd that acts as if an hangin' is a deeply religious experience."

Simon shuddered, nervously fingering his Adam's apple. "They don't be sailor boys do they? I do hope not."

"No, not sailors, but one's a soldier... A common sergeant no less, and t'other's a sort of scrivener from the Customshouse. Anyway they're both murderers. "

Simon was aware that he was starting to redden and had begun to nervously finger his own throat. He gulped hard twice. The sound to him seemed deafening, but the woodcarver carried on talking, oblivious to his discomfort.

"Murderers?" he managed to blurt out.

"That is what they are, common murderers and they'll perform a merry dance for it tomorrow."

"But who'd they murder?"

Simon thought of the dead captain. Had his weighted body been found? Was somebody else, even that vile sergeant, going to swing for a killing that he had had a hand in? The sweat began to trickle down his body and the side of his face. He wiped it away with the back of his hand.

"Are you well lad? You look flushed, as if you're about to burst into flames... Don't tell me, you're one of those that can't stomach a hangin'. Am I right?"

Simon nodded. The woodcarver smiled smugly.

"Don't you be ashamed, lad. I was once like you, couldn't abide crowds, but after a while, it gets easier. Watchin' an hangin' is good for a man... it's his duty so's to speak. Lets him

315

know how fortunate he is to have both feet firmly on the ground. However short his span may be."

"Ere mister, wha' you mean?... Who'd they murder anyhow? Do you know or not?" Simon snapped impatiently.

"Here, steady on now, lad, no need to get flummoxed, specially with one who has offered you gainful employment, even though it be for a short while. But who knows, it could be for longer... I'm not promising anything, but I might be looking for an assistant. Ah, yes now, who was it they murdered? Well, if my recollection is correct, it was the manservant of the Customshouse Collector himself that they killed."

"What? Thomas Croft's manservant?"

"That's right. Thomas Croft... Don't tell me you know The great Thomas Croft?"

"Well I don't knows 'im like, but I bin on ' one of 'is ships. Met 'im, even cleaned the seagull shit off 'is cloak."

"Yes well, they cut his man into little pieces, fed them to the pigs they did. Only for some reason the pigs turned their snouts up at the prospect."

Simon laughed with relief that no mention was made of the dead captain.

"I don't think that it is particularly funny, young man!"

"No I'm sorry, but why did they do it? Do you know?

"Well the story goes that this fellow Rudkin, yes that's his name, Rudkin, had it in for the servant. Bubbling up for years it was, came to a head over a black pudding of all things. Anyway, the sergeant owed Rudkin money on a wager and so Rudkin offered to forego the payment if he helped him do away with the poor unfortunate servant. Now they're to swing, and all for a blood puddin'. Which reminds me, are you hungry? Of course you are, young growing lad like yourself is always hungry. Well, when we get inside the gates, providing the Eremites haven't robbed us blind, I knows a little puddin n' pie shop that keeps its back door ajar on a Sunday. What do you think to that then, lad?"

Simon nodded his head and mumbled, content to let the old man ramble on. Food was the last thing he was thinking of. He knew now that he would get through the gates and once inside and past the beggars, he would make for the Frome quay and should anyone care to listen, declare himself a mariner once more.

CHAPTER 21
The view from the Island

It had been the long, outraged cry from the main bank that had wakened them all. Tyrell lurched blindly for the gun, then remembering it was lost, had nonetheless rushed forward unarmed. Clambering up the rise that formed the backbone of the island, he saw through the pre-dawn murk that he was not the only one with empty hands. How many bows had been lost or ruined? What was happening? Were the ones whose fate it had been to remain on the bank being attacked by the Paquatuogs? Mimicking the movements of his savage companions, he crouched low as they made the ridge. A hand tossed him a long wooden club and with it his courage returned.

The same cry from the same throat rang out. Tyrell caught the glimpse of a figure waving frantically from the shadows of the opposite bank. A cry of rage came from his right. He looked to see first Tidesso, then the others, mount the ridge and wave in return. Open-mouthed, perplexed, he watched them sweep diagonally across his front, hurtling down through the clumps of trees to the rocky edge. He felt he had no choice but to follow and brought up the rear, doggedly racing along in their wake.

Dawn took him by surprise in the same manner that dusk had done previously. Then it had been the helpless relinquishment of light into darkness. Now it was the reverse;

and with daylight came the equally painful revelation that this would in all probability be his last day on earth. There had been no time to count his companions when first waking, but he remembered having the distinct feeling that there were fewer of them. Where was the angry young Winnecowet who had wanted to brain him last night as they huddled around the fire? Where, for that matter, were the others who had stayed their kinsman's hand? Guessing then what had happened, he let out a roar of frustration and swiped the air with the club. They had absconded, probably taking the bark boats with them.

As if in confirmation, from the ones ahead came a chorus of piercing yelps, and despite the rush of the much swollen river it echoed from the opposite bank. At first Tyrell thought that indeed it was an echo, but in a glance he saw the handful of last night's stranded Pennacooks was also racing along the river's edge. In another stolen glance he saw one of them stop momentarily to loose an arrow down into the channel. Though it fell short, the arrow's flash served as a pointer. He ran as close to the edge as he dared, saw ahead of him his own single column of Pennacooks and, just ahead of them in the river below, the two canoes and the four Winnecowets - their long hair like black guidons flapping out behind them as they tore into the flux. From his vantage point above he could see by the lie of the shoals and its submerged boulders why the canoes had not made better progress. It was only now, as daylight penetrated all, that the Winnecowets felt confident enough to start their full stroke. Imitating the canoes' surge, the pace of his companions quickened. Tyrell tried his best to keep up, but the gap between himself and the others opened inexorably. The gap between the canoes and the lead runner was also widening. In the thinning of trees up ahead Tyrell knew that the body of the island was coming to an end. The Winnecowets were going to get away, leaving them stranded. Again he roared and wondered why more arrows were not being loosed. There were at least six bows and plenty of ammunition. So what if they damaged the boats. What did it matter? They were going to get away.

He heard a loud splash, closely followed by another, then a third. Again he ran to the edge. The swirling river surface was much closer, barely a dozen feet below. He saw the canoes; and bobbing like windfall-apples close behind them, the bare, glistening heads of three Pennacooks. From the opposite bank he saw two more launch themselves into the water, their legs still furiously treading the air. Hitting the surface at a run, just beyond the rocks, he watched them swiftly strike out for midstream, amazed at their speed and the way they appeared to claw at the water with powerful overarm movements. Never had he seen such ease in the water even though they were swept along at a furious rate. Tyrell was reminded of the play of dolphins rather than the efforts of humans. But they were no match for a canoe with two paddlers, though reaching it seemed their only salvation from being swept away.

Directly across the channel, Tyrell recognised Managnon. He felt momentary pleasure at seeing him still alive and waved the club in salute, receiving the briefest of nods in return. Like himself, Managnon had been the rear runner. Unlike himself, the Pennacook had an excuse for lagging. As the tribesman ran to the rock edge, Tyrell noticed he betrayed no hint of the twisted leg that had appeared to trouble him so the previous day. But his attention was straightaway drawn to the bow in Managnon's hands. An arrow was nocked and it was raised in readiness. Tyrell could not believe that he would risk such a shot. Whatever his chosen target, in between bobbed the heads of his fellow tribesmen. It was much too risky. In a flash the tribesman's bow was drawn, the arrow barely kissing his lips before being released and no sooner had it been loosed than another shaft had taken its place on the string. Tyrell was panting with the effort of running, and through his watering eyes he missed both arrows' flight, but he saw where they struck.

"Oh yes!..Arrers! shooting! Good shot!" Tyrell yelled out.

Managnon banged his chest with pride and waved the bow above his head, then both raced on, the better to view the result of his marksmanship. The Winnecowet in the stern of the rear craft was rocking back and forth, his back twisted and arching in agony, his empty hands tearing at the canoe's side where the fletching stood proud. It had pierced the bark and pinioned him by the rear upper thigh and the harder he tried to free himself, the more the canoe wavered. The man in the prow fought furiously to keep the canoe midstream on an even keel, but it was apparent by the gap opened up by it and the lead craft that in his attempt he was relinquishing speed. Tyrell cheered again when one of the swimmers grabbed the stern and the canoe shuddered. The pinioned Winnecowet became suddenly animated, flailing out at the bare head with the paddle, before it was wrenched from his fingers. The Pennacook fell back and the Winnecowet fought to release himself from the arrow. Tyrell saw then that it was the same young savage who had confronted him the night before. He was conscious of grinding his teeth and snarling with anger. Although his eyes never left the canoe, he found himself running again, this time onto the sloping tail-end of the island, where a group of Pennacooks stood with nocked shafts, shouting out advice to their submerged kinsmen. One of the swimmers had again managed to grab hold of the canoe, and even the combined efforts of the forward man, to both steer and strike out with his paddle, could not stop another swimmer from grabbing hold. Tyrell guessed that the swimmers were trying to retrieve the canoe in one piece and that was why they simply did not capsize it. But all five swimmers had now managed to either grab hold of the boat's gunnel or each other and, in consequence, slow it down considerably. Seeing that he had lost control, the forward Winnecowet threw himself into the water. A hail of arrows followed, but he surfaced momentarily further downstream, shouting out to the distant lead canoe before disappearing. Tyrell's attention returned to the recaptured craft; it was being steered to the opposite bank. The still pinioned Winnecowet was writhing and howling in desperation. He was finally silenced when one of the Pennacooks rushed into the shallows, crushing the unfortunate man's head with a single club blow, sending out a halo of red spray from the long hair. Tyrell joined in the howls of triumph, then remembering the lost gun, he straightaway turned and started back along the rock edge, his eyes combing every crevice, every crack.

At one point he clambered down the slippery rocks and retrieved a sodden bow. It was Tidesso's. Knowing that it would probably be of no use again, nonetheless he risked life and limb to get it, his mind half thinking that it would in some way compensate for the lost gun. As he started his way back along the lower level of rocks, his toes stepping onto something soft made him reel backwards in terror. Stifling a cry, he prodded at what he first took to be a rock, only to find, to his horror, that he had stood on the debris-covered back of a drowned Pennacook. Tyrell had seen drowned men before, bloated and fish-bitten, but he had never seen such contortion of flesh. The twisted body had been rammed into a rock cleft in such a way that it was nigh impossible, unless stood upon, to discern it as human remains. At once Tyrell realised he was faced with a dilemma. If he should alert the others, they would be duty bound to retrieve the body, wasting precious time.

Tyrell had gleaned enough from their profuse hand gestures and the small amount he understood of their speech to know that they were in deadly danger, with a large enemy force liable at any moment to come screaming through the woods. He understood well enough that somehow they had to get off the island and cross to the far bank of the river. What happened after that he was not sure, but he sensed that once across, they would be within easy reach of their people and safety. But how were they going to cross with only two small canoes? The last thing that was needed was a stinking corpse to carry. Remembering, then, how they had forced him to abandon the unburied remains of Dodds to the foul depredations of the enemy, he spat with frustration and angrily prodded the corpse once more. He instantly experienced a pang of guilt, crossed himself, and quickly looked all around lest he was being spied upon. As far as he could ascertain, no one saw him. The bank's rocky overhang would hide the body from those on this side. The ones on the other side of the channel were too concerned with retrieving the canoe. Even if one of them was watching his every move, it would be well nigh impossible to see what he saw.

Tyrell had made up his mind. Retracing his steps, he immediately clambered up the low cliff edge, mounting the rim as the others came along. He saw they were combing the rocks below and swallowed hard as Tidesso rushed forward to snatch the bow off him. There was no hint of gratitude to ease the tension he now felt. Tidesso looked at his returned bow, then at Tyrell, as if he were in some way responsible for the sorry state of it. Then with a growl of disgust, he cast the bow back into the water.

Tidesso felt his heart grow heavy as a rock. The medicine was deserting him. It was all unravelling like a frayed string of wampum and the beads of fate were trickling through his fingers. The thunder lance had been taken by the water spirits, as were two of his band. They now had his favourite bow and the bows of four others. How were his band supposed to defend themselves from their enemies? They were trapped. What should he do? The rushing of the water filled his head so that no space was left for clear thought. At least Managnon, his right hand, had survived the breaking up of the big canoe. Managnon would soon be beside him, he would speak and plans would be formed. All Tidesso would have to do was choose and act. But first, he had to get Managnon and the others over to the island. It had to be attempted now. The enemies were close, he knew it. All, even the curly one, knew it. Only a few moments past he had seen five deer come running down to the opposite bank. They had not come to drink, but almost threw themselves over the edge in desperation to cross the water and get out of the path of many moving feet. The deer had turned upriver even though Managnon and his companions had returned to the crossing place. Yes, he guessed the enemies were but a handful of pipe-smokes away.

They ran back along the edge to the crossing place. Getting the others and the two canoes over to the island was the first thing to do. The water had risen overnight, but Tidesso could not tell for sure whether it would rise further. He furiously beckoned them over. The water spirits would keep the thunder-lance as tribute. There was no way to locate it and claim it back. He wiped it from his mind and concentrated on the immediate problem.

As the first canoe edged into the channel, he prayed to the water spirits, reasoning with them. After all, hadn't they claimed enough tribute from his people? They had taken the big canoe, the thunder-lance and the lives of two of his band. Surely they would not require more?

"Oh great Glooskap, I ask you to intercede on our behalf.

Ask these Hobbamock to impede us no longer... Let them know that should they require more tribute, there will soon be others, a great host passing this way. Let the spirits ask 'these ones' for tribute. We have already given enough."

Was this the same stretch of river? They were all astounded at the relative ease with which the first canoe was poled across. Nonetheless, Tidesso positioned some with the long saplings on the rocks below, to be ready to fish anyone out, should the second canoe be capsized. In the first canoe had been two Winnecowet quivers and bows. Shorter than the bows of the Pennacook, they were backed with rawhide, powerful and most welcome. But it was the cargo of the second canoe which held the greatest surprise. Overjoyed as he was to be re-united with Managnon, it was the object in the bottom of the craft that caught his whole attention and set him howling with joy. Tyrell was also beside himself with pleasure. Laughing, pointing, jumping up and down, and, before any thought to stop him, he had thrown himself into the beached canoe and was brandishing the returned thunder-lance high above his head. Laughing also, two of the tribesmen lifted Tyrell out of the canoe, lest his dancing feet render it useless; and turning it over, lifted it onto their shoulders and followed the other canoe up through the trees. There was still much required of these canoes. They would have to make four journeys back and forth across the main stretch of river.

"Managnon, my friend, it gladdens my heart to behold you again... You shot well... Twice you shot your arrows well... But tell me, why did you wait so long? Why did you not save us all such a chase and shoot from over there?"

Tidesso chuckled as he pointed to the opposite bank and affectionately patted the back of Managnon, who, though much pleased with himself, simply shrugged his shoulders.

"I needed to exercise this twisted leg, that's why."

"I see too that the water spirits decided to relinquish the thunder-lance, and they chose you to bring it back."

"This is true. When the canoe broke under my weight, the thunder-lance became entangled in the Mateoulin's cape; and instead of me being washed away downstream, it kept me safely on the river bottom. I attempted to acquire the skill of breathing underwater like the fishes, but it eluded me. So I reluctantly came to the surface. The cursed thunder-lance insisted that it come also."

As they clambered up the bank, their attention was drawn to the curly one, who, having ceased his celebration, was now seething with frustration. They watched in silence as he examined the gun. As if chewing unripe, green berries, they screwed up their faces as a long stream of angry-sounding noises emanated from his twisted mouth.

"God's Hooks! Satan's fiery shit... Bollocks... Tis ruined! Look! What am I supposed to do with this? See, the lock is broken, the serpent is buckled, and when I pull the tricker... look, nothing happens, does it? And the flamin' barrel's bent too! Look down it. Go on! Take a look for yourself!"

Tidesso recoiled as the muzzle of the gun was pushed under his nose. By his gestures Tidesso guessed that the Curly-one wanted him to look along the length of the lance, as one would check an arrow shaft for straightness. He did as bidden, relieved at the respite, however brief, from the foul-sounding chatter; and lifting the heavy gun, gazed along the barrel, first from the muzzle-end, then from the stock. Compared to any arrow or spear that he had yet examined, it was perfectly straight. This was wasting time. Already one pipe had gone. He tossed the gun at Tyrell, ignoring his protests, and bounded up to where Managnon stood at the top of the slope.

"You saw the running deer?" Tidesso enquired, at the same

time testing the draw of one of the Winnecowet bows, sighting and sweeping it down across the river.

"Did I see them? They came as close as I am to you... We all took steps to chase them, but forced ourselves to let them go... My tongue still waters to think of it... A hunter could go a long time without seeing the like."

"The enemy host is very close... If it weren't for the chatter of the river, I think we would hear them..."

As he spoke, a raucous flock of ravens angrily took to the air.

"We must waste no more time. Let's start to cross straightway."

For Tidesso, even more welcome than the return of the gun or his friend was the confidence to make a decision. It seemed that his medicine had not deserted him after all. Even if he were soon to look death in the face, it would be with a glad heart.

"They will be upon us before the canoes return from the first journey."

"Half will go now. Those that remain will have all the arrows. Curly will stay too. Quick! Make a flame. He will need it for his weapon... It will make us enough time for those that cross over to warn our people."

"How much time before they overrun us? As long as it takes to smoke a pipe? Or maybe longer? As long as it takes to make an arrowhead?"

"Yes, at least. They will have to cross in the same place that we did. Besides, they will have seen the glow from last night's fire and be drawn to it like moths. We can pick them off as they swim, if they are foolish enough to try. For as long as we have arrows we can sting them. But if they have many canoes at their disposal, then it will be as long as a man takes to eat a dog and smoke a pipe... Which reminds me, do you still have the Squakheag's pooke?"

Managnon nodded and began rummaging among the fire's embers for a light.

"Hi yi! This is good. I would not like to pass over to the spirit world without tasting the smoke mixture one last time. The curly one can take his thunder-lance flame straight from the pipe."

CHAPTER 22
Behold the Enemy

Tyrell had drawn the wet charge and was now frantically reloading the gun. Although overjoyed at first to be reunited with the cumbersome weapon, he also viewed it with a resigned resentment - as a prisoner views the ball and chain that keeps him rooted to the spot. If only the gun had not been saved, he could have been one of those fortunate ones now clambering into the two bark boats. Purposely choosing the smallest ball, he plopped it into the muzzle, sighing with relief when it rolled down the barrel unimpeded. Maybe it was not so bent after all. He let another ball roll down. The first firing would have to be impressive, he mused, letting out a nervous laugh as he withdrew the ramrod. Ripping a piece of shirt-tail for wadding, he rammed the charge home, but due to the damaged lock, left the priming pan empty for the time being. Tyrell did not relish 'firing it off', remembering the time by the big lake when the other gun had split apart. It was just not possible for a man to survive two such accidents.

Clambering up to the island's ridge, Tyrell watched enviously as the canoes slid off from the island's far side. They did not strike out straight across the river, but set out on a diagonal sweep. He was not sure whether this was intentional or because of the current, but it was apparent now that the distance would be doubled, and with it the time taken in returning. It dawned on him then that there was not going to

331

be enough time. He and the several remaining tribesmen were going to stay and fight - and in all probability die. With dread he turned and made the descent to take his place amongst the condemned.

With a sudden tap on his arm, Tidesso signalled him to go with them back to the crossing. Tyrell saw that all the tribesmen were loaded down with arrows. What was he to do when the handful of remaining balls were shot? Shoot stones? He scanned the ground for potential ammunition.

Having returned, each man positioned himself behind a tree or rock and began daubing himself with paint. To Tyrell's continuing discomfort, a cleft boulder of granite overlooking the crossing was designated as his hiding place. It meant that he was the nearest to the landing point. What was he supposed to do? Fire the gun, he knew that much. But when? And most important of all, where was the flame to fire it with? He had caught the whiff of that cursed sorcerer's smoke mixture, seen Tidesso and Managnon passing a smoking tube around. But where was the flame to light his punk? He needed it here and now. Surely these savages understood this much?

Peering through the cleft, he had a clear view of the crossing place. The gap in the rock could not have been better fashioned by a mason, affording him an ideal place to rest and sweep the gun. Careful not to make a grating noise, he slid the long, heavy barrel into place, and sighted along it. Then, with a small amount of the fine powder, he primed the pan. His hand had started to tremble. A few loose grains blew into his face.

The same tap on the shoulder, this time accompanied by a friendly nod, indicated the presence of Tidesso beside him. Immediately the tension lessened. It crossed Tyrell's mind then that the young leader was actually enjoying all this. Tyrell's hand still shook as he pressed the end of the fuse into the glowing pipe bowl, earning him a good-natured rebuke from

Tidesso. The saltpetre-impregnated punk spluttered into life. Tyrell sighed with relief, thankful that he had had the foresight to put aside a short length of it. Now all that had to happen was that the enemy would fail to materialize within the next half hour and the taper would burn through to ash. He knew then that he wanted it to begin. He had whispered a prayer and a semblance of calm had entered him, but he did not know how long it would last. If it should start soon, then he would not show fear; delay would be his undoing.

Again, Tidesso tapped his shoulder. He looked up and was powerless to stop the tribesman from daubing his face with paint. From his fingers, Tyrell could see it was the same mixture of yellow and green that the others had used. He then knew why. The others had all but melted into the undergrowth, making him think for a moment that he and Tidesso had been deserted. Now, above and beneath the mask, he too was a savage greenman intent on taking blood.

Leaning with his back against the rock, he blew gently on the taper, then with a glob of spittle dampened it a little to arrest its progress, He wondered whether the glow would outlive him. An urge to piss was beginning to nag at him. He remembered an age past, when in the company of this same, naked savage, he had wet himself like a babe, yet here he was looking death in the face, able at least to control that bodily function. The taper in his fingers still trembled, but only slightly.

"Come on! Come on you, heathen bastards!" he hissed. A look from Tidesso froze him rigid. Then, instead of a tap, Tidesso grabbed his upper arm tightly, and Tyrell knew that it had begun.

Spinning round, he gazed down the gun barrel and what he saw framed in the rock aperture alone made his heart lurch. From way back in the dappled light of the trees opposite, all the way down to the water's edge, there was a writhing mass of painted warriors.

How in heaven's name had they appeared so suddenly, so silently? Only a handful of minutes earlier he had looked along the gun and seen nothing. But this now was like peering through a window into hell. Hell could not conjure up a more demonic host than the glistening press of savages.

After a few brief moments where his brain struggled to accommodate the swell of the multitude, his eyes began to focus on the varied appearance of the different bands that comprised the whole. Some were not unlike the Pennacooks in appearance, breech-clouted with tufted hair strip. Others had long, skin shirts, bare skulls but for a lock at the back in the fashion of Tartars. A small number had long hair that, cascading from beneath caps of skin and feathers, reached way down their backs like the manes of horses. He had seen the stick armour of the Paquatuogs before, but that had been on dead men, and he had foolishly thought of travelling play actors in Saint George costume, intent on slaying cloth dragons. But seeing them now, bristling with long lances and arm-thick bows, he knew that dragons would run far, far away. Why, oh why weren't they doing the same? These Pennacooks could have swum across to the far side. They were like fish in the water. They could have helped him across. He would gladly try it now himself. Drowning, anything, would be better than facing the enormity of this spirit-crushing horde.

Again, the hand of Tidesso grabbed him. This time it firmly restrained the wrist of the right hand that held the taper. In the fearful distraction, Tyrell had let it come perilously near to the priming pan. Tidesso put down his bow and took the taper, indicating with a pat on his chest that he would be the one to choose when the first shot was fired. Tyrell looked at his companion's face. There was not the slightest indication of fear or anxiety. If anything, beneath the paint, he wore an expression of determined enjoyment, as if some secret wish was about to be fulfilled.

Tyrell was relieved that the responsibility for the first shot was no longer his. He could now concentrate on wedging the stock firmly against his shoulder with both hands. But what was he to aim at? The choice was enormous. It would be like shooting into a flock of pigeons. He could not help but hit something. The answer came almost straightaway. The tap to his shoulder was superfluous, for he was already marking the progress of the three canoes down the slope. Even Tyrell knew by the shape and the markings that they were the remaining craft of the Winnecowet. Had they been given or taken, he wondered?

At the water's edge the canoes were overturned and those that had carried them were revealed to be Winnecowets. He heard himself hiss, then above the noise of the river he heard a series of orders being given. They act as if they do not know we lie in wait...Tyrell could not believe this was possible. He watched as five enemy warriors got in the first canoe, two of them with the long lances as poles, the others, though cramped with knees almost touching chins, had bows drawn. He aimed at the foremost of the two. The taper came closer, the heat of it causing his right eye to blur with tears. Come on! Now! Now! Damn you! The prow of the canoe had edged into midstream and the taper descended.

Even though he screwed his eyes tight, the flash of the priming still penetrated his retina, but the memory of it was at once erased by the thunder-crack and the kick of the charge. Tyrell opened his eyes wide then, but could see nothing for smoke. The curtain was lifted and the opposite slope appeared eerily empty. Then all was pandemonium. In mid-channel, a blood-splattered canoe was in the process of spilling its screaming occupants. Had two balls done so much? he wondered. What Tyrell did not know was that he had entirely missed the foremost polesman, instead hitting the one in the rear, knocking him overboard, making it impossible for the canoe to be steadied by one man alone. The arrows of Tidesso and Managnon had hastened the inevitable result, but as far as Tyrell and the enemy was concerned, one shot had done much damage.

For a few moments he was rendered deaf; the rush of the water was like the tinkle of a child's voice. He turned to see the gaping mouth of Tidesso. His war cry registered faintly. When the roar of the opening battle eventually reached him, he was halfway through reloading, the air was thick with the zip of arrows, and he too was whooping at the top of his voice in the manner of the Pennacooks.

Emboldened by the result, he sighted along the gun once more. This time he had control. The taper hung poised to strike, steady in his hand. From the vantage point he could see the enemy were starting to come out of hiding, and once again the slope was starting to crawl like a maggoty cheese. A running Paquatuog drew his attention. This slat-bound savage came screaming down the far slope in a suicidal charge. Armed with shield and whirling club, he recklessly launched himself into mid-air. Before Tyrell could shoot, an arrow appeared in the man's exposed armpit and his warcry became a scream of pain as he smashed into the surface. In frustration Tyrell swung the gun around, firing it into where the enemy was thickest. Before the smoke again impeded his view he glimpsed virtually the entire horde flinching as one single organism - just like he'd seen shoals of fish start. The battle was suddenly held in abeyance whilst all peered to see the damage done. The low groan of fear rose to become a full-throated scream of rage once more. A clatter of arrows smacking into the rock above his head disabused him of any smugness he may have been tempted to feel, and an agonising cry from one of the Pennacooks served to concentrate his mind on the fact that maybe now they were only a handful against two hundred.

No sooner had he finished reloading the gun, than Tidesso led him scurrying along the bank edge to another position. As they raced along, crouched low, Tidesso let fly three arrows without once checking his gait. The long barrel was again poked over the grey stump of a fallen tree. Tyrell swung it round, searching for a likely shot, knowing that, once spotted, he too would present an irresistible target. In the swing he spied the second canoe being steadied in the water and pressed the taper into the pan. The flash of priming followed, but that was all, there was no shot. A moment's silence and then a roar of derision came from over the water. An arrow glanced against the withdrawing gun barrel in a mocking clunk! Tidesso growled with frustration whilst Tyrell tried desperately to unclog the touch hole. For the first time Tyrell saw a hint of fear and confusion in the savage's eyes.

The war cries from this side told him that the Pennacooks had gone towards the crossing point and were concentrating their attention on the oncoming canoe. With a grunt of disgust, Tidesso raced off to join them. Swiftly stealing a glance, Tyrell saw that once again a canoe had gained midstream. Nonetheless, he glimpsed the craft and its occupants bristling with arrows, and wondered how it still floated. As he crouched low to replenish the priming pan, triumphant whoops from the Pennacooks and howls of rage from the Paquatuogs and their allies indicated that this attempt had also failed - this was too easy. Crawling behind another boulder, he again stole a glance, searching first for a target before sliding out the tell-tale barrel. With the lengthened delay between gunshots and the apparent failure of the last attempt, the enemy had become emboldened, with warriors vying with each other in an attempt to draw the Pennacook shafts, howling with delight as those shafts rattled like hailstones against their wooden shields. He watched open-mouthed as two warriors - armed only with clubs, cords attached to their waists - attempted to swim across the torrent. He jeered with relief when they were hauled ashore like limp bait.

In a swift sequence of movements he pointed the matchlock at a particularly large, vociferous brute who stood at the water's edge, flapping an arrow-studded shield, taunting and tempting with glimpses of his overhanging belly. With tongue clamped between teeth, Tyrell lowered the taper. The blast knocked the wind from him, bruising his shoulder, and nearly severing his tongue to boot, but he was more than willing to pay any penance exacted from this end of the gun, just as long as it perform its task. Even through the smoke he saw the man cut down, blown off his feet, a fist-sized opening in the shield. He could not fail to notice the groaning mouths of the victim's comrades as first they sprang back, then rushed forward to probe with bloody fingers and examine such devilish destruction.

Once more the battle seemed to draw to a momentary halt and again, for a fleeting moment, Tyrell was made to feel like an avenging deity casting thunderbolts from above.

There were only three more lead balls left, and one of those he knew would be a tight fit. What was he supposed to do when they had gone? Fire stones? Wampum-shells? Pouring a measure of powder down the muzzle, he guessed, by the weight, that the flask was still a third full. That, at least, was some consolation - he would shoot sticks if needs be. A ball and wad were rammed down tight, and with the gun laid across his chest he squirmed along on his backside towards another rock - mindful of the continuous zip of arrows overhead. Suddenly, as if dropped from the clouds, a large, fist-sized stone thudded into the bank behind him. He froze, waited and watched as another even larger missile completed a high arc over the water to come crashing down through the trees directly behind where two of the Pennacook marksmen still crouched. With cries of fear they came tumbling down the slope to huddle behind the rocks. What was happening? Did those wicker devils possess some kind of war machine? No human hand could hurl such a large missile. He judged the distance to be at least sixty paces. Choosing a lull in the swarm of arrows, and after marking the course of two more large missiles, he chanced a look. Though most of the enemy force had managed to find some sort of cover - and for the time being seemed resigned to loosing arrows and howling insults - Tyrell noticed the same bold gathering of armoured Paquatuogs amongst the waterside rocks, jeering as the Pennacook arrows struck their shields. He saw also that one of their number waved a long, forked pole, from which dangled a missile-filled pouch.

"A sling! That was it, some kind of giant sling. It had to be!"

Fascinated to the point of foolhardiness, with arrows humming in his ears, he watched as the pole was whirled around, once, twice, three times, each time moaning louder with the increased momentum, until the heavy pouch swung out in a blurred extension of the pole. Then, finally, on the fourth rotation, there was a whipcrack sound, the pouch opened as a thong was released, and from it flew the missile.

From the moment it left the pouch, Tyrell knew that it was no ordinary stone as the others had been. It made a different sound as it sped through the air towards him. Moments later, as the blood welled in a gash in his arm, he knew why. It had not been a single missile this time, but rather a bladder filled with many small, jagged pieces of chert and gravel, exploding on impact. In blind rage, with the dust and grit still in his eyes, he fired off the gun. Even before the smoke cleared he knew that he had hit nothing. The moment the gun barrel appeared, the enemy were alerted, and by the time the priming had set off the main charge, they had dispersed, only to reconvene in the exact same positions as if nothing had happened. Tyrell was beside himself with rage as they let off their mocking whoops.

Behind him he was dimly aware of a wounded Pennacook shuffling from tree to tree, collecting enemy shafts. At least there was no shortage of arrows. The lower slope behind bloomed with their vaned stalks. Either side of him the small band was still holding its own, sending volley after volley, milling about to give the impression that there were at least twice their number. But how long could it last? The enemy would find some way of crossing. Even above the warcries, the taunts and the eternal rush of water, the unmistakable clatter of tree trunks being hacked rang out.

Where were those goddamn bark boats? Surely they would return soon? From his customary crouched position, Tyrell angrily rammed home the smaller of the final two balls, covering his eyes with an arm as another stone-filled bladder burst nearby. Again, a jagged piece drew blood, this time his shin, but of this he was unaware, all his attention drawn by a dull strike to the top of his head that sent off an explosion of pink and purple stars somewhere behind his eyeballs. Rubbing his skull until his hand burned with the friction, he growled with pain and rage, resolved to do his utmost to slay the perpetrator.

Slithering back to his first position behind the cleft boulder, he was again within ten paces of Tidesso, and amidst the rocks on the other side of the short slope that led down to the crossing place, he glimpsed Managnon and another tribesman. Both glistened with blood and the rocks around them shone red and slippery. Though both warriors seemed oblivious to their wounds, Tyrell detected in the diminishing curve of each bow shot a lessening of strength - he started to feel panic returning. This was madness! Where were the boats? They must have returned by now? One last shot and then I'm going up to take a look, he told himself. Just one last shot at that bastard with the big sling and then... The blur of another bladder missile striking close by caused him to go into a crouch. He waited for the angry spray of flints. Nothing. Only a faint thud indicated that it had landed, and from over the channel came loud hoots of laughter. Thinking it strange, but paying it no more attention, he turned and began slowly feeding the gun barrel between the rock fissure, searching for the savage responsible. He had vanished; not even the forked pole betrayed the hiding place. The entire group of Paquatuogs had gone from their position at the water's edge. Only one remained, fallen and twisted in death. Cursing with frustration, Tyrell spat and waited. In his hand barely a two finger length of taper remained.

But they were still there, flitting from rock to tree, taunting with a brief flash of skin, howling with delight when retaliatory arrows flew within a hair's breadth of their contortions. Tyrell was driven to distraction as he squinted along the barrel, trying to train it on one of them, but always, as he was about to fire, the target would vanish into thin air. The air around him seemed suddenly abuzz with flies.

In an effort to arrest the progress of the taper, he dampened it with spittle once more, aware that the shake in his hand had returned, aware that his heart rattled like the tattoo of a drum beating time to the unmistakable hack of stone blades.

Hitherto, the odour of burnt powder, the saltpetre-laced punk, had monopolized his sense of smell - there was a crumb of comfort to be had in its pungent familiarity. But now, even as a wisp from the taper curled round his nose, a sickly stench of corruption began to insinuate itself into his consciousness, demanding that he turn around at once. Turn he did, and the sight before him was straightaway seared into his brain. All strength and pretence of courage drained from him. The gun slid back from the cleft with a clatter and the taper slipped from his fingertips. The sight made his skin crawl with horror, made him bellow like a wounded bull. There in the dust at his feet, grinning, staring at him with one unseeing eye was the putrefying head of his dead friend Sam Dodds.

A rush of bile seared his gorge, causing him to retch bitterly. In terror he ran screaming along the bank, then turned up the slope, indifferent to the arrows that bit at his heels. Only his stumbling saved him. Crawling behind a tree, he tore at the earth with his fingers, wanting it to swallow him up, wishing he could burrow his way into it like a rabbit. The boom of the gun made him jump like a rabbit nonetheless.

"What?...In the name of God! What?"

He whipped around in time to see a stunned Tidesso lying on his back, the barrel of the still-smoking matchlock pointing skyward. Scurrying backwards, Tyrell gained a better vantage point, and from this higher position upon the slope much was revealed. It appeared that some of the enemy, on spying him fleeing away unarmed, had leapt out from hiding to screech and taunt. Tidesso had forsaken any misgivings he may have harboured and fired the piece into the midst of this group; and though he was as yet unaware of it, the single ball had passed through two of the enemy. When, moments later, the young leader saw for himself, the whoop of triumph was unmistakable.

It was the cessation of the wood-chopping that drew Tyrell's attention away from the scene directly below. To him now it seemed more ominous than all the screams, all the stones and arrow shafts, even more deafening than the gun's roar.

From somewhere opposite the end of the island, an authoritative voice was calling out in a wailing summons. In the tone, Tyrell detected an order to assist, and from where he sat, he could see part of the enemy force silently melt away, stealing off towards the call.

Tyrell gained his feet. The trees blocked his view. He found himself suddenly hurtling between them, drawn in the direction of the voice. Already, an inkling of what had been set in motion had occurred to him. They were felling trees to make a bridge. He had to see for himself; and if it were true, warn the others. He knew the exact spot to make for. It was overlooking a position where the opposite bank rose higher than the corresponding position on the island. There the channel was narrowest, but the water was more turbulent in consequence. The wood-chopping had come from the slope above, where the tall trees stood. Skidding to a halt above the narrow section of channel, he edged his way into a clearing and stared at the blanket of green directly opposite. Tyrell did not have long to wait before spying a tell-tale shudder in the uppermost branches of one of the trees. The same voice echoed out again. The chopping resumed and the tree shook, this time more violently than before. Even before the crackle of splitting wood sounded, he knew that all his previous assumptions were proving correct. The combined strength of many hands was hastening the process begun by the axes. Tyrell had never seen a tree felled by a stone blade before. He guessed that it would be a long, laborious undertaking. But a deep enough notch cut into a trunk and the added power of many hands pushing would make shorter work of it. They would also make short work of carrying the tree down to the gap and laying it across. Then it would be all over for the defenders.

Not waiting for any further confirmation, he started back. The creak and groan of the tree continued. Two turns of a sand glass, three at the most, he reckoned, was the time that was left before the tree was felled, carried down the slope and laid across the gap. He had a feeling that the tree would not quite reach all the way across, but could, nonetheless, slope down to be jammed tight into the lower rocks on the island side. He pictured the enemy crawling along the tree-trunk like ants along a grass stem. There was nothing that could be done to stop them crossing over. Tidesso and the others had to be made aware of the futility of staying to fight. Getting off the island was the only possible answer.

Tyrell changed his course, striking upwards for the ridge. Even if the canoes had not yet returned, they would surely be in view. Breathless, his chest pounding with the effort, he made the top, frantically weaving in and out, searching for a clear view. From this part of the island a clear view was not possible unless he returned almost to the position of last night's camp ground. Time was running out. He contented himself with following the ridge and catching tantalizing glimpses of the shining river and the sanctuary of the far side, but the two bark boats were nowhere to be seen. Before he turned off to join the Pennacooks, he caught a glimpse of the beach where they had embarked. It too was empty. Tyrell's heart sank and his legs became leaden as he started down the other side.

"They've abandoned us... Left us to perish... Curse them all!"

He felt like a sinner returning once more into the gates of hell.

Single arrows marked the outer boundary of the conflict,

becoming more numerous with each descending step. Harvesting a bundle of these enemy shafts, he zig-zagged from tree to tree, waiting to gather both his wind and his courage before making the final dash down to the rock edge. From the safety of a tree he looked down the slope. It was very quiet. The howling had ceased. Even the rushing of water seemed to have receded. Was that a voice singing? he wondered, cocking his head like a bird. Surely not! Something strange was definitely happening. Something had caused the conflict to be held in abeyance. What could it be? Whatever it was, he still had to rush across ten long paces of open slope and make the Pennacooks understand that it was time to retreat.

Downwards he charged, making straight for Tidesso, spying the gun beside him. Again he thought it strange that not a single missile came his way. The bundle of arrows Tyrell carried clattered in the dust as he collapsed into a heap against the rock, thankful that Dodds' rotting head had disappeared. Tidesso signalled him to be silent with a dismissive sweep of his hand. Tyrell's voice started to rise, as with frantic gestures and grotesque contortions of his face he attempted to describe what was happening towards the far end of the island. Tidesso growled and pushed him back against the rock, immediately censoring the flow of information. Angered, hurt, in utter confusion, Tyrell resisted the urge to scream it out and instead did as the others, turning his face towards the enemy and the eerie sound of singing. Something strange was definitely going on over there. He shuddered as he turned.

It took a while before his eyes registered what was actually happening. On a clear part of the opposite slope, a rude, wooden framework had been set up. Bound to this framework was a figure, the naked skin criss-crossed in a crimson, lattice work of deep slashes. In the figure's writhing, the framework creaked a mocking accompaniment to the ululating song.

Was it a madman singing out like that? Tyrell had witnessed martyrdom before, heard the stubborn singing of psalms from behind a jacket of flames on St. Michael's Hill. This was no different. He did not want to watch. He wanted to go to the other side and, if needs be, swim - anything to get away. Again he thought of interrupting, but bit his tongue when he saw the solemn, straight- ahead stare of each of the Pennacooks. None moved. Each appeared hewn from the granite.

Who was the poor victim over there, whose passing held such fascination? Tyrell strained to see, wondering if Wadowagwa had been caught, and it was he who sang the death song. But even though the distance was long, Tyrell was sure it was not his former tormentor. No, the body was more lithe, midway between boyhood and manhood. Who could it be, to have such an effect as to stop the conflict? Why, if they aimed a volley high enough, they could easily reach the poor wretch, put him out of his misery, and maybe puncture one or two of his torturers. Tyrell decided he loathed all executioners; and the blood-smeared ones who now pranced around the youth with mussel shells and firebrands were no exception.

The song soared into an even higher falsetto as the youth's legs began to blacken and bubble under the flames. Tyrell found himself fumbling, loading the gun with a stone, inhaling through his mouth, lest the smell of burning flesh reach across. He attempted to raise the gun to the parapet, but knowing that over that distance not even the most perfectly spherical bullet could be relied upon to hit what it was aimed at, he let it slide back. And then it came to him who the poor wretch was, and why his companions were simply looking on like a bench of shit-bound magistrates. It was the one who slew the deer, the first meat that he and poor Dodds - God rest his soul - had tasted since being first captured. It was the one who, for some reason or other, had been made to stay behind. Tyrell had thought no more of it until now. He looked again at the stone-faced ones. In a way they were judges, bound by their tribal pride to oversee the slow death of one of their own, to see that he did not bring shame down on the heads of their people by begging for mercy. If they maintained their stance for much longer, he thought, they too would have the chance to prove themselves, for the bridge across would soon be completed.

The song became a full-throated scream that none could deny. Tyrell caught a flinch in the mask of Tidesso. He did not want to look, but found himself bent forward, peering to see if indeed it was the same one, and what unspeakable depredation was happening to him now. A new horror eclipsed even the image of Dodds' head and caused him to contemplate putting the gun's muzzle in his own mouth and somehow blowing his brains out. The taste of bile again singed his throat as the once proud ridge of hair was peeled from the victim's skull and with the most hideous yell, brandished for all to see. But what followed dwarfed even this horror, making him stumble then retch. Both torturers began to cut and tug the skin down over the head, until the whimpers were finally suffocated by the folds of skin from the victim's own face.

Barely an inch of taper remained. It was now or never. To delay any longer would mean certain death for them all - surely as gruesome an end as the one just witnessed.

The gun's bang was deafening. The irregular stone had whined angrily through the trees, and even though it struck no enemy down, nor rendered a merciful release for the captive, it thawed the frozen movements of the Pennacooks sufficiently to allow them to shoot a volley of arrows into those who had been irresistibly drawn from cover to gloat at the still-bucking body.

Tyrell counted three down. One of the torturers, screaming defiance, tugged a slippery red shaft from his stomach, as if giving birth to a snake, and came hurtling down the slope. At the edge of the rocks his legs failed and face-first he tumbled over - the still-clutched firebrand hissing as he smacked the surface. And then it seemed to Tyrell that everywhere he looked, that space was occupied by the blur of an arrow, followed by another, then another, and yet more. The enemy had been holding back, knowing that only a fraction of their missiles would be returned. But now they had opened up with the full force and again Tyrell made himself into a ball, waiting for the swarm to pass - waiting for one to bite. He looked up. It seemed that every piece of ground, tree trunk, even the cracks in boulders had become the roosting place of an arrow.

"Don't you understand what they are doing?" He was shouting at the top of his voice now, not caring that his words were, to them, just a blather of random grunts and whines - of less meaning than the enemy war-whoops. He carried on, fingers and arms stabbing the air. "Over there! Over there! They make a bridge... cut down a tree... They cross now... We must go over the top to the river... Tegu! Tegu! Coos! Coos!"

He screamed their word for river and tree. "Swim... Now! Now!...Losada! Understand!"

His words trailed off, completed for his benefit alone. All seven faces had glanced his way, the blood-shot eyes expressionless as if he no longer inhabited their world, but harangued them from a dream. One of the mouths moved, a sound escaped.

"What was that?" he whispered, but the beginnings of a song left his question hanging in the air. In despair he turned away. They were expecting to die; almost, it seemed, relishing the prospect. All had been struck by arrows, some more than once, yet they bore their hurts with a stoicism bordering on indifference. How had he escaped this far with nought but a graze? He experienced a fleeting twinge of guilt, then reality. His reality intruded again and his skin began to crawl with fear. He was going to die. If he did not attempt to flee now, he would very soon be dead. Not that he relished the prospect of thrashing about in the water. But maybe the bark boats had returned? Anything was better than this.

They were each one singing now, each his own mournful song; some hardly able to lift a bow, let alone draw the string. Tyrell knew that they would not be leaving this place; but for him, this was the time. Now, whilst the arrows came in small groups of ones and twos again. Something held him back. It was Tidesso. Tyrell needed to say goodbye. Raising his hand to tap the blood-stained back, he stopped short, barely an inch away from the other's skin. An arrow zipped between them as if to censure any final contact and Tyrell found himself haring off up the slope once more, the crack of the spent shafts splintering beneath his feet as he beat a path from tree to tree. Yet more arrows hissed their eagerness to join those already spent, humming for his blood alone, and on leaving the safety of one tree trunk to dash to another, the thudding tattoo, like a stone-beaked woodpecker, rang in his ears.

The stone point that pierced his right hand as he reached out towards one of the looming trunks, also bit deeply into the soft wood, jerking him to a painful halt. The rest of his body found adequate cover, but his arm was now exposed, wrapped around the trunk. Stealing a deep breath, he attempted to tug the pinioned hand free. The deeply-embedded arrow refused to budge, but his hand slid along the shaft, causing him to groan as he exhaled.

"Oh please Jesu, not now! Don't leave me dangling here for them! Let me get to the water, Lord. Water, the water, Lord!"

He was made aware of other arrows thudding into the tree by the vibrations in this barbed divining rod. Suddenly another pain in his forearm, dull at first like a blow from a blunt hammer, then sharp with a searing heat, forced his hand back against the bark. This time the whole forearm was secured, and when he summoned up enough strength to try to move, the pain made his legs buckle and his free hand grasp around the trunk to tear at the bark. It was as he feared. Two arrows now held him to the tree: one through the palm of the hand, the other through the forearm. The loose hand, reaching round, had become wet with blood, slipping from the slimy shaft as he attempted to snap it. Had an artery been severed? There was so much blood. He became frantic. The arrow piercing the hand finally snapped, but it made no difference. It was the other one that held firmest, and this one was only reachable by the fingertips.

"Oh Christ! Why now, Lord? Why?"

What was he to do? A wild animal would gnaw through its arm to free itself from a snare. For that is what had happened. He had been snared like a helpless animal, but it seemed that every time he exposed part of his body, a flight of arrows would send him clinging to the unforgiving bark. They had the range of him now, knew that he was trapped. How long before yet another shaft secured his arm to the trunk? The ones making the bridge would be across soon. They would find him hanging there, helpless as a squirming maggot on a hook. He could almost hear their laughter; feel the slash of shell and the burn of fire - for they would surely take delight in seeing his pale skin pucker and blister.

"Oh sweet Jesu, don't let it happen like this, give me strength to free myself! Give me the strength to get to the water!"

Tyrell realised then that the pain he was going through was akin to that experienced long ago by the one he begged salvation from, but he took no succour from it. Instead, the resolve to somehow tear himself free grew. Again he braced himself, filling his breast to bursting. After three... One... Two... Something stayed him, made the hair all over his body prickle. That sickly stench of bear's grease and woodsmoke had invaded his lungs. It was the Devil's own breath.

There had been no sound, but they were here. He felt the presence of many. He knew that a multitude of eyes bore into his back. And then he heard the malevolent chuckle, almost felt the hiss on the nape of his neck. He knew he recognised that mocking laugh, but before he could turn, a finger rudely jabbed his right shoulder, causing him to lurch and send a further wave of pain coursing through his body. Again, the finger jabbed. This time the finger-nail was twisted into his skin, and the unmistakable chuckle uttered once more. Tyrell turned then. He had not wanted to, but his reflex demanded it. He felt the scream growing deep within him, but before it erupted, he glimpsed the painted bodies pouring over the ridge; and as his head turned further round, he saw the leering face of the one called Wadawagwa.

The scream started then, as if something deep within had finally snapped. Mathew Tyrell was now a falling man, falling deep into the bowels of hell. A crashing blow caught the side of his head, sending him slamming face first into the tree, rough bark gagging the scream. His own scream had been stolen, eclipsed by the roar of the pressing multitude. The pain in his arm caused him to attempt to rise. He caught the shimmer of bodies hurtling past, and then he was falling into blackness once more.

CHAPTER 23

In the Company of the Guard

"What's your 'urry, my babby?"

Simon felt the power of the great meaty hand as it slammed onto his right shoulder, and froze. The one thing he had dreaded, the one thing he had lately grown careless of, was now happening. He had been recognised and was being arrested. Without turning to see who apprehended him, Simon strained to dash forward and somehow lose himself in the dwindling crowd, but a tweak of the giant thumb and forefinger alone held him steady.

"'old on now! 'old your 'orses."

He thought he recognised the voice as belonging to one of the original guards who had chased him all those weeks back. He was done for. Soon to be dangling himself, like the pair he had seen 'turned-off' less than an hour ago.

He had not wanted to come to the hanging, but the woodcarver had insisted he go, even forcing him into helping to sell the remaining crucifixes. He had, after all, received a cot and bowl of porridge thanks to him. Much to his surprise, the woodcarver had been right. Business had been brisk, and in his sweaty fist Simon still held the four coppers the old man had given him as commission. Simon bade the man goodbye and the man had seemed surprised and a little hurt at the termination of their union. He wished now that he had not been so hasty in leaving the woodcarver's company.

"There's someone as wants a word wiv you," the voice boomed in his ear. "Someone important, someone who don't like to be kept waiting."

The hand steered him round so that he was face to face with its owner. He had been right. It was one of the original guards. The man smirked and gave an exaggerated wink. Goddamn! thought Simon. It had all been going too well. There had not been a second glance from the guards at the gate, and one shake of the woodcarver's stave had sent the two decrepit Eremites scurrying back to the shadows. He had even received a passing nod and 'how are you?' from an older seaman he knew - the man not displaying any hint that he was acknowledging a wanted murderer. He had all but convinced himself that it had all been a bad dream, but now before him appeared proof that he was about to enter a living nightmare.

"Would you be so kind as to walk this way, my sailor babby?"

Simon felt his knees turn to jelly. He was dimly aware of faces in the crowd turning to stare as the man nudged him forward. Across High Cross square they went, heading towards Corn Street, the man, purposely it seemed, steering him close to the gallows. There was still a large number of people in the square. They all seemed to be either laughing or stuffing their faces with some titbit or other. Simon remembered how the mass tension and excitement dissolved the moment the two men stopped kicking. It seemed that everyone had a quip at the ready. Though noisier, the crowd had thinned considerably, with nothing like the earlier press of bodies. Simon and the guard easily threaded their way through, coming to a halt no more than twenty feet from the ladders.

Not wanting to look up, Simon could nevertheless not help seeing the dangling feet. Both men had kicked loose a shoe in their terrible dance. A wave of pity engulfed him, quickly turning to dread at the double twitch of Sergeant White's exposed big toe. Surely not still alive after all this time? Nothing could stop him from looking up at the two faces.

"Ha! I wondered 'ow long you could resist afore lookin' up."

The great hand momentarily released its grip of Simon's shoulder to give a great, playful slap on his back, before announcing its return with a vicious tweak. Simon squirmed, squeezed his eyes tight, to block out both the pain and the sight of the contorted faces, but could not help himself opening them again.

"Ol' Sergeant White up there don't look 'appy, do 'e, my babby? But then, 'snot surprizin', 'e weren't a very 'appy man at the best o' times. And as for Customhouse Keeper Rudkin up there aside 'im, well 'e were every bit as objectionable if you ask me. So good riddance, is wha' I says."

And with that the man spat into the straw at the foot of the gallows. The hand remained on Simon's shoulder, but instead of the iron grip, it now turned into a constant succession of friendly pats. Simon was more confused than ever.

"That's enough o' that. Come on now, lad, best not keep him waiting."

"Who be 'e, then?" Simon croaked, struggling to find his voice. "Where you takin' me?"

"Just come on an' you'll find out." The iron grip returned and away from the two wafting corpses they went.

"Over there. Look! Over there 'e is. Look! 'im on the 'orse."

Simon looked over the almost empty part of the square leading towards Corn Street, and there on a sleek, black horse, sat a finely dressed, though portly figure of considerable import. Simon saw too that the horse was being steadied by another figure attired in servant's clothes of blue and white stripes. The man who held him was dressed in the same coloured livery. Simon stopped dead in his tracks.

"God's wounds! Wha' now?" growled the man.

Simon looked him up and down.

"You be no guard no more. Do you?"

"Not on your life, my babby. I 'ad enough o' that lark chasin' 'arter the likes of you."

"But, but I..."

"No, Whitey 'ad me flung out o' the force so 'e did. It were the biggest mistake 'e ever made, cause I 'eard 'im braggin about wha' 'e'd done to Roberts. And where the body was put... Well parts of it, tha' is."

"So you don't be takin' me off to no dungeon?" blurted Simon at last.

"Good 'eavans no! Wha'ever gave you tha' idea? We got someone else for tha' job arter you got clean away. Someone wha' deserved it an all."

"Wha'? You mean I aint no wanted murderer?"

The man looked down at Simon, as if he were stupid for even asking.

"Hang about. You mean to say I been in the woods wiv all they cutroats an' lepers for nuffing?"

"We aint got time for all this. Come on now."

"Well then, where be you takin' me? An' who be 'e on the 'orse?"

"The Customs Collector, Master Thomas Croft, of course. 'E be my master now. An a good one too. It were 'e wha' spied you in the crowd and told me to come an get you. Not to lose you under any circumstances. 'e said sumfing about owin' you a debt of gratitude."

"Wha' me?"

"Yes, sumfing to do wiv a cloak and seagull shite. Now 'urry along, I just felt a spot o' rain, an' I don't want t' get me new suit wet, do I?."

His swollen eyes swept the observation room in the Customs House as if for the first time, even though he had moaned, paced and sat therein for the best part of an hour. He gazed across at the smiling face of Thomas Croft and smiled sheepishly in return. There would be no weeping in the presence of the great man. Outside, rain was beginning to drum against the window. Croft came closer and opened his hand. On the outspread palm glowed a fist-sized orange ball. He walked to the table, placed the orange ball on a silver platter, then taking up a knife, cut it into four segments. Without saying a word, he gave one of the pieces to Simon.

"No sir, I know 'e ain't dead."

Simon bit into the quartered orange ball. Even his deep grief could not undo the pleasure of the sweet, sharp nectar. It was the first such fruit he had ever tasted, and the juice, like surrogate tears, ran freely down his chin. Opening a hand to display the crumpled kerchief he had been given, he wiped away the juice and loudly blew his nose one more time.

"Well Simon, is that not a little better? No, don't eat the skin, lad. Whenever I myself feel a little vexed or anxious, I find the very zest of an orange revives wonderfully. Is that not so, my boy?"

He took a quarter of the fruit himself, breathed deep, then after consuming it, handed Simon one more piece.

"Yes sir."

He sniffed and once more squeezed the kerchief in his fist into a ball, determined, despite the dread information, not to weep in the presence of Thomas Croft. He had been alone in the great man's company for less than an hour and in that time he had learned of the loss of the Swallow and with it his brother Mathew.

"Forgive me, sir, but I just don' feel he be dead. Not in my 'eart I don't."

"Well Simon, I've told you all I know. As I said before, Master Spycer found the wreck, by the grace of God, and on the shore were all the er... er remains."

"Yes sir, I knows sir an' thank you, but I just don' feels it in my 'eart. You said yoursel' that 'e couldn't account for all the bodies."

"Very well, I see you will not be satisfied by my word alone."

Sensing Croft's irritation at being questioned, Simon made a move to apologise, but was silenced by Croft's raised hand.

"No, my boy, you are quite right. He was your only brother and something tells you that he was not slain, but lives yet. I will not gainsay that. Maybe it's the voice of God himself? Well now, what I propose is that when the Cornucopia returns and it should be within the week - she's only sailed to Lisbon after all - I summon Master Spycer and his boatswain here and they can tell you personally. Maybe there is something more to learn. But in the meantime, I want you to carefully consider my other offer."

'What does he want?' wondered Simon. The last time he had seen Thomas Croft, he had not been acknowledged, simply brushed aside by one of his men. Yet now this important man wanted to become Simon's benefactor. The youth could not help but feel suspicious. He was dizzy with the speed of events and the extreme emotions he experienced, elation at his salvation and sorrow at the apparent loss of his brother. On top of all this, he was expected to make a decision that on the face of it almost amounted to adoption.

"Well sir, about this readin' an' writin' stuff sir? Don' get me wrong, I knows it be a good idea, but it took our Mathew nigh on three year to master. An' 'e always said it were done mostly by bein' beaten into 'im like."

"There'll be no beating. For pity's sake, just think of the

doors that'll be opened once you accomplish it. Do you appreciate what is on offer here?"

"Yes sir, but three year. I'd be a full seaman by then, an' tha' be all I wants to be."

"Yes my boy, you'd know all the fancy knots, every inch of rigging, but your fingers would always reek of fish guts, you'd never get your hands on an astrolabe, unless it were to polish it. You would never make Master. Mathew would have done, and you owe it to his memory to try!"

"But sir, he aint dead, I knows it. An' sides, if I can get myself onboard one o' they stockfish ships, well sir, I might get to 'ear somefing."

"Look here now. And this, mark you, is my last word on it. You give me two years - two, not three, mind - two years of hard study, maps n' charts as well as books and then I'll guarantee you a place onboard one of my ships. In the meantime, if any word of your brother reaches me, you shall be the first to hear of it. And if, God willing, it is discovered that he still lives, then I shall do all in my power to find him and bring him back. I give you my word. Now, what say you to that?"

Simon Tyrell raised the piece of orange to his nose and after breathing deeply, sucked at the juice. Nothing in his life had ever tasted so good. Despite his initial reticence, the thought of fine new garments to wear, a fine feather bed, white bread and above all, the promise of more oranges - he knew that he would say 'Yes'.

"Yes sir, Master Croft, I'll give it a go. But one fing I 'ave to know. Why me? I mean, it don' 'ardly seem right, you doin' all this on account me jus' cleaning bird's doin's off of your cloak."

Thomas Croft fingered the light stubble of his chin. Why was he so intent on dragging this youth out of the bilge and putting him firmly in the helmsman's castle? True, something in the lad's honest face appealed, but there had to be more to it than that. Was it simply because it lay within his power to do so? To perform this apparent good deed would certainly confirm this power.

"Well now, my boy, I don't fully understand it myself. It had something to do with spying you in the crowd and thinking you dead. You see, I'd already made up my mind to do something for yourself and Mathew. I wasn't sure why or what. But suffice it to say that, that day on the Swallow's maiden voyage was a very special day for me. So, don't you see? When the Swallow was subsequently wrecked, I naturally assumed that you and Mathew had both perished. You see, by some strange error, your name was included in the ship's list. And when the Cornucopia returned, one of the items retrieved was a red, woollen hat. Of course, I took it to be yours."

Simon scratched his head, then brushing a lock of hair from his eyes, got up and shuffled over to the window. Outside it was beginning to pour with rain, and the pane revealed little more than a dull grey light. He was glad not to be out in it, glad for the promise of a roof over his head. He thought of the two hanging men, they would be sodden now, dripping into the mud and straw beneath them. He shivered briefly, then licked at the piece of orange once more.

"No sir, I lost my own hat a while back. In a game of football."

CHAPTER 24
Death and Redemption

With a loud gasp, Mathew Tyrell was jolted awake, all senses in a whirl of confusion and pain. The rumble of a loud boom was engulfed, then forgotten in the squall of a thousand imagined seagulls. Had he fallen from the rigging? There was a mainmast pointing to the midday sun. Where was he? The deck suddenly stopped its lolloping, becoming instead the hard, earthy slope, and images from a different world came crashing back.

It took a while before realizing that, indeed, he was laying on his back staring at the sun through the broken branches of a dead spruce. What was happening? Why did his arm hurt so? He fought to remember, managed to sit upright and after squinting all around, his focus returned and with it his memory began to stir. There before him stood the blood-splattered tree that had held him in such cruel custody. However, someone had taken the trouble to release him and withdraw the arrows from his hand and arm. Would such a thing be done for a prisoner, one marked for torture? Maybe so. He examined the bark and moss bandage. Would those intent on doing him hurt have gone to such trouble? The arm throbbed with a dull pain and was much swollen. He could barely close his throbbing fingers. And what about that bastard Big-Ears... Wada-goddamn-wagwa? A shudder engulfed him as the image of the leering face returned.

Aagh! Bastard clouted me. Must have... Lump the size of a pigeon's egg... What was his part in all this?. Tyrell shuddered again and attempted to get to his feet.

There were no seagull cries now, never had been, other than deep within another memory. It had been the continuous shrieking of crueler throats. A battle was going on down below. There was no mistaking the din of war. The roar and clatter of hand to hand fighting began to permeate his consciousness. Tidesso and the six remaining warriors could not produce such a noise alone. Any close combat would simply annihilate them in a few moments. No, this was the clash of two larger forces.

Tyrell peered through the trees, his eyes trying to focus as, barely fifty paces away, the dashing colours of fighting men crashed, enmeshed, withdrew, then crashed together again. It was nigh impossible to see how his companions fared. All below was a screaming mass of stabbing, slashing and banging. At one point he thought he saw Managnon hurled aloft as if attempting to fly, but he blinked and the figure was lost in the melee.

Despite the din, a rustling sound over to the right sent him rigid with fear again. From behind one of the trees appeared an armed, painted figure. The figure advanced swiftly, a bow in one hand, a club swinging from the other. With much effort, Tyrell made a feeble fist and waited. Only when the figure had come to within six feet, did Tyrell realize that he was confronted with an adolescent savage of not much more than a dozen years of age. Not even the fiercest face-paint or stiffened scalp-lock could conceal the fact. Even so, the young tribesman was tall, as tall as himself. Tyrell forced a smile, receiving the briefest flash of white teeth beneath the firm, set lips in return. Then the mask hardened, causing Tyrell to take a step backwards. The youth raised his arm. There was a resultant sloshing of liquid. Tyrell was much relieved to see that it was not a club that was brandished after all, but rather a long leather water flask. Tyrell now took two steps forward, and greedily snatching the bag with his left hand, emptied the contents down his throat and onto his face and breast - only in the doldrums had he known such thirst. He stood there swaying, content to let the spilled water trickle beneath his shirt and breeches. Not even the throbbing pain of his arm or the sound of battle could dampen the feelings of relief that were beginning to engulf him.

Even though he had never seen this youth before, there was a familiarity about his physical stamp, about the hard, black eyes set in a wide-boned face, the clay-encrusted hair lock, buckskin breech-clout, black and red paint. The wide, flat bow and the duck-fletched arrows peeping over his left shoulder confirmed it. Here was a fellow kinsman to Tidesso and the others. Here was a fledgling Pennacook warrior. Of course, now he understood. It had not been the enemy that had surprised him, but Pennacooks, come across the river - and not a moment too soon. Wadawagwa must have gone ahead to warn them. God bless the big-eared bastard. This was better, much better than he had hoped for.

"Oh sweet Christ. Jesus, Jesus. Saved!... We're saved!"

He was pounding the earth with a foot, humming tunelessly and chuckling. This time it was the turn of the youth to step back. Tyrell wanted to thank him, hug him, but the youth had abruptly turned away, his eyes anxiously scanning the slope. A hand was raised demanding silence. Tyrell swallowed the protest and indignation he felt at being censured by a mere boy, no matter how big. But when the youth crouched low behind the same bloodstained tree, nocked an arrow, and trained it down the slope, it dawned on Tyrell that with his right arm out of action, he was near helpless and his life could depend on the actions of this mere boy.

Only moments later the slope became alive with figures dashing in frantic retreat. Tyrell peered down to see a body of enemy tribesmen hurtling in a diagonal course through the trees below, the shafts of sunlight bouncing off their stick armour and glistening copper skin. Grim-faced, fearful, panting hard, they were obviously in rout, heading for the end of the island to take their chances with the current. Tyrell grunted with encouragement as the gleeful youth began sending arrow after arrow into the mass. Then, in horror, he watched a handful of the enemy break off from this body and come charging up the slope towards them. The youth screamed defiantly, but when it became apparent that he had only three remaining shafts, he turned to Tyrell and Tyrell saw a child's fear. It seemed that the youth had suddenly become frozen, unable to shoot even these shafts, only able to stare ahead and accept the inevitable fate. Tyrell began to berate the youth and readied himself for a dash.

"You pea-brained fool! Don't just stand there! Get an arrow! Do something, for Christ's sake!"

The youth turned his face skyward and struck up a reedy doleful chant. The four enemy warriors, unable to resist such easy prey, rushed up to within thirty paces, when suddenly a deafening roar from the trees to their right made them stop, turn, then race off in the direction of their retreating comrades.

A high-pitched whoop in Tyrell's right ear indicated that the youth, having abandoned his last prayer, resumed his ill-fitting mantle of courage, and lost no time in sending the last shafts winging after the enemy. Tyrell saw one of the enemy clutch at his back, then go tumbling down. Two of the others stopped, attempted to lift him, but seeing the proximity of the pursuing Pennacooks, were forced to drop the unfortunate man and down the slope he slithered. The youth gave such a howl of glee that Tyrell's teeth were set on edge and then he was gone, whooping, hurtling down to the fallen warrior in an effort to claim his prize before others beat him to it. Knowing full well what grisly trophy the exultant youth was intent on claiming, Tyrell set a course back down the slope away from his cackle, but before he had got half way, the exultant youth was beside him again, chattering, dangling the slippery hair under his nose, acting as if he expected Tyrell to lavish praise upon him. It became apparent to him then that the youth had been assigned to guard his person. Tyrell wanted rid of this overgrown child who had begun to remind him of Tom Black, a bully boy from his own childhood, one who had taken great delight in tearing small animals limb from limb - one who now made his gelt from tormenting poor souls in the Bristol Castle dungeon. He felt an overriding desire to cuff the youth about the ear, to kick his arse and send him sprawling.

But then they were no longer alone and the boy was gone, lost in the greasy press of panting tribesmen. He knew them to be Pennacooks, but what did they make of him? Their black eyes revealed nothing other than the excitement of their victory. Bloody fingers began to probe his hair and skin, some deliberately pressing his wounded arm. Tyrell flinched, but did not let himself cry out. He was reminded of that first group that had jostled him and poor Dodds by the beach. But there he had been shackled by his own fear. Now it would be different. For the time being, all fear had been squeezed from his body.

Indicating with a sweep of his left hand that he wanted to walk forward, the surrounding circle, much to his amazement, parted, taking their places behind and either side of him, silently following when he moved forward down the remainder of the slope. From the corner of his eye he noticed the raw and mangled remains of the recent butchery. Everywhere the grass, the rocks, the trees, was splattered with blood and gore. Bloated flies smacked against his skin, but onward he strode, across the short distance to the edge.

The moment he beheld the shattered matchlock, the memory of a loud, disembodied boom came echoing back. Tidesso must have loaded and fired it himself. Too much powder, barrel's peeled back like a peapod... Or had he found and attempted to load that last ball? It would have been a tight fit at the best of times. If he hadn't succeeded in placing it fully home, it could have had this effect. How could he have known? Tyrell thought anxiously. Where was Tidesso? Where was he? A sickening feeling grew within. He spied the cleft rock that they had both defended, it now shone a sinister red; and in the dirt, the stain of a large, congealed puddle still remained. From this slop of maroon, Tyrell noticed twin, parallel lines, indicating that someone had been dragged away, their bloodied heels marking the trail. Was it Tidesso? He felt his stomach tighten. Again the throng had begun to press close, always the black eyes observing every move he made. Anxiously he searched the faces for one who might have exhibited a degree of authority, but these were all young men, seemingly more interested in sizing up this stranger, than volunteering information or assistance .

"Tidesso... Tidesso!

He croaked out the name. The faces stared back uncomprehending. Tyrell cleared his throat and slowly repeated the name, emphasising the first syllable.

"Tid-esso...Ti-."

This time his upper arms were firmly grasped, and through the crowd he was steered by two of the tribesman. Over to a group of huddled figures he was taken, the sound of low chanting greeting his approach. Off to the side of this group he noticed four shrouded bodies and quickly turned his head away. A supine figure jerked and moaned in the midst of the group. Straightway he recognised who the protruding legs that flexed and twitched belonged to; and a great emptiness engulfed his body. Here was Tidesso. There was no doubt about it. The grip on Tyrell's arms was released. He sank to his knees and crawled forward.

The huddled group was comprised of older men. A thickening around each greased belly indicated this much, yet even though they exuded an imagined semblance of acumen and solidity absent in the young men, Tyrell could not help noticing the fresh, slimy trophies of hair that most appeared to have tucked in their girdles. Two of the group moved aside, affording Tyrell a clear view. What he saw made his good hand rise to cover his mouth. The cry was stifled, but the eyes instantly filled with tears. Was this really the remains of a human face he beheld and not the remains of some fly-blown, over-ripe fruit?

Turning away, he breathed deeply, and holding the breath, steeled himself to look again. The tongue and bottom jaw had gone completely, leaving the throat exposed where the faintest sound of life rattled and bubbled. Grabbing the hand of what was once Tidesso, Tyrell felt the faintest twinge of pressure against his own. A single eye looked deep into his. Tyrell held the gaze, hoping that somehow his depth of sorrow would be communicated, but the eye seemed to burrow deep into his very soul. Was there anger, reproach? Did this savage, heathen man blame him for this calamity? How was he to know that Tidesso would try to load and fire the cursed gun?

It was not the tears alone that forced Tyrell to look away. He knew before his sight had cleared sufficiently for him to look again that the thread between them had been severed. The hand was limp in his own, and even though he met the stare, the single eye was fixed on a point far, far away.

The silence was shattered, no sooner had the last breath departed the broken body. One of the group of older warriors stood erect and commenced a wailing chant, starting with a single, high-pitched note that seemed to glide, then swoop low like an angry hawk. The remainder of the group also got to their feet. One of them, Tyrell was not sure which one, had closed the eye of Tidesso. He turned away then, not wishing to gaze on the destroyed face a moment longer lest his memory always be tainted by the image. The loss of this savage captain, who had been instrumental in his own capture and removal, the death of all his ship mates, and one he had been unable to communicate with in anything remotely approaching a conversation, was greater than he imagined possible.

From the harsh laughter that wafted over from the younger warriors, he guessed they were already rehearsing their bragging speeches, each feeling uniquely invincible at having looked death in the eye and possessing medicine strong enough to turn it aside. Tyrell felt it too. He was greatly saddened by the passing of Tidesso, but the appreciation of his own deliverance was beginning to outweigh the sorrow. Like everyone here, he was glad to be alive - glad to have come through.

More triumphant calls from over the island's ridge announced the return of those who had pursued the enemy. Down through the trees they hurtled, waving their scalp-tangled spears and bows high above their heads. In their wake, dragged along by halters of rawhide, came a handful of dejected captives. Down into a choking heap they were dragged, to be set upon and beaten. Tyrell was howling and jeering too, though he was unaware of it. For these captives he felt not an ounce of pity. His eyes searched the ground for something to beat them with, but as he knelt down to pick up a broken spear shaft, the anger evaporated, and a great weariness engulfed him. Where did he fit in all this? Was he not himself a captive? Was there anyone left to intercede on his behalf? What was his own life worth, now that the gun had been destroyed and, worse still, had been responsible for the death of one of their own?

Picking up the spear shaft, he used it to steady himself and watch, not daring to let the feelings of wretchedness and despair overtake him. That would be the end of him. A sign of weakness would render him truly useless to these wild tribesmen. He had come thus far; he had to survive.

From the corner of his eye he saw one of the older warriors run forward and begin haranguing the younger ones. The more extreme torment of the captives ceased. Suddenly all became respectfully quiet as the bound body of the slain Tidesso was borne aloft.

He needed a familiar face. Surely they were not all slain? Where was Big-Ears? Tyrell had looked for him, not wanting to admit it, but realizing now that his life had been saved by the actions of that tribesman. Again he scanned the battleground, the scattered enemy dead that littered the slope, each corpse bristling with arrows like preening hedgehogs; feeling nothing at the sight of a reddened crow flapping out of a gaping torso, a shiny snake of gut trailing from behind.

The lesser numbers of Pennacook dead were laid in shrouded rows. The 'victorious quick' were still too exultant to mourn their passing - that would come later. Under the shade of trees the main group of wounded were huddled together. Two of these were sat apart leant against a boulder. Though the gestures of each were laboured, Tyrell saw that they were able enough to converse; a water skin was passed between them. He recognised them both. One was Big-Ears, and much to his relief, when the empty bladder was cast aside, the drawn features of Managnon were revealed. It appeared that of the ones that stayed behind, he and Managnon were the only survivors.

Tyrell relinquished the spear-shaft, picking up an empty water skin in its place, then walking from the bustling scene, he went down to the waterside, and after drinking his fill, he submerged the vessel, made his way back up the bank, the filled skin knocking against his shins. They both seemed pleased to see him, briefly nodding with gratitude as the bladder was offered and accepted. Through laboured breath Managnon stared to say something, but remembering that Tyrell did not understand the tongue of the people, shrugged and addressed the words instead to Wadawagwa. Tyrell swatted at the flies, shuffled his feet, feeling stupid and embarrassed that he could understand so little. Eventually, it was Wadawagwa who managed to bridge the gap in communication by pointing to Tyrell's wounds. He mimed a man screaming with pain, then mimed the scream being brought to an abrupt halt by a knock on the head. Tyrell found himself rubbing the back of his head and laughing nervously. Wadawagwa briefly lifted his club, pointed to it and began to chuckle himself. The effort made him wince, though he tried to pass it off as a dry throat. Tyrell noticed his eyes were very bloodshot, as if a fire raged behind them. With much difficulty, both he and Managnon dragged each other to something resembling a standing position, and were proudly pointing out their wounds, chuckling as they did so. Suddenly, as if part of the mime, Wadawagwa growled, dropped the club, stared at his own empty hand, then pitched forward. Tyrell rushed to catch him, nearly collapsing under the weight, and, in the process, starting the blood flowing from his own wound. He knew then, the moment he made contact with the fallen man, that he was dead. A stunned Tyrell let the body down as gently as he was able; but as the head lolled forwards, and the tail of the scalp-lock fell aside, he saw the neat hole of exposed bone and clotted blood, where a club spike had pierced the skull. This was the one wound Big-Ears had not pointed out. The wound that had eventually killed him.

Tyrell looked up at Managnon, wondering if he would be next to collapse, but instead Managnon gained his full height and raising his face skywards, began a triumphant chant, his glistening chest heaving with the strain. Soon they were both surrounded by tribesmen. Once again hands were reaching out to tug and turn him this way and that, and then, like a dream-walker, Tyrell was being led away up the slope by the same, overgrown boy who had watched over him earlier. And in his ears the chant of Managnon resounded, even haunting him midstream as he huddled exhausted in the prow of a bark boat and trailed his swollen fingers in the cold, swift water of the river.

CHAPTER 25
Mkazas

The crow flapped her insolent way across the river, the small feathers of her head still crowned with tiny jewels of blood. She had supped well on the carrion of the two-legged ones, but as always when they were close, she had been obliged to leave the choicest morsels and take to the skies. She saw that directly below her was a big fish on the back of which rode more of the twolegs. These ones were alive, moving, splashing. Today these twolegs were everywhere making their noise.

In disgust, she shat and climbed higher, until the big fish-shape was a forgotten minnow. In the climbing it was all forgotten. Even the recent feasting was wiped clean from her memory, as, for the time being, was hunger. But she was forever driven to this restless flight, attracted to the course of a glittering tributary with no less curiosity in her bones than any creature that breathed, for all that glittered was truly irresistible.

Over the sward-like green of the trees she flew, away from the main river, always with the smaller watercourse in view, mindful of its meanderings, but steering a straight line, looking, looking, always looking, above and below.

Hardly had she left the main water-course than hunger stirred within her once again, and down towards the water she glided, turning once to torment an ungainly heron with her vicious grace, as it dared to lumber through the margins of her range. Although contemptuous of the heron's laboured flight, she was wary of that stiletto beak, jealous of its ability to pluck fish from the shallows faster than she could blink. That was something she could never do. Fish glittered and fish were good to eat.

A great heart was beating in the wide clearing below. The twolegs were making noise again in their upturned nests of sticks and bark. A triumphal chorus ruffled her ear feathers. This was a different noise, not the squawk of conflict, but the melodious sound of celebration. She too felt the promise of success, knowing that it lay in the beckoning rows of yellow sweetness that surrounded the smoky nests. There was fear, too. With the twolegs there was always fear, for though they were earthbound, they were unpredictable creatures; and they would try to frighten her away from the rows. But they would not kill her. They would have the power to kill most other creatures, with the sharp beaks that flew from their flightless wings. She had watched them do it often and been glad of their leavings. But they would not kill her. Was it not Mkazas the crow that had carried to them the gift of the yellow sweetness? But, of course, she could not possibly know that.

EPILOGUE
Dreams of Sleeping Bears

It is nearing the end of February, the Snow-Blind Moon. A dozen years have run their course. Many generations of crows have criss-crossed the skies above the tree-bark town of the people. And many of the people boldly strode through the palisade gates, never to return. Old war-captains have stumbled as old wounds they thought long since healed have finally demanded due attention. And as they have learned to sit closer to the hearth coals and embrace a different perspective, others have rushed forward to take their place on the war trail. For life murmurs on, in spite of this newly assumed wisdom. So goes the song. For the song of war is the most vibrant of sounds; more so than the song to conjure the moose or the bear, or even to give thanks for the ripe corn. And there are always new rhymes to add and new throats eager to join in singing. But this being the end of the Snow-Blind Moon, and soon to be the Bear-Waking Moon, there is little talk of war, and the young men bide their time, set aside their untried war arrows and try to guess which one will fly truest, which barb will bite deepest.

There is always the majority amongst men who, in their prime of life, hold sorrow and joy to be equal guests in their lodges. One, they will court and eagerly clear space for by the hearth-side; the other will come unannounced, demanding all the warmth and turn the heart to ice in thanks. Haii Yaii! Let none say to their faces that they hold back or shirk in any way, for the opposite is true. These significant men are not yet ready to gather up all their tales and trophies, for there are more to be gained, though they know it will be accomplished more by cool cunning than by hot-blooded passion.

"This one is a friend."

The voice outside the bark lodge was familiar.

"Truly I am your friend."

Curly had eagerly uttered the required rejoinder to the greeting and squinted a smile as the mat covering the low entrance was raised. A stooped, fur-clad figure waddled forward. The blinding white of snow caused Curly to shield his eyes. The kiss of a few snowflakes made it through the fire's spiralling smoke to lightly anoint the back of his hand and the mat fell back, returning the wigwam to its usual smoky murk. Outside it was so bitter that, but for a small chink, even the smoke flap had been pulled tight. In the past four nights it had been so cold that trees had exploded down by the lakeside, causing him to imagine the guns of ghost ships being fired in his sleep, but then this had happened nearly every winter. Curly knew better than to wake or dwell on it. He had long resigned himself to having dreams peopled with faces and events from his past life. At first, it had filled him with such a yearning to return - if not across the Ocean Sea , maybe somehow to step back into the dream - that he thought he would perish or go mad from the pain of it. But then one day he surprised himself by telling a jest to some of the menfolk. It was not until they had all stopped laughing that he realised that not only was he conversing fluently, but also thinking in the language of these once strange people. From that point on, he began to divest himself of the unwanted baggage that his previous life had heaped upon him and began to cherish the advantages this new life offered. These were his people now.

Their constraints and taboos had seeped into his pores like the songs, the smoke, the vivid colours and the lice. They were now his code, as were the inherent freedoms. And there were more freedoms now than ever there had been in his old life. Why, even the great Sequasis, who was calculated to be over a hundred years of age, regularly summoned him to the great wigwam to sup sagamite. No such honour from one of corresponding importance would have been bestowed upon him in England.

"It gladdens my heart to see you, Managnon." He bade his guest sit opposite. "Take off your mittens and take some soup with me, it is thin enough to peer through, but there are a few pieces of squirrel meat floating in it somewhere. Maybe you will be lucky and land a piece."

Managnon blew air through his fingers, held them momentarily over the steaming rim of the earthenware cooking pot, then, when they were sufficiently warmed, into the broth he dipped a wooden bowl and with a clamshell scoop began to slurp the greasy liquid.

"Hi Yi! I see you have discovered some meat?"

"My son says that his blunts took them, but they were so thin I think they offered themselves for the soup just to be warm. Attitash was good enough to cook them for us...She has been very attentive."

Managnon chuckled, and obscuring his face with the bowl, drank it dry.

"Take more."

Managnon held up his hand and nodded.

"More will make me sleepy, Nammos."

Managnon addressed Curly by his more formal name, "Nammos the fishcatcher". He had long ceased to think of himself as Mathew Tyrell.

"It is for men to stay awake whilst other creatures sleep. Unless, of course, they wish to dream for waking guidance."

A long silence ensued. Finally Managnon spoke again.

"I have dreamed of where a bear sleeps. A big one, plenty of sweet fat for all. Do you want to come?"

Curly's heart leapt. To dream of a kill's whereabouts was still beyond his comprehension. At first he had dismissed it as sorcery, but in the many winters he had dwelt with the people and tasted bitter hunger, that same hunger had been assuaged by the yield of such dreams. He cleared his throat to speak, trying at the same time not to appear too eager.

"I will come gladly. I have mourned my woman's death sufficiently. She would want me to help get a bear. I'll burn some of its fat in her honour."

"You have good, snow moccasins. I know this because you won my best ones from me. What about your stout lance? Ah yes, I see you have it still."

Curly grunted and began to retrieve the lance from under the raised sleeping platform. To reach the blade, the end of the shaft had to be manoeuvred past Managnon and under the entrance mat. The ensuing chink of light glistened off the iron point. Curly examined the blade for rust, rubbing his finger along the greased metal of what was once part of a gun barrel. Managnon reached across and nodding with satisfaction, patted the lance.

"Good. Yes, this lance will come in handy. I wish I still had mine. There's little chance of the point breaking off. Any bear would appreciate the beauty of it. Yes, how I regret throwing my lance at that Etechimin. You would think he would have the good manners to throw it back instead of running away with it."

"When do we go?" asked Curly, chuckling at the memory of the past encounter.

"This snowfall is light. It will die off soon and the coming days will be good. I will go and gather the others. Mikshish and Sabatis, as you know, are good, dependable hunters. I will come and call you in the first light of the new day."

"This is good. I'll be ready."

Curly watched Managnon leave the lodge, and then, standing fully erect, stretched his arms to open the smoke flap further. He blinked at the flood of light, once again feeling snowflakes fall on his cheeks and eyelashes. Visibility in the dome-shaped bark lodge was much improved. He located his bow and quiver and the rush basket, where his mooseskin shirt and cape of beaverskin were neatly folded. Swiftly peeling off the reeking skins of mourning, naked save for a breech-clout, he ventured outside, and grabbing handfuls of fresh snow began to rub his body down. From the surrounding lodges he was greeted by the rhythmic pulse of maize kernels being pounded. With a wild yelp, he jumped high in the air and to the accompanying tattoo began to improvise a song in the fashion of his adopted people, although the words were in English.

"Hiyiii! Tell me who gives a hoot
That I'm clothed in nought but soot!"

He scrubbed and scraped as he sang, yelping and prancing round the wigwam.

"Hiyiii! Though none may give a damn
Once I was a Bristol man
Once I was a Bristol man."

The pounding stopped. Coming to an abrupt halt, he quickly scanned the Pennacook town. The central longhouse where, over the continuous passing of smoky pipes, all the important tribal business was conducted. Clustered around it, the domed wigwams - of which there were over fifty - spread out across the large, palisaded compound like the up-turned eggs of some great, mythical serpent, waiting for a more propitious moment to hatch forth their occupants. How snug

379

it all appeared in its coverlet of white, the individual threads of smoke disappearing skyward.

In the corner of his eye he noticed entrance mats being pulled aside to see what all the noise was about. None censured his outburst. One by one the mats fell back into place and the mortar pounding was resumed. Apart from a couple of older women, their backs bent under huge bundles of firewood, only children and dogs appeared to be up and about. He saw his son - named Tidesso, the Bluebird, in honour of the dead war captain - was amongst them, and beckoned him over. The children scampered forward in a laughing huddle. Swiftly he ran round the wigwam and reappeared with an arm full of snowballs. The children shrieked and scattered like goslings, tangling their feet with the yelping dogs as he pelted them. Then when his ammunition was exhausted, the older ones, his son amongst them, advanced and pelted him in return. With teeth chattering he made his retreat.

Back inside the lodge he dried himself and after rubbing his body with bear oil, thankfully pulled on his leggings and shirt. The soft caress of the fur inside swiftly banished the shivering from his body. It was cold out there. He would never be like these true people, seemingly inured to its bite. Maybe he had been foolish to stay out naked in it for as long as he did, but it was too late for regrets. He was starting to feel alive for the first time in ages.

He calculated roughly that it had been nigh on two months since his wife had been slain by the Asagunticook - a month spent trailing her killers almost to the salt sea, but to no avail - two months confined to this hovel. He missed her more than he thought possible, but found comfort that he had mourned her both as a lapsed Christian and an adopted Pennacook. Now though, life's distractions were what he craved - life itself would heal him. It had not been easy, an age spent inside the bark lodge with nought but a lobster claw pipe to suck on, and regurgitated dreams for distraction. Maybe that was the true intention, to imbue the bereaved one with a zest for life through deprivation. It had certainly done that. Two days ago Attitash had relieved some of this deadening abstraction by raising her best doe-skin dress to sit astride his middle and do her best to grind him into the ground. He had done nothing to encourage her, not even taking suck on a proffered breast as it was brushed back and forth across his lips. She had been angry yesterday when he refused to return her advances. This, he surmised, was why the soup was so thin.

"Father, I have heard that you are going with my uncle to get a bear?"

Curly spun around, startled. He had not heard his son enter the wigwam. It seemed that his wife's people were all born with the gift of stealth. Curly envied their oneness with their surroundings. Though he had acquired some of the art of silence, still he was always aware of his comparative clumsiness when abroad in the forest. It seemed to him that only his ability to hit game at a greater distance with his arrows avoided him being a huge embarrassment. In fact, despite his own misgivings, he had become something of a lucky mascot. Whenever he was taken on a hunting trip, it was almost guaranteed to return successfully laden. As well as Curly, another name for him was "Shoots-Far".

Regaining the archer's skill had not taken him long, but although he searched everywhere he went, he never came upon a yew tree. He experimented with many woods, but in the end settled for the hickory wood favoured by the Pennacooks. To their bemusement, he fashioned a heavy longbow in the English style. Although no equal to that special mix of the Yew's sap and heartwood, none of the tribesmen could come close when it came to distance shooting, or for that matter at a target. But when it fell to loosing many shafts in quick succession, or pulling off a shot at a moving animal, however small, he was outclassed. None chose to emulate his method of release, or way of making bows and arrows. Their method had served them well for centuries and would continue to do so. To the people, his was nothing more than a gifted aberration. After all, he had to approach them for his stone points - no matter how hard he tried, the flaking of stone was beyond him. His son had chosen to emulate the true people's way with the bow. Curly was proud of this nonetheless. Though only ten years old, more often than not he could knock a pigeon from the summer sky, or a squirrel scampering along a high branch - the lad was also, under the watchful eye of his grandfather, Tolba, starting to produce the finest stone points.

Curly gazed at the dark, eager eyes set in their almond lids, the chestnut, wavy hair that seemed bent on inexorably turning a little darker each winter, as if any of his own blood passed on to this only child were being slowly purged from his being.

Even before the request was formed, Curly knew that it would be to accompany the bear-hunt. Correspondingly, his own eyes and mouth were already forming the refusal. The child saw this and, in place of the request, issued a sigh of frustration and turned to leave.

"Soon, Tidesso, you will come with me, but not this time... Maybe next winter... You grow so fast. Every time I turn to look at you, you have grown a little taller, but do not be too impatient. It will be at least three more winters and then a summer before they give you the bitter drink and turn you out into the forest to return a man. Before that happens, I will take you on a bear- hunt."

The boy had turned to face his father. As he spoke, his eyes were lowered.

"Plausawa has been with his father on a bear hunt... Natanis has been with his uncles... Most of my clan friends have been. Why am I the last?"

"Plausawa happened to be with his father when a bear cub fell from a tree and blocked their path. Besides, I have spoken!"

Again Tidesso made as if to leave. Curly's voice took on a hard edge.

"Where are you going? Did I say you may leave? Come back and eat some soup."

With lowered head, the boy shuffled over to the bubbling pot, and, dipping in a bowl, began to slurp noisily. Curly knew that he was doing this to annoy him, but let it pass.

"Truly it is not as tasty as the soup your mother made, but nonetheless we should be thankful to Attitash for making it... She might not come again for a while. When I am away, add some corn and beans to it, or even better another squirrel. Oh, and add snow, don't let it boil away."

Curly stopped talking, having noticed tears dripping down the boy's cheeks into his bowl, but even though the eyes glistened, the face was set hard. Why had he mentioned the boy's mother? It was not right to talk of the dead so soon - not the way of these people. It was also not the way of these people to scold their children over virtually anything. No matter how hard he tried, Curly could not be like this. It seemed that he was forever denying his son something. He felt a pang of regret. When the boy's mother was alive, there existed a counterbalance. She would delight in spoiling him. Now it was obvious that this balance had been taken away. Curly thought of himself as Mathew Tyrell once again. He felt a yearning for his own mother, the softness that always lurked behind even the sternest of faces. Did she still live a world away across the 'Ocean Sea ', or had she pined for him, giving him up for dead and herself perished of a broken heart? His own yearning became a red-hot blade, twisted between the short ribs, as both his mother and wife were before him in the most vivid of images. Did this combined apparition signify her passing also? Suddenly weakened, he stumbled to his knees, his face momentarily suspended over the rim of the steaming pot. Opening his eyes, he half expected to see the same image shimmering in the greasy surface of the broth, but all that appeared, apart from the lazy swirl of yellow beads of maize and a single piece of meat, was a fleeting hint of his own wild reflection.

Taking a breath of savoury steam deep into his lungs, he pulled himself away, fingering the long-neglected whiskers that adorned both his cheeks and the side of his head, and with great difficulty he ran the fingertips through his twisted scalp lock - this would not do.

A different image presented itself, this time one that teased a brief chuckle from between the tightly drawn lips. It had been long ago, at the site of the old town - two day's walk further up the big river that flows from the lake. He had not been there long and was still recovering from the wounded arm, fretting about his fate - the nightmare image of the tortured prisoners freshly branded on his mind - when an incident happened, which, though causing him much physical discomfort, went some way to setting his mind to rest. He had been wandering by the riverside to watch the rising fish, when he had been suddenly set upon by a group of women, both young and old. They had stripped him completely naked, cast him in the shallows, and jumped in around him. Though they laughed and chattered, he could not help noticing the mussel shells each one brandished. Had not these same women, armed with blades of shell, only days before coaxed cries of mercy from the mouth of the youngest Paquatuog prisoner as they cut him to shreds?

Were they intent on performing the same hideous task on him also? As he had been pulled spluttering beneath the surface, Curly noticed the growing gathering along the bank and had mistaken laughter for howls for blood.

Another guffaw exploded from Curly's lips as he thought of it again. His son peered tentatively over the rim of his empty bowl, as if loath to lower it fully and be forced to confront the crazy man beyond. Curly recalled going as rigid as a tree trunk when all these hands started setting about him. Apart from his armpits, eyebrows, eyelashes and scalp lock, they plucked every hair from his body. Despite his squeals of protest that he was swallowing half the river, they had held him on the surface and a large, matronly hand had grasped his privates, held him firmly like a tiller, whilst his balls were painfully denuded.

When it was over, they had borne him up onto the bank. All the people lined in two rows, grinning and reaching out to pet him as he had staggered like a child taking its first footsteps. And, in a way, it had been a prelude to a new beginning, for only a day later he was again led into the river as part of the ceremony that announced his adoption into the tribe.

Over the dozen or so years he had lived as one of the true people, he too had learned to love water. Though he had spent much of his old life upon it, he had always viewed it with a terror born of ignorance. Now he thought nothing of slipping beneath the surface to grasp at the silver flanks of fishes. He had also proved himself a fearless warrior. Many times in the intervening years he had been called to spill the blood of other men. Did he not carry still, part of a broken arrowhead in his shoulder, and a chipped elbow joint that ached in this cold weather as reminders of his bravery? In this matter of learning the skills of war there was no choice, for the people's enemies always seemed to outnumber their allies and twice more the Paquatuogs had come against them in force. Both times they had been beaten back, and once he had been a prominent member of a two hundred strong warband going to the very gates of the Paquatuog lair and setting light to their maize fields. They had not returned for over five summers. Instead, the Maquaks and others of the Hodenasaunee confederacy had taken their place as the main protagonists, and almost every spring their warbands would come over the Green mountains to wreak depredations on the true people and their allies. But this was his life now, the saltwater had ebbed from his blood and in its place flowed a oneness with life that only an enemy arrow or tomahawk could gainsay. He knew full well that should he ever find himself back on the deck of a English bound ship, the pull to return to this land and these people would be so great that he would jump overboard and swim back, no matter how far the land.

Lurching suddenly against his sleeping platform, fumbling in the blackness beneath it, Curly retrieved a beaver skin bundle, which was duly unrolled, and onto the floor mat clattered the long knife of Sam Dodds. He gazed at it for an age, then, venturing a finger towards the leather-bound handle, he rolled it towards his knees.

"Do you see this blade, boy? This is the sharpest edge you may ever see in your life. It belonged to Dodds, my uncle. He was of the same clan as me - the Fishtakers."

The boy looked puzzled. There was no such clan among the people.

"I'm talking a long time before you were given life, before I became one of the people. When my name was Tyrell. Mathew Tyrell."

"What does the name mean? Tirl! Tirl!"

The boy tried his best to imitate the sound made by his father. Curly held up his hand, indicating that it was a pointless exercise.

"The name means..." He paused for a long moment conscious of the eagerness in his son's eyes. "It means He-who-steps-from-the-saltwater." He was relieved to see the acceptance in the boy's eyes. "Yes that's what it means. Anyway, when you have drunk the bitter drink and return a man, I will make you a present of this knife. Here, take it in your hands. Does it not feel powerful? Good, well, I will make a trade with you. I'll cover my face with grease and you will scrape all the grease and all the ugly hair away. If you do this well and do not cut me more than er...five times, then you can come with us on this bear hunt - providing of course Managnon agrees. After all, it is he who has dreamed where the bear nests."

His son's face lit up in a smile. "Now I also want to see where you stepped from the saltwater into the life of the people."

Tyrell rolled his eyes and let out a sigh. "First, the bear, boy. Then we'll see."

That night as he slept, Curly also dreamed of the bear. In this dream the other hunters had scattered, but he had stood firm, and his iron-tipped lance had pierced the bear through the heart. In the dream's periphery he was aware of his son being among the group, but when he had called to him, the lad had become Simon his own brother. He awoke knowing that he had called out his brother's name, as if the echo of it still hung in the smoky lodge space. But beside him young Tidesso and his dog slept soundly. All was dark. Outside, nothing stirred. He must have shouted, only in the dream. Why Simon? He looked nothing like Tidesso. He felt guilty, knowing that he hardly ever thought of his younger brother.

'Well Sim, what's up lad? What are you doing now?' he whispered to himself in between yawns. The dog sniffed. He calculated that Simon would now be a full grown man of twenty-eight years. No longer the gawky boy, forever following his every move. Good luck, Sim. God be with you wherever you may roam. Curly found himself mumbling a prayer and once more he was Mathew Tyrell. But before the prayer had ended, his mind was elsewhere, enticed by the memory of the dream. Hi yi, he was going to slay the bear. There was no doubt in his mind.

Managnon led them for two days across the flat pans of frozen lakes, up into the foothills of the great mountains, at times their bandy, snowshoe stride taking them through engulfed forests, where the squint of their soot-banded eyes were level with the treetops. Despite his unflinching effort, the boy Tidesso was always in the rear, but not so far behind that he could not be seen or heard - Curly made sure of that, himself lagging just that little bit behind the others, reaching the campground as the kindling began to crackle, in time to hold out a bowl of hot, chokecherry bark water as the steaming boy waddled in.

Nothing was said. No words of encouragement were given or expected, but on the second day, as Managnon indicated their imminent approach at the bear's sleeping place, the boy was given the iron-tipped lance to carry, lest lurking wolves decided to accompany him.

They camped for the night in a shallow cave, and before the coming of dawn Managnon led them to where he had dreamed of finding the bear.

"Brother, I too dreamed of this very place," Curly whispered.

Managnon nodded, smiling knowingly, but did not say a word. Solemnly they converged on a single, giant spruce. But for the creak of the snow beneath their shoes and the curls of breath, they were as a congregation of ghosts gathered to bless the dawn. They all saw beneath the lumpen snowline where branches had been dragged amongst the roots by the hibernating bear, and with the iron-headed lance the boy indicated the animal's melted breathing hole. Curly lightly touched his son's shoulder and when the boy looked up, nodded his satisfaction. The boy shivered with fear and excitement. They all did. Slowly they withdrew, and a small fire was kindled. Around this fire they all squatted and into the flames were crumbled dried tobacco and sumac leaves as an offering to the Grandfather, for this was how Managnon addressed the bear.

"Grandfather, we have walked for two sleeps to come to this place and are all so weary that we can barely lift our snowshoes. Also our bellies are cold and need the warmth of your good, sweet flesh and our children cry out for your fat... We beseech you to offer up yourself to us. Now we must come."

Curly took back the iron-tipped lance, motioning for his son to remain in the rear. Again, the four men advanced, Managnon carrying a lighted brand, a low chant accompanying his breathing. The snow was scraped away, the bark and branches parted, and into the lair was pushed the brand. They stood for an age, watching wisps of smoke tease up from the hollow, waiting for the bear to show signs of waking. Managnon reached forward to twist the brand further. Even before his fingertips touched the haft, it vibrated and an angry coughing noise erupted forth. As one they took a step backwards, then without conferring, regained the step, each man's lance tip almost touching, twitching like divining rods - searching out the spark of the bear.

"Grandfather," Managnon whispered. "Grandfa..."

The roar they all expected, when it finally came, shook the fibre of each man nonetheless, and once more they sprang back. Managnon was the first to charge forward, lunging, twisting with his stone-tip, until it was contemptuously wrenched from his grasp. One by one they rushed forth. Curly felt the iron blade slice deep, lodging itself into bone. Holding on to the shaft, he was whirled around, as the head and shoulders of the bellowing animal broke forth and the heavy entrance branches were tossed aside like dried cornstalks. The sight of the maddened eyes, the gaping jaws and the blast of foetid breath filled him with such terror that he felt his heart would explode. But still he hung on to the lance, his bare hands sticky with the rivulets of warm blood that ran down the shaft. Managnon had grabbed one of the other weapons and even though the tip had snapped, was stabbing at the snarling jaws. The beast appeared bigger than in his dream. It bore few signs of the usual winter wastage, and less sign of wanting to volunteer its life, even though Managnon was still gasping for permission in between lunges. They were all trying desperately to keep the beast from fully evacuating its lair, terrified at the thought of it running amongst them. Mikshish darted forward in an attempt to retrieve his own lance, but instead fell back with a raked arm, his blood and that of the bear blossoming in the snow. And then Curly's hands were not alone on the spearshaft. His son was beside him and they were snarling and lunging as one. Out of the earth womb it reared, determined to display the power of its full height, but frustrated in its attempt by the long, jagged thorn that would not withdraw; one last, mighty heave was all that its breath would allow. Curly stumbled as if performing a gesture of obeisance, and in so doing, the butt end was lodged into his midriff, and down towards them slid the crushing blackness of the dying bear.

When they finally managed to roll the dead bear aside and pull the boy out from under it, he too seemed devoid of spark. Bathed, as Tidesso was, from head to toe in gore, it was hard for Curly to grasp that it was the bear's and not the boy's blood.

Managnon detected a pulse, but held Curly back, lest he lurch forth and embrace the lad, causing both of them more hurt. Curly collapsed in the pink snow, speechless with pain and yearning, knowing that his own hurt was a mortal one, knowing that he would never raise himself from this ice shroud. Suddenly, as if waking from a refreshing nap, the boy opened his eyes and sitting up, enquired where he was, looking at the great black mound beside him as if it had dropped from the heavens. Curly tried to smile as the boy beheld his father's sorry state.

He thought he heard the roar of the ocean, felt its swell, felt his toes flex to ride the imagined ship's deck. He was Mathew Tyrell for a few moments more. They crowded round him then. He half expected to see Bristol shipmates, but was more than glad to behold his son and Managnon. He grabbed at his friend's wrist. "Take him to the saltwater where you found me. Will you do this for me?" Managnon nodded. He felt his grip loosen. There was no more strength in his fingers or any other part of him.

He saw the boy's look of horror turn to anguish and heard them all weeping; but then, that was the way of these people. They always wept over the slaying of a bear.

JULY 1498
Under the flag of Cabot

The longboat was midway between ship and shore when the painted men were first glimpsed seeping from the trees. The oars were momentarily raised as each of the ten man crew waited on Boatswain Simon Tyrell's decision. On the shore, one of the painted ones hallooed and waved in a most harmonious manner. Simon thought he caught the glint of sun on metal, and fingering the pommel of his hanger, he gave a curt nod, eight oars dipped as one, and forward they skimmed. The sea was calm, with only a perfumed, offshore breeze blowing and as they neared the land, he counted a naked congregation numbering just a brace more than themselves. He was, however, mindful of the proximity of the trees and the fact that countless others might be lurking. In consequence, he bade the two nearest seamen rest their oars and look to the priming of the four arquebuses.

In truth, there was no choice but to advance. Men would soon be dying of thirst if he did not get fresh water back to the ship. Already, one had lowered a pail to quaff at the sea, and in consequence had been consigned raving to the hold. Others would have followed. He had known men drink their own piss or even bilge water before now, but yesterday it had rained a little, thank God, and they had managed to catch enough to ease the swollen tongue of the lookout, allowing him moisture enough to croak out 'Land ahoy!'.

Turning about, he scanned the horizon. There was nothing. No sign of any of the other ships. What fools they all were to have listened to the Venetian's blandishments and set sail with him for a second time. What had he known that was not common knowledge amongst all the mariners and merchants of Bristol? The Venetian had overridden them all, successfully petitioned the King and received his letters Patent. How had he done it? Did the King curse himself for a fool for not having taken a bite at the titbit the two Colombo brothers had dangled before him? And what a tasty morsel that had turned out to be, with the jaws of Spain and Portugal now firmly clamped on either half... Ah yes, that was how, Johnny Cabotto had shown King Henry the topside - as yet not divvied up by Papal bull of a Spanish Pope, if you please. And when the King had learned that in return for a fifth part of all profit, and dominion over all as yet unchewed morsels, he would not have to part with a penny, the royal jaws had bitten good and hard.

What of that first voyage? To Cipangu was it? Of course they had reached land. Did anyone expect otherwise? Cabotto was sailing with a Bristol crew, after all. But what did he have to show for it? Part of a red-painted stick. A grass snare - and a whispered glimpse of a skin-clad shadow? If only he had known that there, drunk and puking in the city gutters, had been Johnny Bowlegs, once an ignorant native from these very shores, once an outlaw in Stokeleigh woods. Ah, but the Venetian - the 'Great Admiral', if you please - had had the last laugh, receiving a pension from his gracious majesty on return and finance for this voyage to boot! Dressed in the finest silk he goes, and we all clamoured to enlist... Well, where in God's name are you? Have you floundered in the tempest? Where now, Great Admiral Cabotto? Do you apportion the ocean bed to your cronies? God knows there was precious little dry land left. Why, even your Genoese barber learned to strut and call himself count of an island none have yet seen... No favours for the lads of Bristol though, eh? Other than the privilege of showing you what's where. Well, we be here waiting. Where in God's name be you? In the court of the Great Khan, perhaps?"

"Wha's tha', Mist' Simon?"

The nearest man looked up, his blistered face pursed in a look of mock fright. Someone behind sniggered. Simon could see the arquebus's exaggerated shaking, the raised muzzle of which brushed past his own chin, the fore-sight snagging at his beard.

"Tis nothing, Crank, just look to your piece. Don't point the damned thing at me, and don't let the water get to your wick."

"Wha' you say, Mist' Simon?"

Simon Tyrell could see the smirk on Crank's face. His own recent promotion to boatswain, over the heads of others, had brought him much derision and not a little resentment from the older hands, and Crank, in particular, delighted in causing him unease.

"I says don't get your wick wet!"

His words were lost in the waves' rake of the shingle fifty feet beyond. Guessing the bottom was but a fathom below, Simon relinquished the rudder to another, clambered over the grumbling rowers to the prow, withdrew his sword and braced himself for the coming leap. On the beach the painted tribesmen had spread out and were moving cautiously forward, no sound coming from their tread. He noted, with a little relief, that none had arrows nocked. Most even held unstrung bows. Now there was trust!

There was a lurch as the keel cut into the shingle and over the side he vaulted. Stumbling briefly in the calf-deep spray, as the pebbles rolled and receded beneath his boots, he grabbed the gunnel, righted himself, and ignoring the jeers, marched his way up onto dry land.

"Don' you be gettin' your wick wet, Mist' Simon."

It seemed like an age standing there alone, gazing into the broad, painted faces, waiting for the others to reach his side, wanting to chivvy them along with a shout, but not daring to turn round. Despite his own broad grin, the painted faces now revealed little more than a row of impassive masks. Only the young adolescent who carried the metal-tipped lance displayed any sign of acknowledgment. Simon was confused. They had been quite demonstrative in their desire for the boat to land, but now, face to face, they appeared different. They were also much taller than he had thought. Even the adolescent looked down on him. He noted a slight difference in the facial cast of this youth. True, he was not painted in the same uniform black and red ochre of his older companions, nor did he have his head shaved into a tufted strip. Instead, his long locks flapped free. Simon detected a slight kink and lighter hue to their sheen and, despite the paint, there was a familiarity in this face.

The otherwise sweetly-scented breeze blew a new sinister odour off these wild men, reaching deep into his throat. He fought not to gag. Was this a trap? Where were the others? Come on, you dodderin' laggards! He began to feel a flicker of fear. His mouth was devoid of all moisture. Suddenly, amidst the crunching shingle, the clang of metal and panting of nervous lungs indicated the arrival of the others, and into the beach beside him were thrust gun rests and a limp banner depicting the Venetian's newly assumed crest. What was he supposed to say? There were special words of great solemnity, devised for this very occasion, but they were not supposed to have come from such as his lips. Then whose? Admiral

Cabotto's other three ships were nowhere to be spied, and the Genoese master of the Beatrice was flat on his back in the stern castle, caulked up with the bloody flux - and any words that issued from his mouth held no import for Englishman or pagan alike.

Simon Tyrell cleared his throat to speak, but was silenced by the forward advance of one of the savages. The man held out a belt of white shell beads. Nodding solemn thanks, Simon took the beads and drawing a long knife from his own girdle presented it haft first to the savage. The man accepted it with equal solemnity, but no sooner had his fingers curled around the handle than he turned, chattering to his fellow tribesmen, waving the knife above his shaven head as if it were a wizard's sceptre

"Big beggars, haint they?" a voice whispered, close to his ear.

"Steady now lads... Keep it steady."

Simon found himself croaking the command, more than a little uncomfortable at calling hands old enough to be his father 'lads'.

"I gotta' 'ave a drink, Mist' ...Ask 'em fer some water."

"Me an all."

"Stow it Crank, Johnson!" he barked.

The foremost savage spun round to face them once more. He was grinning now, grinning and chattering excitedly. Another stepped forward. It was the young one. All eyes rose to take in the metal point of his spear and then dipped again as from an otter-skin sheath he withdrew a long metal knife - but for the signs of age and wear, almost identical to the one just offered.

"Look a tha' then...'e do 'ave a Bristol blade."

"Yerz, 'owz 'e get tha' then eh?"

"I ant 'eard of no Bristol ship comin' this far south for over ten year or more."

"Stow it, I said! I can't hear myself think."

The exasperation in Simon's tone was noticed by the savages, who once again stood in silence. Tyrell knew that before all else he must ask them for fresh water - a man needed moisture to think straight. With wriggling fingers, he mimed the action of water cascading into his gaping mouth. Understanding immediately, the same foremost tribesman spoke to the youth. Relieving him of the spear, he sent the boy and one of the others scampering off into the woods. After a short while, wherein Simon passed the time examining and complimenting with effusive gestures the workmanship of the beaded belt, the two returned laden down with slopping bladders. These containers were handed to the gasping mariners, who jostled and gurgled until not a drop was left other than the pearly drops of moisture shining in their beards.

"Ere mist' Simon," whispered Crank. "Look at tha' there point on tha' there 'og sticker... It be rounded, like it's off of a gun barrel."

Simon Tyrell took a casual step nearer to the youth, smiled broadly at him then looked up at the point. Without being asked, the youth obligingly lowered the spear shaft to let it be examined. Simon saw straight away that indeed it was a broken piece of gun metal ground down into a long tapering point, but with a section of the inner channel very evident. And beneath the layer of grease was the maroon stain of recent bloodletting.

"Where did you get this point, and that there knife, lad?"

The youth looked on, baffled at the barrage of strange sounds. Simon pointed at the knife and the spear tip. The youth shook his head and once more raised the spear to a vertical position, then suddenly breaking into a broad grin, began to speak.

"Tirl.. Tirl... Fader me! Fader me!" He thumped his chest as he spoke.

"Wha's he jabberin' on about... Damned 'eathen tongue."

Ignoring Crank, Simon once more pointed to the knife. "Where did you get it?... From a mariner? One such as we?" He pointed to the sea.

"Tirl!...Tirl gib!...Tirl gib me!"

"Off of the Swallow... I'd put gelt on it," Crank piped up again.

Simon's ears pricked up at the mention of the Swallow. Was Crank being serious, or was he purposely trying to get him worked up into a lather? It was common knowledge that Simon had lost an older brother on the Swallow and was obsessed about any possibility of a connection. But Crank was a piss-taking joker, not to be trusted. Simon breathed deep, with a mind to tread easy, not to fall for any of his mischief.

"You don't know that! That was years ago, Crank, before he was born."

"Well, I realises tha' you yoursel' would only be a young un', Mist' Simon, but even so, old enough to know wha' 'appened to the crew... Or maybe you was too busy wiv your 'ead stuck in a book in tha' there rich merchant's place... too busy learnin' your readin' an' writin' to give a dribblin' shite about wha' went on outside them walls?... Well, I lost a lot o' good mates on tha' there ship... a lot o' good mates cut to pieces by 'eathen savages such as these 'ere babbies. An' one or two of 'em looks old enough."

"Wha' you say about the Swallow, Cranky?"

Johnson and one of the other older crew members sidled up. With a gruff command Simon sent them smirking back to their previous position. Of course, that was their game. They were taking him for a fool, wanting to get him wound up like a crossbow prod, of this Simon was now certain, but he would deny them the satisfaction. He knew that, above all else, he must maintain control. He knew, too, the tribesmen were becoming restless, aware of the sudden mood change. But what if Crank was right?

"There must 'ave been other ships put in down here. Or maybe they could 'ave bartered 'em?... God knows... It don't matter right now."

"Well, it matters to some of us, Mister Tyrell... Matters a lot."

"Look, you gobby bastard. It matters to me too. I lost my brother on the Swallow and you damn well know it. So, shut your mouth, and let me think."

Simon Tyrell could feel the sweat beginning to pour down from his hairline and well above his brows. Forcing a grin, he turned once more towards the savages, brushing away the sweat with his tunic sleeve before it deluged his eyes. The smile froze. Even though no arrows had been drawn, he saw in an instant that the previously unstrung bows were now tensioned. It had happened so fast. He turned to Crank and knew that he too had seen it.

"Well tha's it then, ennit."

Crank spat and shouldered his arquebus. With a groan, the savages leapt back, reaching over their shoulders for arrows.

"No Crank... No!"

Uttering a roar of disbelief, Simon stared helpless as the lighted serpentine clicked downward and a heartbeat later the arquebus jolted in a deafening blast. Two more explosions from behind made him crouch and swivel on his haunches; past his right ear an arrow whined. Though the sword had appeared in his hand, he knew not what use to put it to. His first inclination was to slash at Crank, but the drumming of a great flock of pigeons rising from the trees - eclipsing even the screams of the fleeing savages - momentarily occupied all his thoughts. The gunsmoke cleared to reveal a single, broken body on an empty beach, and beyond, an empty wall of trees. Simon opened his mouth, but before the anguished groan could escape, Crank fired off another shot, contemptuously ignoring all orders to the contrary.

"I said no more!"

Crank looked at Simon as if he were a peevish child and proceeded to pour powder down the gun's muzzle and ram home a ball. In his growing rage, Simon swiped the barrel with his sword. A dull ring ensued.

"You butcher! I said no! I said no!"

Crank let go of the arquebus. It fell towards Simon, coming to rest on his chest. Silenced for a moment, Simon watched him pick up the discarded knife, walk towards the bloodstained body of the young savage, and stoop down beside it. Fighting to keep himself from becoming hysterical with rage, his hand tightened on the sword and with the flat of the blade Simon slapped at his still damp breeches.

"Turn round when I'm talking to you, you whore's bastard!... Turn round, I said!"

Crank ignored him. Simon could see the vile creature's arm moving in a sawing motion. It was too much. He ran forward, catching Crank a blow to the back of the head with the gun's stock. Crank slumped forward over the desecrated body of the youth. Simon raised the gun to strike him again, but an agonised cry from behind set him spinning around.

"Johnson's down, be hurt bad. Spitted through 'is middle. What's to do?"

It was Thomas Smith who called out from the group now gathered round the wounded man. Why in God's name are they bunched together like that? thought Simon. Surely they know that much?

"Anyone else down?" he called. They all shook their heads.

"Well, get him to the boat. The rest of you spread out. An' load them pieces."

"Wha' about us, then? Wha' if they savages come back? Wha' if there be more of 'em?"

The possibility had never left Simon's mind, but there were other considerations.

"We must get water t' take back to the ship."

"I aint a goin' in them there woods up there."

"Nor me an all."

"You'll do as you're told, John Fuller...By God, you will!"

He had screamed the order, his voice breaking into hysterical falsetto, and feeling somewhat ridiculous, braced himself for their derision. But any possibility of further argument was abruptly terminated by a hail of arrows rattling amongst them. Two of the guns were hurriedly fired at the scream-filled trees. And then, with no command needed, those that were able rushed back to the ship's boat. Cursing in pain and frustration, they tried to get the boat off the shingle, but it was proving too firmly lodged. Soon every one of them had sustained wounds. Some, with several shafts bristling in their flesh, squealed like whipped dogs as shipmates buffeted against them in the struggle to budge the craft. In the end, it was the sheer terror at the sight of the yelping tribesmen pouring forth that lent them the final impetus, and only the gun that Crank had so contemptuously pushed into Simon's hands earlier, stopped the two foremost tribesmen from reaching them as they laboured in the shallows.

Four of their number did not make it into the boat at all. Crank was amongst them. As they pulled away, Simon watched through tears of rage as the cause of all their distress was discovered, feigning death, and raised up pleading and squawking in the midst of a howling throng. Somehow he broke free and made it to the surf, but was again captured, cursing and thrashing wildly. Again Simon fired the arquebus, but the hastily-laid charge sent him sprawling back amongst the cries and curses of the wounded crew.

"We saw what you done back there to Crank. Tis you what's good 'as killed 'im!"

When the broken shaft in his own side finally allowed Simon to right himself and look once more, the unfortunate rogue had been stripped naked. As the laboured oarstrokes slowly dragged them away, he watched the distant, jerking, lilywhite object turn to glistening red.

The End

Five ships set out in John Cabot's third expedition.
Earlier in the voyage, one of these ships returned badly damaged to Ireland.
Of the other four, nothing was ever heard again.